PART ONE:

1977 – YOU MAY NOT BE AN ANGEL

ONE

They stopped him as he was coming through customs. Why wouldn't they stop him? Terry looked like trouble.

His skin pale from too many sleepless nights and God knows what else, the second-hand suit jacket from Oxfam, the CBGB's T-shirt, Levi's that hadn't been touched by water since the day he bought them and wore them in the bath (his mother telling him he would catch his death, his father telling him he was bloody mental), Doctor Martens boots and – the crowning glory – his short, spiky hair dyed black, and badly, from a bottle of something called Deep Midnight that he had found at the bottom of the ladies' grooming counter in Boots.

'One moment, *sir.*'

Sir used like a weapon, like a joke. As if anyone would seriously call someone like Terry *sir.* Two customs men, one of them knocking on for thirty, with mutton chops and a mullet, like some King's Road footballer trying to keep up with the times, and the other one really prehistoric, maybe even as old as Terry's father, but lacking the old man's twinkle.

'Been far, sir?'

This from the elderly geezer, ramrod straight, all those years in uniform behind him.

'Berlin,' Terry said.

The younger one, as hairy as a character from Dickens, was already in Terry's plastic Puma kitbag, pulling out his God Save the Queen T-shirt, his silver tape recorder, a spare pack of batteries, a microphone and a change of Y-fronts.

As Terry's mum always pointed out, you never knew when you were going to get knocked over.

'Berlin? Must be lovely this time of year,' said muttonchops, and the old soldier sniggered. They thought they were funny. The Eric and Ernie of Terminal Three.

The old soldier flipped open Terry's thick blue passport and did a double take. The pale-faced, black-haired youth before him bore little resemblance to this incriminating snapshot from Terry's previous life, his mousey-haired and baggy-flared life, the living at home with Mum and Dad life, the working at the gin factory life when he walked around lost in dreams, and all his dreams were of getting out.

In the mug shot Terry peered out at the world from under a failed feather cut, trying to look like Rod Stewart but coming out more like Dave Hill of Slade. He even had the start of a suntan. It was a snapshot from when Terry was still waiting for his life to start, and his cheeks were burning as the old soldier closed the passport.

Then muttonchops was digging deeper in the kitbag, making Terry flinch now, because he was touching the things that really mattered to him, pulling out a two-week-old copy of *The Paper* with Joe Strummer on the cover, looking as beautiful and doomed

4

as Laurence Harvey in *Room at the Top*. He flipped the big inky broadsheet open, gawped blankly at the news pages, at headlines that meant nothing to him.

This Year's Costello. Talking Head Cases. Bachman Turner Overdrive Disband. Muddy Waters – Hard Again. Fanny to Warm Up Reading?

Quickly flicking through *The Paper* now. Not even glancing at the double-page centre-spread cover story on the Clash by Skip Jones, the greatest music writer in the world, but pausing – as if that's what it was all about! – when he got to the classifieds.

'*Dirty Dick's Records – get yourself a dose,*' muttonchops read out loud, pulling a face. 'That's disgusting, that is.'

He tossed *The Paper* to one side and rummaged deeper, producing Terry's battered copy of *The Kandy-Kolored Tangerine-Flake Streamline Baby* with entire paragraphs underlined, and then the truly irreplaceable – cassettes from Terry's recent interview with the legendary Dag Wood, the only man to be booed off stage at Woodstock.

Terry watched the priceless cassettes being handled as though they were something that they gave away with the petrol and he felt like telling the bastards to do something useful, like go and catch Carlos the Jackal.

But he thought that might be an invitation to a full body search, so he bit his lip, clenched his buttocks and wondered how long his girlfriend would wait for him.

'And was your trip business or pleasure, sir?' said the old soldier.

'I'm a journalist.'

It still gave him a kick to say that – nine months into the job and it gave him a thrill to see his name in a by-line, especially next to the postage-stamp picture you sometimes got. Small things, but they signified that Terry was becoming the someone he had always wanted to be. They couldn't stop him now.

'A *journalist?*' said the man, a note of suspicion in his voice, as if a real journalist should be wearing a suit and tie, or carrying a briefcase, or old or something. 'What do you write about then?'

Terry smiled at him.

It was the end of a summer day in 1977 and there was something in the air, and in the clubs, and pouring out of every radio. Everything was suddenly good again, the way it had been good ten years ago, back in the Sixties, when Terry was a child, and his parents still thought that the Beatles seemed like nice boys.

What did he write about? He wrote about the way everything was changing. From haircuts to trousers, and all stops in between.

What did he write about?

Oh, that was a good one.

Terry thought of something that Ray Davies had said recently, about how he felt like sobbing his heart out whenever he looked at anyone's record collection, because it was just so moving to see that personal soundtrack laid out before you, naked and open and fading with the years, because if you cared about this kind of thing then it was all there among the scratched vinyl and the cracked gatefold sleeves, as plain as could be, all the hopes and yearnings of someone's private universe, and everything that a young heart could possibly want or need or yearn for.

'I write about music,' Terry said.

Misty was waiting for him at the arrivals gate.

He saw her before she saw him. He liked it that way. It was one of his favourite things in the world – to see her before she saw him.

Misty. His honey-haired, cat-faced darling. Tall and slim in a simple white dress matched with a pair of clonking great biker boots.

Girls were starting to do that all the time, pairing something undeniably feminine – mini-skirts, fishnet tights, high heels, Misty's simple white dress – with something brutally male – DMs, spiked dog collars and wrist bands, Misty's motorcycle boots. Throwing their sex in your face, Terry thought, demanding to know what you were looking at, and silently asking you what you were going to do about it. It was a new thing.

Slung over her shoulder was a bag with her camera equipment. Dangling from one of the straps, where you might expect to find a little plastic gonk or perhaps a figurine of the Fonz or Han Solo, there was a pair of handcuffs – pink fake mink handcuffs. You couldn't tell at first glance if they came from a toyshop or a sex shop.

Misty and her pink fake mink handcuffs. Terry sighed at the sight of her.

She was like a girl from a book. No, a *woman* – you couldn't say girl any more, that was another of the new things, it wasn't allowed to say girl, you had to say woman, even when they were still – technically, legally – girls. Misty had explained it all to Terry – it was something to do with what she called *the suffocating tyranny of men*.

Funny that, thought Terry.

Yes, she was like the bird – *woman* – in the Thomas Hardy novel they read at school, the year he dropped out and went to work in the factory. *Far from the Madding Crowd*. Misty was like the woman in there – all female softness, but with a thread of steel you couldn't guess at by looking at her. Bathsheba Everdene. That was Misty. Bathsheba Everdene in a white dress and biker boots, Bathsheba Everdene with a pair of pink fake mink handcuffs.

She still hadn't seen him, and the sight of her face scanning the crowd full of strangers made his soul ache. Then she caught his gaze and started jumping up and down, so glad to see him again after being apart for so long.

Over a week!

She ducked under a sign that said STRICTLY NO ENTRY and ran to him. She wasn't the kind who cared about signs, she moved through the world as if she had a right to be there – anywhere, everywhere. Like a woman in a book, like a girl in a song.

'Look, Tel,' she said.

She had the most recent copy of *The Paper* in her hands. Almost a week old, and somehow the ink was still damp, and her fingertips were black, and there on the cover was a gaunt, grim-faced man with platinum blond hair standing in a trench coat by a great wall with a sign that said, *Achtung! Sie verlassen jetzt West Berlin.*

Terry's story on Dag Wood, written on a hotel laundry bag and phoned in from Berlin.

'So what's he like?' Misty said, and he had to laugh, because normally the question drove him nuts.

You wrote a 3,000-word piece about someone and then everybody asked you, *What's he like then?* What he was like was in the story, it was always in the story, or the story had failed. When Tom Wolfe wrote about Muhammad Ali, or Phil Spector, or Hugh Hefner, did people say, *Yeah, Tom, but what are they really like?* Probably. But Terry didn't mind. As it was her. As it was Misty.

'He's the greatest,' Terry said. 'I'll introduce you tonight, okay?'

Then Misty had that look in her eye, that sleepy, faraway look, and she was tilting her head to one side, so Terry placed his mouth on her mouth, and felt her fingers running through his dyed black hair, and the cameras that were stuffed inside her shoulder bag pressed through his Oxfam jacket and against his heart.

Their kisses tasted of Marlboro and Juicy Fruit, and as they snogged at the arrivals gate, completely wrapped up in each other, oblivious to the smirks and stares and snide comments – 'What are that pair supposed to be dressed as, Dad?' – neither of them doubted that their kisses would taste that way for ever.

Leon Peck was doing the singles.

He sat in the review room, the little corridor-shaped cubby-hole with a stereo where they went to listen to new music, and all around him were the week's releases, maybe a hundred or more seven-inch 45s, some of them in the new-fangled coloured vinyl and picture sleeves.

Convention demanded that Leon found something to rave about – The Single of the Week – and then picked twenty or thirty other singles that were worthy of a cheap joke that could be told in one pithy, piss-taking paragraph.

A kind of spiteful irreverence had always been a part of *The Paper's* appeal, and just under the title of every issue the readers were promised, 'Hotsies, groovies, goldies and a rootin', tootin' tab of vicious controversy'. That was exactly what Leon needed to conjure up for his singles page. A rootin', tootin' tab of vicious controversy.

Except he couldn't be bothered.

Something had happened to Leon at the weekend that made slagging off – let's see, what do we have here? – 'Float On' by the Floaters or 'Easy' by the Commodores or 'Silver Lady' by David 'Starsky' Soul – or was he 'Hutch'? – seem beneath him.

Something had happened at the weekend that had changed the

way Leon looked at the world. So he picked up 'Silver Lady' – Starsky or Hutch grinning like a lobotomised Osmond on the picture sleeve – and flung it across the room like a Frisbee. The seven-inch slice of vinyl shattered with a satisfying, surprisingly loud crack against the far wall. It felt good.

So good in fact that Leon did the same with 'Float On'. And then 'Easy'. And then 'You Got What It Takes' by Showaddywaddy. Leon picked up 'Fanfare for the Common Man', the new single by Emerson, Lake and Palmer, and that was tossed with particular venom. Soon the review room was covered in shards of splintered vinyl.

Leon pushed back the stacks of singles and began leafing through the most recent issue of *The Paper*, sighing at the soul-shrivelling trivia of it all. Didn't these people know what was going on in the world?

There was Dag Wood on the cover, doing his tired old heroic-junkie routine by the Berlin Wall. Leon was pleased for Terry – could imagine him puffing up with pride at the sight of his story on the cover – but *come on*. As if Lou Reed hadn't done it all first and better! As if Dag Wood actually knew the difference between Karl Marx and Groucho!

Terry's such a sucker for all that rock-god schtick, Leon thought. They all are up here.

Leon yawned, and turned to page two, sighing at the sight of the charts. Mindless disco crud ruled the singles – Donna Summer faking multiple orgasms all over 'I Feel Love' – and, top of the albums, music to help tranked-out housewives hobble through the menopause. *The Johnny Mathis Collection*.

Leon snorted with derision. He flicked through *The Paper*, his fingers, like his mood, becoming blacker by the second.

Eater to record first album during school holidays . . . new singles by Pilot, Gentle Giant and the Roy Wood Band . . . new albums by Ry Cooder, Boney M and the Modern Lovers . . .

And then – finally! – at the bottom of page 11, jostled into a corner by a massive ad for Aerosmith at Reading and a world exclusive on the break-up of Steeleye Span, there were a few brief paragraphs that held Leon's interest and made his heart start pumping. The piece had his by-line.

The National Front plan to parade through a black neighbourhood this coming weekend. Hiding their racist views behind an anti-mugging campaign and countless Union Jacks, the NF plan to leave from Clifton Rise, New Cross. Their route and the time of the march remain undisclosed.

A peaceful counter demonstration planned by local umbrella group the All Lewisham Campaign Against Racism and Fascism (ALCARAF) will assemble in Ladywell Fields, next to the British Rail Ladywell Station, at 11 a.m.

Be there or be square.

The magazine had appeared on newsstands nationwide the previous Thursday, and in London as far back as last Wednesday. A lifetime away, thought Leon. Because last Saturday the march and the counter demonstration had combined to produce the biggest riot London had seen since the war. And Leon Peck had been there.

I was there, he thought, touching the bruise on his cheekbone where he had been clipped by the knee of a policeman on horseback. I saw it happen. While many of his peers were dreaming of seeing Aerosmith at Reading, Leon had been in the middle of the riot at Lewisham, crushed in with the protesters being forced back by the police and their horses, and he had felt as if the world was ending.

Flags waving, bricks flying, policemen on horses riding into the crowds, the battle lines ebbing and flowing – screaming, righteous chaos all around. Orange smoke bombs on Lewisham High Street, the air full of masonry, dustbins, bottles and screams, taunts, chanting. The sound of plate-glass windows collapsing.

What he remembered most was the physical sensation of the riot, the way he experienced it in his blood and bones. His legs turning to water with terror as the air filled with missiles and the police spurred their horses into the crowd, his heart pumping at the sight of the loathing on the faces of the marchers, and the raging anger he felt at the sight of these bigots parading their racist views through a neighbourhood where almost everyone was black.

He had never felt so scared in his life. And yet there was never a place where he was so glad to be.

It mattered. It mattered more than anything. Leon Peck, child of peace and prosperity, had spent his Saturday afternoon doing what his father had done in Italy during the war, in Sicily and Monte Cassino and the march on Rome. Fighting Nazis.

Leon didn't kid himself. Lewisham had been one Saturday out of his life. It couldn't compare to what the old man had done in World War Two. But the experience had been like nothing he had ever known.

When he was younger than today, Leon had been involved in student politics at school and at university. But this was something else. The Pakistani shopkeeper at the end of the road where Leon was squatting had had his face opened up by a racist with a Stanley knife. The Nazis were coming back. It was really happening. And you either did something about it, or you went to see Aerosmith at Reading.

Later that sunny Saturday, just when the riot was starting to feel like one of those visions he'd had when he was dropping acid in the lecture halls of the London School of Economics, Leon had stopped outside an electrical shop on Oxford Street and watched the news on a dozen different TV sets. The riot was the first story. The only story. A quarter of the Metropolitan Police Force had been there, and they couldn't stop it.

Leon wondered if any of the readers of *The Paper* had gone to Lewisham because of his few measly paragraphs. He wondered if he had done any good. He wondered if soon the – he had to consult his own article here – the ALCARAF would be the name on everyone's lips. But then he turned the page and the classified ads brought him back to reality. This was what their readers were interested in.

LOOK SCANDINAVIAN! Scandinavian-style clogs – £5.50 ... Cheesecloth shirts for £2.70 plus 20p postage and packing ... Cotton Drill Loons. 'A good quality cotton drill in the original hip-fitting loons.' Still only £2.60.

Leon's thoughts turned reluctantly to fashion, and he wondered, *Who wears this crap?* Leon himself looked like a shorthaired Ramone – a London spin on a New York archetype. A style that said – I am making an effort, but not much of one.

Leon's face and body had not quite caught up with the greasy machismo of his clothes. At twenty he was still whiplash thin, frail and boyish, looking as though he only had to shave about once a week.

His Lewis Leather biker's jacket sported a plastic badge on the lapel featuring the Jimmy Hill-like profile of Vladimir Ilyich Lenin. He wore drainpipe Levi's, a threadbare Thin Lizzy T-shirt and white Adidas trainers with three blue stripes down the side. Pretty much the standard uniform for the enlightened urban male in the summer of 1977, although Leon had topped off his look with a trilby hat from a charity shop. Funnily enough, you couldn't buy that look in the back of *The Paper*, where they were still packaging what was left of the spirit of the Sixties.

Cannabis leaf jewellery. Solid silver leaf pendant on real silver chain – £7.

Leon closed *The Paper*, shaking his head. He adjusted his trilby. It was as if nothing had changed. It was as if there wasn't a war on.

It seemed to Leon that everyone he knew was living in some old Sixties dream. The people he worked with at *The Paper,* all of the readers, his father – especially his father, a man who had belonged to CND for a few years but who now belonged to a golf club.

What was wrong with them? Didn't they realise it was time to take a stand? What did they think the National Front was doing marching in South London? He touched the bruise on his cheek again, and wished it could stay there for ever.

This wasn't about some little style option – the choice between long hair or spiky, flared trousers or straight, Elvis or Johnny Rotten. It was about a more fundamental choice – not between the NF and the SWP, who were daubing their rival slogans all over the city, like the Sharks and Jets of political extremism – but the choice between evil, hatred, racism, xenophobia, bigotry, and everything that was their opposite.

The memory of Lewisham still made him shake with fear. The rocks showering down on the marchers. The faces twisted with hatred. The police lashing out with truncheon, boot or knee. The sudden eruption of hand-to-hand fighting as marcher or demonstrator broke through the police lines, fists and feet flying. And the horses, shitting themselves with terror as they were driven into the protesters. Leon knew how those horses felt. Lewisham had been the first violence that he had been involved in since a fight in the playground at junior school. And he had lost that one.

Mind you, Leon thought, she was a very big girl for nine.

He thumbed through the singles until he found something worth playing. 'Pretty Vacant' by the Sex Pistols. He put the record on the turntable, placed the needle on the record, and pulled the arm back for repeat play. Then, as the stuttering guitar riff came pouring out of the speakers, he set about destroying the rest of the singles. The Jacksons, Donna Summer, Hot Chocolate, Carly Simon and the Brotherhood of Man – all of them were thrown to their doom across the review room, all of them perished in a dramatic explosion of vinyl.

Leon was about to launch Boney M's 'Ma Baker' when the door to the review room opened and standing there was an elderly black cleaner with a Hoover in his hands, staring open-mouthed at the destroyed vinyl that littered the carpet.

'What the goodness you doing in here, man?' the cleaner said.

'I'm doing the singles,' Leon said, his face burning with embarrassment. 'I was just about to clear all this up.'

Watched by the cleaner, Leon got down on his hands and knees and began picking up the smashed records, his mouth fixed in a smile that he hoped showed solidarity, and some sort of apology.

*　　　*　　　*

'I hope you like curry,' Terry's mum said to Misty.

'I *love* curry,' Misty said. 'In fact, my father was born in India.'

Terry shot her a look. He didn't know that Misty's dad had been born in India. It seemed there were a lot of things he didn't know about her, despite being together since Christmas.

Misty and Terry and his parents crowded awkwardly in the tiny hallway. Misty was making some rapturous speech about the glories of the Raj and something Kipling had written about the correct way to cook chicken tikka masala. Terry's parents smiled politely as she babbled on. His father took her photographer's bag. Terry noticed that she had unclipped her pink fake mink handcuffs, and stuffed them in the bag. It was her first visit to his home and everyone was making an effort. Misty had turned the charm up to ten and Terry's dad had put his shirt on. Terry's mum had prepared a special menu and Terry hadn't brought any of his laundry home.

They entered the front room where an old film was blaring from the telly in the corner. For a moment it commanded all their attention. Tony Curtis and Sidney Poitier were runaways from a chain gang, a white racist and a proud black man, still handcuffed together.

'*The Defiant Ones*,' said Terry's mum. 'He was lovely, Tony Curtis.'

'I'll turn that thing off,' said Terry's dad. That was a sure sign that royalty was visiting. They never turned the TV off until it told them to go to bed.

'What was it that Truffaut said about life before television?' Misty said, her lovely face frowning with concentration.

'I don't quite recall, dear,' said Terry's mum, as if she had been asked the name of Des O'Connor's last single, and it was on the tip of her tongue.

'Truffaut said that before television was invented, people stared at the fire.' Misty looked very serious, as she always did when relating the thoughts of one of her heroes. 'He said that there has always been this need for moving pictures.'

They all thought about it for a while.

'Cocktail sausage?' said Terry's mum, holding out a plate of shrivelled chipolatas bristling with little sticks. 'Take two, love. They're only small.'

Terry thought it was so strange to see Misty parked on the brown three-piece suite in the front room of the pebbledash semi where he had grown up. When Terry was small, his father had worked at three jobs to get them out of rented accommodation above the butcher's shop and into a place of their own, but he knew that what was a dream home to his mum and dad must have seemed very modest to a girl like Misty.

There was flock wallpaper and an upright piano in the corner and a wall-to-wall orange carpet that looked like the aftermath of some terrible car crash. There were matching pouffes for them to put their feet up on while they were reading *Reveille* (Mum) and *Reader's Digest* (Dad). Misty perched on the middle cushion of what they called the settee in what they called the front room about to eat what they called their tea.

Strange for all of them. Front room, settee, tea – it even felt like his parents spoke a different language to Misty.

Terry's dad stared bleary-eyed at the dead TV, a cocktail sausage on a stick forgotten in his hand. He had just woken up, and was getting ready for another night shift at Smithfield meat market. Even if he had been more awake, small talk wasn't really his thing, unless he was around people he had known for years, like the men at the market. But Terry's mum could have small talked for England.

She busied herself in the kitchen, conversing with Misty through the serving hatch, like a sailor peering through a porthole.

'I do like your frock,' Terry's mum said, her eyes running over the white dress and down to Misty's biker boots. 'It's a lovely frock.' She passed no comment on the biker boots. 'Would you like chicken or beef curry, love?'

Misty almost squealed with delight. 'I can't believe that you've gone to all this trouble!'

But Terry knew that the curry was no trouble at all. His mum would just drop the bag of Birds Eye curry in boiling water for fifteen minutes. He knew that wasn't the kind of curry that his girlfriend was expecting. He knew she was used to real Indian takeaways.

Waiting for tea, Terry had the same sinking feeling, that preparation for humiliation, that he had once felt after PE in the junior school when Hairy Norton had hidden his trousers. Unable to locate his missing pair of grey shorts that were stuffed behind the urinal (thanks, Hairy) Terry had made the long walk into the classroom, fully dressed apart from his trousers.

'Please, miss . . .'

The rest had been drowned out by the mocking laughter of thirty eight-year-old children. That's how he felt waiting for his mother to serve them their curry. Like Hairy Norton had hidden his trousers in the toilets all over again.

And the funny thing was his mum was a good cook.

When Terry had been living at home, tea (Misty would have called it dinner) and Sunday dinner (Misty would have called it lunch) was always meat and two veg, with a nice roast on the Sabbath.

Apart from Sundays, the meal was always consumed in their

favourite chairs, the toad in the hole or shepherd's pie or pork chops and their attendant soggy vegetables wolfed down in front of *Are You Being Served?* or *The World at War* or *Fawlty Towers* or *Nationwide* or *The Generation Game.*

'Nice to see you, to see you – nice!'

But something had happened since Terry had left home. Now it was all convenience food – Vesta chicken supreme and rice, Birds Eye Taste of India, *'For mash get Smash'* – spaceman food, dark powders or a solidified brown mass that required either the addition of or immersion in boiling water.

When Terry was a boy, his mum had baked bread, and it was the most wonderful taste in the world. The smell of a freshly baked loaf or rolls had made little Terry swoon. Now his mum no longer had time for all that business. Terry's dad blamed women's lib and Captain Birds Eye.

But his mum had pushed the boat out tonight, or at least as far as the boat would go in these modern times, and Terry loved her for it, even though it seemed he never had much of an appetite these days.

They sat themselves at the table that was usually reserved for Sundays and Christmas, paper napkins, folded into neat triangles, by best plates, the prawn cocktails in place. A bottle of Lambrusco had already been unscrewed.

'So you work at night,' Misty said to Terry's father. 'Just like us.'

Terry's dad shifted awkwardly in his seat, considering the prawn drowning in pink sauce on the end of his teaspoon.

'Hmmm,' he said. 'Night work. Working at night. Yes.'

'You hate it, don't you, the night work?' Terry's mum said, prompting him. 'He hates the night work,' she told Misty in a stage whisper.

'Why's that then, Dad?' Terry said, rearranging his prawn cocktail with his teaspoon. His father had been working night shifts for as long as Terry could remember. It had never occurred to him that he would have preferred working during the day. 'Why do you hate working nights, Dad?'

The old man snorted. If you stirred him from his silence, he could be brutally frank. 'Because you're working when everyone else is asleep. And you're asleep when everyone else is awake. And then you get up when the day's gone, and you don't get cornflakes or a nice fry-up for your breakfast, you get prawns.'

He smiled at his wife with a mouthful of prawns, to draw the sting from his words and show her that he was grateful for her efforts. Misty smiled and nodded as if everything was wonderful.

'Salad, anyone?' said Terry's mum.

'Not for me,' said Terry.

'I'll have a bit of salad,' said Terry's dad.

'He likes his salad,' said Terry's mum.

Terry knew it wasn't real salad – he knew that what his parents called salad was really just tomatoes and cucumber and lettuce, with a radish or two chucked on top for special occasions, such as today. He knew that Misty would expect a salad to come with some sort of dressing. Vinaigrette or thousand island or olive oil or something. He knew this because joining *The Paper* had been a crash course in food and restaurant lore, as every press officer on every record label in Soho Square had rushed to buy the new boy lunch on their expense account, until they realised that he was going to slag off their rotten acts anyway.

But here was another thing he was learning about Misty. Salad dressing didn't matter as much to her as making his mum feel appreciated, and that touched his heart. By the time his girlfriend had pronounced his mother's boil-in-a bag beef curry to be delicious, Terry was more deeply in love with her than ever, if that was possible.

'So how did you like Berlin, Tel?' his mum said, sinking a bread knife into a Black Forest gateau. If she had noticed that her son was only force-feeding himself enough to be polite, she gave no sign.

'It was incredible,' Terry said.

His mum waved the bread knife expansively. 'Lovely to go travelling all over the world and get paid for it. You were in Germany, weren't you?' she said to his dad. Terry realised that many of his mum's observations ended with a question to his dad, as if she was afraid the old man's natural reticence might mean he was left out of the conversation.

'Bit different in my day,' said Terry's dad.

'Why's that, Mr Warboys?' Misty asked.

Terry's dad grinned ruefully. 'Because some bugger was always shooting at me.'

Misty shook her head with wonder. 'You've had such an interesting life,' she said. She touched the hand of Terry's mum, the hand where she wore her engagement ring, her wedding ring and the eternity ring she had got last birthday. 'You both have. Depression . . . war . . . it's like you've lived through history.' She looked at Terry. 'What has our generation ever seen or done?'

Terry's parents stared at her. World war, global economic collapse – they thought that was all normal.

'Lump of gateau?' said Terry's mum.

They took their Black Forest gateau to the settee, and Misty perched herself on the piano stool, lifting the lid on the old upright.

'I had lessons for ten years,' she said. 'Five to fifteen. My mother was very keen for me to play.'

Terry smiled proudly. He had no idea she played piano. His smile began to fade as it became clear that she didn't, not really. Misty picked out the worst version of 'Chopsticks' that he had ever heard.

'Ten years?' Terry's dad chuckled with genuine amusement. 'I reckon you want your money back, love!'

'I'm a bit rusty, it's true,' Misty smiled, seeing the funny side.

'Don't listen to him, darling,' said Terry's mum, and she sat next to Misty. 'Shove up a bit. Let me have a go.'

The piano had belonged to Terry's grandmother – his mum's mum, back in the days before television when every sprawling East End family had their own upright in the corner and a chicken run out back. You made your own entertainment and your own eggs. There wasn't really room for a piano in that little front room, but Terry's mum refused to get rid of it, especially now that Terry's nan was no longer around.

His mum cracked the bones in her fingers, smiling shyly, then began to play one of the old songs, about seeing your loved one's faults but staying with them anyway. She had the easy grace of the self-taught and she started singing in a soft, halting voice that made them all very still and quiet, although Terry's dad wore a knowing grin on his face.

> *You may not be an angel*
> *Angels are so few ...*

Terry's mum paused, but kept playing, and Terry's dad guffawed with delight.

'She's forgotten the words,' he said, embarrassed at his fierce pride in his wife and her gift. But she hadn't forgotten the words.

'But until the day that one comes along . . .'

And here she gave a rueful look at Terry's dad.

'I'll string along with you.'

Misty stared at Terry's mum with an expression of total seriousness, as if she was in church, or in the presence of Truffaut saying something profound.

Misty had once told Terry that she'd never tasted instant coffee until after she had left home. And he knew that his mum would end the dinner with coffee that came out of a jar from Nescafé. He also knew that his mum would probably add sugar and milk without asking Misty if she wanted any or not, the way you were supposed to, and he knew that someone was going to have to wash up those prawn cocktail teaspoons before they could stir their Nescafé.

But as he watched his girlfriend watching his mum pick out that old song, Terry felt for the first time that none of that stuff mattered very much.

The train shook Ray Keeley awake.

He brushed a veil of long blond hair out of his bleary eyes and stared at the harvest fields, the scattering of farm houses, a couple of mangy horses. One hour to London, he thought.

Ray knew those fields, could read them like a clock. He even recognised the horses. He had been passing through this part of the country for three years, since he was fifteen years old, heading north to see bands on tour in Newcastle and Leicester, Manchester and Liverpool, Leeds and Glasgow, and then coming back to London to write about them.

He realised what had woken him. There were voices drifting through the carriage, loud and coarse, effing and blinding. A bunch of football fans were approaching, on their way to the dining car. At least they looked like football fans – long floppy feather cuts, short-sleeve shirts that were tighter than a coat of emulsion, and flared trousers that stopped some distance from their clunky boots. Feeling a familiar shiver of fear, he sunk deeper into his rock-hard British Rail seat, allowing his fringe to fall over his face, hoping to hide from the world.

Ray knew their type, and knew what they would make of him with his long hair, denim jacket, white jeans and cowboy boots. But they were more interested in finding lager than tormenting a lone hippy kid, and guffawed their way out of the far end of the carriage.

Ray closed his eyes. He didn't feel good. He couldn't remember sleeping last night, although he knew he must have at some point, because he couldn't remember when the woman had left his hotel room.

She was the press officer from the record company, there to make sure that Ray got into the shows and got to interview the lead singer while they were travelling from one town to the next. He liked her a lot – she looked a bit like the girl in *Bouquet of Barbed Wire,* and she knew her music. But Ray knew that the next time they met she would act as though nothing much had happened. That's what it was like. You were meant to take these things lightly.

Ray ran upstairs to his room, hardly registering the presence of his younger brother sprawled on his bed, reading a football magazine.

After chucking his bag in a corner Ray knelt before the stereo on his side of the room. The pose made him seem like a religious supplicant, but when he ran his fingers along the spine of his record collection, it was like a lover – familiar, loving, taking his time, and knowing exactly what was there before he had even looked.

The records were alphabetically filed. The As were sparse and unplayed for years – Alice Cooper and Argent and Abba and Atomic Rooster – but B was for *The White Album, Abbey Road, Revolver, Rubber Soul, Let It Be, A Hard Day's Night* . . . B was for Beatles galore.

He pulled out *Abbey Road*, and the boys marching in single file across that zebra crossing brought back twenty melodies. Ray knew that street in St John's Wood better than he knew the road where he lived.

The white VW parked on the pavement, the curious passer-by in the distance, and the unbroken blue of a cloudless summer sky. And the four of them, all with a role to play. George in denim – the gravedigger. Paul barefoot – the corpse. Ringo in his long black drape – the undertaker. And John in white – the angel.

Ray replaced *Abbey Road*. Almost idly, his index finger fell upon the Ds – *Blood on the Tracks* by Dylan, *Morrison Hotel* and *L.A. Woman* by the Doors, *The Golden Hour of Donovan, The Best of Bo Diddley* and . . . *For Your Pleasure. For Your Pleasure?* Ray's handsome face frowned at the cracked cardboard spine. What were Roxy Music doing among the Ds?

Ray glared across at Robbie.

His twelve-year-old brother was reclining on his bed with a copy of *Shoot!* It was double games on Tuesday afternoons and there was a smudge of mud running right across the bridge of Robbie's nose, like war paint on the face of a Red Indian.

'You been touching my records again?' Ray said.

'No way, José,' Robbie said, not looking up from a feature on Charlie George.

Ray furiously filed Roxy Music next to the Rolling Stones, where they belonged. Then he turned back to his kid brother.

'Don't touch my records, okay? And if you *do* touch my records – *don't*, but if you *do* – put them back in the *right* place, okay? You don't put Roxy Music in with Dylan and the Doors.'

Robbie mimed a yawn. 'I've got my own records,' he said.

Ray laughed. 'Yeah, *Disney Favourites* and *Alvin Stardust's Greatest Hits.*'

Robbie looked up, stung. It was the brutal truth. Robbie only owned two records.

'I'm getting *In the City* for Christmas.' His brother had recently seen the Jam on *Top of the Pops*. It had been love at first sight. 'Mum's getting it for me.'

Ray ignored his brother. Bickering with a kid was beneath him. He pulled out *Pretzel Logic* by Steely Dan, the cover – that old man selling pretzels, that frozen American street – as familiar as the bedroom he shared with his baby brother. It was as if his record collection was the real world, and the place where he lived was the dream.

He loved the way that albums demanded your attention. The way you held them in both hands and they filled your vision and all you could see was their beauty. For a moment he thought of the girl last night, the *Bouquet of Barbed Wire* press offi ... .

There was a girl on the cover of *Pretzel Logic*, in the background, walking away, hair long and trousers flared, a girl that probably looked just like Ali McGraw in *Love Story*. He wondered about her life, and who she loved, and how he could ever meet her. Ray Keeley ached for a girl of his own. Holding that album was like holding that girl. Or as close as he would ever get.

'Ray! Robbie! Your tea's ready,' his mother called up from the foot of the stairs. Ray sighed with appreciation as he closed the sleeve.

His father was sitting in his favourite armchair like some suburban sultan while his mum carried plates of bread and jam into the front room. Ray's parents were an unlikely match – his mother a small nervous woman, jumping at shadows, his father as broad as he was tall, a bull of a man in carpet slippers, and these days always on the edge of anger.

Above the new fireplace – the real fire had just been ripped out and replaced with a gas job that had fake coals and unlikely-looking flames – there were photographs in silver frames.

Ray's parents on their wedding day. Ray and his two brothers John and Robbie on a sightseeing junk in Hong Kong harbour, three little kids – Robbie small, Ray medium and John large – smiling and squinting in the blazing sub-tropical sunshine. Their father grinning proudly in the light khaki of the Hong Kong Police Force, looking like an overgrown boy scout in his shorts and woolly socks, his bony knees colonial white.

Somewhere in the middle Sixties the photographs turned from black and white to colour. And among the colour photos there was John, eighteen years old now, in the darker uniform of the British Army, taken just before he was killed when an IRA bomb went off on a country road in South Armagh. It was the most recent photograph. Nothing had been right since then.

On the television, young women in swimming suits and high heels were staring ahead with fixed smiles as Matt Monro moved among them singing 'Thank Heaven for Little Girls'.

Ray and his mum sat on the sofa and Robbie sprawled between them on the floor. Everybody drank diluted orange cordial apart from his father, who had a cloudy glass of home-made beer by his feet.

'Now how can you compare some tart from Bongo Bongo Land with some tart from England?' he asked. 'It's not fair on them, is it? The darkies. Completely different standards of beauty.'

Ray rolled his eyes. The same old stuff, on and on, never ending. They said that travel broadened the mind. They had obviously never met his father.

'I might marry a black woman,' Ray said through a mouthful of Mother's Pride and Robertson's strawberry jam, the one with the smiling Golliwog cavorting on the jar. 'Your grandchildren might be half black. Did that ever occur to you, Dad?'

A cloud seemed to pass across his father's face. 'What about the kids? The little half-castes? Did you ever think about them? Not belonging to any group. How do you think that feels?'

'If we all got mixed up together then there wouldn't be any more racism,' Ray said. 'Because then we would all be the same. Got any more blackcurrant, Mum?'

It was one of the things he argued about with his father. Along with the volume and value of his music, the length of his hair and John Lennon. It felt like they argued about everything these days. Ray wished he knew a black woman just so he could marry her and show his father that all men were brothers.

'Birds of a feather,' Ray's father said, pointing his knife at Ray. 'You don't see robins flying about with crows, do you?'

'Are you a crow, Dad? Are you a robin?'

'She's nice,' his mum said. 'Miss Korea. What one do you like, Robbie?'

'I don't like any of them!' Robbie said, blushing furiously. Ray laughed. He knew that his brother liked all of them. He wasn't fussy. He had heard Robbie fiddling about in his stripy pyjamas when he thought that Ray was sleeping.

'Enoch's right,' his father said. 'Send them all back.'

'What if they come from here?' Ray said, pushing the last of his bread and jam into his mouth. 'Where you going to send them back to, Dad?'

With his father still ranting about birds of a feather and beasts in the wild, Ray got up and carried his plate out to the kitchen and went upstairs to his bedroom. He knew what he needed, and put on the Who as loud as he dared – '5.15', sad and angry all at once, to match the way he felt.

> *Why should I care?*
> *Why should I care?*

As he made sure that he had enough tube fare to get him back to the city, Ray remembered something he had heard at *The Paper*. Skip Jones had told him that taking heroin was like stepping into a golden bubble – your troubles melted away when you were in there. That was how Ray felt about his music. It made the world go away.

But from downstairs came the rank stench of home-made beer – bitter hops, liquid malt extract and priming syrup, the whole sorry mess fermenting in the huge metal vats for weeks at a time – and it almost made him gag. That was the problem with living at home with his parents.

Ray's floor would always be his father's ceiling.

Leon stood at the hermetically sealed windows of *The Paper*, watching the sun going down and the crowds leaving the tower block, scuttling to Waterloo station and home.

When he was certain that most of them had gone, he went to the washroom and stared into the mirror above the sink. He waited for a few moments, heard a cleaner clatter by, and then slowly removed his hat.

Leon's hair was thick and wiry, like something you would use for scrubbing pans, but what was most striking about it was that a few hours earlier it had been dyed a virulent orange. Autumn Gold, it had said on the packet.

Leon winced as if he had been slapped. He quickly replaced his hat, gripped the brim with both hands and firmly pulled it down over his ears. It was a disaster. As always.

Leon hated his hair. And Leon's hair hated him right back.

There was a line from a Rod Stewart song, back when Leon was fifteen years old and Rod was still big mates with John Peel and playing the working-class hero – kicking footballs around on *Top of the Pops*, pretending he was fresh off the terraces, before he developed that embarrassing taste for straw boaters and blazers and high-maintenance blondes and Art Deco lamps, and everyone had to pretend that they had never liked him in the first place.

It was the first line of the first track on *Every Picture Tells A Story* – the line that rhymed 'mirror' and 'inferior'. Leon always felt like that song had been written about him.

He knew there were battles to fight now. The middle ground was collapsing, and the Fascists were getting stronger. Not the public-bar bigots, the Alf Garnetts ranting on the sofa, but real Jew-baiting, Paki-bashing Fascists. Out there right now, getting bolder by the day, their numbers swelling, the hate spreading like a virus. Leon had seen their faces at Lewisham, clocked their proud Nazi salutes, and glimpsed what was inside them. There was nothing remotely funny about them, these dreamers of repatriation, these would-be builders of new ovens. Something had to be done.

So why the fuck, Leon asked himself, was he still worried about his hair? You didn't need a good haircut at the barricades.

He slung his record bag over his shoulder. Inside it was the latest edition of his fanzine, *Red Mist*. Too valuable to leave lying around the office, Leon believed. Someone might steal it.

The fanzine – a Xeroxed mix of radical politics, new music and cut up kidnapper's graphics, hastily stapled together – had landed Leon his job on *The Paper* eighteen months ago, reminding some of the older guys of their radical youth. But there were sighs and rolling eyes when Leon tried to sell *Red Mist* in the office, and when he said they should have more politics and less showbiz.

'We're a music paper, man,' they told him every day, as if the music could ever be separated from what was going on in the street, as if music wasn't a part of the real world but just some playpen that they climbed into for light entertainment.

Leon believed that the new music could be a force for social change. The fire still burned. The audience just needed to be radicalised. And the musicians just needed to be educated. Basically all you needed to change was everything.

Most of the new groups just didn't get it. They dreamed of the same old stuff – sexual opportunities, uncut white drugs and driving a Rolls-Royce into a swimming pool. They thought that anti-Nazism was just a cool brand name to be dropped in interviews, just another pose to be struck, as empty as Mick Jagger marching to Grosvenor Square to stop the Vietnam War in the Sixties.

But Leon knew this was real. The Labour Government wasn't going to last for ever. Jim Callaghan wasn't going to be around for much longer. And then what would happen? Fighting in the streets, Leon reckoned. Struggle. Civil unrest. More riots. Read your history books, he thought. Ask A. J. P. Taylor. See what happens when the centre is too weak to hold. A Lewisham every day of the year.

And when it was all over, from the ashes would rise a better world where racism was defeated and Leon's hair did exactly what it was told to do.

THREE

'I tell you, Dag Wood is hung like Red Rum,' Terry said. 'When he gets it out, it's like – I don't know – an Indian snake charmer . . . or a sailor with a rope . . . he sort of has to *unfurl* it.'

This was one of the best parts of the job, Terry thought. Coming home and telling your mates what had happened, all the interesting stuff that you weren't allowed to put in a magazine that they sold in sweet shops. He loved it. He looked over at Misty sitting on his desk and she smiled encouragement. He knew how to tell a story.

'Now are you sure it was Red Rum?' Leon said, slightly bashful in the presence of Misty. He had only recently learned how to be around her without blushing. He was sitting on his desk, knees drawn up to his chin, smiling as Terry paced their little office, holding his hands out like a fisherman measuring the one that got away. 'Are you sure it wasn't Arkle he was hung like?'

'What's Red Rum?' Ray said, swinging back and forth in his chair, fiddling with his tape recorder, his hair falling in his face.

'Famous racehorse,' Leon said. 'Won the Grand National lots of times. Despite being built like Dag Wood.'

'Definitely Red Rum,' Terry said. 'I got a good look. We were standing at these traffic lights, right? Just me and Dag, in the middle of the night. And he's asking me about the scene in London – how good the bands really are, what the audience are going to make of him – and this VW Beetle pulls up at a red light, and Dag whips it out – *unfurls* himself – and then . . . takes a leak on the Beetle with this enormous thing.' Terry shook his head. He still couldn't believe it. The outrageous act had been done so casually, so naturally, that he still couldn't work out if Dag had done it to shock him, or if he was truly that untamed. 'I'll never forget the look on that Beetle driver's face.'

Misty slid off Terry's desk and half-raised a hand in salute, leaving their office with a wry smile and a raised eyebrow, like a wife of twenty-five years who enjoyed the story, but who had heard it before: Dag taking cocaine until his ears bled, Dag reducing a woman reporter from Fleet Street to tears, Dag banging groupies two at a time after his girlfriend had left town.

There were things about Dag that had made Terry uncomfortable – the cruelty, the casual, almost gluttonous infidelity, the choice of drugs – everybody in London under the age of twenty-five believed that cocaine was the chemical equivalent of a feather cut. But Dag had been like every rock star that Terry had ever met – a great seducer.

Dag had gone out of his way to make Terry love him – giving him a book of Van Gogh's letters to his brother Theo that Dag had been given by David Bowie – there was a neatly written inscription at the front – borrowing some instruments in a West Berlin jazz bar so that Dag and his band could play a few of their greatest hits, showing him his extraordinary cock – and so Terry did.

In fact, Terry loved Dag so very much that there was one thing he had left out of both his piece and the other story he told his friends. Dag looked old.

Really old. Horribly old. If you could imagine Rip Van Winkle as a porn star, then you were getting the general idea about Dag Wood and the way he looked.

Terry had been so eager to hero worship Dag, so desperate to lionise this man that all the new bands name checked as a major influence, so hungry to be his best friend that he hadn't had the heart to say how prehistoric Dag looked.

Dag's body – which he showed off at every possible opportunity, habitually tearing off his shirt not just on stage but during interviews and at sound checks and at the hotel's buffet breakfast – was still in great shape, lean and pumped, like one of those Charles Atlas ads at the back of DC and Marvel comics.

But the ravages of ten thousand nights of debauchery and depravity were in every deeply ploughed line of Dag's face, like Dorian Gray in silver lamé trousers with his hair dyed white. Dag Wood looked like a recently deceased bodybuilder. But Terry kept that to himself. Because it didn't fit his story.

The three of them looked up as the editor of *The Paper* appeared in their doorway. Kevin White was twenty-nine years old, and every inch a grown-up version of the Mod he had once been. The only man in the office who came to work in a suit. White was tall, powerfully built, with curtain-parting hair, like one of the Small Faces around the time of 'Lazy Sunday'.

'Can I see you in my office, Ray?'

Ray shoved his tape recorder in his desk and followed White to his office. Leon pulled a copy of *Red Mist* out of his shoulder bag and began thumbing through it. Terry sat at his desk, closed his eyes and sighed with contentment.

It was good, yes, telling his friends was good. Almost the best part.

But when Terry introduced Dag Wood to Misty later at the Western World, and they both saw just how much the other one loved him, then it would be perfect.

'So how's it going?'

Kevin White slumped into his chair and put his feet on his desk. The editor had the only corner office in *The Paper*, and Ray could see what seemed like all of London stretching out behind him.

'It's going okay,' Ray said, making his fringe fall forward over his face. Even after three years, he couldn't quite get over this shyness he felt around the editor. Ray had known White since he was fifteen years old, turning up in the reception of *The Paper* with a handwritten think piece on the Eagles when he should have been writing about *An Inspector Calls* for an English Literature paper. White had never treated him with anything but kindness. But somehow that only made Ray's shyness worse. It was funny. Ray had never yet met a rock star that he felt in awe of, but he was in awe of Kevin White.

'Your mum okay?'

She's on the Valium, Ray thought. She cries in her sleep. Sometimes she can't get out of bed in the morning. If you mention John she looks like she's been given an electric shock.

'She's all right,' Ray said.

White glanced at the photograph on his desk of two smiling toddlers, a small boy and a smaller girl. He was the only person in the office who had a photo of children on his desk.

'I can't imagine what she's been through,' White said, more to himself than Ray. 'No parent should ever have to bury their child.'

Ray didn't know what to say. Unless they were talking about music, he always felt tongue-tied around the editor. Like every other writer on *The Paper*, Ray thought that White was touched with greatness. Everybody knew the story. Even the readers.

In the early Seventies *The Paper* was a pop rag in terminal decline, called *The Music Paper*, if anything could ever be that corny – but then all music papers had corny titles, from *Melody Maker* to *New Musical Express* to *Sounds* to *Disc*, they all had names that had sounded groovy back when dinosaurs walked the earth – and Kevin White had saved it.

White had left school at fifteen, working on the print at the *Daily Express* with his father, his uncles, his brothers and his cousins until some bright spark above stairs asked the teenage Mod to write 500 words on a Motown revue – a dream ticket with the Four Tops, the Supremes, Stevie Wonder, Martha Reeves and the Vandellas and Smokey Robinson and the Miracles all on one bill. White never looked back, and he was a junior reporter on *The Music Paper* when the big chance came. The suits upstairs gave White three months to increase advertising revenue and double the circulation, or they were going to put *The Music Paper* out of its misery.

White dropped the *Music* from the masthead, fired all the old farts who were nostalgic for the days when the big news was the Tremeloes' tour and Herman's Hermits' secret heartache and whether Peter Tork was going to leave the Monkees. In a daring last throw of the dice, White kept the title alive by hiring heads, freaks and hairies from what was left of the underground press, because the underground press was dead or dying too. It felt like everything was dying in the early Seventies.

Ray could imagine the looks on their faces at *Horse and Hound* when the new writers started turning up for work, all those refugees from *Oz* and *Red Dwarf* and *Friendz* and *IT* who filled *The Paper* with tales of bands that all the other heads, freaks and hairies knew by affectionate abbreviations. Heep. Floyd. Quo. Lizzy. Tull. Zep. And those writers loved Kevin White, just as Ray loved him, because White had the guts and the vision to do something that nobody else in this entire tower block of magazines would ever do – he gave you your first chance.

'You just got back, didn't you?' White said.

Ray nodded, on surer ground now the talk was moving on to bands. 'Thin Lizzy,' he said. 'Leicester and Birmingham. Two thousand words. Centre spread.'

'Good tour?' White said.

Ray nodded, smiling. Thin Lizzy had been the first band he ever went on the road with, and they would always have a special place in his heart. When Ray had been a bumbling schoolboy with absolutely no idea how to conjure a two-page feature out of forty-eight hours with a band, Phil Lynott, the band's black Irish frontman, had taken care of him – showed Ray that on the road it was okay to drink screwdrivers at breakfast if they calmed you down, coached Ray on how to conduct an interview, and even turned on Ray's tape recorder when it was time to talk.

'You've written about them before, haven't you?' White said.

'This will be the third feature,' Ray said.

White sighed, and something about that sound sent a sense of dread crawling up Ray's spine. For the first time since entering the editor's office, he felt that this was going to be bad.

'Yeah, you've been doing this for a while, haven't you?' White took his feet off the desk and looked out the window. 'And that's the big problem with this job. You can only do it for so long.'

Ray felt sick to his stomach. That was the flip side of White's fresh-blood policy – it meant some guy at the far side of his twenties quietly being put out to pasture.

But surely not me, Ray thought. I'm young. And I've got nowhere else to go. Nowhere else I want to be.

'It's like this, Ray,' the editor said, talking more quickly now, wanting to get it over with. 'We can't send you to interview the new groups.'

'But – Thin Lizzy!'

White held up a hand. 'Hardly new. And that's different. We all love the first band we went on the road with. You can't do that every week.' Then White was leaning forward, almost pleading. 'I need writers who I can send to interview Johnny Rotten and Elvis Costello and Dag Wood.' White sighed with exasperation. 'And that's not you, is it? Look at your hair.'

Ray suddenly saw himself in White's eyes and – beyond the paternal affection and friendly chitchat – Ray saw that he looked ridiculous.

The music had changed, as the music always will, and Ray had not changed with it. Suddenly *The Paper* didn't need a young head who was still hung up on the flowers-in-your-hair thing. It was a joke, *man*. Ray still believed in the whole peace and love and acoustic guitars thing that everybody was sneering about now. How could you send someone like that to talk to John Lydon? What would the Clash think?

He was no longer the little star. The world had changed while he wasn't looking. It was like Ray – Beatles fan, California dreamer, the hippy child who was born ten years too late – was a star of the silent era, and talkies had just come in. He watched the editor pick up a copy of *The Paper* and turn to the section for album reviews.

'Listen to this,' White said. '*Another slice of New Nihilism for all you crazy pop kids, and it's like staring into an abyss of meaninglessness.*'

Ray listened to his words being read. His mood improved. He had been reasonably pleased with it, especially the bit about *the abyss of meaninglessness*. That sounded pretty good. That sounded like something Skip Jones might write.

'What's wrong with it?' Ray said mildly.

Kevin White scowled at him, and Ray flinched. The editor could be scary when he wanted to be. For five years he had bossed an office full of precocious, overgrown adolescents, all of them high-IQ misfits, many of them habitual users of illegal substances. He knew how to control a meeting.

'*The abyss of meaninglessness?*' White threw the paper on his desk. 'It's KC and the Sunshine Band!' Then his voice softened. White had seen it all before. Writers who were once part of the *zeitgeist* – a word that was freely bandied around in the offices of *The Paper* – but now belonged to yesterday, writers who had done their stint on *The Paper*, their bit for rock and roll, and didn't realise that it was time to be moving on. Writers who had lived for music suddenly discovering that everything they heard disgusted them, suddenly discovering that the music didn't live for them.

'This new music . . .' Ray shook his head, and a veil of yellow hair fell in front of his face. He brushed it away. 'Tear it down, smash it up. No words you can understand, no tunes you can hear.'

'Who are you?' White said angrily. 'My maiden aunt from Brighton?'

Ray hated it when the editor raised his voice. It reminded him of home.

'What's happening?' Ray said. 'I don't understand what's happening.'

But he understood only too well. He should have been writing ten years ago, when it really felt like this music was going to change the world. 1967 – summer of love, year of wonders, the year of *Sgt Pepper*, when music was still pushing back the boundaries, when people still believed in something. He should have been in London when heads and hearts were still open, when there was still the possibility of glimpsing the Beatles playing live on a rooftop in Savile Row. He should have been tooling around and taking notes when the world still believed in love, enlightenment and John Lennon. And he should definitely have been at Woodstock, chanting *no rain, no rain* in the mud, with flowers in his hair and a California girl in his sleeping bag, a mellow smoke on the go, good acid in his veins turning everything the colour of sunshine, and maybe Arlo Guthrie up on stage singing. Instead of having to wait until the film came out in the grey light of a colder, drabber new decade. Yes, those few days on Yasgur's farm really summed it all up for Ray.

Were you at Woodstock?

No, but I saw the film with my mum.

Kevin White took a deep breath.

'Maybe, Ray, maybe a move from the staff to freelance would be good for you, and good for the paper.'

Ray's eyes were hot. 'Would I still have my desk?' he asked.

White shifted uncomfortably. 'Well, probably we would have to give your desk to someone else.'

Ray could see it now. He would be like one of the freelancers who came into the office hoping to be tossed a bone – a minor album to review, a lesser gig to attend – while the stars of *The Paper* wrote the cover stories, while Terry and Leon flew around the world, and got their picture next to their by-line. No desk to call his own, never really belonging, on the way out.

'This is the only job I want,' Ray said, and it was true. Ray could not imagine his life without *The Paper*, without his friends, without the comforting routines and rituals of rock and roll – going on the road, doing the singles, having somewhere to come every day, somewhere that felt more like home than the house where he lived. He had loved it as a reader, and he loved it as a writer. On either side of the looking glass, it was in his blood.

'Then you're going to have to give me something fast,' White said, embarrassed that he had to act like the boss of IBM or something. '*Something I can use.*'

At that moment Leon Peck burst into the editor's office. 'Let me read you something,' he said. 'Sorry and all that – this won't take long.'

White and Ray stared at Leon. 'Don't you knock?' White said. 'And what's with the stupid hat?'

'The Nazis are coming back,' Leon said, tugging self-consciously at his trilby. 'So maybe we should worry a little less about bourgeois convention and a little more about stopping them.' He cleared his throat and read from the copy of the *Sunday Telegraph* he was holding. '*It is a disquieting fact, recognised by all the major political parties, that more and more people are giving their support to groups which believe in taking politics to the street.*'

'What's the point?' White said.

Under the brim of his hat, Leon's eyes were shining with emotion. 'Boss, I was down there on Saturday. Look, look,' he said, pointing at the bruise under his eye. 'Look what they did to me.'

'You'll live,' White said. Ray noticed he was a lot rougher with Leon than he was with him. But then Leon hadn't been just a kid when he first walked into *The Paper*.

'Let me write something,' Leon begged. 'Give me next week's cover. Hitler said that if they'd crushed him when he was small, he would never have succeeded.'

'This shower are just a bunch of skinheads, that's all,' White said, taking the *Sunday Telegraph* from Leon and looking at the picture of the flag-waving mob. 'They couldn't find their own arse without a road map, I can't see them invading Poland.' He handed back the newspaper. 'And Elvis Costello is on next week's cover.' White thought about it. 'But all right – you can give me 500 words on Lewisham. Anybody go to this demo?'

Leon smiled. 'I'm assuming you don't mean thousands of anti Fascist protesters, boss. I guess you mean rock stars. Concerned rock stars.'

White rolled his eyes. 'Anyone our readers might've heard of.'

'No, they were all too busy doing photo shoots and getting their teeth capped to fight Fascism. But I hear John Lennon is in town.'

Ray's jaw fell open. He stared at Leon, not believing a word of it. 'Lennon's in New York,' he said. 'In the Dakota with Yoko and baby Sean.'

Leon shook his head. 'Lennon's in London,' he said. 'For one night only. Someone at EMI just called me. Thought it might make an item in the diary. Passing through on his way to Japan.' Leon cackled. 'Give me McCartney any day of the week. At least Paul *knows* he's a boring old fart who sold out years ago. Think Beatle John would fancy pinning on his Chairman Mao badge and coming to the next riot? Has he still got his beret? Or should we start the revolution without him?'

'Well, he started it without you,' Kevin White said. 'Come on – what are you doing for us, Leon?'

Leon's face fell. Ray knew that's what they always said when they wanted you to get in line. *What are you doing for us?* 'Well, mostly I'll be working on this riot story,' Leon said. 'I thought we could call it *Dedicated Followers of Fascism.* Maybe –'

White consulted a scrap of paper on his desk. 'Leni and the Riefenstahls are at the Red Cow tonight. You can give me a review of that by first thing tomorrow morning – 800 words.'

Leon nodded. 'So that's 500 words for the fight against Fascism, and 800 words for Leni and the Riefenstahls – who less than a year ago were parading around the 100 Club in swastika armbands. Right.'

'We're still a music paper, Leon.'

Leon laughed. 'That's right. We're doing the pogo while Rome burns.'

'A good journalist can write well about anything. Look at that piece by your father this morning. You see that?' White asked, turning to Ray. 'A piece about the cod war – what could be more boring than the cod war?'

'I didn't see it,' Ray said, still thinking about John Lennon. But he knew that Leon's father wrote a column for a liberal broadsheet. He was one of the few journalists in Fleet Street that was read and respected up at *The Paper.*

'It was about the decline of Britain as an imperial power,' White told Ray. 'About how we used to go to war to fight for freedom. And now we go to war to fight about fish. Brilliant.' White shook his head. 'Brilliant. Tell him how much I liked it, would you?'

'Bit tricky that,' Leon said, edging towards the door.

'Why's that?' White said.

'I don't talk to my father.'

They were all silent for a bit. Leon caught Ray's eye and looked away.

'Oh,' White said. 'Okay.'

Leon closed the door behind him. Ray realised that the editor of *The Paper* was watching his face.

'So,' White said. 'Think you can get me John Lennon?'

Ray gawped, feeling the sweat break out on his face. 'Get you John Lennon? Who do I call? How do I get you John Lennon?'

White laughed. 'You don't call anyone. There's no one to call. No press officers, no publicists. EMI can't help you – this is a private trip. You just go out there and *find* him. Then you *talk* to him. Like a real grown-up reporter. Like a real journalist. Like Leon's father. Like that. Think you can do it?'

There was so much that Ray wanted to say to John Lennon that he was sure he would not be able to say a word. Even if he could find him among the ten million souls in that Waterloo sunset.

'I don't know,' Ray said honestly.

'If you find him,' White said, his blood starting to pump, his editor's instincts kicking in, 'we'll put him on the cover. World exclusive – John talks!'

'But – but what about pictures?'

White looked exasperated. 'Not Lennon the way he is now – he must be knocking on for forty! No, an old shot from the archives. Lennon the way he was in Hamburg – short hair and a leather jacket, skinny and pale. You know what that would look like, don't you?'

Ray thought about it. 'That would look like . . . now.'

'Exactly! *Very* 1977. *Totally* 1977. Nothing could be more now than the way the Beatles looked in Hamburg. They were out of their boxes on speed, did you know that? I can see the cover copy: *Another kid in a leather jacket on his way to God knows where . . .*'

'But Leon says he's leaving tomorrow!'

White's fist slammed down on his desk. 'Come on, Ray. Are you a writer – or a fan?'

Ray needed to think about that. He had no idea if he was a real journalist, or if he would ever be. How could you tell? Who had ever dreamed that loving music would turn into a full-time job? He was a kid who had written about music because it was more interesting than a paper round, and because they didn't give you free records if you stacked shelves in a supermarket.

'I don't know what I am,' he said.

But Kevin White was no longer listening. The editor was staring over at the door, and Ray followed his gaze. On the other side of the rectangular pane of glass, there were men in suits waiting to see Kevin White. Men from upstairs, management, bald old geezers with ties and wrinkles who looked like your dad, or somebody's dad. They were waiting for White to finish with Ray. Sometimes White had to smooth things out with them. One time a cleaner found a wastepaper bin full of roaches, and suddenly there were men in suits everywhere, all having a fit. But White worked it out. He was a great editor. Ray didn't want to let him down.

'I'll try my best,' Ray said. 'But I don't know if I'm a real journalist or just somebody who likes music.'

Kevin White stood up. It was time for him to face the men in suits again.

'You'd better find out,' the editor said.

Leon was gone. Terry was sitting on his desk, his DMs dangling, flicking through the copy of last week's *Paper* that Misty had given him at the airport.

'This is what you need, Ray,' he said. '*New! The Gringo Waistcoat.*

Get into the Original Gringo Waistcoat – the new style. You'd loo. lovely in a Gringo Waistcoat.'

Ray dropped into his chair and stared into space. Terry didn't notice. It was an endless source of amusement to him that the classifieds in *The Paper* were always exactly one year behind the times. While the kid in the street was trying to look like Johnny Rotten, the models in the ads still looked like Jason King.

Cotton-drill loons – still only £2.80 . . . Moccasin boots – choose from one long top fringe or three freaky layers.

According to the classifieds, the readers of *The Paper* were wearing exactly what they had been wearing for the last ten years – flared jeans, Afghan coats, cheesecloth galore, and, always and for ever, T-shirts with amusing slogans. Sometimes it felt like *The Paper* would not exist without T-shirts with amusing slogans.

I CHOKED LINDA LOVELACE. LIE DOWN I THINK I LOVE YOU. SEX APPEAL – GIVE GENEROUSLY. And that timeless classic, the fucking flying ducks – two cartoon ducks, coupling in mid-flight, the male duck looking hugely satisfied, the female duck looking alarmed.

Terry leaned back, smiling to himself, his spiky head resting against a picture he had torn from a library book and sellotaped to his wall – Olga Korbut, smiling sweetly, bent double on the mat. After the Montreal Olympics last year, a lot of people had switched their affections to the Romanian girl, Nadia Comaneci, but Terry was sticking with Olga.

They each had their own wall, facing their desk with its type-writer, a sleek Olivetti Valentine in red moulded plastic. On Terry's wall were bands and girls – record company 8x10 glossies of the New York Dolls, the Clash and the Sex Pistols plus images pillaged from magazines of Debbie Harry in a black mini-dress, Jane Fonda in *Barbarella* and Olga Korbut at the Munich Olympics.

Leon's wall was by far the most artistic – an undercoat of favourite bands had been almost obliterated by headlines cut from newspapers, with yet another layer of breaking news and advertising slogans pasted on top. So a record company glossy of the Buzzcocks had a headline about the death of Mao Tse-Tung running diagonally across it, while a yellowing picture from *The Times* of General Franco's coffin was enhanced with an ad for the new Only Ones single. And as Ray swung round in his chair and took out his tape recorder, he was watched by pictures of John Lennon.

There were also dog-eared images of Joni Mitchell and Dylan and Neil Young, but Ray's wall was really a shrine to Lennon. John gone solo, in white suit and round NHS specs, Yoko hanging on to his arm. John when he had just started growing his hair, that golden middle period of *Revolver* and *Rubber Soul.* John during Beatlemania, grinning in a suit with the rest of the boys. And the leather-jacket John of Hamburg, all James Dean cock and swagger, too vain to wear his glasses . . .

This fucking, fucking tape recorder!

The problem was that one of the spools was slightly off kilter. Ray had probably bent it pulling out the cassette after interviewing Phil Lynott with one too many screwdrivers and half a spliff in his system. Now the spool described an erratic circle when it should be standing up straight. You couldn't stick this thing in front of John Lennon.

Terry guffawed. 'Listen to this,' he said. 'Couple of girls trying to get up a petition to get Roxy Music back on the road – they say, *Roxy Must Rule Again.*'

Ray looked over his shoulder, smiling at his friend. The classi-

STORIES WE COULD TELL

Tony Parsons began his career as a writer on *NME*, interviewing everyone from The Sex Pistols, Blondie and The Clash, to the Rolling Stones, Bowie and Springsteen. His novel *Man and Boy* is a publishing phenomenon, selling two million copies in 36 countries and winning the UK Book of the Year prize. His subsequent novels – *One for My Baby, Man and Wife* and *The Family Way* – were all number 1 bestsellers. The film rights to *The Family Way* have been sold to Julia Roberts. Tony Parsons lives in London.

Visit www.AuthorTracker.co.uk for exclusive information on Tony Parsons.

D0424176

Praise for *Stories We Could Tell*:

'Tony's book tells of love, London and leather jackets, of growing up fast in a world where words and music were all we had to hold on to, while the decade crumbled around us. Read it and weep.' Robert Elms

'Characterised by an utterly personal choice of subjects – parenthood, friendship, love, betrayal, men trying to juggle their commitments – and an utterly personal way of telling them.' *Guardian*

'A funny, affectionate and heart-warming page-turner.' *Irish Independent*

'Tony Parsons' blistering new novel doesn't just capture the mood of the time but tells it exactly like it is and reads like the novel he was always destined to write.' *Mirror*

'Parsons manages three fast, action-packed plots like a practised juggler.' *Observer*

'Parsons looks at friendship and love through the eyes of three young men. Set on the night Elvis dies, it oozes rock'n'roll.' *Grazia*

'August 16, 1977 was obviously a good day to be horny and work in music journalism.' *Daily Telegraph*

'Fun, raunchy and touching.' *Good Housekeeping*

STORIES
WE COULD
TELL

Tony Parsons

HarperCollins*Publishers*

HarperCollins*Publishers*
77–85 Fulham Palace Road,
Hammersmith, London W6 8JB

www.harpercollins.co.uk

This paperback edition 2006

First published in Great Britain by
HarperCollins*Publishers* 2005

A catalogue record for this book
is available from the British Library.

ISBN-13 978 0 00 715126 4
ISBN-10 0 00 715126 8

This novel is entirely a work of fiction.
The names, characters and incidents portrayed in it
are the work of the author's imagination.
Any resemblance to real persons, living or dead,
events or localities is entirely coincidental.

Typeset in Minion by
Palimpsest Book Production Limited,
Polmont, Stirlingshire

Printed and bound in Great Britain by
Clays Ltd, St Ives plc

For David Morrison of Hong Kong

He always felt a bit down coming off the road. You were tired. You were hungover. There was a ringing in your ears from seeing two shows and two sound checks in the last forty-eight hours. And there was always some girl you liked who would be somewhere else tonight. And of course you were going home.

The youths came back, swigging from cans of Carlsberg Special Brew, a few of them leering at Ray with amused belligerence. He stared out of the window, trying to control his breathing, feeling his heart pounding inside his denim jacket. They were everywhere these days. But they're nothing compared to my father, he thought. My father would kill them.

Then he must have fallen asleep again, because when he awoke the sun was low, and it took Ray one foggy moment to realise that the fields were gone, there were graffiti-stained walls all around and people were collecting their bags as the train pulled into Euston.

16th August 1977, and here comes the night.

TWO

As Misty steered her father's Ford Capri along the Westway towards the city, Terry laid his right hand lightly on her leg, feeling the warmth of her flesh through the white dress, idly wondering what their children would look like, and loving that little swoon of longing he got every time he looked at her.

Misty was nineteen years old – three years younger than Terry – and although they had grown up within a few miles of each other, he was aware they were from very different places. More like different planets than different parts of the London sprawl. Misty's family rode horses and Terry's family bet on them.

He was born in a rented room above a butcher's shop and she grew up in a house crammed with books, her childhood full of pony clubs and prep schools, her old man some sort of hotshot lawyer – that's where the money came from. She was a bit vague about it all, but then you had to be embarrassed about it now, privilege was nothing to boast about in the summer of 1977.

But she didn't need to spell it out. Terry knew they were different. She knew where she was going and he kept expecting to be sent back to where he had escaped from. It wasn't as bad as it had been at the beginning. It wasn't as bad as his first day at *The Paper*. But then nothing could ever be as bad as that.

The memory of his humiliation could still make his face burn. Even now – with a girlfriend like Misty, with a friend like Dag Wood, with his latest story on the cover – the thought of that first day made him cringe.

This is how raw Terry was – he tried to return a review record. One of the older guys gave him a month-old album that nobody else was interested in, pointed him in the direction of the review room and left him to it. And when Terry had finished, when he had come up with his 300 smart-arse words on Be Bop Deluxe, he walked into the office where a few of the older guys sat, and he tried to give back the album. How they laughed! And how his face burned and burned.

He knew that one of the reasons he had been hired was because of the way he looked – that *On the Waterfront* thing that was back in style. The music wanted to be tough again. And there he was on his first morning, a Be Bop Deluxe record in his hand, his face all red and tears in his ears. He wouldn't have minded their amusement if they had been nothing to him, but these were writers he had admired for years. And they were laughing at him. They thought he was funny.

This was his dream job and it felt like he had just strolled into it. Desperate for new writers to cover the new music, *The Paper* had responded to Terry's carefully typed and Tipp-Exed reflections on *Born to Run* and a review of the Damned at the 100 Club (Bruce Springsteen and Rat Scabies – a nice combination of old and new school). They invited him into the office, where he met Kevin White, the ex-Mod editor who had practically invented *The Paper*, and White was quietly impressed that Terry had already seen some of the new bands live, and he liked the way Terry looked in his cheap leather jacket – luckily the interview was immediately after Terry had just pulled a night shift in the gin factory, so he looked fashionably knackered.

They hired him as a trainee journalist to cover this new music that was just starting to happen, this new music that none of the existing writers liked all that much or could even get a handle on. But getting the job turned out to be the easy bit.

Terry had once had a girlfriend who broke it off outside a Wimpy Bar, so he thought he knew about women. He had once smoked a joint that was more Rothman's King Size than Moroccan Red, so he thought he knew about drugs. And he had left school as soon as he could for a job in the local gin factory – a purely temporary measure until he became a world-famous writer – so he thought he knew about the real world. But Terry soon discovered that he knew nothing.

That terrible first day. He didn't know what to say – this young man who had always loved books, who had always loved words – it was as if he had lost the power of speech. He couldn't talk the way the older guys talked – the way they said everything with that never-ending cynical amusement, the ironic mocking edge that placed them above the rest of the world. Already he felt that he could write as well as any of them – apart from Skip Jones himself, obviously – but Terry didn't know the rules. How was he supposed to know you kept review copies? Until today he'd had to save up for any record he wanted.

It was like everyone else was speaking a language he didn't understand. He had a lot of catching up to do. Maybe too much. Maybe he would never catch up. And then he saw Misty's face for the very first time. And then he really knew that he was out of his depth.

One of the older guys parked Terry in the office he was to share with Leon Peck and Ray Keeley, the other young writers. Neither of them were there – Ray was at a Fleetwood Mac press conference somewhere in the West End, and Leon was on the road with Nils Lofgren. So while Terry waited for one of the older guys to find him something to do after finishing Be Bop Deluxe, he played with his typewriter, and looked in the drawers of his empty desk. And then he heard her, explaining something to the picture editor, and climbed on his desk to see the owner of that cool, confident voice.

The office was divided by grey, seven-foot-high partitions that made up the individual offices. It looked like a corporate maze. But if you knelt on your desk you could see over the top of the partitions. Two offices down he saw her – shockingly gorgeous, although he could not work out why. It was something to do with the way she carried herself. But he felt it for the first time – the little swoon of longing.

'I've gone for a look of emptiness and stillness,' she was telling the picture editor. 'I think you'll find it's redolent of the Gerard Malanga shots of Warhol and the Velvet Underground.'

She had been taking pictures of Boney M.

Together Misty and the picture editor were poring over her contact sheets, these glossy black sheets of paper with tiny photographs – Terry had never seen a contact sheet before – drawing lines in red felt-tip around the shots they liked, then finally choosing one image by placing a cross next to it. Like a kiss, Terry thought, knowing already that it was hopeless. She was way out of his league.

'I know they're ridiculous,' Misty was saying. 'But it's like Warhol himself said, *Everybody's plastic, but I love plastic.*'

She looked up then and caught Terry's eye and he attempted a smile that came out as an idiot leer. She frowned impatiently, and it just made her look prettier, and made him ache with hopeless yearning. And just then the two older guys came for him.

They loped into his office with no door, all faded denim and lank hair, untouched by the changes happening on what Terry and everyone else on *The Paper* thought of as *the street*.

'Smoke, man?' one of them said.

Terry was immediately on his feet, practically snapping to attention, and holding out a packet of Silk Cut. And the older guys looked at each other and smiled.

Five minutes later Terry felt like he was dying.

With the giant spliff still in his hand, Terry shivered and shuddered, the sweat pouring down his face, his back, making his capped T-shirt stick to his skin. He wanted to lie down. He wanted to be sick. He wanted it all to be over.

The older guys had stopped cackling with laughter and were starting to look concerned. Their faces swam in front of Terry's rolling eyes. One of them prised the joint from Terry's fist.

'Are you okay, man?'

'He's *really* wasted, man.'

They were in the shadow of the monstrous grey tower block that was home to *The Paper* – an entire skyscraper full of magazines about every subject under the sun, from stamp collecting and hunting foxes and cars and football and knitting all the way to music, three titles on every floor – loitering in a scrap of wasteland that doubled as a makeshift car park, overlooking a silvery patch of the Thames and the mournful tug boats.

'Don't feel well,' Terry croaked. 'Might sit down. Until I feel better.'

The older guys went, leaving him to his fate. It was ... now what was the word? What was the word that people on *The Paper* had used all morning when something was even slightly out of the ordinary, like the lady who came round with the sandwiches running out of cheese-and-tomato rolls? Oh yes – Terry remembered the word. It was *surreal.*

His thoughts felt like they were being formed in quicksand. He could taste his stomach in his mouth. He pressed his clammy face against the tower block, moaning, and felt the entire skyscraper slide away from him. Surreal didn't quite cover it. Terry had been poisoned.

And then Ray Keeley was standing before him.

Even through the thick fog of industrial-strength ganja, Terry knew it was him. Ray was wearing a Stetson, like Dennis Hopper in *Easy Rider*, and it made him look like a hallucination, a vision of the Old West glimpsed on the banks of the Thames.

Ray Keeley was only seventeen, but Terry had been reading his stuff for years. Every week Terry looked at Ray's by-line picture in *The Paper* – he looked like those early shots of Jackson Browne, the open-faced matinee idol eyes peering out from behind the veil of long, lank, wheat-coloured hair – a teenage hippy heart-throb – and the envy came at Terry in waves, like a toothache.

Ray was the rising star on *The Paper* in the mid-Seventies, a pretty and precocious fifth-former rhapsodising about Joni Mitchell, Jackson Browne and the whole California thing that seemed so very far away now. And Ray liked the Beatles, especially the Beatles, even though they were further away than anything, even though they had broken up a full four years ago, and John was hiding in the Dakota and Paul was touring with his wife and Ringo was banging out the novelty records and George was disappearing up his own Hari Krishna.

You read Ray Keeley and you forgot about the three-day week and the miners' strike and the streets full of rat-infested rubbish that no one was ever going to collect. All the grey dreariness slipped away when you read Ray Keeley on seeing Dylan at Wembley, reviewing Joni Mitchell's *Court and Spark,* even trying to give Wings the benefit of the doubt. You read Ray and suddenly it was yesterday once more, summer in the Sixties, the party that everyone under the age of twenty-five had missed. You forgot about Ted Heath and thought about making love to Joni in the dunes on the beach at Monterey.

But Ray wasn't writing so much lately.

'You all right?' he asked Terry, with the expression of one who already knew the answer.

Terry shook his head, speechless, feeling as if his body was paralysed and his mind was broken and his tongue was the size of an oven glove.

Then Ray did something unexpected. He put his arm around him.

'You've got to take it easy with that stuff,' he said. 'These guys are used to it. You're not. Come on, let's get you back to the office. Before someone shops us.'

'How'd you know?' Terry mumbled. 'How'd you know me from *The Paper?*'

Ray grinned. 'Not from *Horse and Hound,* are you?'

Terry laughed. 'Nah!'

Ray half-dragged and half-carried Terry back to the office, and sat him at his desk, and gave him orange juice and black coffee until the shivering and the sweating and the sickness began to subside. Ray took care of Terry when he had been left to melt in the dirt by a couple of the older guys, and it was a simple act of decency that Terry would never forget. He tried to thank him but his tongue was a dead weight.

'Be cool, man,' Ray told him. 'Just take it easy now.'

All that first morning people had been telling Terry to be cool and take it easy. The music had changed, and most of the haircuts, and people were throwing away their flares and buying straight-legged trousers, but the language was still largely the lexicon of the Sixties.

For all the changes, for all the new things, a different language had yet to be invented. All that old-fashioned jive about being mellow and taking it easy and loving one another was still around. Be cool. Take it easy.

All that first morning these worn-out old words had sounded empty to Terry Warboys. But he found himself giving his new friend a stoned, wonky smile.

Because Terry thought that when Ray Keeley said these things, they actually sounded as though they meant something.

Ray let himself into the house, and was immediately assaulted by the smell of home-brewed beer and the sound of the television.

'*Miss Belgian Congo is a nineteen-year-old beautician who says her ambition is to travel, end all wars and meet Sacha Distel.*'

'Back again, are you?' the old man shouted, not stirring from his chair in front of the TV. 'Like a bloody hotel . . .'

It was true. Ray treated his parents' suburban semi like a hotel, coming and going without warning, never staying long. But the funny thing was he treated hotels like they were home. The last two nights, when he had been in the Holiday Inn in Birmingham and Travel Lodge in Leicester, he could not stop himself from making his hotel bed in the morning. It was as if his home was out there somewhere.

fieds were a magic kingdom of musicians wanted, records wanted, girlfriends wanted, perfect worlds wanted, where ads for Greenpeace and Save the Whales were right next to ads for cotton-drill loon pants and Gringo Waistcoats.

But Ray saw that though there was derision in Terry's laughter, there was also something that he could only identify as love.

This was their paper. This was their thing. This was their place. And soon he would be asked to leave. He didn't know how he could stand it.

'*Badge collectors read on,*' said Terry, and then he looked up at Ray. 'What the fuck's wrong with you?'

'Nothing.' When you grew up with brothers, you learned you always had to come straight back at them. 'What the fuck's wrong with you?'

Ray turned his back to Terry, busying himself at his desk, trying to straighten the bent spool on his tape recorder, and letting his hair fall forward so that his friend couldn't see the panic and pain in his eyes.

FOUR

Leon's squat was in a large, decaying white house on a street of boarded-up buildings.

There was a kind of muddy moat around the perimeter of the house with wooden planks leading across it, like the ramshackle drawbridge of a rotting castle. On the ground floor the cracked and crumbling white plaster was almost obliterated by slogans.

WE ARE THE WRITING ON YOUR WALL. NO DRUGS IN HERE. CATS LIKE PLAIN CRISPS. Someone had changed a scrawled white NF into a bold black NAZIS OUT.

Leon slipped his hand into his leather jacket and felt for his key, glancing over his shoulder before he began negotiating his way across the planks. He had been in the squat for over a year now, ever since he had dropped out of the LSE and started full time on *The Paper*, but there was still a taste of fear in his mouth whenever he came back. You never knew when the bailiffs and cops would be coming. You never knew what was waiting for you.

As soon as he was inside the hallway a hairy unwashed face appeared at the top of the stairs, as Leon knew it would, as it always did. It wasn't just Leon. There was a creeping paranoia about squat life that never really went away. It seemed strangely familiar to Leon, because he thought it was not so different to the suspicion lurking behind the net curtains of the rich suburb where he had grown up.

'Someone's waiting for you,' said the hairy face at the top of the stairs.

Leon was amazed. Nobody was ever waiting for him.

'Some straight,' said the hairy guy. 'Reckons he's your father.'

I *knew* it, Leon thought, his stomach sinking. I *knew* something bad was going to happen.

'The French guys don't like it,' said the face at the top of the stairs. 'We nearly didn't let him in.'

'You shouldn't have,' Leon said, trying to keep his voice calm, trying to pretend he was in control. He began climbing the stairs.

The squat was meant to be some kind of democracy, but in reality it was run by the French and Germans, who were older, who had been doing this for years, who talked about adventures in places like Paris and Amsterdam with such authority that Leon always fell silent, and felt like a kid who had seen nothing of the world. Leon was furious that his father should embarrass him in front of these great men.

At the top of the stairs he heard the usual babble of languages and sounds. The floorboards of the squat were bare and everything echoed and seemed louder than it should have. The Grateful Dead, turned up to ten, an argument about the murder of Leon Trotsky, another argument about a borrowed bottle of milk, and a woman's voice, apparently soothing a baby.

Leon wondered what his father would make of the overwhelming smell, for the squat was full of ripe scents, the trapped air behind the boarded-up windows reeking of dry rot, unwashed clothes, joss sticks and, seeping into everything, the odour of the vegetable soup that was permanently simmering on a big black stove.

The old man. Fuck it. Leon swallowed hard. When would it ever end? That fear of facing his father? That terror of seeing the disappointment in his eyes?

He was by the sash window, his hands behind his back like the Duke of Edinburgh about to inspect the guard, staring down at the street. He was a tall, good-looking man seven days from his fifty-third birthday, calm and regal in his crisp Humphrey Bogart raincoat. He was standing. There was nowhere to sit down. There was nothing in the room but a pile of rucksacks and a few sleeping bags, one of which contained two sleeping teenage girls, curled up like kittens.

'What are you doing here, Dad?'

The old man turned to him.

'Hello, Leon,' he said, as if he could hardly believe their luck at bumping into each other. 'I could ask you the same question, couldn't I?'

The old man seemed perfectly relaxed. Leon had to hand it to him – how many of the boys he went to school with had fathers who could walk into a squat and not bat an eyelid? Leon remembered what his father had said to him when he was a boy, and delirious with excitement because his daddy had taken him to his newspaper office as a special treat during the long summer holiday. *A journalist has to be at home everywhere, Leon. Remember that.*

The old man smiled, and placed a hand on Leon's shoulder, patting it twice, and then let it fall away when his son did not respond.

'Good to see you. Are you keeping well?'

He looked up at Leon's hat but said nothing. Leon's parents had always been very understanding about the vagaries of fashion. Infuriatingly tolerant, in fact. None of his haircuts – the botched Ziggy Stardust, the failed Rod Stewart – had ever troubled them. That's their problem exactly, Leon thought. They can understand a bit of youthful rebellion. But they can't stomach the real thing.

Leon grimaced. 'You really should have rung. This is not a good time. I'm going out – my friends will be waiting – at the Western World.'

His father frowned, lifting a hand to Leon's bruised cheekbone, but not quite touching it. 'What on earth happened to your poor face?'

Leon wanted to say – oh, please don't fuss, I've had twenty years of it. But he couldn't resist – he wanted his father to know. He wanted his father to be proud of him. And when the fuck would *that* ever end?

'I was down there on Saturday. You know – Lewisham.'

Leon relished the frightened look in the old man's face.

'The riot? What – they beat you?'

Leon laughed at that. 'I just got clipped. A cop's knee.'

His father was wide-eyed. Everything amazed him. 'His *knee?*'

Leon sighed with irritation. How could anyone know so little? 'He was on a *horse*, Dad. He was a cop on a *horse*.' Leon waited. He wanted some acknowledgement from his father. A bit of credit, that wouldn't have gone amiss. Some small nod of recognition that Leon had done a good thing by going to Lewisham and standing up to the racists. But the old man just exhaled with frustration.

'Why do you want to get mixed up in all that? A bunch of

bovver boys waving the flag, and another bunch of bovver boys throwing bricks at them. What does that solve?'

Leon's face reddened with anger. 'You should understand. You of all people. They're *Fascists*, Dad. They have to be stopped. Isn't that what *you* did in the war?'

The old man raised his eyebrows. He almost smiled, and Leon blushed. He wished he could stop doing that.

'Is that what you think it was like at Monte Cassino? A punch-up on Lewisham High Street? What a lot you have to learn, my boy.'

This is why I left home, Leon thought, his eyes pricking with tears. The constant belittling. The just-not-fucking-getting-it. The never being good enough. The being told that I know nothing.

'I don't care what you think,' Leon said, knowing he cared desperately. 'And why did you come? Why?'

'Your mother asked me to,' said the old man, and Leon felt that twinge of hurt. So it wasn't his *dad* that was worried about him. It was *her*. His mother. 'Your mother doesn't get it. All your advantages and you end up living with a bunch of dossers.'

'Listen to you,' Leon said, mocking him now. 'The great enlightened liberal – sneering at the homeless.'

'I'm not sneering. I'm just – I'm just happy to see you.'

'Can you keep your voice down, please?' Leon said, indicating the sleeping girls, trying to show the old man that he was on his territory now. 'They've been up all night.'

His father peered at the girls as if noticing them for the first time.

'Who are they?' he said, keeping his voice down. There was a natural curiosity about him, and Leon thought perhaps that was why he was such a good journalist.

'Someone found them sleeping in the photo booth at Euston. They've come down from Glasgow.'

He wanted his dad to understand. He wanted him to see that these were Leon's battles – fighting racism, finding a roof for the homeless, confronting injustice – and they were just as important as the battles that his father had fought.

But the old man just shook his head sadly, as if it was insane for children to be sleeping in photo booths, and it infuriated Leon.

'Dad, do you know what happens to most of the homeless kids who sleep in railway stations? They end up selling their bodies within a week.'

'They might be homeless, but you're not, are you, Leon?' He looked from the sleeping girls to his son. 'You're just playing at it.'

Leon was having trouble controlling his heart, his breathing, his temper. He was at that point in a young man's life when every word from his father's mouth enraged him.

'I'm playing at nothing,' Leon said. 'They can't leave good housing empty. We're not going to stand for it any more. The homeless are fighting back.'

'But you *choose* to be homeless, Leon. Where's the sense in that? You give up your home for a slum. You give up your education for some music paper.'

Here we go, Leon thought. As if writing think pieces about the cod war is morally superior. As if sitting on your fanny and getting a degree somehow validates your existence.

'I've got a friend called Terry. His parents think he's done very well for himself by getting a job on a music paper.'

'I am sure Terry didn't have your advantages. I'm sure Terry wasn't at the London School of Economics until he dropped out in his first year. How can you throw all that away? Your grandfather was a taxi driver from Hackney. Do you know what he would have given for the chances you've had?'

The taxi driver from Hackney, Leon thought. It always came back to my father's father. The old man didn't know how fucking lucky he was – all he had to compete with was a taxi driver from Hackney who never quite lost his Polish accent. And what did Leon have to compete with? Leon had to compete with *him.*

One of the girls in the sleeping bag stirred, opened her eyes and went back to sleep.

'You shouldn't have come here, Dad,' Leon said.

'I came because your mother's frantic,' the old man said, and Leon flinched at the feeling in his voice. 'She's worried sick. Where's your compassion for *her*, Leon?' His father looked around wildly. 'You think whoever owns this place is going to let this last for ever? One night soon someone is going to kick you out – and kick you bloody hard, my son.'

Leon narrowed his eyes. 'We'll be ready for them.'

His father threw his hands in the air. Leon had seen that exasperated gesture so many times. It said *the things I have to put up with!*

'Oh, grow up, Leon. You think these people are going to change the world? Take a good whiff. They have trouble changing their socks.'

'They're committed to something bigger than themselves. They care.'

'They *care*,' his father echoed. 'One day you'll see that the people who care, the people who profess love for the masses, are the most heartless bastards in the world.' Then his voice was almost begging. 'Look – I was like you. Thought I knew it all. You've got so much time, Leon. You don't realise how much time you have.'

Round and round. Never ending. It had been just like this in the last days of home, Leon thought. Bossing him around, dressing it up as reasoned debate. Until one of them – always Leon, now he thought about it – slammed away from the dinner table and went to his room. But he wasn't living at home any more. His father did not understand. That was all over.

'You just want me to be what I was, Dad – a good little student you can boast about to all your friends.'

His father shook his head, and Leon felt a flicker of fear – he looked like he was in some kind of pain. 'No – I just want you to have a happy life. Dropping out – that's not the way, that can never be the way.'

Happiness! Now Leon had heard everything.

'Life's not just about happiness, is it? I can't go back to my old life, Dad. I can't sit around with a bunch of privileged middle-class kids when there are people sleeping on the street, when there are racists beating up Pakistani shopkeepers, when they are marching through the streets making their Nazi salutes. I can't pretend it's not happening.'

'Come home,' his father said.

That's what it came down to in the end. Never hearing a word he said. Wanting things to be the way they were, when they could never be that way again.

Leon shrugged.

'I am home.'

'Oh, you stupid little boy,' his father said, and Leon was shocked to see him filling up with tears, turning his face away, staring out the window at nothing.

Leon couldn't stand it. He couldn't stand to see the old man so upset. He felt like putting his arms around him, but just as he was about to do so a couple of the French guys appeared in the doorway and stood there with their arms folded, making it clear that this man was unwanted in this place.

Leon's father felt their presence, glanced at them waiting in the doorway and nodded, as if he understood.

The old man hugged him and pulled away quickly. Leon felt like patting him, or saying something to reassure him, or telling him it had to be this way, but he didn't know where to start.

Leon walked his father to the door in silence. They shook hands, as formal as strangers who had not really had a chance to talk, and Leon watched the old man turn up the collar of his Humphrey Bogart raincoat and carefully cross the muddy moat.

You were meant to keep the front door shut and locked, but Leon watched his dad as he walked down the boarded-up street, and he kept watching until he had disappeared round the corner, and by then all the anger had faded to this sort of flat, empty sorrow. Leon couldn't see a reason why they would ever meet again.

He closed the door of the squat and began setting all the locks.

The office emptied and the big white clock by the reception desk seemed to get louder by the minute. But still Ray tarried at his desk, fretting over the damaged tape recorder, huddled over it, trying to straighten the deformed spool.

Pressing *start*. Watching the thing wobble. Straightening it with his thumb. Pressing *stop*. Pressing with his thumb again – pressing harder this time . . . and then the spool snapped.

It came away with a crisp, sickening sound and flew across the room. Ray gasped with shock, staring at the jagged black stump that was left behind. Bad, this is so bad. So much for tracking down John Lennon, Ray thought. I never even made it out of the office. Pathetic. I *deserve* to be given the boot.

His friends were gone now and Ray ached for their presence – for someone, anyone, to tell him what to do next. He stared helplessly at the useless tape machine and he realised that he knew this feeling. This feeling of being completely and totally alone.

He was eleven years old and standing in front of a classroom full of children who had already had time to make friends, form alliances and learn how to grin knowingly when they saw a new kid who was trying not to cry.

Too late. Always too late.

It was easy for his two brothers. John was four years older, tough, athletic, afraid of nothing. And his younger brother, Robbie, was only five and just starting school. He wouldn't know anything but this strange new place.

But Ray was at that awkward age. He looked different to the other boys and girls. His hair was still cut in a brutal short back and sides, he was wearing grey flannel short trousers and a short-sleeve white nylon shirt, and he was still sporting the tie and blazer of his old school.

It was the summer of 1969, and Ray Keeley was dressed like Harold Macmillan.

Although his new classmates also wore a nominal school uniform, compared to Ray they were Carnaby Street peacocks.

Long hair curled dangerously over the collars of paisley shirts, or it was cropped to the point of baldness. School ties had knots thick enough for Roger Moore. Many of the girls had hiked their regulation skirts up to just below their knickers of regulation navy blue. And lounging right at the back of the class, there were boys in pink shirts.

Pink shirts! On boys! Flipping heck!

Ray had been in England for a month. Nowhere had ever felt less like home.

'Ray is from Hong Kong where his father was in the police force,' announced the teacher. She picked up a ruler and slapped it twice against a map of the world. 'Now, who knows what Hong Kong is?'

The class chanted as one, making Ray jump.

'One of the *pink bits*, miss!'

'And what are the pink bits?'

'The pink bits are *ours*, miss!'

But Ray felt that nothing belonged to him – not the Chinese place they had left behind, or the army bases in Cyprus and Germany where his family had lived before that, and certainly not this strange suburban town where the boys and girls were dolled up as if they were going to a fancy-dress party.

A skinhead child was assigned to look after Ray but deserted him as soon as the bell went for morning playtime.

On the far side of the playground Ray could see his big brother John kicking a ball around with some of the lads. His kid brother Robbie was running in circles with a pack of little fellows, giggling like crazy. Ray stood there, not knowing where to go, what to do, or even where to put his hands. But then something happened that changed everything.

Someone started singing.

It was the chorus from 'Hey Jude'. On and on. Voices joined in. And then there was another chant – the opening bars of 'All You Need Is Love'.

The children kept on playing. The football and gossip didn't stop, did not even pause for breath. The conkers and hopscotch continued. But they sang as they played.

There were more tunes, more chants – yeah, yeah, yeah – 'She

71

Loves You' – and more children raising their voices in these songs that they all knew better than any hymn, better than the National Anthem.

Songs they had grown up singing, the soundtrack to all those Sixties childhoods. It was only the Beatles. Always the Beatles. As if the times that these children grew up in began and ended with John, Paul, George and Ringo. And soon the entire playground was singing and Ray Keeley stepped out among them, his senses reeling, surrounded by the music, and a world unlike any he had known before. A world of shared feelings.

Years later he wondered if he had imagined it all – the first day at the strange school, the desperate attempt to hold back the tears, the sight of his big brother playing football with his new friends somehow underlining Ray's loneliness, and then out of nowhere the playground full of children singing Beatles songs. Certainly he never saw it happen again.

But he knew that it was real. He knew that it had really happened. He had felt it. The magic that can set you free.

And sometimes Ray felt like his entire life was about trying to get back to that moment, to recover that day when suddenly it didn't matter that he knew no one and his clothes were all wrong, that schoolyard in 1969 where the children sang, na-na-na, yeah-yeah-yeah and love-love-love, love is all you need.

The office wasn't empty. Ray should have known. Their office was never quite empty.

Music thundered from inside the review room, making the panel of glass in the door rattle. Ray pressed his face against the glass and saw that Skip Jones was in there. He would probably be in there all night, writing the lead album review for next week's issue. By hand.

Despite all the modern red plastic Olivettis in the office, Skip Jones always chose to write by hand. You would see him in odd empty corners of the office, or in the review room, his long giraffe-like limbs hunched over a tatty notebook, and the fact that he was left-handed and had to wrap his hand around his leaky Biro made the process seem all the more awkward and tortured and strange.

Yet Skip Jones still wrote the pants off everyone else at *The Paper*, effortlessly constructing this cool, pristine, sceptical prose that seemed perfect for the age, and he was the closest thing *The Paper* had to a legend.

Ray hated to disturb Skip Jones. But if anyone knew where Lennon would be tonight, it was Skip. He paused, working up the courage. Then Ray let himself into the review room with a diffident smile, his hair falling forward.

Skip didn't notice him at first. He was lost in the music, consumed by his writing, surrounded by a forest of dead cigarettes that he had half-smoked and then carefully stood on their filter tips, allowing them to burn down to a bendy cone of ash.

Ray watched him work, wondering what the music was – twin lead guitars, a world-weary nasal vocal that was completely contemporary, but with a dreamy quality that was out of step with what was going on.

Ray loved to watch Skip work. It restored his faith, it made him feel that they were doing something worthwhile and important. Watching Skip made Ray feel that the music hadn't died.

Skip leaned back in his chair, lit a cigarette and noticed Ray. He grinned and motioned him further into the room, not quite making eye contact for, while Skip Jones was the best writer at *The Paper*, he was the shyest man in the world. Looking you in the eye was Skip's personal Kryptonite. Ray smiled gratefully and pulled up the room's other chair.

'Ray Keeley,' Skip said. 'Wild.'

Skip handed him the cover of the album he was reviewing. *Marquee Moon* by Television. Ray shook his head – never heard of it. Skip closed his eyes and nodded emphatically, indicating that this was the real deal.

'Man, what's the biggest selling album of the year?' Skip said.

'Don't know,' Ray said. 'I guess it's still *Hotel California.*'

'Wild,' Skip smiled, carefully standing his newly lit cigarette on its filter tip. 'Laurel Canyon cowboys – cod country that the Byrds did first and harmonies that the Beach Boys did better.' He chuckled, and Ray laughed along with Skip, even though he had always been quite fond of the Eagles, and it felt like a bit of a betrayal. 'Well, sorry, boys – Television are going to kick your LA arses all the way back to the dude ranch.'

Ray's eyes shone with admiration. He thought that Skip Jones looked like a buccaneer. A buccaneer who had been shipwrecked with Keith Richards and a big bag of drugs.

Skip was freakishly tall, alarmingly thin, deathbed white, and if you had seen him loping by, a stack of albums stickered with the words *Promotional Copy Only: Not For Sale* under his arm and about to be sold, you might have thought he was a homeless person, or a genius who could not live as mere mortals did. You would have been right on both counts.

On the rare nights when he actually went to bed, Skip Jones slept on a succession of sofas and floors across north and west London. Skip often lacked a home, but never a roof. Too many people worshipped him.

By day, Skip lurked in whatever spare corner of *The Paper* was free – he had no office of his own, and didn't want one – that's how totally rock and roll Skip was. He seemed to embody the very essence of the music. And on crumpled notepads, scraps of paper, the backs of press releases and the inside of empty cigarette packets, Skip wrote – by tormented hand, in laborious, cack-handed pencil – the most glittering words about music that anyone had ever read.

Skip was wearing the only clothes he seemed to own – torn black leather trousers, a red leather biker's jacket and the kind of ruffled blouson that might be suitable if you found yourself fighting a duel with rapiers at dawn. He wore these elegant rags every day, in every kind of weather. Ray thought Skip looked like some kind of rock-and-roll cavalier, when everyone else was a roundhead.

Skip's trousers were ripped at the crutch and sometimes at editorial meetings his meat and two veg were given an unexpected airing. Hardened rock chicks who thought nothing of giving head to a member of Dr Feelgood backstage at the Rainbow blushed to the roots of their dyed hair, but Skip was oblivious.

When he walked through the streets of London, rough boys with feather cuts and diamond-motif tank tops and flared jeans flapping above their steel-capped boots lobbed rocks at him. The wide world scorned him as a freak. But at *The Paper*, Skip was revered. It wasn't just Ray. Leon loved Skip. Terry loved Skip. He was the reason they all wanted to work for *The Paper*.

Skip Jones had started writing for *The Paper* when he was a bleary-eyed dropout from Balliol and the youngest writer on *Oz*, and his waspish reflections on the music's glorious dead – Jimi Hendrix, Brian Jones, Jim Morrison, Nick Drake – and walking wounded – Lou Reed, Brian Wilson, Syd Barrett, Iggy Pop, Dag Wood – did more than anything or anyone to help Kevin White drag *The Paper* from underground rag to mainstream music magazine.

'You like the new bands?' Skip said. 'Not your thing, right?'

Ray smiled politely. He didn't really have to explain anything to Skip. Skip understood.

'I like them,' Skip said. 'Some of them. But what they're doing, what they're devoting their careers to, Eddie Cochran did in less than two minutes. Check it out, man. "Summertime Blues" – one minute fifty-nine. They want back to basics? Eddie Cochran did it first. And you can't slag off the old guard when you're stealing their riffs. I mean, where did the Clash lift the riff for "1977"?'

'The Kinks,' Ray said. '"You Really Got Me".'

Skip smiled slyly. 'So what are *you* into these days? Not Led Zeppelin?'

'My brother liked all that. I liked – I don't know – the folky stuff they did. You know, "Tangerine", "White Summer/Black Mountain Side".'

Ray didn't say that his brother had died and the records were gathering dust in a bedroom that his parents had locked. He didn't tell Skip Jones that. They didn't talk about their lives. Every conversation they had was about music. Ray supposed that Skip must have a family somewhere. But he never mentioned them. Over the din of the music, what they talked about was music.

'Big Joni Mitchell fans, Page and Plant,' Skip said. 'Everyone ignores that. But if you like that acoustic side of Led Zeppelin, you got to check out some of those folk boys. Davy Graham. Bert Jansch and John Renbourn, the Pentangle boys. Leo Kottke. John Fahey – a mad genius, the acoustic Hendrix. And John Martyn. You know John Martyn? He's our Dylan. Don't be put off because the guy's got a beard, man.'

'Beards don't bother me,' Ray said, struggling to commit the names to memory. He had to listen to these people. There was great music out there that he had never even heard of.

'And then you have to go back further,' Skip was saying. 'To the blues. To the music that's behind our music – if you know what I mean.'

Somehow Ray knew what he meant.

'Check out Son House.' A shy, sideways glance. Ray nodded. He would definitely check out Son House. 'Charley Patton,' Skip said. 'Asie Payton. The Delta Blues. It all comes from the same source. That's what the special ones understand. The blood knot. Where it all gets mixed up – black and white, the city and the country. They get it. All music comes from the same place. Elvis understood it. And Dylan. And Lennon too.'

Ray took a breath.

'I need to find him, Skip. John Lennon, I mean. He's in town. White wants me to find him and interview him.'

That shy, sly smile, looking at a point on the ceiling. 'A world exclusive? A scoop?'

'That's it. Yeah. You know – like proper journalism.'

Skip nodded. 'They're all in town tonight,' he said. 'John Lennon . . . Dag Wood. It's a strange vibe, man.' He smiled, peeking at Ray out of the corner of his eye. 'Spirits are abroad.'

Ray remembered that Skip had once discovered Dag Wood turning blue in an empty bath in Detroit. Or maybe it was the other way round. It was a bad scene, anyway. Skip knew everything. He had met everyone.

'Where should I go tonight, Skip?' There was urgency in Ray's voice now. He saw he still had a faint chance. 'If you were me – where would you go?'

Skip considered. 'If I were you, and I was going out tonight, then I'd try the Speakeasy. Or maybe the Roundhouse.'

Ray was doubtful. 'You really think that Lennon will be in those places?'

Skip frowned. 'John Lennon? I doubt it, man. But you'll be able to buy some great gear in the toilets.'

Ray sighed. He couldn't help himself. He remembered that although Skip had met everyone and knew everything, it was said he had trouble boiling a kettle. The banalities of life eluded Skip. He was operating on some higher astral plane.

'Yes, but where will *he* be? John, I mean?'

But before Skip could hazard a guess, the door to the review room burst open. A small, indignant woman in glasses glared at the pair of them. Ray recognised her, she was from the magazine across the floor, *Country Matters*.

She bustled over to the turntable and angrily pulled the needle from *Marquee Moon*, making the vinyl screech in protest.

'Have some consideration for others,' she said, red-faced with fury. 'You're not the only ones working late, you know.' She strode back across the review room, pausing at the door. 'And get some fresh air!'

When she was gone, Ray and Skip looked at each other for a moment.

And then they laughed until it hurt.

'Get some fresh air!' Skip Jones said. 'Wild!'

Misty drove them to the place where they spent their nights. Terry felt his heart pounding with joy. He loved it here. He thought that it looked like the end of the world.

The old Covent Garden flower market had been torn down and

carted away. Almost nothing remained. Now the area reminded Terry of the bombsites he had seen as a kid, all ploughed mud and smashed buildings and gaping holes in the earth. But every night, something stirred among the rubble.

'Here they come,' Misty said.

Terry and Misty sat on the roof of her dad's car in a scrappy piece of wasteland, watching men in dinner jackets and women in evening gowns emerge from the darkness and carefully pick their way through the ruins. The opera-goers.

Terry and Misty liked to watch this swanky crew on their way to the Royal Opera House on Bow Street – the men suave in their dinner jackets and bow ties, looking all David Niven and James Bond, the women holding up the hems of their long dresses, dripping jewels, every one a Princess Grace of Monaco, and laughing as if crossing the ruins of Covent Garden was a great game.

A woman in a red dress and pearls waved at them, and Terry and Misty waved back.

The opera crowd had a friendly relationship with the feral-looking young people who flocked to see bands play in a basement club on Neal Street. Terry thought that it was because they were all there for the same reason. They were all there for the music.

'This was a garden once,' Misty said. She liked to lecture him. But he didn't mind. He liked it when she told him things. 'Did you know that, Tel? They grew fruit and flowers here. That's where the name comes from. Covent Garden. It really was a garden.'

'And now it's a bombsite,' he said. 'Let's go and see if Dag's arrived yet.'

'It must have been so beautiful,' she said.

Terry let loose a Kung Fu cry and jumped from the roof of the car. Before he hit the ground he lashed out at some imaginary enemy with the side of his foot, and chopped the air once-twice-three times.

'Bruce Lee,' he said proudly, and his girlfriend smiled at him in the darkness.

Then they looked up as the sky cracked, the heavens opened and the rains came down.

Within seconds they were both soaked. A jagged bolt of lightning snaked across the skyline. It was not the weather of summer. The sudden storm seemed to herald something momentous, some elemental force being unleashed, a change in the universe.

Terry and Misty held hands, laughed out loud and turned their faces to the sky, delirious with life.

And five thousand miles away, behind the gates of a great house in Memphis, Tennessee, a forty-two-year-old man was taking his dying breath.

FIVE

The noise – the incredible level of sound – that was what Terry noticed first. It roared out of the basement of the Western World, blasted through the open door where a large bald man in black stood guard, and seemed to rattle the night air, shaking the NHS fillings of the soaked and bedraggled queue waiting to be let inside. Someone was live on stage. And Terry was suddenly aware of the beat of his heart.

He took Misty's hand, feeling giddy with history. Once the Western World had been an illegal drinking joint. Later it was a strip club. Then it was a gay bar. And now it belonged to them. Now it was their turn.

Everyone in the queue was dressed up in the fashion of their tribe, and Terry found something comforting about all those emblems of rebellion – the Fuck-you-to-Hell-and-back heels and torn black tights on the girls, the bollock-crunching skinny trousers and big boots on the boys, the leather jackets and short, spiked hair for everybody, dried out by talcum powder and kept vertical with Vaseline, as though an electric shock had just run through the veins of every one of them. These were his people. Beyond the tribal piercings, the make-up like wounds and bruises – Panda eyes, red slit mouths – Terry recognised many of the faces, and he felt a strange kind of warmth inside. It was good to be among your own kind.

'Or we could go somewhere else,' Misty said, tugging on the sleeve of his Oxfam jacket.

He stared at her. You never knew what she was going to say next. 'What are you talking about?' Even standing outside the Western World, you had to raise your voice to be heard above the din.

Her eyes were huge with excitement. 'We could take the car. Drive all night. Be in the Highlands when the sun's coming up.'

For a second he was speechless. Didn't she understand the importance of tonight? Didn't she get it?

'But *Dag's* coming tonight,' he said. 'He's going to be waiting for me. To meet *us*.'

Terry remembered the moment in a Berlin bar when he had shown Misty's picture to Dag. She was clowning around in a photo booth, sitting on Terry's lap, but you could still tell how special she was. Dag had nodded a restrained approval. 'Crazy lady,' he had said, and Terry's heart had flooded with gratitude.

That's right, Dag. Crazy lady.

'Yeah, yeah,' she said. 'But it would be just like Sal Paradise and Dean Moriarty in *On the Road*.' She thought that would tempt him. She knew how much he loved that book. 'Sal and Dean driving into Mexico as the sun's coming up, Terry. We could drive all night – just *go*.'

She meant it. He knew she meant it. Crazy lady was dead right. And although it was crazy – Dag Wood might be already *inside*! –

Terry couldn't be angry with her. This craziness had been one of the reasons that he had fallen for her so heavily.

He remembered the early days, just before new year, when the rest of the world was still worn out by Christmas, and her ex-boyfriend, the old boy, had stood vigil outside Terry's bedsit, crying his heart out in the snow, and they had sneaked past him giggling, and run around London as if they owned it – jumping over fences, scaling walls, climbing trees in royal parks in the middle of the night, wandering across the pitch in some empty football stadium. She wasn't like any girl he had ever known. But he wasn't tempted to turn and walk away from the Western World. They had the rest of their lives to drive all night.

'Come on, Misty,' he said gently. 'Dag's waiting.'

And she smiled at him, not minding at all, and he loved her.

They walked to the front of the queue, and Terry was proud in the knowledge that their names were permanently on the guest list of this special place. He clocked all the familiar slogans of sedition scrawled on shirts, trousers and school jackets. ANARCHY. DESTROY. CROYDON SUCKS.

A wild-eyed apparition emerged from the queue. He wore a suit jacket that seemed to have been made out of a Union Jack. His two front teeth were missing. 'Terry, Terry,' he lisped, 'he is here! He walks among us! Dag Wood is in the building! I saw him go in!'

Brainiac was one of the veterans of last summer. Terry had first seen him in front of the stage at a Clash gig with blood all over his face, giving him the appearance of a cannibal at teatime. Some dancing partner had just taken a bite out of Brainiac's nose. Brainiac didn't care, he just grinned foolishly, showing his gappy teeth, as if losing the odd limb was all part of the fun. Some said that Brainiac had invented vertical dancing because there was just so little space to move in their subterranean haunts. The only way was up and down. Nobody knew where Brainiac came from – he seemed to appear fully formed, as if the madness and the Union Jack jacket had always been there, as if he had always been Brainiac.

Terry had heard that Brainiac had once been Brian O'Grady, and that he had come to the Western World via a large London Irish family, a scholarship to a public school (apparently Brainiac's IQ was off the radar, and Terry sort of believed it) and then, after his first nervous breakdown, a mental hospital. But nobody knew for sure, and it didn't matter anyway. Brian was gone and Brainiac was here now. They were all here now.

'The great Dag Wood is in the building,' Brainiac insisted, his fingers clawing at Terry's Oxfam jacket, sweat and rain dripping all over his ecstatic face. 'The only man to get up their kaftans at Woodstock. Your piece – extreme gonzo – if I may say so.'

'Is he?' Terry said. 'Is he really in there? Dag?'

It seemed too good to be true. But Brainiac nodded excitedly, and Terry patted him on the back of his Union Jack jacket, thankful for the happy news. Then he stared at his hand. It was covered in grime.

'You may come in with us,' Misty said, and Brainiac fell into step behind them, babbling happily.

Terry spat on his hands and rubbed them together. Brainiac had been wearing the red, white and blue jacket the night he almost lost his nose, and it was filthy beyond belief now. Terry didn't say anything because Brainiac was only about seventeen years old and he liked him a lot. And Brainiac was one of the originals. But as they moved closer to the front of the queue, Terry saw with a sinking feeling that the crowd was changing.

It had been so good at the start. The best time of his life. For the second half of last year and the first half of this one, all through that blazing summer of 1976 and the freezing winter that followed, Terry could come to the Western World and know every face in the club. It felt as if everyone was a musician, writer, photographer, band manager, fashion designer – or at least, that's what they were trying to be, as they all searched for an escape route from their old lives and stifling normality. Their own private gin factory, Terry thought. Brainiac himself talked endlessly about the perfect band that existed in his head. They were all hungry for new experience, starved of life, ready for anything.

There were just a few of them back then. One night Terry had watched the Jam play at the Western World when the only other people in the audience were three members of the Clash and Brainiac. Afterwards Brainiac and Terry had helped Paul, Bruce, Rick and Weller's dad load their gear into the van for the long drive back to Woking. It was a good night. But that was when all of the new bands were unsigned. That was when they were all just starting. Now most of the groups had records out, and some of them – the ones that didn't have any ideological objections to the show – had even appeared on *Top of the Pops*.

Terry thought that what was so perfect about the early days was that it felt like they were all in this thing – whatever this thing was – together. But now he couldn't help the Jam to load their van. They had roadies to do that sort of thing, and he had his fragile dignity to preserve. They were professionals now, or pretending to be.

Terry knew those early days had been strangely innocent, no matter how many outraged headlines there were in the newspapers. Although they had all dressed up as if they were ready for a fight or a fuck or both, there had been a real sense of community. But now there were mean faces waiting outside the Western World, and they glared at Terry and Misty with naked hostility as they bypassed the queue. 'Careful, careful – strangers,' Brainiac hissed at Terry's shoulder, seeming on the edge of tears. 'Strangers are here.'

Out of the corner of his eye, Terry registered three youths who didn't spike their hair but shaved it – ferocious, gleaming bald heads, like extremist skinheads. One of them was tall and sickly thin, the other beer-drinker porky, and the third built like a refrigerator. Through dull, sullen eyes they watched Terry walk by with Misty holding his hand.

'What else you get for Christmas?' one of them shouted, and the others chortled in perfect harmony.

Terry didn't know what it meant exactly, but he knew it was an insult. And he knew now who they were. The Dagenham Dogs.

The tall and thin one was called Junior, and the nearest thing this crew had to a leader. Under Junior's right eye there was a tattoo, or rather three tattoos – a trio of dark teardrops, the colour of melting black ice, small, medium and large, growing in size as they ran down his face.

There were about fifty or sixty Dagenham Dogs, all from the badlands of the East End–Essex border country. They followed and fought for a band called the Sewer Rats the way – less than a year ago – they had followed and fought for West Ham United.

The Sewer Rats were decent middle-class boys – well-spoken political science graduates who gave thoughtful interviews where they talked about oligarchy and permanent revolution, Mao and the MC5.

Terry had gone on the road with them and found them charming. But there was something in the toe-tapping, bitch-slapping brutalism of their music that was irresistible to what Ian Dury had defined to Terry as lawless brats from council flats. Not the ones like Terry, who knew he would never be as tough as he wanted to be. The real thing. The real dead-end kids.

You saw Junior and the Dagenham Dogs at Sewer Rat gigs, slamming into each other in front of the stage – a strange new thing, something that had never been seen at shows before, a violent evolution of Brainiac's pogo dance – fighting with each other, fighting with anyone, shrieking at the moon, covered in gore, nothing to lose. You were seeing more and more of their kind around. They didn't care about the art school rhetoric of the new music, or theories about teenage boredom, or Vivienne Westwood T-shirts. They were here for the riot. They were here to have a laugh, to get out of their heads, to smash the place up if the mood took them.

Terry didn't look at them as they eye-balled him from the queue. They scared him. If they had said something about Misty then his code of honour would have insisted that he confront them, and accept a good kicking, for he knew he had no chance in a scrap with the Dogs. But they didn't, and he was hugely relieved.

'Just ignore them,' Misty said.

'You think I'm scared of them?' Terry said, keeping his voice down.

Ray was waiting for them at the door, looking uneasy.

'Need your tape recorder,' Ray said, his words coming out in a rush. 'Mine's buggered.' His hair fell down and he didn't push it back. 'Have you got your tape recorder? And some batteries. And a C-90 tape.'

Terry looked at him. 'Why's that then?' he said.

'Because I'm going to interview John Lennon.'

'It's in the car,' Misty said, taking out the keys and handing them to Terry.

Terry contemplated the keys. 'Why do you want to talk to John Lennon? In seven years it's going to be 1984. You think anyone's going to remember the Beatles by 1984?'

The queue began easing past them into the club. Make-up streaming, bodies steaming. Ray sighed. 'Can I just have that tape recorder?'

'Come inside for a minute,' Terry pleaded, slipping the keys inside his Oxfam jacket. 'Have a beer. Then we'll go and get the tape. You know who's going to be down here tonight? You know who I'm going to introduce you to? *Dag Wood.*'

Ray was unimpressed. 'What do I want to meet Dag Wood for?'

Terry looked hurt. 'Dag was at Woodstock!'

Ray laughed. 'Yeah, where he was bottled off stage.' He looked at Terry and Misty. He was anxious to get on with it, but in a way he didn't mind delaying his quest. Because even if he found John Lennon, he didn't know how he could ever talk to him.

'All right, one beer,' Ray said, and he had to smile at the delight on Terry's face. The three of them went inside, past the bouncer, through the lager-stained lobby and into the darkness. Terry could feel the music hammering his eardrums, and then the noise began to translate into a song – it was Billy Blitzen who was on stage downstairs, doing his big number, 'Shoot Up, Everybody'.

Juddering Eddie Cochran riffs made Terry's jawbone clench, and his eyes misted over with bliss. It was like getting off the plane in some exotic country. You were hit in the face by this other world – the noise and the heat and the smell of sweat and Red Stripe and ganja. Suddenly there was less air to breathe. And Billy Blitzen was live on stage.

Five years ago Billy had been in a band that Terry had loved – the Lost Boys, native New Yorkers who sang about scoring junk uptown and girlfriends crying in shower stalls, all that Manhattan Babylon stuff but given a sassy mid-Seventies sheen, and stuffed into platform boots. And Billy was a friend of Terry's now, maybe his best friend outside *The Paper* – one of those Americans, a graduate of CBGBs and Max's Kansas City and the Bottom Line, who were flocking to town, actually moving to London, sensing the gold rush to come. They could all hang out together, Terry thought happily. Dag Wood and Misty and Ray and Billy Blitzen. It was going to be a perfect night.

Pierced, painted faces stared out of the gloom. Faces shone in the darkness for a moment and then were gone. There was Brainiac, grinning like a mad man, taking alternate swigs from the cans of Red Stripe he held in each hand. And there was the nearly famous Grace Fury, the girl of the moment. Grace Fury – red hair, black tights, some sort of PVC corset and a tartan mini-kilt that would have just about covered her pants, if she had been wearing any. Terry felt Misty's hot breath on his neck and tried not to stare at where the skirt ended and the legs began. Maybe Grace could hang out with them too.

A crush of bodies pressed against him. Some kid who looked barely into his teens had shredded his school blazer and put it back together with safety pins. Because the grown-up world was too slow and stupid to sell it to them, and because they had no money, most of their stuff was customised or home-made. Like Terry, many of them were wearing a dead man's jacket.

Maybe Grace Fury's gear was from the far end of the King's Road, but all around him were mail-order catalogue T-shirts subverted with rips, pins and slogans borrowed from records by the Clash – WHITE RIOT, UNDER HEAVY MANNERS, 1977 – and rendered with toy printing-press stencil sets or wonky Biro.

As they moved slowly through the crowd, Terry could feel Misty behind him, her arms around his waist, and Ray trying to stick close by his side. According to Terry's calculations, Ray was only the third person with long hair ever to enter the Western World. The other two had been Jimmy Page and Robert Plant, who had turned up on separate nights to check out this new scene. Because nobody knew if this music was going to dominate everything for the next ten years or fade away to nothing, nobody knew if this time next year these bands would all be signed and rich and famous, or signing on the dole, or dead. That was what was so wonderful, Terry believed. Nobody had a clue what was going to happen next.

They went down to the basement, feeling the semi-derelict wooden staircase creaking dangerously beneath them, having to step over a young man in a Lewis Leather and a pink tutu who was comatose at the bottom, and then there it was – the basement of the Western World. Terry had to smile.

In front of the bouncing mob, Billy Blitzen was on a low stage the size of a snooker table – Billy dapper and beautiful in his soiled three-piece suit, his pomped-up black hair flying, letting his Fender swing at his side while he stabbed an imaginary syringe in his arm. '*Whooh!*' Billy sang, and the crowd went stark raving mental. '*Shoot up, everybody!*'

Then Billy grabbed the guitar's neck and tried to do a Chuck Berry duck walk in the confined space. Terry's eyes shone with joy.

Billy's group, the P45s, were a pick-up band of jobbing local musicians, who had chopped their hair off and dyed it metallic silver. This time last year Terry guessed they had looked like pub rockers – all shiny-arsed suits and Dr Feelgood swagger and a snout permanently on the go. Unless Billy got a deal, this time next year they would again have different trousers and haircuts. But Terry knew that Billy was happy with them because they all knew their five chords and where to buy drugs in Chalk Farm, and they didn't matter anyway, for Billy Blitzen was essentially a solo act now, well on his way to perfecting his stage persona as the Dean Martin of the new music.

'*Whooh! Shoot up, everybody!*'

Needles had yet to really surface in London, but to a New Yorker like Billy they were old hat, a way of life, something to brag about, sing about, and a way of pulling rank over all the little London speed freaks and spliff smokers. The Americans already knew how hard drugs could be, and they flaunted that knowledge like a college degree. Terry sang along at the top of his voice to 'Shoot Up, Everybody' and he couldn't hear a word. Needles still had a dark glamour for him. He hadn't seen any yet.

'There's *Dag*,' Misty said, starting to jump up and down. And Terry gawped at her, momentarily stunned. Jumping up and down? He thought she only did that for him.

Yet then Terry was looking at Dag Wood and grinning shyly. It was really happening, the moment Terry had yearned for all the way through Berlin. Dag Wood – hero, rock star, friend – was in the basement of the Western World, looking like an exiled king or something. There he was at the back of the basement, as far away from the stage as he could get, in the only place where the crowd thinned out and you could sit down at a rickety table. Dag's face looking like it had been hacked out of granite, his lank white hair pushed back, his huge bug eyes surveying the heaving basement as if it was his own underground fiefdom. His silk shirt was half off, and his muscles rippled. *Holding court,* that's what he's doing, Terry thought. Dag was surrounded by people – his musicians, his slick chubby manager, a dark-haired German woman called Christa, who was maybe his girlfriend or maybe his drug dealer or maybe both, plus some of the bolder regulars who had worked up the nerve to approach their tables. Everybody else, the ones who were not watching Billy Blitzen, was trying to be cool and not quite managing it. Kids who never changed the bored-witless expression on their face when they spilled a beer over a Buzzcock or peed next to a Sex Pistol or stood on the toe of a Strangler, stared with swoony wonder at Dag Wood – the Godfather, the thorn in the side of the Woodstock generation, the man who had started it all. And Dag Wood saw Terry Warboys and laughed.

'You did it, didn't you?' Dag said, coming over to him, the voice surprisingly deep and booming. He slapped Terry's shoulder so hard it hurt. 'You got me the cover. You are a *good writer,* man.'

Terry's face ached with the grinning.

Oh, he knew how it worked. He knew that he had the ability to make rock stars his temporary friend if he got them the cover of *The Paper.* But Dag was different. He wasn't some snot-nosed opportunist who had been a prog rocker with a mullet six months ago. Dag was the real deal – he was crawling across broken glass in Texas biker bars when the Beatles were sitting at the Maharishi's feet, spitting blood and telling the world to shut its fucking mouth long before it was fashionable. And they had really connected in Berlin, Terry believed. What he had with Dag was like the thing he had with Billy Blitzen. They respected each other's talent.

'Hello, stretch,' Dag said to Misty, who was hovering at Terry's shoulder. 'How are you tonight?'

And Terry thought – *stretch?* What does *that* mean? Is it – what? Because she's tall or something? Terry thought – I don't get it.

'Love the dress,' murmured Dag, narrowing his eyes.

Misty was laughing brightly and Terry was telling Dag her name, and then he was trying to introduce Ray, but his friend hung back, half-turning away with a fixed grin on his face, his hands stuffed deep into his Levi's, letting his fair hair fall into his face, hiding behind it, and Terry felt a twinge of annoyance and disappointment. Ray had a way of just shrinking into the background when he felt uncomfortable. And it was too late anyway, because by then Dag had taken Misty's hand and was guiding her past the sticky tables occupied by his musicians who – Terry couldn't help noticing – casually sized up Misty as they sucked from cans and rolled joints and scanned the club to see who they might take back to their hotel tonight.

As if, Terry thought bleakly, she was just another girl.

Dag's manager – a greasy New York type with cropped white hair who Terry now realised he had always disliked – vacated the seat next to Dag so that Misty could sit down. 'Welcome to London, Dag,' Terry said, having to almost shout it. 'You want a drink or something?' He paused, trying to be a good host. This was all so new. 'They got Red Stripe and Special Brew.'

'Man,' Dag said, drawing it out, not taking his unblinking eyes from Misty's smiling face. 'I'm going to have exactly what you're having.'

Dag's manager laughed at that, and Terry flushed in the darkness, and he did not like that laugh at all. But he was paralysed, standing there like an idiot, uncertain what he should think, let alone do. He was off the map and in uncharted waters. Then Dag did this thing that made Terry's blood freeze. Dag lifted his legs as if in slow motion, and eased them across Misty, so that his black leather-clad calves were resting on the top of her thighs. The pair of them looked like a weary man of the world about to give a lesson in life to a bright head girl. And Terry thought – now what the fuck does *that* mean? Is that like a *sex* thing? What's going on here? He looked at Ray, but Ray looked away.

Billy Blitzen and the P45s had left the stage and dub reggae was playing. Prince Jammy, maybe. You only heard two kinds of music at the Western World – the live stuff slashed out by the bands on stage, which was the fastest music in the world, and the dub reggae records played by the DJ, which was surely the slowest. It put you in a trance. Misty was still talking to Dag. Terry didn't know what to do. He glanced up at the DJ box and the DJ seemed to stare back at him, impassive and unreadable behind giant Superfly shades and a huge matted tangle of dreadlocks. Misty always claimed that there was an affinity between the white kids in the Western World and young Jamaicans, and that's why there was always dub reggae on the sound system. But Terry knew that it was because when the club had first opened none of the new music had yet been recorded. The DJ played dub reggae because they were the only records he had. Misty didn't know what she was talking about.

Then Billy Blitzen was by his side, the sweat streaming down his dark Italian face. 'That A&R guy from Warners is coming down later,' Billy said. 'Warwick Hunt. For our second set. It's our big break.'

Terry placed a hand on Billy's shoulder. He felt for him. They all loved Billy Blitzen at the Western World, they were still in awe of him because of the Lost Boys, but somehow he was being left behind. While the musicians who had worshipped him from way back recorded their first or second albums in New York or Nassau, Billy was still playing basements for pin money.

'Man, I need you tonight,' Billy said. 'A review. Even just a mention . . .'

'I'm there,' Terry said, nodding emphatically. 'I'll do a review. No problem. You want to say hello to Dag?'

Billy stared at Dag and shook his head, grimacing with distaste. 'I already met that asshole,' he said. Then he was gone. The dub reggae thundered on. The bass line rang in Terry's head like an echo from the underworld. Misty was talking to Dag. He was listening patiently. Someone touched Terry's arm.

'You all right?' Ray said.

Terry nodded blankly.

Look at her face, he thought. She looks – what is it? Happy. Fucking happy. He had felt closer to her than to anyone on the planet. Now he felt like he didn't know her at all. And he didn't know what to do.

Wild maniac drumming came from the stage. Terry tore his eyes away from his girlfriend and Dag Wood. Brainiac had occupied the empty drum kit and was attacking it with fury, his red, white and blue arms flying. At first nobody stopped him. There were no more fans. That was the idea. The old barriers between the act and the audience had been obliterated. No more heroes and everyone a hero. But when Brainiac began kicking the snare and throwing the cymbals around, the drummer of the P45s came back on stage and grabbed him by the throat. It was all right obliterating the barriers between the performers and the audience, but you didn't want some toothless idiot destroying your Sonor drum kit, did you?

Terry gave Ray a push. 'Let's get some drinks.'

Grace Fury was standing at the foot of the stairs, smoking a cigarette and basking in the glow of her recent TV appearance, frowning over her guitar on *Top of the Pops*, plucking out the bass line to 'Baby, You Kill Me'. She had that glow about her, that glow they always got when success finally happened. She smiled at Terry and he liked it.

'Terry Warboys,' she said in that gently mocking way she had, touching the lapel of his Oxfam jacket. 'Still rocking and rolling?'

He laughed and didn't know what to say. He wondered if she was trying to catch Dag Wood's eye, even though everyone knew that her band's lead singer was her boyfriend. Grace ran her long fingers down Terry's Oxfam lapel as if she was stroking an erect penis, and he caught his breath. Everybody wanted her now. But not me, Terry thought. I already have a girlfriend.

'Got a little something for me, Terry?' Grace said.

'Catch you later,' he said, easing past her. He knew she wasn't talking about sex. She was talking about amphetamine sulphate.

'Not if I catch you first,' she laughed.

Terry wanted to get back to Misty as quickly as possible. But at the top of the stairs, someone stepped in front of him, barring his way. Terry pulled up and Ray clattered into him. It was Junior. The other two Dagenham Dogs, the fridge and the fat boy, were behind him, the cans of Red Stripe in their fists looking like offensive weapons. Terry's heart sank when he saw that Junior had a rolled-up copy of *The Paper* in his hand. He knew they were easily offended.

Terry was aware that a gap in the crowd was opening up around them. He felt the dryness in his mouth. The old playground terror when faced with someone who can take you to bits.

'You work with that Leon Peck, don't you?' Junior said.

Terry didn't have to ask what Leon had done. He already knew.

He watched Junior lick his index finger and slowly open *The Paper* at the albums page. There was lots of space around them now, and everybody was watching, excited by the promise of violence. Some community, Terry thought. He knew what was coming. Leon had slagged off the first Sewer Rats album in flamboyantly bitchy true *Paper* fashion. He had criticised the band for their music, their politics and their choice of trousers. Even upside down, Terry could read the headline of Leon's review, *REBELS WITHOUT A COCK.*

'He doesn't write the headlines,' Ray said over Terry's shoulder. The refrigerator scowled, came in closer and Terry felt his testicles shrivel. But he took half a step to his right, placing himself between Ray and the fridge.

'We're not talking to you, hippy.'

'Leave him out of this,' Terry said.

'What about this bit?' said Junior. '*You would need a very small penis to make or listen to this exy-exer-execrable –*'

'That means shitty,' said the fridge, not taking his eyes from Terry's face.

'*– this execrable debut? Only that sad hunch of sub-Fonzie thugs who have blighted every Rats gig from the Red Cow to the Nashville. The likely lads who couldn't tell oligarchy from Ozzie Osbourne.*' Junior closed *The Paper*. 'Did he write that bit?'

Terry reluctantly nodded, conceding that Leon had probably written that bit.

'Well, you tell him,' Junior said, 'that we are going to break his fucking neck.' His gaunt face reddened, a vein in his temple began to throb. He began screwing up *The Paper* tighter and tighter, as if throttling it. 'And then we are going to break his fingers.' *The Paper* began to disintegrate, and so did Terry's bowels. 'And then we are going to shove his typewriter so far up his anus he'll be writing his next review with his electric toothbrush.' He threw the shredded magazine in Terry's face. 'Can you remember all that?'

Terry nodded. 'Think so.'

Junior pressed his sloping brow against Terry's forehead. 'Good.'

The three Dogs shoved them aside and headed downstairs. Terry watched scary-looking kids with metal pushed through their cheeks and steel-toe-capped boots on their feet flatten themselves against the wall to let the Dogs pass.

'They'll kill him,' Terry said simply. 'They'll really do it. They're not like everybody else down here. They mean it.' He suddenly felt more sad than scared. 'Let's get those beers.'

'I better get moving,' Ray said. 'I'd better start looking for Lennon. Can we get your tape recorder?'

Terry would be glad to get Ray out of here. Earlier he had entertained visions of Misty and Ray and Leon all happily hanging out with him and Dag Wood, talking about music, getting off their faces, sealing Terry and Dag's friendship. But Terry could already see it wasn't going to work out like that.

They stepped outside the club. It was raining harder than ever. Terry looked up at the monsoon sky. There was something *wrong* with this weather. The middle of August and thunder rumbled, lightning flashed and cracked directly above their heads. The sodden queue pressed itself against the tiled wall of the Western World. They didn't use umbrellas.

And then there was Leon, patrolling the pavement with a stack of fanzines under his arm, chanting like some old geezer selling the *Evening Standard,* water streaming from the brim of his trilby.

'Nazis are back. Fight the Fascists with *Red Mist.* Only ten pence, five pence for the registered unemployed. Nazis are back. Fight the Fascists with *Red Mist.* Only –'

Terry took his arm and quickly pulled him round the corner, away from the flickering neon to where there were no lights, just the rubble and ruins stretching off into the darkness.

'They're waiting for you in there,' Terry said. 'They're going to get you.'

'Because of your review,' Ray said. 'The *REBELS WITHOUT A COCK* one.'

Leon hefted the fanzines under his arm, tugged on the brim of his hat, thinking about it. And then he smiled like a naughty child.

'The Sewer Rats are waiting for me?' he asked. 'Those middle-class tossers? That bunch of bloody students? What are they going to do? Debate me to death?'

Terry shook his head. 'Not the band. The nutters that follow them. The Dagenham Dogs.' He watched the colour drain from Leon's face and he felt for his friend. Terry knew it was so much easier to be brave on the page than in real life.

'The ones you said haven't got any balls,' Terry reminded him.

Leon bristled at that. 'That's a complete misreading of my review,' he insisted. 'I didn't say they have no balls. I said they have *small cocks.'*

He wasn't smiling now. He hugged his fanzines close to his chest, peering around the corner. 'They're waiting in there, are they?' And then he saw something that changed everything. 'Bloody hell! Leg it!'

The spike-haired gang outside the Western World had started

to scatter in every direction. Fanned out across the ravaged street, a group of grown men were sauntering towards the club, and even in the gloom of Covent Garden, you couldn't mistake their silhouettes for anything other than their tribe. Long drape coats, thick brothel creeper shoes, skinny strides and greasy hair swept back in what was more of a Hokusai wave than a quiff.

'Teds!' someone screamed.

Terry was aware of Ray taking off and running, surprisingly fast, he thought, and he was just about to do the same when he realised that Leon was on his hands and knees, pulling copies of his fanzine from a puddle.

'Leave them, Leon!' Terry said, a disbelieving laugh rising from somewhere in the back of his throat. 'You mad bastard!

'It's the new issue!' Leon said, and Terry cursed and stooped and snatched up handfuls of *Red Mist*. He looked up and saw that the Teds had broken into a trot. And then he saw the thing that he had been dreading.

In the middle of them all there was a freakishly large man, a sumo wrestler of a Ted, a heavyweight in a drape coat that seemed to strain at the seams, huffing and puffing a bit, and sweating a lot, but with the kind of dopey, murderous look on his face that reminded Terry of the shark in *Jaws*. Terry knew that he was called Titch.

'Leon – I mean it – *come on.*'

And then they were off, breathless and gasping with fear and flight, Terry with a fistful of his friend's leather jacket in his hand, dragging him on, making Leon keep up. Fanzines scattering all around them, and Leon was still babbling about the new issue, and Terry's blood was pumping and he felt the wild, mad laughter well up inside him.

Titch! Fucking hell!

Terry had once seen five cops trying to arrest Titch for throwing some Johnny Rotten lookalike through a Dunn & Co. window down on the King's Road, and the only way they could do it was by beating him unconscious. Terry could still see their truncheons bouncing off that enormous greasy head. If you saw Titch coming, then you ran. He looked as though he could snap you in half if he could ever catch you. Titch and the Teds were on their tails now – they had spotted them. Terry and Leon were running across rough ground, no sign of Ray, the darkness all around, the lights of the West End shining in the distance, Leon swearing and Terry almost choking with panic-stricken laughter, both of them running for their lives.

The Teds were their great tormentors. And it wasn't like the Dogs – this was nothing personal and it made it all the more insane. They didn't need an excuse to batter you.

The Teds seemed like old men. Not just the ones who had been there in the Fifties, tearing up seats to *Rock Around the Clock*. Even the younger ones, the second- and third-generation Teds, seemed prematurely middle-aged. They had sentimental tattoos on their arms and elaborate sideburns on their chops and blunt instruments inside their drapes. So the kids from the Western World fled, like a herd of terrified antelopes dispersing before a pride of lions, and Terry laughed like a lunatic because he knew it was all a game, a lark, and nothing personal, but he ran because he knew the game could put you in hospital.

They tore across rough ground, tripping and stumbling through the blackness, over the rubble, and Terry could feel his heart pounding as if it would burst, could taste the salt of his sweat on his lips, feel his breathing start to burn. He could hear screams in the distance, and it made him stop laughing and concentrate on running and then suddenly there was another scream right by his side as Leon went down a water-filled hole and clattered flat on his face.

Panting hard and muttering a quick prayer, Terry pulled Leon to his feet. The hat was gone. Even in nothing but pale moonlight, Leon's hair gleamed metallic orange.

'Fucking hell, Leon,' Terry chuckled. 'What happened to your hair? What is it – ginger?'

'Autumn Gold.' Leon shoved muddy copies of *Red Mist* into his shoulder bag. He was in a grumpy mood. 'Where's my hat?'

Terry scanned the ground and shoved Leon's trilby back on his head. He shushed Leon, and they half-crouched, watching the shadows of Teddy Boys hunting across the wasteland, passing nearby but spreading out, losing the scent. Terry gulped hard, put an arm around Leon's shoulders, pulled him close. The Teds looked like throwbacks, missing links, their feet enormous in brothel creepers, their torsos abnormally long in their Edwardian drapes, their shortened legs unnaturally skinny. And topping it all, that crowning glory of Elvis '56 hair, wilting now in the unseasonable weather.

'Come on,' Terry whispered.

They ducked inside a building with two of its walls gone. Terry guessed that it was once some sort of storehouse. Maybe they kept flowers here, back when it was a market. Now it looked like a bomb had hit it.

'Titch is not with them, is he?' Leon babbled. He was shaking. 'I didn't see Titch. I don't think Titch is with them.'

'Titch is with them,' Terry said. He straightened Leon's hat, patted him twice on the shoulder, trying to calm him down. 'How could you miss the great ape? Come on.'

The ground floor was nothing but rubble, crushed bricks and splintered wood. They climbed a broken staircase to the first floor, and Terry was shocked to find the sky was still above them, the roof half gone, the rafters like a mouth full of broken black teeth.

'Everybody always wants to kick our heads in,' Leon whispered, and there was something about his plaintive voice that made Terry smile.

'Everybody always wants to kick *your* head in,' he hissed. 'Especially me. Next time, leave your rotten fanzine –'

Suddenly they froze. Something was stirring in the darkness. They were not alone. They pressed themselves against the angle of gaping walls. A stone skittered across the bare floorboards. Terry and Leon looked at each other, and Terry picked up a heavy piece of wood, thinking of Bruce Lee in *Enter the Dragon*, Bruce walking into the room full of mirrors, confronting his destiny. Then Ray stepped out of the darkness, his blond hair soaked and matted and plastered to his filthy face.

'This floor safe?' he said. 'Feels a bit wobbly.'

'Jesus Christ, Ray,' Terry sighed, dropping the piece of wood. They stared at each other and laughed nervously, woozy with relief. The Teds still hadn't caught them. They huddled under a piece of the remaining roof and slumped against a wall with bare bricks showing. Terry saw they were all exhausted. And it was still early. It was time to jump-start the night.

'Titch is with them,' Ray said. 'I saw Titch.'

'We saw him too,' Terry said, reaching inside his jacket pocket. He took out a small cellophane bag and, shielding it from the rain with his free hand, he held it out to Ray. But Ray shook his head, no, and gave Terry a disapproving look. Terry felt a flicker of annoyance. Ray would never let him forget getting messed up on his first day.

103

Leon was peering out of a shattered window frame. 'They're still down there,' he said. 'Those fucking dinosaurs.'

Terry laughed. 'If anybody's going to be extinct tonight, it's you.'

He unwrapped the bag and dipped in the car key. When he pulled it out, the tip was covered in white powder. Terry placed an index finger on one side of his nose and the snowy key-tip under his open nostril. Then he sniffed hard, throwing back his head, tasting the chemical numbing the back of his throat. He blinked at Ray, his eyes filling up, and gave a satisfied cough.

'You keep taking that bathtub sulphate and you'll be extinct before anyone,' Ray said, and Terry knew that what he meant was – *the first time I met you, you never wanted to see another drug for the rest of your life.*

Terry did the same to his other nostril. 'It helps me work.' *Makes me strong,* he thought. *Makes me fearless.* 'Keeps me awake,' he said. 'Makes the music sound better.'

'The music shouldn't need anything to make it sound better,' Ray said. 'Or there's something wrong with the music.'

'Oh please,' Terry said. 'As if the bloody Beatles weren't out of their Scouse boxes from one end of the Sixties to the other.'

'That's different,' Ray said, though he didn't quite know how it was different. He started pulling wet strands of hair from his face.

Terry smiled at him in the darkness. 'Getting an early night tonight, are you?'

Ray shrugged. 'Probably not tonight.'

'You better give me some of that,' Leon said. 'I've got a long night myself. Got to sell the fanzine and then review Leni and the sodding Riefenstahls at the Red Cow.' He crouched before Terry and then hesitated. 'Not coke, is it?'

Terry laughed. 'Sixty quid a gram? I can't afford coke. And

wouldn't want it if I could. I might turn into a Fleetwood Mac fan.' He dipped his key into the bag. 'This is the good stuff. Amphetamine sulphate from Fat Andy.'

Leon nodded approvingly. 'It's a proletarian drug. Soldiers took it in the war. To stay awake and fly bombers and fight Fascism.'

'Twelve quid a gram,' Terry said. 'It doesn't get much more proletarian than that.'

Leon noisily snorted the speed, a rhino at the watering hole. Terry and Ray both laughed and shook their heads, and told him to keep the noise down. 'What?' Leon said. Then Terry once more held out the tiny bag to Ray.

'Come on,' he said, his voice gentle now. 'It'll help you to stay awake. While you're looking for John Lennon.'

'You interviewing Lennon?' Leon said, sounding more impressed than he would have liked.

Ray nodded, seeming to say yes to everything. Terry watched him almost delicately sniff the speed, and he was once again aware that Ray had been doing this for longer than all of them. They smiled at each other in the darkness.

Terry crept to the empty window. Through the pouring rain he could see the neon sign of the Western World flickering in that ocean of blackness. He thought of Misty and wondered if she would wait for him to come back. And then he quickly stepped back when he saw the misshapen shadows moving around in the wasteland, still hunting their prey.

'We're here for a while,' he said. He stared up at the sky through the ruined rafters. 'I'll get you that tape recorder as soon as it's safe.'

Ray was silent for a second. He could taste the speed on the back of his tongue, feel it lift his mood. Then he said, 'Okay, thanks,' as Leon excitedly pushed his face in their faces and said, 'Is-it-having-any-effect-on-you-because-I-can't-feel-a-thing-and-I-wonder-if-it's-really-working?'

Ray and Terry laughed at him, and Terry shoved him, and Ray turned his hat back to front.

'What?' said Leon, genuinely baffled.

In the angles of the remaining walls, where the floor was driest, Terry kicked some splintered wood out of the way and lay down on his back. Ray stared at him for a moment and then lay down beside him. Leon lay down on the other side, moved around and got comfortable for a bit, and then he was calm at last.

Then they lay there in silence for a while, listening to the rain, watching it come straight down, feeling it cool their sweating faces. You couldn't avoid all of it, not with that missing roof, but after being chased by Teds, it was so refreshing that Terry sighed. And he thought how good it was to be still, to be quiet for once, to be with people you knew so well that there was no real need to talk, and to just feel the sweet kick of the sulphate in your veins, to enjoy that rush of pure euphoria, and to let it all go for a while.

Because, despite all the trials of their youth, summer was here, they were just starting out and when Terry Warboys looked up at the night sky, he couldn't tell where the stars ended, and where the lights of the city began.

SIX

The singing brought Terry out of his dreams.

A woman's voice, drifting across the wasteland, holding a note that could shatter crystal, and then another, and then another – these heavenly sounds that pierced his soul and seemed to know every corner of his heart.

What was it? Italian? A song of loss and yearning – Terry knew that much. A song about the love of your life turning to dust in your hands. There was something about the unknown song that made his heart flood with sorrow. As if he had already lost her.

'Puccini,' Leon said by Terry's side, startling him. '"One Fine Day". Very nice.'

Terry felt Leon get up on one side of him, and then Ray on the other. But he just lay there, staring up at the stormy dome above his head, the rain on his face, listening to the woman's voice, paralysed by the unearthly sound, finding the beauty of it almost unbearable.

It was the most glorious music that he had ever heard, and as it was punctuated by the thunder and lightning, it made him despair, made him feel numb with stupidity for giving himself so totally to a girl who would so casually let some old rock star rest his legs on her lap.

Maybe it was crazy to have a girlfriend at all. To be courting, as his mum would call it. Maybe it was crazy to have someone special in this world, at this time, in this new life, when everyone was trying to be special. Maybe it was mad to have one woman when there were suddenly women all around, when every female in London under the age of twenty-five was flocking to the Western World with dreams of writing about music, or designing clothes, or taking photographs, or playing bass like Grace Fury. But the voice of the unknown singer gnawed at him, wouldn't let him be, and made him bitterly aware that Misty was the one he wanted, madness or not.

Yet what did he really know about her? He knew that she was nineteen, that she tasted of cigarettes and bubble gum, that her favourite photographer was Man Ray, that men looked at her in the street, and not just because she never wore a bra.

As 'One Fine Day' drifted across the black night, Terry knew with complete certainty that you didn't have to know someone to love them, and he also knew that he had never felt like this before, not with the girls in the Mecca and Locarno dance halls and the butcher's doorway of his old neighbourhood, or even the girl he had gone out with at the gin factory, Sally, the one he had liked so much, the one his parents had liked so much, the one they thought he might have ended up marrying, if he didn't have these dreams about another life as a writer waiting for him.

Unlike the girl at the factory, unlike Sally, Misty didn't want him to meet her parents, or talk about their feelings, or their future, and all that crap. She didn't want the things that he expected her to want. She wanted other stuff. He didn't really know what it was, though, and maybe she didn't either. The girls he had known talked about engagement rings and getting serious. Misty talked about *The Female Eunuch* and the suffocating tyranny of men. It drove him nuts. Maybe he should be like everyone else. Just screw around. Take his pleasures where he could. Not act like some old married man. Why not? You could sleep with everybody in the world if you wanted to. It wasn't as if sex had ever killed anyone.

But something in the Puccini drifting across the ruins made Terry realise that he wanted her, he wanted this one, and she was the only one he wanted. He got to his feet and joined his friends at the window.

'It's the aria from *Madam Butterfly*,' Leon said. 'There's this Japanese chick and she falls in love with this American – I don't know – naval captain or something. Then he goes home and marries someone else. But she still loves him. And she says that one fine day her love will come again.'

Terry and Ray waited. Leon laid his folded arms on the window frame and rested his chin on his arms. He sighed.

'Then what happens?' Terry said.

'And then he comes back, but it's too late.'

'That's lovely, Leon,' Ray said, clawing wet hair from his face.

Terry angrily wiped his eyes. 'How do you *know* all this stuff?' he said.

'I just know it,' Leon said, embarrassed and glad it was dark. He couldn't say – my father loves opera, I grew up with this stuff on the music system. That was not the kind of thing you admitted to.

Terry didn't push it. He knew it was a sore point with Leon, this store of knowledge he carried with him. People came to the new music from all sorts of places – factory, dole queue, prison, private school, state school, and the army. Even the London School of Economics. Nobody asked too many questions. Reality was up for grabs, their lives were still waiting to take shape. Terry was glad that there was one of them who knew about Puccini.

The three of them squinted into the darkness. In the distance, walking towards the lights of the West End, they could make out figures in dinner jackets and evening gowns, returning from the opera, umbrellas up, the rain lighter now. It was one of the women who was singing. They listened until the party hailed a taxi and 'One Fine Day' stopped and all you could hear was the rumble of the diesel engine. The yellow *for hire* sign went out and the cab pulled off into the night, a glossy black on a deeper black. They turned away from the window, and that's when Terry heard the voices beneath their feet.

'Are you sure that sulphate wasn't just talcum powder?' Leon was saying, unwrapping a thick pink slab of Bazooka Joe bubble gum and throwing it in his big gob. 'Because I can't feel –'

Terry clamped a hand over Leon's mouth. Ray had already heard them, and had sunk into a kind of protective crouch. Leon struggled, muttered a brief protest and then froze. Now he heard them too. Terry could feel the stickiness of the Bazooka Joe on his sweating palm.

'It's human nature,' someone said downstairs, and the voice – thoughtful, high-pitched, almost lisping – came up through the wrecked floorboards. 'It's because there's been no war for thirty year. All that aggression has to come out somehow.'

The three of them eased into the shadows, back into the angle of the two remaining walls, suddenly aware of every creak in the rotten floorboards. *Thirty year.* It reminded Terry of the way his uncles talked, the way his father talked. That old London habit of making everything singular.

'Don't know about that, Titch,' said a deeper voice and Terry felt his stomach curdle. Ray and Leon were both looking at him. *Titch.* Fucking hell! 'I just hate the fuckers and want to give them all a good hiding . . .'

'There's always been wars,' Titch was saying. Terry could hear them poking around, throwing aside pieces of abandoned furniture. Hunting their prey. 'The English and the French. The Germans and everybody. The Mods and the rockers. The skinheads and the Pakis. The Vikings.'

'Tony Curtis and Kirk Douglas,' said the deeper voice.

Ray smiled. Terry shook his head. There was a splintering of wood.

'Fuck are you talking about?' said Titch.

'*The Vikings,*' said the deeper voice. 'Good picture. Tony Curtis and Kirk Douglas.'

More smashing wood. There was a fury and violence in the squeaky voice now. 'Kirk fucking Douglas? Tony fucking Curtis?' More destruction. 'You think the Vikings were a bleeding film, do you?'

'I'm just saying.' There was something pitiful about the deep voice – a big man humbled. 'I'm just *saying*, Titch.'

There was a rustling sound at his feet and Terry saw a rat the size of his Auntie Elsie's cat poking its snout into Leon's newspaper bag. It made him shiver. Leon poked at the rat with his foot and Terry furiously seized the collar of his leather jacket and shook him

'I don't like them either,' Titch was saying, conciliatory now.

'We've been around a lot longer than anyone. They look like they're not men. Just weird. Strange. Very odd. They nick our clobber – they'll wear a drape – but they'll rip it up. What's that all about? Or they copy bits of our music – it's rock and roll – but it's not done right. They say they're going to wipe Teds out. And we're not having it. It's out of order.' More wood being thrown, smashing to pieces, and the violence in the voice. 'It's a diabolical liberty.'

'They're taking the piss, all right,' said the deeper voice. 'Dog collars and dustbin liners and stupid coloured hair.' Terry and Ray both looked at Leon. 'We're not having it.'

The rat emerged from Leon's bag chewing a mouthful of *Red Mist*. It scuttled noisily into the darkness.

'Fuck's that?' squeaked Titch.

You could almost hear them listening.

'Want me to look upstairs?' said the deeper voice.

'No, I'll go,' said Titch. 'You round up the others.'

They heard heavy footsteps coming up the stairs. Then Terry felt the grain of amphetamine sulphate lodged somewhere between his nose and his throat start to stir. He fought to control it but it was no good – a giant sneezing cough needed to explode from his mouth and he couldn't stop it. His mouth opened. His nostrils flared. The terrible snorting sound rose in Terry's throat – and Ray gripped his nose between his thumb and forefinger and the noise came out in a silent gasp. They stood there with Terry's hand on Leon's mouth, Ray's fist wrapped across Terry's nose, their hearts pounding, the footsteps getting louder. They pressed back into the shadows, up against the wall, until they could retreat no further.

A giant form appeared at the top of the stairs. Terry felt his breathing stop. A flash of lightning and Titch was suddenly illuminated, the massive face frowning with effort, scanning the room, the quiff standing up on his head like medieval plumage. Then he chuckled. The enormous rat was at his feet, sniffing a brothel creeper the size of a landing craft.

Titch was still chuckling as he went back down the stairs.

'It was just a cute little mouse,' they heard him say.

They didn't speak until they were sure the Teds were gone.

Downstairs now, staring into the blackness from the empty door, Terry listened to the voices drifting away towards the West End. 'We should get cracking,' he said.

'Yeah,' Leon said, stuffing wet copies of *Red Mist* into his shoulder bag. 'I've got to sell all these before I go and see Leni and the Riefenstahls.'

Terry smiled. 'You really think you're going to flog all these fanzines before Leni and the Riefenstahls come on? Who's going to buy them?'

'I'll have one,' Ray said, and Terry felt a stab of shame. It had never occurred to him to buy a copy of Leon's magazine. He watched Ray counting out the coins with hands that were still shaking.

Terry pulled out a handful of coins. 'Better give me one too,' he said.

Leon laughed with delight as he gave them their fanzines and pocketed the cash. 'This is turning out to be a bloody good night!' he said, hefting his shoulder bag. 'Okay – I'll see you back at *The Paper*.'

With their copies of *Red Mist* in their hands, Terry and Ray watched his slight figure making off towards the lights of the West End, moving across the flattened surface of Covent Garden like the first man on the moon.

Terry looked at Ray. 'Want another line?'

'No, I'm cool.'

Ray could already feel the euphoric buzz wearing off, and being replaced by a tight, jangled feeling. This was why he disliked speed. There was always a price to pay for the heady bliss of the first rush and your blood bubbling with pleasure. There was always a come-down. He wanted something to take the edge off the speed, but not more of the same. He said nothing as Terry dipped his key into the little bag, bobbed his head and came up sniffing like a man with a fever coming on. Terry didn't need saving any more.

'We should go,' Ray said. 'Get that tape recorder.'

'Yeah,' Terry said, although he was afraid to return to the Western World, uncertain what he might find. But the sulphate burned away the doubts, filled him with a kind of cocky elation, and made him feel like he could conquer the world. 'Misty will be waiting,' he said.

They walked back towards the club in silence, watching their footing for the potholes and muddy trenches that pockmarked the area. The rain was easing off, but it didn't make much difference. They couldn't get any wetter.

'Before you joined *The Paper*,' Ray said, 'when you were a reader, did you ever buy it a day early?'

Terry was distracted, trying to remember where Misty had parked the car. So much had happened – Dag Wood, the drugs, the Teds, getting chased, that bloody rat – that it felt like weeks ago. He could see the lights of the club in the distance.

'You mean come up to the centre of town on a Wednesday?' he said. Now he thought about it, he could remember it well. 'I did it all the time. I did it every week. I got off my shift and caught the tube down to Tottenham Court Road. The stall outside the station. They always had it there.' He remembered the excitement he had felt every Wednesday, the new issue of *The Paper* damp with ink. Reading Skip Jones. Reading Ray Keeley. 'How about you?'

'Wednesday,' Ray said. 'It meant so much to me. My family hadn't been back in the country long. School wasn't going great. I didn't really have any mates. And *The Paper* – it was a window into this world that I loved, that I wanted to be a part of. That's why I went up there when I was fifteen with my little think piece on the Eagles.' Terry laughed. 'That's how it started,' Ray smiled.

'*The Paper*,' Terry said. 'It just made you see that there was something more than the drab misery of everyday life. All the greyness and disappointment. Know what I mean?'

Ray nodded. He knew exactly what Terry meant.

'So I worked up the nerve to walk in there,' he said. 'Didn't know anything about making appointments. Spoke to White. He was great – asked me what music I liked, who I read – it really surprised him, how much I knew. Got a couple of albums to review – stuff nobody else wanted. That's how I got in there. Because it was the only thing I really cared about.'

'I still sort of feel the same way,' Terry said. 'It's different, but it still gets to me. When I walk into the office in the morning I always wonder what's going to happen today. Maybe I'll talk to Skip and he'll have found some great new band. Maybe there's going to be Debbie Harry or Joe Strummer sitting on my desk. And I know Leon will be arguing with people, and White will be laying out the cover, and the older guys will be shouting for the dummy, and all those kids out there will be waiting for the new issue – maybe even coming up to town to get it a day early.'

'Like we did.'

'Yeah. Like we did.' Terry stopped, scratching his head. 'Car's somewhere over there,' he said. 'I'm sure it is.' He looked at Ray. 'What made you think of all that? Buying *The Paper* on a Wednesday?'

Ray took a breath, let it go. 'I might be leaving soon,' he said. 'I might be out.'

Terry was stunned. 'I can't believe it.' Somehow he had always assumed that the world would become how he wanted it to be, and then just stay that way for ever. He couldn't imagine the offices of *The Paper* without his friend. And suddenly he understood the importance of Ray finding John Lennon. 'White,' he said. 'That bastard.'

'It's not his fault,' Ray said. 'It's not Dr Barnardos.'

They were at the car. Terry snapped open the boot.

'Wow,' Ray said, contemplating the Ford Capri. 'Misty's got a great car.'

'It belongs to her old man,' Terry said, embarrassed, for this was a time when you boasted about being on the dole or living in a tower block, not possessions or privilege. If you came from any kind of money, you kept quiet about it. 'He just lets her use it sometimes, that's all.'

'Nice wheels though,' Ray said. None of them had cars. They used the bus and tube, unless a record company or their expense account was paying for the ticket. Terry zipped open his kitbag and took out the tape recorder.

'If I can find him, I reckon he'll be easy to talk to,' Ray said. 'But I might puke up before I meet him. That's okay, isn't it?'

Terry nodded, slamming the boot shut. 'Yeah, I puked up before I met Bowie.'

Ray thought about it. 'It's just – you don't want them to think you're a dickhead, do you?'

'That's right.' Terry locked the boot. 'But of course your big problem, Ray, is that you *are* a dickhead.'

'Yeah, well. Takes one to know one.'

They laughed and Terry shoved Ray, and then he was serious. 'They can't get rid of you.'

Ray shuffled his feet, hugging the tape recorder. 'I don't know why not,' he said. He tried to make his hair fall in his face but it was far too wet. 'Everything ends. It does. Sooner or later. This – all this – it has to end sometime. It's a music paper, not the civil service. Sooner or later, everything comes to an end.'

Terry looked at him and he thought that Ray wasn't just talking about his job.

'Yeah, maybe everything ends,' Terry said. He could hear the buzz of traffic, the distant boom of a live band, the city calling them to their fates. He gave Ray a final push, not smiling now – encouraging him, telling him to get moving, but mostly just for friendship's sake. 'But not yet.'

Leon's senses felt heightened, alive, and awake to every detail on the top deck of the bus. He could smell cheap aftershave and beer breath and vomit and chips drenched in vinegar and, permeating all the other top-deck scents, the choking fog of cigarette smoke. He lit up a snout and sucked on it hungrily.

Beneath him he saw the pubs with their red, white and blue Silver Jubilee bunting, shabby and frayed now after a few months in the elements, and he wondered if they would ever take it down. He narrowed his eyes against the smoke and the light, and began composing his review.

He loathed Leni and the Riefenstahls with a passion – all that flirting with swastikas, all that art school pretension, all that po-faced bollocks done up as though it actually meant something. He knew he could write a great review. Which meant a great bad review, a hatchet job of distinction.

Christ, he thought, if you *must* have Teutonic end-of-all-we-know nihilism then listen to Kraftwerk, or the Velvet Underground before Nico had to flee New York. At least the mad cow was the real thing. Yeah, get Nico references into the review, he thought, bury the bastards with unfavourable comparisons. *Attempting to recreate the Weimar Republic when you are from the Home Counties.* Oh yes, he could use that too. Maybe he should be writing some of this stuff down. White would love it – would see that he was the rising star.

Leon wasn't looking forward to seeing the band – or being surrounded by all their pea-brain fans in their Mister Byrite jack-boots – but he was really looking forward to slagging them off.

His plan was to write the review in his head on the bus, see the gig for a bit of local colour, then go back to *The Paper* in the early hours and knock out his review before they all started arriving in the morning. Then he saw something from the top deck of the bus and all his plans went out the window. Leon pressed his face against the glass, and although it steamed up with his breath, he could still make out the club shining through the mist and rain.

The Goldmine. The name picked out in sickly yellow neon that resembled Birds Eye custard far more than any precious metal. It was a Leicester Square disco that they were queuing around the block to get into, all these suburban kids in their High Street flares.

Leon stared with wonder at the strangeness of their clothes.

The boys in trousers that held their crutch in a leech-like grip but then exploded around their ankles, shirts that were either plain short sleeves in this stretchy, clingy material, their young male nipples sticking through, or elaborate long sleeves with abundant collars – all of them open to the hairless chest with a St Christopher swinging around their neck, the patron saint of wankers in flared trousers, and the girls with those overdone mumsy haircuts, everything flicked up at the ends, every one of them a Charlie's Angel, and wearing lots of white to look good under the lights. A riot of wide trousers and hairspray and flicked feather cuts.

Leon had to laugh.

Now *that's* truly a world without meaning, he thought. Nihilism? Blankness? A rejection of all values? Leni and the Riefenstahls should take a look at this scene. This is real world-negating numbness – not some rock-and-roll approximation.

But despite his reflex sneering, there was something about these boys and girls outside the Goldmine that touched him deeply, just as he always felt inexplicably moved when he was standing outside the Western World, trying to sell *Red Mist*. In the whole of battle-grey Britain, with its fading Silver Jubilee bunting in washed-out red, white and blue, it often felt like the only splash of true colour was the young.

Leon began dropping copies of his fanzine out of the bus window. They fluttered to the street among the disco kids like propaganda leaflets being parachuted into an occupied nation. Leon felt a warm glow inside as he imagined these culturally malnourished youngsters reading his thoughts on the Lewisham riot, the new Tom Robinson single and the MPLA. But then something terrible happened. The disco kids completely ignored the copies of *Red Mist* that were falling all around them. They chatted and laughed among themselves and fumbled in their tight clothes for the entrance fee to the Goldmine. They walked all over *Red Mist*.

Leon clattered down the stairs of the bus and jumped off into the traffic. Then he was among the disco kids, picking up the unwanted copies of his fanzine, cursing to himself about ungrateful bastards. He straightened up as he heard some sort of ruckus in the crowd. Voices raised in protest, muttered threats, a girl's scream. Violence was very close. And then he saw them.

More Dagenham Dogs were passing by, on their way to the Western World. Twenty of them, maybe more, a private army of shaved heads and pierced faces, all of it clumsily done – the shaving, the piercing – and caked with dark, dried blood. They roughly shouldered through the disco kids, heaving them out of the way when they didn't move fast enough, and asking anyone who protested if they wanted some.

'You want some? You want some?'

Leon didn't want any. He knew if they saw him he'd be dead.

He bolted into the lobby of the Goldmine, ignoring the protests of the girl at the door, ducking past a large black bouncer too slow to stop him, and down the wide, red-plush staircase. Leon stopped at the foot of the stairs, staring at the heaving dance floor as if he was an explorer who had stumbled upon some lost tribe. He had never seen anything like it.

It was another kind of music in a different kind of basement.

They were getting ready to leave without Terry.

And then he comes back but it's too late.

Dag and his entire team of flunkies were piling into three cars lined up outside the Western World with their engines running. Misty was standing by an open door of the lead car while Dag, already reclining in the passenger seat, talked to her, the palms of his hands held upwards, as if he were praying, or selling something. She had the decency to look undecided.

'Misty?' Terry said, and she looked at him over the roof of the car.

Then one of the brothers in the band intercepted Terry – the beefy, meathead drummer with bad tats all over his back – and gently took his arm, steering Terry towards the end car.

'Don't worry, man, we saved you a slot.'

'I'm not worried,' Terry said, shrugging him off, and then Misty was in front of him. He shook his head. 'What's going on?'

'Dag's inviting us back to his hotel.' *Dag* – as if she was the one with the relationship, not Terry. 'We're going to hang out.'

'It's all cool, man,' said the meathead drummer, suddenly there again, placing a large paw on Terry's arm. Terry pushed him off, not so gently this time. And he looked at Misty with eyes that said, or tried to say – *this is me.* That face he loved so much broke into a smile, but there was something behind it that he had never seen before. She was holding something back. He could tell.

'Why don't I see you there?' she said lightly. It wasn't a question.

Then before he knew what was happening Misty was climbing into the passenger seat of the lead car, easing herself on to Dag's lap. Terry heard laughter and a squeal before the door closed and the car pulled away. He stood there sick to his stomach with a feeling that threatened to eat him alive.

The drummer had drifted away to the second car.

And then some other woman's voice, calling his name. 'Terry?'

The back door of the last car was open. He saw a beautiful, smiling face, but couldn't place it for a moment. Oh yes – Christa. From Berlin. Dag's girlfriend or drug dealer or whatever. Black hair, white teeth, and skin that looked as though it had never been exposed to daylight.

'You can come with me if you like,' she said.

The second car, containing the drummer and his bass-playing brother and their pick-ups, had already left. And that was good because Terry felt a murderous rage towards the drummer, who had conspired with Dag to separate him from his girl. *Like some kind of pimp,* Terry thought, visions of Bruce Lee on the rampage in his head. Kicking, smashing, destroying. Fucking bastards, he thought. Fucking bastards, the lot of you.

But nobody had held a gun to Misty's face, had they? No, whatever got held to Misty's face tonight, Terry thought, it wouldn't be a gun.

So he got into the back seat of the final car. The woman – Christa – gave him the same easy, empty smile that she had given him in Berlin, as mechanical as a stewardess, a lovely smile that was strained from overuse, all its natural beauty drained away by faking it too many times.

Dag's manager, Warhol blond and fifty if he was a day, was in the passenger seat, next to a chauffeur with a peaked hat. Without turning round, the manager said something in German and Christa laughed. Terry didn't like any of it – the old boy who knew more than he did, the language that he didn't understand, the joke that he suspected was at his expense, and his girlfriend gone. That's what he liked least of all.

Then Terry felt expert fingers exploring the top of his thigh.

And the car began to move.

SEVEN

There were no good places to come down, but the underground was the worst.

The speed had left Ray with his nerve ends rattling, fighting off sweating claustrophobia and obsessively loading and unloading the cassette into Terry's tape recorder.

This wasn't the time to be on the Piccadilly line.

Again and again, he made sure the red *record* light flicked on as it should, ensuring that it would capture Lennon's words when the time came. If it ever did. And he tried to batten down the mounting dread inside him, knowing it was only the other side of the drug. Speed always did this to him – showed him a great time and then threw him out the window.

When the three of them had been looking up at the lights and the drama of the storm, the amphetamine sulphate had felt like molten joy running in Ray's veins. But the euphoria wore off as time wore on, and now it had been replaced by a nagging, unnameable anxiety. He felt like crying. Everything seemed washed out and fucked up. Including him. Especially him.

The tube train thundered west, crammed with office workers with loud voices, all Take Six suits and Glitter Band hair, still stinking of the Rat & Trumpet, and the noise and the smell and nearness of all those other lives made Ray's head throb like a fresh bruise.

The office workers were rolling to their mainline railway stations and the last train home. Ray still had a job to do. Concentrate, concentrate. What's the plan, Ray? There was no plan. Licking lips as dry as the Gobi Desert, he suddenly knew he couldn't interview John Lennon feeling as bad as this. Interview him? He couldn't even find him.

He had got on the tube with the vague notion of staking out the lobby of the Hotel Blanc and waiting for John to show. The Hotel Blanc, tucked just behind Marble Arch, was the obvious choice – visiting American musicians almost always stayed at the Blanc when they were in London. A thousand cowboy boots had ambled past the palm trees in its lobby, a hundred bands had enjoyed its aura of slightly decadent affluence, dozens of music writers from the *NME, Sounds, Melody Maker* and *The Paper* had turned up with their notepads, dreaming of good quotes and free cocaine. By the time he was seventeen, Ray knew the lobby of the Blanc better than he knew the sixth-form college that he was still technically attending. Yes, he liked the idea of going to the Blanc. It calmed him down. It felt almost cosy.

But in his heart Ray already knew that going to the Blanc was hopeless. Just because Nils Lofgren and Fleetwood Mac and the Eagles stayed at the Blanc when they were in town, that didn't mean John Lennon would be there. In fact, it almost certainly meant that John would be somewhere else. John went his own way. I have to be like John, Ray thought. I have to go my own way. This is a lesson I must learn . . .

The tube train stuttered to a halt between stations, and the office workers jeered as an Asian voice came on the intercom to apologise for the delay. Stopping between stations when you were coming down – this was not good. This was the pits.

In response to the Asian voice, some of the office workers started singing some Peter Sellers hit – '*Oh, doctor, I'm in trouble.*' – '*Well, goodness gracious me.*' – while Ray fought to control his breathing, battling down feelings of panic. His left arm began to tingle and he felt his heart hammering like it would burst. A heart attack? Death was so close, it was always so close. They didn't realise that – Terry and Leon and the rest of them at *The Paper*. Everything you love will die and rot. All of it. Maybe very soon. Ray thought he might die tonight and that threatened to tip the panic over to hysteria. But he couldn't lose it. Not down here, stuck between stations. Not here.

He needed something to take the edge off the speed. He needed a different kind of drug. If he got off this train alive, the first thing he would do was score a nice mellow smoke. But he fumbled in his pockets and came out with only loose change and a Polo mint. Not enough to score. He fiddled with the tape recorder again, still enough speed in his veins to get caught up in the action, to become obsessed with it. That was the thing about speed, he thought. You lost yourself.

'Testing, testing,' he said as quietly as he could, pulling the tape recorder as close as a lover's face, and the office workers saw him and mocked and scoffed, saying things like, 'Do you read me?' and 'Come in, Houston,' and 'Beam me up, Scottie,' and 'Exterminate, exterminate.' Ray saw the little red light responding to his voice, and he tried to concentrate on that, aware that he was panting like an exhausted dog.

Then, as he watched the red light and tried to shut out the

office workers, he suddenly knew what he wanted to do before he could talk to John.

He wanted to go home. He wanted to get straight. He wanted to soften the come-down with what he had hidden in his old Doctor Who lunchbox.

And most of all Ray wanted to see his brother, and to make sure that he was okay.

It was easier to sneer on the outside.

Down in the Goldmine, Leon was on their territory, and it made him pause, check himself, feel painfully aware that he was carrying a shoulder bag full of fanzines and wearing a funny hat. As he moved along the crowded bar he got a twinge of that old crippling self-consciousness that he'd had in front of mirrors when he was young, when you were just so burdened by how different you were to everyone else that you thought maybe you would never move again. He thought it was lucky that he was out of his mind on drugs.

Everything in here was strange, new, different.

The dancing. The moves that Leon was used to seeing hardly qualified as dancing at all. Just this piston-like movement, up and down for ever, letting off steam. But here in the Goldmine they had these intricate steps and secret, hard-earned moves – they could really dance, the way Gene Kelly and Cyd Charisse could really dance. They made it look as though it was as natural as breathing. And Leon thought – why can't I move like that?

And the clothes. In the Western World they dressed as if they had salvaged some rags from the aftermath of a nuclear holocaust. In the Goldmine they dressed as if they were going to a wedding. In the Western World the clothes were shades of black. Here in the Goldmine their clothes were tight and white, their hair permed and teased, and everyone looked as though they had just had their weekly bath. And then there were the lights.

The Western World was always in almost complete darkness apart from the bare bulbs above the upstairs bar and the downstairs stage. The Goldmine was constantly alive with streams of piercing sci-fi lasers and twirling disco balls and pulsating strobes. Leon shyly bought a screwdriver and tossed it down, tasting the orange juice at the back of his throat, feeling the kick of the Smirnoff, fascinated by the intricate swirls of colour of the lights above the heaving dance floor, trying to work out when blue would change to red, positive he could work it out if only he watched carefully enough. There was so much colour in here. He had never known there could be so much colour.

And then there was the music. No bands here. No lads in Lewis Leathers slouching on stage and saying something like, 'This one's about pensions. One! Two! Three! Four!' Here there were records and records only, with the DJ up in his booth, but nothing like the impassive natty dread at the Western World, there to provide mood music between the main events. Here the DJ bossed the night. And the music!

For some reason Leon had expected the Goldmine to be full of sappy romance and chart pap – but it was more narcissistic than that, more esoteric – all these exhortations to move it, get down on it, make it funky now. It wasn't like any mainstream music Leon had ever heard. It was harder, tougher, funkier – the DJ proudly boasted of white labels, imports, rare grooves. They were as elitist as any kid at the Western World.

This wasn't his kind of place. Not at all. What was the point of the fanzine in his bag? Why was he alive? He dreamed of fighting racism, defeating injustice, changing the world. And in the

Goldmine they dreamed only of leaving the world behind. Yet he ordered a second screwdriver, and didn't want to go.

Because there was something about the scene – the lack of pretentious bastards on stage, the ever-changing colours of those epileptic Christmas lights, and above all the seamless, endless beat – the sheer mindless joy of the music, the way the records just flowed into each other, like a river of music – that he found hypnotic, and thrilling, and oddly comforting.

Leon began to sway at the bar, watching the dance floor, wishing he was brave enough to do that. Brave enough to get out there with the well-scrubbed kids in their tight white clothes. Brave enough to dance.

And then he saw her.

She was in the middle of the dance floor.

The most beautiful girl in the world.

Surrounded by a group of her friends, all of them responding to some new record as if it was the news they had been waiting for. They whooped, they raised their arms above their heads, their dancing stepped up a gear. Someone blew a whistle and it made Leon jump.

At first the record they were responding to seemed like any other record in the Goldmine. This rolling, tumbling funk punctuated by a waterfall of piano and then a burst of lonely brass started wailing and then, finally, after an age, the voices came in.

'*Shame!*' cried the back-up singers, and then this woman with a perfect voice sang, '*Burning – keep my whole body yearning!*' and then she muttered something that Leon couldn't quite catch, and then the chorus girls shouted, '*Shame!*' again and then the singer was saying that her mama just didn't understand, and the chorus was moaning like love-sick angels – '*Back in your arms is where I want to be . . . want to be . . .*'

Leon had never heard anything quite like it.

Never heard anything so full of life.

It made wanting someone, and not getting them, seem like the most important thing in the world. More important than . . . anything. The real reason we are alive. Leon's head was spinning.

He wanted to push through the crowds and talk to the most beautiful girl in the world and say – I get it, I understand, I feel the same way. But his tongue was a hopeless knot, his feet felt like they were in concrete. He knew he could never talk to a girl like that. And Leon dancing seemed about as likely as Leon levitating.

'Oh yeah, baby,' said the DJ, before this perfect record was even over, 'Evelyn "Champagne" King there with a little thing called "Shame" . . . and before we get down and dirty with Heatwave, we have some breaking news . . .'

Heads on the dance floor were turning towards the DJ in his booth. Leon kept looking at the most beautiful girl in the world.

'Ladies and gentlemen, boys and girls,' the DJ said, uncertain of the tone he should adopt, and sounding both solemn and facetious. 'The King is dead.' No reaction on the dance floor. 'That's right – we just heard that Elvis Presley died tonight.' The DJ slapped down a record.

'Thought you would like to know,' said the DJ. 'That's the end of this newsflash.'

They cheered. Leon stared at them in amazement. They were fucking cheering.

Not all of them. The most beautiful girl in the world and her friends looked puzzled, briefly conferred, as if they were not quite sure who this Elvis Presley person was, as if they had heard the name somewhere but couldn't quite place him.

But most of the dancers seemed to think that they owed the news some sort of reaction. And many of them whooped as if their side had scored, or as if one kind of music had just triumphed over another. And all of them started dancing again.

But by then Leon, emboldened by the speed and a sense of outrage that came naturally to him, was pushing his way across the dance floor and climbing into the DJ's booth, snatching up the microphone – the DJ took a step back, raising his hands in compliance, letting the madman in the funny hat have it – and then Leon was staring out across the dance floor, trying to find the words. He knew that this was important.

'No – wait – listen,' Leon said, and the DJ helpfully turned off 'Boogie Nights'. 'Testing, testing. Hello? Elvis – right? Respect to Elvis Presley. Elvis is – was – more than the ultimate rock star, right? Elvis is – was – where it all begins.' His voice was rising, it was coming to him now. 'Elvis broke down more barriers than anyone in history. Racial barriers, sexual barriers, musical barriers. I mean, the personal is political, right? Elvis – what Elvis Presley did – he dared to see the world in a new way . . .'

'Right on, baby,' said the DJ, leaning into the microphone. He smiled at Leon and nodded encouragement. 'Carry on.'

'Thank you,' said Leon. 'Black and white music – it was like apartheid before Elvis.' He was warming to his theme. 'Music was like one big fucking South Africa. White radio stations. Black radio stations. Music, all types of music, it was kept in a ghetto. Elvis made all of this possible.' Leon stared at them helplessly. They were all watching him. Maybe he had gone on too long. Maybe he could have expressed it better. 'I'm just saying,' he said, and there was a pleading in his voice now. 'Don't cheer his death. Please don't do that.' He tugged nervously at the brim of his hat. 'Forget about cheeseburgers and Las Vegas and, you know, white jump suits, B movies in Hawaii or dressed up as a soldier. Whatever. That's not it. You have to look at the way things were, and everything he changed. He was a great man. Flawed – yeah. Corny at times – well, all right. But Elvis Presley . . . he fucking set us free, man.'

There was a moment of complete stillness and silence. The crowd stared up at Leon, and Leon stared back at them, and nobody knew what to do. Then the DJ snatched his microphone back and Leon felt the air move as he slammed down a 45 like a short-order cook slapping a raw meat patty on a grill.

'Yeah, respect to the King, baby,' said the DJ, 'and respect to . . .' his voice dropped to a sultry baritone, '. . . the Commodores!'

Leon thought they would throw him out. There were bouncers at the Goldmine who were far meaner looking than any security at the places he was used to, these bouncers who looked like they treated violence as a profession, a calling, but he felt oddly calm about the prospect.

Leon wasn't a coward, not where physical violence was concerned. He could never be as afraid of bouncers or the Dagenham Dogs as he was of dancing. Or of talking to a girl he really liked, such as the most beautiful girl in the world. A quick, impersonal beating didn't scare him as much as the prospect of that incredible girl looking at him with pity.

But in the shadows of the Goldmine, the bouncers just stared right through him with hooded eyes and folded arms, not moving. One of them – a tough-looking forty-year old with a silvery quiff – even nodded at Leon. An Elvis fan, he thought.

The DJ just smiled at Leon, patted him on the back as if he

was some kind of floor show, and turned up the volume. The dancers were already lost in the music.

Leon self-consciously started from the booth, feeling awkward and clumsy and tight in the presence of all those habitual dancers, all those loose-limbed groovers getting down with the Commodores. He was depressed about the death of Elvis, and felt like his words were useless and inadequate.

Nobody knows what I'm talking about, he thought, and then he stumbled badly on the bottom step of the DJ booth and pitched forward like someone trying a reckless new dance move.

Leon was getting up off his knees and looking around for his hat when he was aware that someone was standing over him. It was the most beautiful girl in the world.

A journalist is at home everywhere, Leon thought, as she took his hand. At home everywhere. Remember that, Leon.

'Like the hair,' she said, the sound of the suburbs in her voice. 'Autumn Gold?'

Terry loved speed because it helped him to think clearly.

The cold white conviction of the drug helped him to stay focused, to deal with the job at hand, to forget about all the things that didn't matter.

That's why on the short journey across the West End he was able to pretty much ignore Christa's hand resting on the top of his thigh, to shut out the mindless babble of Dag's manager in the front seat, and let the crowds beyond the car window just melt away. The speed helped him to give his complete attention to Misty, and what he was going to say to her when they got there. Oh yes.

The car pulled up in front of the Hotel Blanc, and Terry felt

Christa's fingernails increasing their pressure. He looked at her as if for the first time and she smiled at him with her smooth, practised smile, and the funny thing was, he really liked her face, he had liked it from the moment he first saw her in Berlin.

He liked the red slash of her mouth, the pale skin, the unearthly, un-English whiteness of her teeth. The way she dressed more formally than what he was used to – like a businesswoman, he thought. All that was good. But he already had a girl, and he needed to find her.

Christa said his name but the door was open and he was already gone, out of the car and into the hotel, which he knew well from interviewing various longhairs from Los Angeles in his early days at *The Paper*, before he could pick and choose who he talked to, who he wrote about, but he still came here from time to time, most recently to interview a steady stream of shorthair musicians from New York. American groups at the Hotel Blanc was one of the things that never changed. The first thing he saw was Brainiac being ejected by a uniformed doorman.

'It is imperative that I speak to Mr Dag Wood immediately,' he was saying. 'Terry! Tell them!'

Terry was already at the staircase where Dag's rhythm section, the two brothers, were lazily ascending with a couple of girls from the Western World. The girls had seemed fashionably undomesticated in the gloaming of the club, all torn stockings and hair stiff and spiked with Vaseline, blinking out at the world from big black Chi-Chi and An-An circles. Under the harsh lights of the hotel lobby they looked like dumpy vampires, or overgrown children on Halloween. But Terry knew there was no man less choosy than a musician on the road.

The drummer brother, the dumber brother, all bulging tattooed biceps in his sleeveless vest, held out a meaty arm, hailing Terry like a long-lost friend. Terry wished he would stop doing that. It was really starting to get on his nerves. He walked past the drummer, and carried on up the stairs, two at a time, past the bass-playing brother, who he had actually liked, who he had spent time with in Berlin, who he had thought was some kind of friend. Terry was starting to learn that you could never really be friends with these people.

There was a door open at the top of the stairs, a party going on inside, and a waiter was trying to get a signature for a tray of drinks. He held out the pen to Terry as he approached and Terry scribbled on the chit, gave the waiter back his pen and entered the room without breaking his stride.

The room was full of people. Some of them he knew. The rest of Dag's band. Faces from the Western World. Other musicians who must have been lodging at the Blanc. Somebody that Terry had seen dealing little blue pills in the toilets at the Roundhouse. And then there was a familiar face at last. Billy Blitzen was sprawled on the sofa, short, dapper, hair everywhere, his immaculate waistcoat unbuttoned, smoking a joint the size of a Mr Whippy cornet.

'I thought you had a gig tonight,' Terry said. 'I thought Warwick Hunt was coming down for your second set. I thought it was your big break and I was going to do a review.'

Billy looked insulted. 'There's plenty of time. Who are you? My mother?'

'And I thought you didn't even *like* Dag Wood,' Terry said, scanning the room. No sign of her. Where the fuck *was* she? 'I thought you said he was an arsehole.' Terry's face twisted with a parody of transatlantic vowels. 'An *asshole*.'

Billy sucked on his Mr Whippy spliff, and didn't need to explain a thing. That's one thing I've learned about these New Yorkers,

Terry thought. They follow the drugs. And then he saw Misty.

On the far side of the room, she came out of what had to be the bathroom followed by Dag Wood. Then she was leaning against a wall and Dag was standing in front of her, his hands resting on the wall either side of her head, almost pinning her there. Terry flew across the crowded room.

'Hey, man,' Dag said to Terry, slowly removing his hands, as if it was no big deal. 'What kept you?'

Terry stared at Dag, then at Misty. He realised he didn't know what to say. He didn't know what to do. He didn't know what was happening. All he knew was that he didn't like it, and his confidence was ebbing away with the kick of the sulphate.

'Is that my JD and coke over there?' said Dag, as smooth as a Foreign Office diplomat. *'Finally.'*

A big cheesy smile and then he was gone, and Terry was alone with his girl again, alone with her in that rented room, and he waited for her to say something.

'What?' she said.

All wide-eyed and innocent.

Terry was speechless. 'What?' he said. 'What?'

'Yeah – what?' A bit of a fishwife tone creeping in now.

'Why'd you run off like that?' he said, more hurt than angry. 'What's going on? I mean – fucking hell, Misty!'

Misty examined her fingernails. 'I didn't run anywhere.' She sighed as if he was her bloody father. 'Chill out, will you? Please, Terry.'

'Chill out?' he said, suddenly agitated. 'Chill out? How can I chill out? What's wrong with you tonight?'

Her hands clawed at the air, grasping at nothing, trying to find the words. As if the way he was drove her insane. It scared him. This was even worse than he'd thought.

135

'Nothing,' she said. 'Everything.'

'I want to know what's happening here.' Trying to keep calm now. Wanting to understand, to make it right. To get things back to where they had been only hours ago. Trying to avoid sounding like one of those men that Germaine Greer had warned her about. 'I just want to know . . .'

He struggled to express what he wanted to know. What had happened to the girl who had met him at the airport? And was it all over between them? And was she going to fuck Dag Wood? Yes, he wanted to know all of these things. But a part of him would prefer not to know.

And he wondered how he was meant to deal with the changes in his life. It was less than a year ago that he had lived in a world where you could get your head caved in for looking at someone's girlfriend the wrong way. For *just looking*. But now he was somewhere else, some weird place where you were meant to chill out and be cool and take it easy when someone was trying to actually fuck your girlfriend.

'You can't steal a woman,' Misty said, reading his mind, making him start with surprise. 'Don't you know that yet? Haven't you learned anything? You can't steal a woman. A woman is not a wallet. You know what your trouble is, Terry?'

Now she was making him tired. 'Why don't you tell me?'

'All right then – you don't want a strong, independent woman. You want the girl next door.'

He almost took a step back. 'What's wrong with the girl next door?'

Misty laughed in his face. 'She's a boring little cow.'

He thought of his ex-girlfriend, the girl from the gin factory. Sally. The one he had left behind with his old life. He missed her tonight. He knew Sally wouldn't be a sucker for Dag Wood. Sally liked Elton John. Especially *Goodbye Yellow Brick Road.*

'There's nothing wrong with the girl next door,' he said.

She shook her head, examined her nails. 'You don't want me to have a career,' she said. 'You can't handle it.'

It was his turn to laugh. 'This is a career? Some old rock star jumping on your bones? That's your idea of a career?'

She almost snarled at him. 'You don't think Dag might be interested in *my work*? Did that even cross your mind? That he might want to look at my portfolio?'

'Oh, I've got no doubt that he wants to take a look at your portfolio, love.' Then his voice softened. 'Come on, Misty. I saw him in Berlin. Dag fucks anything that hasn't got a knob. You think you're special?'

She looked stunned. 'Well, don't you?'

He didn't know what to say. Of *course* he thought she was special. He thought there was no one like her in the world. But wasn't that obvious?

'And why have I never met your parents?' he said.

It was all coming out now.

'Oh, what's that got to do with anything?' she said. 'You're just an old-fashioned guy, Terry. You want me to stay home and – I don't know – bake bread or knit socks or something. You want to hide me away from the world.'

He wanted her to understand. 'No, I don't – I just want to protect you. I just want to stop bad things happening.'

Misty tried to be reasonable. 'Look, Terry – he's a legend. We're just ... talking, that's all. Really. We're just spending some time together. Like the pair of you did in Berlin. What's the difference? That I'm a woman? But why should that stop us? It might be 1955 in your head, but it's 1977 in here. We're just *talking*,' she said, and he felt horrible to see her so unhappy. 'And if not now – then when?'

'I know him,' Terry said simply. 'You don't.'

'But I want to,' she said, and they looked at each other with something close to loathing. A weight seemed to settle on Terry's shoulders. They had never looked at each other like that before. 'You'd like to chain me to a pushchair until my brain melts,' Misty said. 'Admit it!'

Pushchairs? Melting brains? He had no idea what she was going on about. He stood there dumbfounded, lost for words, offering no defence, as if guilty of crimes that he now realised he had committed by accident. Then suddenly Dag was back, his JD and coke in one hand, draping his free arm around Terry's shoulder.

'Look at that,' he chuckled, contemplating his glass and the thin frozen sliver floating on top of his drink. 'They call that ice. Say, man, you got any of that crank left?'

Terry stared warily at Dag. He still wasn't completely sure what was happening. He seemed to be the only one who felt that every-thing had gone wrong. Maybe he was overreacting. Maybe this was how things were in the new world, and you had to live with it. He wished he had more experience of these things. He wished he had seen more. He wished he were older. Maybe everything was innocent after all. How could Terry know? He felt like he knew nothing.

Misty acted as though hanging out with Dag was a cross between harmless fun and a kind of job interview, fascinating but also vital for her career prospects, while Dag acted as if nothing unusual or untoward had happened – as if draping your leather-clad legs across another man's girlfriend and then whisking her off into the night and taking her into a fucking toilet in a hotel room and offering his own girlfriend as fair exchange – but was that really what had happened? – was socially acceptable.

Christa approached their little party and slid her arm around Dag's waist, smiling 'Hi' to Misty, who smiled 'Hi' back, and Dag's big lizard lips placed a wet kiss on Christa's ear. The tip of a fleshy tongue teased her lobe. Her smile never faltered. But, her hand in the car – that was surely a come on, wasn't it? Or was she just being friendly?

Terry gawped at them all, his face red, then fumbled for his speed, a fool who didn't know what to do with his hands. Perhaps he was making a big deal out of nothing. Be cool. That's it. He had to be cool. They would all have a line together and everything would be fine again, even better than Berlin because now Misty was with him.

But the cellophane bag of speed was almost empty. Just a few flakes were left, hardly enough for one decent line. They must have taken more than he realised when they were under the stars, hiding from the Teds. Terry held the bag up apologetically.

'That's okay,' Christa said, her accent more American than German. 'I've got some good stuff up in the suite.'

Dag's huge blue eyes shone. 'Not the Keith blow?'

Christa nodded, and Dag kissed his fingers, a debauched-looking sommelier recommending the Chassagne-Montrachet, assuring Terry and Misty that they were in for an experience they would never forget.

The two young people laughed nervously, like children on Christmas Eve who had just been told that Santa was stuck halfway down the chimney. And they smiled at each other, as if something had been restored between them, healed and mended, and the atmosphere was so cool, meaning relaxed, that when Dag urged Terry to go with Christa and collect the good stuff, he could hardly refuse to go, could he? Because they were all friends here.

So Terry left Misty with Dag and found himself walking out of the party with Christa and catching the lift up to the very top of the hotel. She slipped the key in the lock, smiling her dazzling red and white smile.

'This is it,' she said.

It wasn't like any hotel room that Terry had ever seen. It was more like some rich man's house. He wandered through all that space in a daze, shaking his head – what would his mum think? There was a huge living room with a grand piano and a bedroom with a four-poster and a spiral iron staircase leading up to somewhere else. Net curtains shifted in the wind by the open windows, and Terry stepped out on to the balcony, catching his breath in the chilled summer night air, the rain falling gently now, and it felt like the best of the city was spread out below him.

He saw the lights of the West End, Marble Arch gleaming white and gold, the taillights and headlights of the traffic on Park Lane streaming past the big hotels and car showrooms all the way down to the Playboy Club where right now Bunnies would be dealing cards and spinning roulette wheels with their backs turned to the floor-to-ceiling windows one flight up, and from the street you would be able to see their fluffy rabbit tails shining. Terry smiled to himself, and let his eyes drift beyond all the noise and lights and promise to a great silent expanse of darkness that framed it all. Hyde Park. He breathed in, and it was like inhaling the air on a mountaintop.

When he turned away from the window Christa was sitting on the sofa, naked below the waist apart from a pair of high heels, with her legs crossed. She must have removed her shoes, taken her businesswoman's trousers off, and then put her shoes back on. That's a lot of trouble to go to, Terry thought.

She was opening a carefully folded paper packet that was the size of a book of stamps. He watched her use a razor blade to ease a small mound of white powder on to the large glass-topped coffee table.

'Just a quick one,' she said. 'You've got time for a quick one, haven't you?'

She expertly hoovered up one long mound of cocaine into her perfect nose, and then another. She held out a short silver straw to Terry.

'It doesn't have to be a quick one, *liebling*,' she said soothingly. 'You can take as long as you want.'

He watched her get up from the sofa and walk towards him, felt her place the silver straw in his palm, felt her lips on his mouth, her fingers in his hair, was aware of kissing her back, his hands on her rear, still holding the straw. And he felt himself start to want her, and then start to really want her.

For a moment he thought – why not? Why not just take her now and then go back to the party? Who does it hurt? Then he abruptly pulled himself away, a drowning man fighting for his life, and he was on his way out of the room before he could think about it, her voice and his erection urging him to stay.

'No, I've got to go,' he said, unsure if he was talking to Christa or himself.

She said his name again once, but didn't try to stop him, not really, and then he was in the lift impatiently punching the button for the first floor, but when he got there it was all quiet, the party was over, or had moved on, and the door where he had signed for room service was closed with a *Do Not Disturb* sign outside. He had thought that was Dag's room – wasn't it? But the suite had to be Dag's – didn't it? He looked down the corridor, but all the doors were closed, and the signs all said that nobody wanted to be disturbed. The anger began to boil up inside him. Where is she? Where's my girl?

He banged on the room they had been in, calling Misty's name, ignoring the American voice inside that told him to go and fuck himself. Finally the drummer brother threw the door open, sighing and buck-naked and as intricately mapped with tattoos as a Japanese gangster, and he wearily told Terry to go home, man.

'She's not here, okay?'

Over his shoulder Terry could see one of the dumpy vampires from the Western World kneeling on the floor, as if waiting to pray.

'No, it's not okay,' Terry said. 'It's nowhere near okay.'

'Well, that's too fucking bad, sport,' said the drummer, slamming the door in his face.

Then Terry was moving down the corridor, calling Misty's name again and again, his path impeded by the ruins of room-service deliveries left out for collection. He began banging his fist on door after door, until the ridge from his wrist to his little finger began to pulsate with pain, and voices beyond the locked doors were raised in threats and protest. At the end of the corridor Terry saw his face in a long wall mirror and was stopped in his tracks. He looked like some monkey-faced kid, pale from the speed and wet-eyed from losing his girl. Not a proper grown-up. Nowhere near it. He didn't want to be this way. Everything was out of control.

So from the nearest trolley he picked up a champagne bucket

and hurled it with full force at the mirror. It felt like the glass was still breaking when the two security guards came running up the stairs. Terry stood there hypnotised as the mirror fell away in long shards that shattered and splintered to sparkling pieces as they hit the floor with this tinkling sound that was almost musical. Then they had him.

Then they were dragging him away.

'Misty!' he shouted, trying to dig in his heels. 'Misty!'

But there was no Misty, only people he didn't recognise peeping from beyond doors that never risked releasing the safety chain.

The hotel guards pulled Terry down the stairs and through the lobby, the late-night tourists staring at him as if he was a madman, and he felt the fight going out of him. And he heard the guards laughing at him.

Then he was through the big glass doors and out into the night, dumped on the seat of his pants on the pavement, the security guards turning away as he called her name one last time, shouting up at the hotel rising above him, searching the windows for his Misty. But he saw only darkness and a few fleeting shadows up there. They could have been anyone.

He slowly got up, knowing he wasn't Bruce Lee, knowing he was weak, knowing he had lost her at the first hurdle, knowing the girl he loved was being fucked by some other man. Somewhere far away, the church bells were chiming midnight.

On his feet now, the rain on his face, the loss of her pressed down on him like a physical weight. He had never felt like this before. He had never been brought so low by another human being. All that misery, jealousy and rage, all that dark stuff, all of it wrapped up in the shape of a nineteen-year-old girl.

He shouted her name one last time, knowing it was useless,

and it came out like a cry of pain. The love song of Terry Warboys.

And as he stood there feeling all the places that he hurt, they came around the corner and the blood seemed to freeze in his veins.

Teds.

An entire pack of those terrifying, unmistakable silhouettes – the sharks' fins of their greasy quiffs, the torsos abnormally long inside the drape coats, the skinny Max Wall legs and the feet enormous inside their rubber-soled brothel creepers. And at their head was the monstrous form of Titch, Frankenstein's Teddy Boy, his limbs so large that the act of walking seemed to require a super-human effort.

It seemed to be an entire tribe of them – three generations, from pimply, pale-faced teens to the scary forty-year-olds with a quarter-century of manual labour behind them, all the way up to the granddads, the elders of the tribe, those pitiless old lions with missing teeth and thinning quiffs and silver shining through their Brylcreemed ducktails.

Terry stood there awaiting his fate, unable to leg it, with no heart to scrap, knowing that anything he did was pointless. Resigned to being battered senseless, and not caring much with Misty in some new bed.

And then something remarkable happened.

The Teds walked by, they just walked on by, passing either side of Terry like a school of flesh-eating fish with no appetite. Titch himself passing close enough for Terry to smell his perfume of tobacco and brown ale and Brut splash-it-all-over cologne.

But they didn't touch him.

They didn't even look at him.

They let him be.

And as the Teds passed, the only sounds that Terry could hear were the drum beat of his heart, the soft tread of their brothel creepers on the wet pavement, and the muffled chokes of their sobbing, as the warrior tribe mourned their dead king.

PART TWO:

1977 – ANGELS ARE SO FEW

EIGHT

Terry stood in the middle of Oxford Street with the Ford Anglia hurtling towards him.

Its lights were flashing and the driver was leaning on the horn. Terry took off his mohair jacket and brandished it like a bull fighter's cape, crying a bit. Hemingway, he thought. *Death in the Afternoon.* She'll miss me when I'm gone.

Terry could see the driver's face now, twisted with anger and fear, a girl by his side, a woman, long hair flicked up at the ends. The clean hippy look that you saw about ten million times a day. She had her hands to her face. She seemed to be screaming.

'Come on then,' Terry said, shaking his jacket as the Anglia came towards him. He felt himself stop breathing.

The car swerved to avoid him, scraped against the side of the pavement and hurtled past in a blur of metal and noise and green and cream paint. A wing mirror caught Terry's jacket and whipped it out of his hands. It fell off outside Ravel's, and as Terry went to retrieve it he could hear the driver shouting abuse. But the Ford Anglia didn't stop. They thought he was a nutter.

Terry left his jacket where it lay and stared at the shoes in the window of Ravel's. They all seemed to be some new colour that Terry had never heard of – this sort of bruised purple. Aubergine, they called it. *Our aubergine range of Oxford heels now in stock.* Terry shook his head. He felt like he didn't understand anything any more. He felt like there was lots and lots of stuff going on that he just didn't know about. He thought – what's going to happen to me? Who's going to love me? He punched the window as hard as he could. Then he punched it again.

It must have been some kind of reinforced glass, because the blow did far more damage to Terry's hand than he did to the window. He stood there like a lemon, inspecting his skinned and throbbing knuckles. Then he heard the bus.

A big red double-decker, a number 73, was barrelling down Oxford Street on the wrong side of the road. That's a bit off, Terry thought, collecting his mohair jacket and dusting it down. Then he brandished it in both fists, placed himself in the middle of Oxford Street and waited for his bus.

The bus didn't slow down, it didn't sound its horn and it showed no sign of altering its course. Either the driver hadn't seen Terry, or he just didn't care if Terry got hit by a bus. Terry's life was clearly nothing to the driver. He licked his lips. The bus was getting closer. And closer. Jesus, it was big. And closer still. And Terry didn't want to die.

Terry threw himself out of the way and landed on his belly and elbows with a grunt of pain as the bus careered by, swerving sickeningly now, suddenly seeming top heavy as it bounced off the kerb on one side of the street and then the other with a screech of rubber and hubcap. Then it was up on two massive wheels, and then up on the other two massive wheels, holding that pose for what seemed the longest time before it keeled over, this great hulking red beast toppling over in slow motion, hitting the ground with a whoosh of air and cracked glass but still not stopping, still moving but on its side now, screeching down Oxford Street with a sound of metal on concrete that seemed to split the night.

Terry was on his knees, his breath coming in short, terrified gasps. What had he done? *Oh God – don't let them be hurt. Please – I'll do anything.* He slowly rose to his feet and took half a step towards the stricken double-decker. And then he saw them.

Junior was the first to appear, his terrible shaved head popping out of the driver's cab like it was a trap door, the tattoo of three teardrops looking like a black wound. Then another Dog appeared from the same opening – there must have been two of them at the wheel – and then Dogs were pouring out of the stricken bus like rats from a burning barn, crawling out of the long emergency window at the back, tumbling over the upended platform, kicking side windows out with their murderous boots. And as the police sirens wailed in the distance, they ran and hobbled down Wardour Street and Dean Street and Poland Street into the dark sanctuary of Soho.

Terry sprinted east, away from police and Dagenham Dogs, and he didn't stop running until he reached the British Museum, where, covered in sweat and lungs bursting, he held on to the railings with the giant white columns lit by moonlight like a vision of some lost civilisation.

And as Terry stood there steeped in the mystery of the ages, he asked himself, as he would ask himself so many times in the years ahead – how the fucking hell do you steal a bus?

The train rattled north, heading for home, and Ray could feel the spirit being sucked out of him. Home always did that to him. He pressed his face against the window as they passed the twin towers of Wembley, lit by moonlight. Nearly home.

Ray always thought that home was like some dream of England that his father had on a bad day in Hong Kong. One of those bad days when you opened the wardrobe and found that the humidity had grown mildew on your clean shirt, or the crowds in Kowloon made the place seem like one great big screaming nuthouse, or there was some old man in a vest and flip flops gobbing on the pavement and scratching his crutch.

Ray and his brothers had loved Hong Kong. Loved every second, and wept when the ship left for home. There was endless adventure for three small blue-eyed boys among the secret islands, the unexplored hillsides, the swarming backstreets where you could stuff your face at a *dai pai dong* street stall. And their mother, who had seen nothing beyond the Home Counties, had loved the markets, the temples, the exotic glamour on every street, the lights of Central seen from the Peak, the excitement of every plane coming through the skyscrapers to land at Kai Tak Airport, the reassuring sight of the Star Ferry, and the unadorned friendliness of the Cantonese.

But not Ray's father. His father hated the crime, the stink, the great press of humanity. All the foreign faces and their resentment of a pale Englishman in a policeman's uniform. His father dreamed of England, his father dreamed of home. White faces and green gardens, clean cars and neat children, never too hot and never too cold. A tepid sort of home. And that's what he brought them back to.

Home was always there. All through the night, the trains carried milk and papers and the last of the drunken commuters out to the endless suburbs. You could always get back, no matter how late it was and no matter how pissed you were, you could always get home even if it was only on a train that stopped at every half-baked hamlet on the line.

Ray knew that they had once called this place Metroland – a salesman's term, a marketing brand name from the first half of the century when the areas north-west of London in Middlesex, Hertfordshire and Buckinghamshire had first been sold to the public as some kind of suburban dream. Ray's father had bought the dream. The rest of them had to live in it.

The train pulled into a gloomy station surrounded by scrubby fields and an almost empty car park and an estate of box-shaped houses. Ray was the only passenger to get off.

He walked through streets of pebble-dashed semis where everyone was tucked up and dreaming, and paused at the gateway of a house that looked just like all the rest. No lights were on. Good. He wouldn't have to see his father.

But before he had let himself inside he was aware of a man's voice coming from the living room. The television? No, it was past midnight, the telly had finished hours ago.

'*The resolution of the British people is unconquerable,*' rumbled the voice. '*Neither sudden nor violent shocks, nor long, cold, provoking, tiring strains can or will alter our course.*'

It was an album. One of his father's records. Winston Churchill. His dad's favourite recording artist.

Ray trod lightly down the hallway. The living-room door was slightly ajar. He peeked through the crack and took in the familiar scene in a moment. He saw his father comatose in his favourite chair, the one that faced the TV, an empty glass at his slippered feet. The smell of tobacco and home brew. The LP still turning on the Dansette.

'No country made more strenuous efforts to avoid being drawn into this war,' Churchill said. 'But I dare say we shall be found ready and anxious to prosecute it when some of those who provoked it are talking vehemently of peace. It has been rather like that in old times. I am often asked to say – how are we going to win this war?'

Ray's father had always listened to this stuff. Even when they were in their flat in Hong Kong, before they lost John and it all went so wrong, Ray could remember having to play quietly at the weekends because his father was listening to Churchill's speeches, eyes glistening with emotion. But since John's death, it had got worse. Now the old man was mixing home brew with the speeches. Ray headed down the hall, the God-like voice rolling through the house, wondering how his family could ever be happy again.

'I remember being asked that last time,' said Churchill, 'very frequently, and not being able to give a very precise or conclusive answer.'

Ray went up the narrow staircase, his footsteps creaking on the worn Cyril Lord carpet, and he crept past his parents' bedroom, hearing the sound of his mother's breathing, and her muttering in her sleep, despite the pills the doctor was dishing out like Smarties, and then past John's old room, untouched since the day he died, and finally to the room at the end of the hall that Ray shared with Robbie.

He eased himself inside, silently closing the door behind him, and was immediately frightened by the stillness of his brother's body. Ray knelt by the bed, the palm of his hand in front of Robbie's mouth, smiling to himself when he felt warm breath on his skin. Then suddenly Robbie was sitting up in bed, gasping with shock.

'Shut up, dummy,' Ray hissed. 'It's only me.'

Robbie rubbed his eyes. 'I thought you was a ghost. *Dummy.*'

'Ghosts don't exist. I told you. And don't call me dummy. Go back to sleep.'

But Robbie was awake now. 'Dummy, dummy, dummy,' he hissed, keeping his voice low. Then he yawned. 'Why did you wake me up?'

'I was just checking on you.'

Ray went over to his side of the room, for Ray and Robbie's bedroom was as segregated as East and West Berlin. Ray's walls were tastefully decorated with a few select images of the Beatles – a *Yellow Submarine* poster, a *Magical Mystery Tour* flyer and the four big glossy pictures that were given away inside the gatefold sleeve of *Let It Be*, the boys looking beardy and wise. Even Ringo. The posters were fraying around the edges now because Ray was really too old for all that kid stuff. The real John Lennon was waiting for him. Somewhere.

Robbie's walls were plastered with any rubbish he could get his grubby hands on, mostly posters given away with the one-shot magazines he somehow persuaded their mother to buy. Bands he probably hadn't even heard. But mostly pictures of the Jam. Robbie came across the room and squatted by his brother as he flipped through his record collection, looking for his Doctor Who lunchbox.

'You haven't touched these records, have you?' Ray said.

'No way, José.'

'Can you stop saying that? Nobody says *No way, José* any more.'

'What did you do tonight?' Robbie said. Ray could smell his brother's clean breath. Colgate Dental Fresh. 'Did you meet Paul Weller yet?'

'I told you. They're not going to send me to interview Paul Weller. They'll get Terry to do that.' He kept flicking through the

records. 'I was at the office. Then I was in a club with my friends.'
Ray looked at his little brother. 'And now I'm here with you.'

'It's all right for some,' Robbie said. Sometimes he talked like
an old woman. And he was only a kid. Their mum still washed
his face with a flannel.

'What did you do tonight, Rob?'

Robbie shrugged. 'Watched telly. Did my homework. Counted
my pubic hairs.'

'Yeah? How's that going?'

'Thirteen. One fell out. I think I must be moulting.' Then he
almost squealed with excitement. 'If you meet Paul Weller –'

'I won't, okay?'

'But if you do meet him, get him to sign something for me,
will you?'

Ray smiled at his brother in the darkness, and patted him on
the shoulder of his pyjamas.

'Maybe I'll get Terry to do it. How's that?'

Robbie rocked with delight, hugging his knees. 'Wait till Kevin
Wallace sees my brother knows Paul Weller!'

Ray pulled out a fistful of albums topped with *Exile on Main
Street*, reached through the gap in the record collection until he
felt the leatherette of his old abandoned school satchel. He fished
out a scratched Doctor Who lunchbox, flipped it open and pulled
out a short, stubby, slightly squashed hand-rolled cigarette. His
emergency joint. Robbie's eyes were wide.

'I know what that is,' he said. 'That's drugs, that is.'

'You're a genius, aren't you?'

'Dad will *kill* you.'

'Then I'll be dead.'

Then they were both silent, thinking about the room down the hall that no one was allowed to touch, that no one was allowed to enter, and the brother who you were not allowed to mention in this house. The brother you couldn't even fucking *mention*. Ray thought of those unseen, untouchable walls, dedicated to the glory of Led Zeppelin and Muhammad Ali and Charlie George, and his brother's strength and kindness, and that country road near the border in Northern Ireland. Ray heard Robbie starting to snivel, and put his arm around his shoulder.

'It's okay, Rob.'

'1 miss him, that's all.'

'We all miss John. Come on.'

Ray went over to their window and gently pulled it open. Cool air rushed in, the smell of newly cut grass after rain, that summer softness. He could hear Robbie by his shoulder, sucking up snot, drying his eyes. His little brother, being brave.

Ray stuck his head out of the window and lit up, took a long drag and held it. His brother giggled as Ray exhaled.

'Dad will marmalise you,' Robbie said.

But Ray already felt better. Seeing his brother, holding the joint. He let the jangled nerve endings relax, felt his breathing slow down, and the anxiety seep away. Finding John Lennon – how hard could it be? He had hours to go before dawn. He took another hit, narrowing his eyes at all the patches of garden below with their sheds, their flowerbeds, and the occasional bomb shelter.

'Let me have a go then,' whispered Robbie. 'Go on. Don't be a spoilsport. I won't tell anyone.'

Ray shook his head. 'No way, José.'

'Go on then,' Robbie said, lunging for the joint. 'Let me have a go. I'm only here for the beer.'

Robbie had this annoying habit of quoting commercials. Ray held the joint away from him. 'You're too young.'

'I'm almost thirteen!'

Ray laughed. 'Exactly.'

'It's okay,' Robbie said. He fanned the air towards his face. 'Because I can get high just standing next to you.' He closed his eyes. 'I can feel it . . . I'm stoned . . . I'm freaking out . . .'

Ray felt the smouldering roach in his mouth, stubbed out what was left on the window sill and flicked the charred remains into the garden of Auntie Gert and Uncle Bert next door, who were no relation whatsoever. Then he put his Doctor Who lunchbox inside his satchel, shoved it under his bed and headed for the door.

'You're not going out again, are you?' Robbie said.

'I'm going to interview John Lennon.'

Robbie was impressed. 'The bloke that was in the Beatles? Paul Weller likes the Beatles. But they were not as good as the Who – any dummy knows that.'

'Go back to sleep, okay?' Ray said. 'I'll be back tonight.'

'Promise?'

'Yeah.'

'Okay.'

Ray waited until his brother had got back down under the sheets, and then let himself out of the bedroom. His mother was standing on the landing, her hair in curlers, clutching a pink polyester dressing gown at the neck.

'Thought it was a burglar,' she whispered.

We have spent a lifetime keeping our voices down, thought Ray. Because of him. Because of the old man.

'It's only me, Mum. Sorry I disturbed you.' She was always antici-pating disaster. He kissed her on the forehead, her skin as parched and white as old paper, although she wasn't even fifty yet, and he saw that she was trembling. My nerves, she always said, as if that explained everything. Her nerves had been fine until John died and the quack started filling her up with pills and Dad got into the home brew.

'You're not going back out again, are you?' she said, as if he was planning to climb Everest rather than catch a train back to the city. 'Do you know what time it is?'

She peered at her gold Timex, but couldn't read the face without her reading glasses. She held the watch at arm's length, squinting, but it was still no good. 'It's flipping late,' she said.

'Got to go to work, Mum.' He hugged her, felt the frail body. All skin and bone, she would have called it. 'Please go back to bed. Don't worry about me. I'm fine. I'm always fine.'

He started down the stairs while his mother fretted to herself about the lateness of the hour, and the danger of the world. In the living room Churchill growled on.

Ray reached the bottom of the stairs and then the door of the front room flew open and his father was standing there.

'*We did our duty,*' said Churchill.

'Where the bloody hell are you going?' said the old man. Fuming at nothing. As always. 'You treat this place –'

'Like a bloody hotel,' Ray muttered. A mistake he immediately regretted.

His father's face reddened. 'Your lip now, is it? Do you think you're too big and too ugly for a good hiding?'

His mother had a kind of strait-laced decency, a sense of propriety. But his father had never seemed far from violence, even before his eldest son had been lost. Beyond the net curtains of their little semi, his father still carried the bite and bile of the South London slum where he had grown up. The old man frightened Ray. Especially when he could smell the home brew on him.

'I'm going to work,' Ray said. 'I'm going to interview John Lennon.'

His mother's voice called from the top of the stairs. 'There's no more Northern Line. I told him. It's the mainline or nothing.'

The old man shot her a withering look. His contempt, that was what you noticed most about him, Ray thought. He acted as if he despised the people who shared his life. Then he looked back at Ray.

'John Lennon? That weirdo? That bender?' Pushing Ray now, starting to enjoy himself a bit. 'The long-haired beatnik with the mad Chinese bird?'

Ray tried to get past him, but the old man blocked his path. Ray felt weak in his father's presence. He didn't want to fight. But his father always wanted to fight.

'*Now we have to do it all over again,*' Churchill said. '*We have to face once more a long struggle, the cruel sacrifices, and not be daunted or deterred by feelings of vexation.*'

'That drug addict?' said the old man.

Ray flared up. 'Don't worry, Dad. You can't teach John Lennon anything about getting out of his head.'

Then the old man had Ray by the lapels of his denim jacket and was swinging him around, banging him hard against the wall, clipping the table that was home to the telephone and some cherished souvenirs, rattling the ornaments that Auntie Gert and Uncle Bert had brought back from Benidorm, the plastic bull and the set of maracas, before he held his son close to his face, screaming at him. 'And what does that mean? What does that mean?'

'Nothing!' Ray shouted, as his mother sat down halfway down the stairs, moaning that her nerves couldn't take any more, and

Robbie sat beside her and started to grizzle, burying his face in his mother's pink dressing gown.

'Tell me what it means!' Ray's father bawled.

'It means you getting stoned every night on your crappy home-made beer,' Ray shouted back, and felt the palm of his father's hand crack across the side of his mouth, his bottom lip splitting on his two front teeth, and then everyone was crying, apart from the old man, who released Ray with a snort of scorn.

'I'm not fighting you, Dad,' Ray said, shrinking into himself, leaning against the wall. There was a fleck of blood on the floral wallpaper.

'Of course you're fucking not,' said the old man, and he went back to the living room, settling himself in his favourite chair and pouring himself a glass. The record was still playing.

'*I have never given you any assurances of an easy, or cheap, or speedy victory,*' warned Churchill. '*On the contrary, as you know, I have never promised anything but the hardest conditions, great disappointment and many mistakes. But I am sure that in the end all will be well for us in our island home. All will be better for the world.*'

And Robbie was whimpering at the top of the stairs, having retreated when the old man got physical, while his mother had Ray's face in her small, bony hands, pulling it this way and that, making the stinging red flesh hurt even worse, and Ray told her through his tears that everything was fine.

'You're weak,' said his father. It was the worst thing he could think to say. 'You're all gutless.'

'*And there will be that crown of honour for those that have endured and never failed which history will allow them for having set an example to the whole human race,*' said Churchill.

Ray pulled himself away from his mother's embrace, and stumbled to the door. His mother's kindness and concern humiliated him as much as his father's violence. The record was spinning on an empty groove. It was over.

'It should have been you,' Ray's father said, not stirring from his favourite chair, not even looking at him, just staring into the empty fireplace that they no longer used because of the central heating while the end of the record crackled and hissed. 'He was worth ten of you. With your long hair and your drugs. Oh, you think I don't know about that? I know all about it, my lad. *It should have been you.*'

He hadn't said it before. But it didn't hurt Ray as much as he thought it would. Because he knew that his father had always thought it.

'I'm going now,' Ray said, to nobody in particular.

He opened the door, his mother on the stairs fiddling with the neck of her pink dressing gown, his little brother peering through the banisters like a pale-faced prisoner.

And as he walked back to the railway station through those comatose streets, his mouth pulsed with the smack his father had given him, his bottom lip was torn and swollen thanks to the old man, and Ray wondered if his dad would have been a better man if his life had been easier, if the dreams had all worked out. Thinking about his father made Ray think of John Winston Lennon, born on 9th October 1940 during one of the Luftwaffe's night raids on Liverpool, and the feckless ship's waiter, Freddy Lennon, who so soon abandoned baby John and his mother. Yes, thinking about his old man got Ray thinking about his hero, and how John grew up without the presence of a father in his life. And Ray thought – oh, you lucky, lucky bastard.

His face hurt and he knew from experience that it would hurt for a long time. Getting smacked wasn't like the movies. In real life it was amazing how much mess your father could make of your face with just one punch.

Then his stomach seemed to rise up to his mouth and Ray had to hold on to a lamppost until he choked it down. Here was this other thing that violence did. Violence made you sick. Violence made you feel like puking, as though just being on the wrong end of it gave you some kind of illness. Ray knew all about it.

His dad had taught him.

Nobody understood why he wouldn't cut his hair. Nobody got it. Not even Terry. Not even Leon. They didn't understand why all the violence of the new music appalled him.

Ray thought – I can get all that at home.

Terry walked east along the great artery that links the city's entertainment area and its financial district, the fun and the money, his DMs tramping down New Oxford Street, High Holborn, Holborn – nothing open, everything closed, apart from the odd Dunkin' Donuts and, somewhere to the south, the meat market where his father was working through the night.

And every step of the way he thought about her.

He should have seen it coming. Should have seen the end in the beginning. That guy crying in the rain outside Terry's bedsit, he was a married man called Acid Pete. What kind of a girl has a married man crying in the rain? What kind of a girl knocks about with someone called Acid Pete?

A girl like Misty, Terry thought. A wild girl. I should have seen the pink fake mink handcuffs and run a mile. The very first time

I heard her recite some second-hand tosh about 'exploring my sexuality', I should have bailed out. I should have known there were too many miles on the clock when she said the doctor had told her to take a break from the pill before her ovaries exploded or something. I should have made my excuses as soon as I saw a copy of *The Female Eunuch*.

The girls he had known didn't mess with married men, especially married men with names like Acid Pete. The girls he had known read *Cosmopolitan,* if they read anything, not seminal feminist texts. And they started taking the Pill when they started going steady, then stopped when they got married – always a white wedding, always in church – unless they were still saving up for their first mortgage and the baby had to wait a while. They didn't have to take a break from the Pill because they had been on it for so long.

The girls he had known might let you explore their breasts if the night was full of Blue Nun and romance, but they certainly didn't explore their sexuality. And, without an engagement ring on their third finger left hand, they weren't too keen on you exploring it either. Regular sex was for steady boyfriends. A blow-job was like getting eight draws on Littlewood's football pools, and when it happened, you had to break up with the girl immediately and tell all your friends. That was a drag, because you missed the girl, but witnessing the miracle of a blow-job was just too momentous to keep to yourself.

A large part of Terry's life felt as though it had been dedicated to trying to get a hand inside some girl's bra in the back of some dad's Ford Escort. It wasn't like that with Misty.

She had her own wheels. And, being a wild girl, she never wore one.

*   *   *

He remembered the first time he spoke to her.

He had joined *The Paper* as the blazing summer of 1976 drew to a close, but didn't exchange a word with her until the end of the year when he was sitting under a twinkling Christmas tree at Heathrow, rereading *The Subterraneans*, when Misty entered the airport lounge. They were meant to be doing a job together.

She was wearing one of her Alice in Wonderland dresses with a man's jacket over the top, and even behind her mirrored aviator shades, you could see that she was crying. Really crying. Sobbing her heart out.

'Are you all right?' he said, closing his Kerouac and standing up.

'I'm fine,' she told him.

She flopped down on the hard airport chair, crying even harder, and he sat beside her. She partially lifted the enormous sunglasses, dabbing at her eyes with a screwed-up piece of toilet paper. Terry had no idea what to say or do, so he went off and bought two plastic cups of boiling hot tea and offered one to her.

'Never fuck a married man,' she said, taking the tea. 'They make a big fuss if you turn up at their home.'

Terry tried to process this information.

'I didn't know if you took sugar or not,' he said. 'So I only put one in.'

Misty took a sip of the brown liquid, flinching at the heat. 'You're sweet,' she said. Then she wiped her nose with the back of her hand, sniffed loudly and seemed to brighten. 'Any idea if our flight's on time?'

When Terry had joined *The Paper*, Misty had seemed as distant and glamorous as a pin-up.

He saw her around the office, her cameras swinging from her

neck, laughing with one of the older guys or talking to the photo editor as they looked at contact sheets of Generation X and Patti Smith and the Buzzcocks. She said hello to Ray if they bumped into each other, but stared right through Leon and Terry and avoided their office. One time Leon caught Terry watching her.

'Way out of our league,' Leon laughed, and Terry blushed and threw a wastepaper bin at him.

Terry learned from Ray that she was the full-time assistant and part-time girlfriend of an older photographer, a stringer for *The Paper*, a minor Sixties legend called Acid Pete who had taken pictures of Cream at the Albert Hall, the Stones in Hyde Park and Hendrix at the Isle of Wight, just before the end.

Acid Pete was a married man, and sometimes when he came by to see the photo editor his wife was in tow – Misty made herself scarce – one of those constantly smiling hippy chicks, the type who seemed both beatific and brainless. When Terry met Acid Pete in the office and shook his limp, hippy hand, Acid Pete seemed endlessly amused, impossibly experienced and as though he had taken just a few too many drugs.

Terry was intimidated by Acid Pete. He had seen so much and taken so many great photographs, and even at an age when the Queen must be getting ready to send him a telegram – forty-one? forty-two? – he was still seeing – *screwing*, Acid Pete would have called it – the best-looking girl – *chick*, or possibly *lady*, Acid Pete would have called her – in the office. The only thing that made Acid Pete bearable for Terry was the knowledge that the older man's glory days were gone.

Acid Pete didn't get on with the new music, didn't dig what he called 'the aggressive vibe' in places like the Western World, and soon he was seen looking forlorn in the photographers' pit of the

Roundhouse, huddled inside his greatcoat, the buttons gone, and Misty was the one who was getting the assignments. Towards the end of the year, one of them was with Terry – flying up to Newcastle to join the Billy Blitzen tour, covering two dates in Newcastle and Glasgow for a centre spread.

'Kerouac,' she said, drinking her tea and clocking Terry's copy of *The Subterraneans*. 'He's a real *boy's* writer, isn't he?' Wet-eyed and smiling now. 'I bet *all* the writers you like are boy's writers.'

Terry felt like one of those cartoon characters with a question mark hovering above his head. 'What's a boy's writer?'

'You know. A boy's writer. Go on – talk me through it.'

He had no idea what she was going on about. 'Talk you through what?'

She laughed happily. 'Your life in books, silly.'

So he did. Or at least the ones he could recall.

'Well, I can remember my mum reading me Rupert the Bear for hours on end. And then there are the books at school that got to you. *Treasure Island* and *Robinson Crusoe* and *Kidnapped*. And *To Kill a Mockingbird* and *My Family and Other Animals* and *Travels With My Aunt*. I loved *My Family and Other Animals,* I wanted to live on Corfu . . . And then you get a bit older and you start making your own reading list – I remember Ian Fleming at eleven, all the Bond books. *"The scent and smoke and sweat of a casino are nauseating at three in the morning."* The first line in the first 007 book.'

She smiled, took off her aviator shades, nodded. Her eyes were a shade of green he had never seen before. Maybe it was the tears.

'And then this funny period,' he said, 'when you're in your early teens and you're reading what's supposed to be trash – Harold Robbins, *Airport, Valley of the Dolls* – and the big bestsellers – *Zen and the Art of Motorcycle Maintenance* and *Alive!* – and you're also getting into Hemingway and F. Scott Fitzgerald and J. D. Salinger and *Catch 22* and *Lolita* and Norman Mailer. And then you realise there are all these great journalists out there – Tom Wolfe and Hunter S. Thompson and . . .'

They called their flight. Terry felt a stab of disappointment. He enjoyed talking to her.

'Well,' she said, pressing his chest with her boarding card. 'At least you like Rupert the Bear.'

'I am going to nail that little picture snapper before she gets off the bus,' said Billy Blitzen's manager. 'What's her name? Foggy? Smoggy? Well, boys, I'm going to nail Foggy's sweet little ass to the fucking *carpet*.'

The band all laughed, apart from Billy himself. They were at the sound check for the gig, and Misty hadn't come along, had stayed at the Holiday Inn making heated calls to London. And Billy swung his guitar on his hip and led Terry to the side of the stage.

'She with you, man?' said Billy. 'This Misty with you?'

He was a sweet man. A good man. Terry's favourite musician. Because of what he had done with the Lost Boys, and because he was still great on stage. But mostly because he was the only one who cared enough to ask Terry that simple question. But what could he say?

'No, Billy,' Terry said, attempting a smile. 'Misty's not with me.'

Billy sighed. 'Well, I guess that's all right then.'

Despite the Aerosmith and Kiss cassettes the band listened to on the bus, Billy Blitzen and the P45s conformed to the dress code of Max's Kansas City and CBGBs – ties as thin as liquorice, drainpipes tighter than a coat of emulsion, second-hand suit jackets and fluffed-up Beatle cuts that could have been worn by the Byrds in 1966.

But their manager was old school, a lawyer from LA in cowboy boots who had graduated from Harvard Business School and cocaine. He had been around for years and he knew how it worked.

Now he raised his voice in the empty student hall, for Billy's venues were getting smaller by the month, and the P45s laughed and clapped.

'Nail her *ass* to the fucking *carpet!*'

It was a great show that night – the longhaired students out of their minds on real ale as Billy mimed jamming a spike into his arm and the entire student union hall sang along to 'Shoot Up, Everybody'.

They went back to the bar of the Holiday Inn. The band and the manager and Terry and Misty and the few local kids of both sexes who always managed to tag along, offering drugs, sex or flattery.

Terry didn't talk to Misty. It was different on the road. They both had a job to do. And by the time he gave up, realising that she was not for him, the drugs were all gone, the bartender had started mixing the screwdrivers with orange cordial, and Misty was in a corner talking to the LA cowboy.

Terry never found out what happened in the bar after he turned in. He didn't want to know. But Misty knocked on his hotel room door just after midnight, unafraid but seeking refuge, and that was the start of it all for Terry Warboys and his cat-faced darling.

That first night was the best night, at least for him. He would never forget the sight of her when he woke up just before dawn, sitting on a sofa in her pop socks, smoking a black cigarette called a Sobranie. And they did it again, getting their hat trick, because there was something about the combination of the pop socks and the Sobranie that drove him wild.

And then in dawn's early light he found her standing above him, naked now, the pop socks gone, and holding the pink fake mink handcuffs.

'Are you into submission?' she said.

Terry stared up at her with bleary eyes.

'I don't know,' he said. 'What label are they on?'

They took it from there.

If he was going back to his bedsit, he needed to head north, find a night bus. But he couldn't face the poky little flat and his lumpy mattress tonight. Not with the speed still in his veins, not with Misty in some hotel room, exploring her sexuality. Everything in his life made sleep unthinkable.

I believed, he thought. Believed in her, believed in him. Listened to his records when no one was buying, when no one cared – loved Dag Wood before he was cool. Terry had believed, even when Bob Harris sneered, 'Mock rock.' Believed and was betrayed.

And believed in her too, Terry thought. Believed in her most of all. Saw something in that face that made me want to give up on every other woman in the world. How fucking stupid can you get?

He tramped on through the night, turning up the collar of his dead man's jacket against the chill, and it was only when he veered left at London Wall that Terry realised where he was going.

With the big white buildings and the statues of men on horses behind him now, he headed up the City Road, and suddenly he could feel the poverty among all those blocks of council flats, those ramshackle boxes that some dumb architect had thought was a clever idea ten or fifteen years ago, stretching off into the darkness all the way to the Angel.

The blackness was broken by one colossal building. It stood there halfway up the City Road, every light blazing, the night air reeking of the product it made. The gin factory.

Why had he come back here? To the place he had tried so hard to leave? He knew it had something to do with life becoming more complicated than he had ever imagined.

A regular girl bored you, but a wild one made you miserable. One made you feel like a prisoner, and the other made you feel like you were nothing. One of them wanted to marry you, have babies, and keep you locked up for ever. And the other one wanted to fuck strangers.

He wanted his old life back. The simplicity of it, the modest comforts. A girl who loved you and stuck by you, even if the price you paid was the prison of marriage.

He had thought that this new life would set him free, and yet every day there were new rules to learn. *Don't be too heavy. Don't be too macho. Don't care too much.*

In the giant shadow of his old job, Terry punched a lamppost as hard as he could. Then he hopped around for a bit, sucking up the pain.

He was going to have to stop doing that.

NINE

It was a different kind of club.

'Members only,' the man on the door told Ray.

He was one of those teak-hard old Cockney geezers, blurred navy tattoos displayed under the short sleeves of his drip-dry bri-nylon shirt, and what was left of his hair brushed straight back.

A bit like Henry Cooper, thought Ray. But he couldn't imagine this one smiling his way through a Brut commercial with Kevin Keegan. Here was the anti-Henry. He looked as though he would fill your cakehole in as soon as look at you.

Ray peered over his shoulder at the dingy, bamboo-clad bar. Loud, laughing people moved through clouds of cigarette smoke, the men in suits, the women in flared denim. Somewhere Matt Monro was singing.

'I came here once with Paddy Clare,' Ray explained. 'Paddy, who writes the pop page in the *Daily Dispatch*?'

The doorman looked exasperated. 'Look, sonny, I don't give a flying toss if you came here with Princess bleedin' Margaret and all the fucking corgis. It's *members only*. Got it?'

Ray nodded, but he was reluctant to turn away. He touched his bare wrist anxiously. He didn't own a watch. Hadn't needed one until tonight. He had never really seen the purpose of a watch. To Ray, a watch was something belonging to his father's world – like ties, and shined shoes, and the speeches of Winston Churchill. A watch meant work. And what did Ray know of that? *The Paper* wasn't *work*. *The Paper* wasn't *a job*. He could see his old man now, synchronising his Omega to the chimes of Big Ben coming out of a tinny transistor radio. But with the night running out, he began to see the reason for watches at last. How long before John caught the plane to Tokyo? How much time did he have?

Touching his wrist again, Ray peered over the shoulder of the keeper of the door. This wasn't his type of place – there didn't appear to be anyone under the age of forty in the room, or anyone who wasn't wearing a cheap suit stained with food and drink, but he didn't know where else to go. All he knew was that the Empire Rooms never closed.

Ray had once spent an alcoholic afternoon in there. He had been sent to cover an Art Garfunkel press conference as one of his first jobs for *The Paper* and found himself sitting next to a sweating man in a crumpled three-piece suit. It was Paddy Clare, author of the Sounds Groovy! page in the *Daily Dispatch*.

He smelled a bit – a strange brew of Guinness and fried food and Fleet Street sweat – but he was very friendly to Ray, this fifteen-year-old wearing a denim jacket with school shirt and trousers, and he politely wondered if the younger reporter would fill him in on the artist's recent career.

'So what's this curly-haired cunt been doing since Simon and Garfunkel split up?' was how Paddy put it.

174

Ray took a breath and told him. He knew this stuff inside out. The career of someone like Art Garfunkel had been stored away without even trying. So he told Paddy about the two solo albums, the two giant hit singles – the exquisite 'All I Know' and the unconvincing 'I Only Have Eyes for You' – plus some very interesting work as an actor. *Catch-22, Carnal Knowledge.*

'Also, he's pitch perfect,' Ray said, warming to his theme, 'and he has a degree in mathematics and they say he is going to record the theme tune for that cartoon about rabbits – what's it called?'

Paddy Clare looked thoughtful. *'Bugs Bunny?'* he suggested.

Ray shook his head. *'Watership Down.'*

Paddy Clare's yellow teeth glinted with delight. 'I owe you one, kid,' he said, seeming genuinely grateful. But Paddy had a notepad with *Art Garfunkel* scribbled at the top of a blank page, and Ray couldn't help noticing that nothing he said was considered worthy of writing down. Perhaps Paddy had a photographic memory.

Then Art Garfunkel appeared, a tall, beaky, bookish-looking man surrounded by the usual record company flunkies and management, and Paddy Clare raised his chewed Biro, the mangled blue plastic gleaming with spit.

'Art,' he said, 'is it true that you and Paul hate each other?'

Art Garfunkel looked pained. The record company flunkies frowned and flapped.

'Any chance of a reunion then?' probed Paddy. 'Did *romance*' – Paddy Clare bared his yellow fangs at the word, and made it sound like anal sex with a barnyard animal – 'bloom with any of your co-stars? Are you really doing a remake of *Bugs Bunny?*'

It was a different kind of writing.

But Paddy Clare took a shine to the boy by his side, and after the strained press conference was cut short the old hack invited Ray for 'a swift one at this little place I know'.

The Empire Rooms was billed as a private club, which made it sound very grand to Ray, but the shabby reality was a basement with a bar in a dustbin-strewn yard off of Brewer Street on the eastern side of Soho. Frayed curtains permanently drawn, potted plants wilting in the gloom, plastic Pernod ashtrays overflowing with fag butts. And all these pissed old people with no special place to be.

Paddy told Ray that there were hundreds of these places dotted around Soho, skirting the licensing laws by restricting entry to members only. And Ray wondered who were the members? Anyone the despot on the door decided was a member, Paddy said. They stayed for six hours.

When it was over, and unbelievably the Soho night was just beginning, Paddy – still sober but sweating more heavily than ever – went back to Fleet Street to write his column while Ray staggered the length of Brewer Street before puking up from one end of Old Compton Street to the other. From Wardour Street to the Charing Cross Road, heaving all the way.

'Still here, are you?' said the anti-Henry. 'You a member yet?'

Ray shook his head. 'Not yet, no,' he said politely.

The doorman's eyes blazed. 'Go on, you little herbert – fuck off out of it before I give you a good hiding.'

Ray trudged back up to the top of the filthy staircase, peering out at the soft rain falling on Soho. What time was it anyway? When did the planes start at Heathrow? And then he heard someone call his name.

Paddy Clare was laughing at the bottom of the staircase, gesturing for Ray to join him. The hawk-faced bruiser on the door was still glaring up at Ray, but Paddy indicated that it was all right. Ray smiled shyly and came back down the stairs. Paddy Clare put a protective arm around his shoulder as the man at the door shoved a thick finger in Ray's face.

'No bluies, no reefer,' he said. 'Or I'll give you a fourpenny one.'

'Why is he so nasty?' Ray asked Paddy as he led him into the smoky gloaming.

'Albert? Well, the Empire Rooms are not really a club. It's more like a private cocktail party. Or a fiefdom. Yeah, that's it – it's a fucking fiefdom. Nobody – none of the regulars – calls it the Empire Rooms. They call it Albert's Place. And Albert doesn't usually get your type in here.' Paddy's yellow teeth shone in the ill-lit room. 'You know – the flower people.'

Ray breathed in a lungful of cigarette smoke. He rubbed his bare wrist. This wasn't where he needed to be.

'I'm looking for Lennon,' Ray said, pushing his hair back. At least he was drying out a bit. 'You know? *John* Lennon of the Beatles?' Although Paddy Clare wrote the Sounds Groovy! column, Ray was never sure exactly how much he knew or didn't know about the contemporary music scene. Sometimes it felt that Paddy's interest in pop music had ended with Billy Fury, Jet Harris and the Shadows, and other times it felt like Paddy had never had any interest in music in his entire life. 'He's in town for one night.'

Paddy nodded thoughtfully. He lifted his glass to his lips, but it was empty. Paddy seemed surprised.

'On his way to Tokyo with Yoko,' Ray said. 'My editor wants me to interview him. It's really important.'

Paddy considered Ray for a moment, then slapped him on the back. 'Don't worry, son, I'll give you a job on Sounds Groovy! when you're ready to join the big boys.'

Ray felt a wave of despair. 'Thanks, Paddy.' He smiled wearily and scanned the dark room, touching his bare wrist. Paddy led them to a table where fag butts were spilling out of an ashtray with Pernod written on it. He signalled to the barman and two glasses full of transparent liquid were slammed down in front of them. Ray took a sip and it was the most disgusting thing he had ever tasted in his life.

'Tastes like that stuff my mum used to give me for toothache,' Ray said. 'Clove oil.'

'Yeah, good, innit?' Paddy said. 'You can't beat a G and T.'

Ray gulped down another mouthful, grimacing, but not wanting to appear ungrateful.

'As for John,' Paddy said, 'the last I heard, he was down at the Speakeasy.'

Ray gawped, the gin halfway to his mouth.

'I've got a couple of snappers down there.' Paddy Clare chortled into his drink. 'Never know what the pair of them are going to do next, God bless 'em. Staying in bed for peace. Sending back his MBE because "Cold Turkey" was going down the hit parade. Eating chocolate cake in a bag to stop the war – now what's all that about?'

Ray stared at him in wonder. Paddy was a product of the old Fleet Street. Sometimes you felt like he knew nothing. And other times you believed that he knew all there was to know. He was on his feet, scrambling, suddenly aware that he still had Terry's tape recorder with him.

'Thank you, Paddy.'

Paddy looked pleased with himself. Ray could tell he was happy to help. Under that stained suit, there was a kind man.

'Told you I owed you one. Yeah, my editor's very excited – he loves John and Yoko – they're his two favourite weirdos. Fucking loves 'em, he does!'

Ray gulped down the remainder of his drink, not wanting to abuse Paddy's hospitality. He scanned the room for a clock. But there was no clock in Albert's Place.

'What time is it anyway?' Ray said.

Paddy looked at the younger man with sorrow and pity, gin-sodden tears in his rheumy eyes.

'Oh, it's very late,' Paddy said, and Ray's fingers touched his naked wrist.

What was it about that face?

It was as though you could see her whole life in it. She would be a beautiful old lady one day, and she must have been a beautiful baby. There was something otherworldly about her face – something angelic. The face was alarmingly symmetrical, the face of the most beautiful girl in the world, as though God had placed everything exactly where it was meant to be. She looked like an improved version of the girl in *The Last Picture Show*. That was it. Like God's second attempt at Cybill Shepherd. The wavy blonde hair, eyes that could see into your soul. And a mouth built for snogging.

Everything's just stuck on so nicely, Leon thought.

'My dad liked Elvis,' she said, shouting over Kool and the Gang. 'I remember watching him as a little girl – the films, you know, they would show them on Sunday afternoons. And he always seemed to be either in Hawaii or the army.' She smiled, and Leon's heart fell away. 'I thought he was a film star – like Steve McQueen or something. Clint Eastwood. Like that. I never realised he's a *singer*.' Then her lovely eyes brimmed with grief, as though all those Sundays watching Elvis films with her dad were gone for ever. 'That he *was* a singer, I mean.'

Leon nodded enthusiastically, leaning close to her so she could hear, his mouth just inches from that face.

'We have a strange relationship with the music that our parents love,' he said, and she thought about it, smiled politely, and Leon cursed himself – why do you always have to try to say something clever? Now she thinks you're a pretentious wanker!

'Oh, I know what you mean,' she said. 'Because my mum likes Frankie Vaughan so I always sort of liked Frankie Vaughan.'

And when the talking was done, Leon did this impossible thing – he danced. Leon danced, and the world slipped away. He danced, forgetting about the Leni and the Riefenstahls gig he was meant to be reviewing, forgetting about the copies of *Red Mist* – abandoned on a table sticky with spilled alcohol – and almost but not quite forgetting about the Dagenham Dogs who were hunting him down. They would never find him in here. He would be safe in the Goldmine.

So Leon forgot about everything except the music and the dancing and the most beautiful girl in the world.

Leon danced – which in his case was a modest bobbing movement, his head nodding thoughtfully under his trilby, the index finger on his right hand raised, as if he was about to make an important point – but nobody cared! That was the glorious thing about the Goldmine. Nobody cared if you were cool, or doing the right thing, or just treating dancing as though it was another form of breathing! That's what he liked – oh, he really liked it – about this place.

It was its own kind of underground. He could see that. There were the dancers and the hard men and the peacocks, all with their own rituals. But they left a little space for someone like Leon.

He could sense that there was room for a non-dancing nerd such as himself. You just needed the confidence to take that giant step on to the dance floor. But Leon found that it was like stepping off a cliff. Once you had done it, there was no going back.

Dancing – which to Leon had always seemed as physically impossible as flying – seemed like a normal part of human endeavour in the Goldmine. He danced through the anxious, frazzled feeling you get after one line of speed and no more, he danced through his come-down, and he danced out the other side.

Leon danced to records he had never heard – this wonderful music! Full of thick, meaty funk and strings as light as gossamer and voices that were as ecstatic as some heavenly choir – singers who could really sing, voices trained in church choirs and on street corners – and he was totally in thrall to the face of the girl in front of him. She stunned him. She paralysed him. Just being in the presence of that face made him pause, his tongue tied with self-consciousness. But she made it easy for him.

During a break in the dancing, when they went to the bar for a screwdriver (him) and a Bacardi and coke (her), she was just so unaffected and natural that his tongue, like his feet, could not stay tied for ever.

'Autumn Gold brings out a person's bones,' she said, and it turned out that's what she knew about, that's how she earned a living – cutting, crimping and dyeing in a salon called Hair Today. She gently lifted the brim of his hat to consider the merits of Autumn Gold. Leon took a half-step back.

'Oh, come on,' she said, smiling in that way she had. Leon couldn't tell if she was flirting or just being nice. 'Don't be shy.'

'Okay,' Leon said, grinning like a loon.

181

And then – how easy she made it seem – Leon found himself following the most beautiful girl in the world back to her natural habitat. Back to the dance floor.

And time just slipped away, time was meaningless out here. Lights struck the crystal globe slowly twirling on the ceiling, throwing flashes of colour across a face he knew he would remember on his deathbed.

She danced with this gentle swaying motion – taking small steps on high heels – almost not moving at all – but somehow it looked to Leon like *great dancing* – her hair falling in her face, then shaken away with a smile, a secret smile, as if she had just remembered where she was, as if something mildly amusing had just occurred to her. She was perfect. Much better than Cybill Shepherd, Leon decided.

And there was this other thing – she was inseparable from the music. Leon danced for the first time in his life and those incredible songs – tales of a world devastated, or made complete, because of one love – would be impossible to hear again without thinking of that fabulous face.

'*If I can't have you . . . I don't want nobody, baby . . . If I can't have you . . . oh-oh-OH!*'

'Here,' said the most beautiful girl in the world. 'Have you got a cold?'

Leon didn't want to lie to her.

'No,' he said. 'No, I've been taking drugs.'

She raised her eyebrows. He was terrified she was going to turn away. For the first time that night, he knew real fear. The fear of never seeing her again.

'Oh, you shouldn't take drugs,' she said. 'You're not yourself when you take drugs.'

Leon had never thought of it like that. And he suddenly realised that there was something he desperately needed to know.

'What's your name?' Leon said, when what he meant was – may I love you for ever?

And she told him.

Terry felt like a tourist in his own life.

The factory hadn't changed. The metallic rumbling from the guts of the place, like some great ship in the night, the reek of malted barley and juniper berries that turned your stomach.

And he wondered what would happen to her stuff. In the past, breaking up was easy. The girls he had known lived with their parents. When it ended there was nothing to sort out. You went your separate ways and then, months later, you maybe saw them with some other guy and an engagement ring. Seen in a park, glimpsed in a car, and then gone. It was more complicated when you lived together. There was all this *stuff* to sort out.

Her bags full of camera equipment, rolls of film, contact sheets, big cardboard boxes with ILFORD printed on the front. Her records by Nick Drake and Tim Buckley and Patti Smith. Her coffee-table books of Weegee and Jacques-Henri Lartigue and Dorothea Lange. Floaty dresses, skimpy pants, big boots. Some cracked tableware from Habitat. It had all arrived at Terry's bedsit stuffed into her father's Ford Capri, taking up every inch of the boot and the back seat and the passenger seat. Terry wiped his eyes, staring up at the factory. He supposed that her things would leave the way they had arrived. He didn't want to see it. He didn't want to be around for that.

He remembered the night she had moved in. The evening had begun the way every evening seemed to begin as 1976 became

1977 – with a trip to see a band. It was a few weeks after being on the road with Billy Blitzen. A few weeks after the midnight knock on his door. He was trying to stop thinking about her. They had both gone back to their lives in London. She had her married boyfriend, he had his one-night stands and his friends. There was plenty to do. Terry never stayed home. There was nothing to stay home for.

'Grab your kaftan,' he told Ray one night. 'I am going to take you to see some new music you'll love.'

At the foot of the tower there was a dusty little shop that sold sad souvenirs to the few tourists who made it across the river to Southwark Cathedral. Terry and Ray saw Leon in there, arguing with the Asian owner, pointing at a sun-bleached T-shirt in the window.

'But you can't *sell* this rubbish – it's racist,' Leon was saying. 'Do you understand?'

The offending item was designed to look like a band's promotional T-shirt. 'Adolf Hitler – European Tour: 1939 to 1945', it said, and under a picture of Hitler looking pleased with himself there was a list of countries resembling dates on a tour. 'Poland, France, Holland, Italy, Hungary, Czechoslovakia, Rumania, Russia'.

'This only fashion,' protested the owner. 'Only trendy.'

'It's not remotely trendy!'

'You bad for business,' the owner said. 'You a trouble boy. You get out shop.'

'Come on, trouble boy,' Terry said, taking his arm. 'I'm going to take you to see some new music you will love.'

They caught the tube to the Hammersmith Odeon where Terry's name was on the door plus one. He talked to the press officer from Mercury and managed to get a plus two. And it was a great night – Tom Petty and the Heartbreakers, one of the few bands they could all agree on. Fast and furious enough for Terry, jangly and longhaired enough for Ray, and enough like Dylan to keep Leon happy. They punched the air and sang along to 'American Girl' and 'Breakdown' and 'Hometown Blues' and 'Anything That's Rock and Roll' and even though Terry said that the *real* Heartbreakers were Johnny Thunders' band, there was something beautiful about this lot – it sounded like the kind of thing they would have heard on the pirate radio stations of their childhoods, but it was undeniably new music. In a black cab back to Terry's bedsit, the three of them argued all the way.

'It's too trad for me, Dad,' Leon said, and the other two jeered at him because the little fucker had been screaming 'American Girl' louder than any of them.

'But you hate hippies,' Ray said to Terry as they trudged down the musty hall to the six-quid-a-week bedsit. 'You hate all hippies!'

'I like lots of hippies,' Terry insisted. 'And Tom Petty's not a hippy.'

'Name me one hippy you like,' Ray said, turning on the electric fire in Terry's room. They would be here all night now. Talking about music, listening to music. Drinking vodka until it ran out, smoking until the cigarettes were all gone. Maybe grabbing an hour or two's kip just before dawn, and then catching the bus to *The Paper*.

'John Sebastian,' Terry said. 'I love John Sebastian.'

'The Lovin' Spoonful,' Ray said. 'Looked a bit like John Lennon.'

'One of the greatest songwriters of all time,' Terry said. '"Didn't Want to Have to Do It", "Summer in the City", "Nashville Cats", "Younger Girl".' He cracked open a bottle of Smirnoff and poured shots into three filthy teacups. 'Incredible writer. "Do You Believe in Magic?" "Rain on the Roof" – I love this geezer! He's better than Dylan!'

'Oh, bollocks, he is,' Leon said, kicking off his DMs and lying down on Terry's mattress.

'"Warm Baby", "Never Goin' Back",' Terry said. 'One of those Americans who fell in love with the Beatles but never stopped loving their own music. Blues, country – it's all in the mix, buried deep. And he slept with thirteen women at Woodstock.'

Leon sat up, impressed at last. 'Who did? John Sebastian? Thirteen in three days?'

Terry nodded. 'Had sex with thirteen women at Woodstock and still had time to perform a solo set.' He began excitedly flipping through his record collection. 'And then, when the Lovin' Spoonful was over, John Sebastian was still writing great songs, when he was a working musician, a writer for hire. He wrote this great song for the Everly Brothers – "Stories We Could Tell". All about being on the road and sitting on a bed in a motel and talking about all the things you've seen and done. The Everly Brothers did an okay version – but John Sebastian's version, that's the one . . .'

Terry dug out a battered old album called *Tarzana Kid*. The vinyl was scratched and worn, and when Terry put the needle on the track he wanted, Ray could tell that this was a record that had been loved. They all had records like that. And the three of them sat there listening to this understated little song, slide guitars sighing under John Sebastian's voice, and Ray thought that it was the best song he had ever heard about friendship.

Talking to myself again
and wondering if this travelling is good . . .
Is there something else a-doing we'd be doing, if we could?

Then there was a knock on the door.

It was the guy down the hall, the manager of a couple of unsigned bands. Misty was behind him, breathless and laughing and lugging a tatty suitcase. They all helped her to carry her things in, even the guy from down the hall, because Misty was the kind of girl who men did those things for, and Terry did his best to hide his surprise that she had suddenly decided to move in without feeling the need to talk about it. They sat around awkwardly when all her things were in, and then Ray and Leon finished their drinks and slipped away.

And later, after she had cried for a bit, and they had made love and she had fallen into an exhausted sleep, he saw the marks on her body, all these dark marks on her arms and legs, just about visible in the light seeping into his bedsit, bruises in the moon-light.

He had seen marks like that in Newcastle, the first night, and he had even asked her about them, and believed her when she said, 'I mark easily, I just bumped myself,' because he wanted to. It was too hard to think of anything else. But now he could see that they were not the marks you get from bumping yourself, no matter how easily you bruise.

Nobody knew they were together then. Apart from Ray and Leon, nobody knew. Not until Terry went into the picture editor's office the next day and hit Acid Pete so hard that he broke Acid Pete's jaw and two of the fingers on his right hand. Then they knew.

Minutes later, in the office of Kevin White, woozy with the pain in his smashed hand, the editor was almost in tears of frustration and anger, asking Terry how he could do anything but sack him.

'I can't stand it when men knock around women,' Terry said.

187

They stared at each other for a long while. 'For whatever reason,' Terry said.

'Get out of my sight,' White said, and at first Terry thought he had been fired. Then he realised he was being sent back to his desk. And he knew that he would owe Kevin White for ever.

Now nobody knew they were apart. But they would know soon. And they would all have a good laugh, and they would be right to laugh at him, Terry thought. What else did he expect? How else could it end when the start was such a miserable fucking mess?

Terry walked through the iron gates of the gin factory and the security light snapped on, blinding him for a moment, making him raise his hand to his eyes, and he saw the shadow that he cast looked just like a bruise in the moonlight.

Ray was shocked to see the pack of photographers outside the Speakeasy. Somehow he had imagined that he would be the only one looking for Lennon. But there must have been twenty of them, jostling for position behind both sides of a roped-off scrap of red carpet, laughing and complaining, craning their necks at the rock and rollers who came and went from the Speak.

They were a curiously old-fashioned crowd. Longhaired girls in skin-tight leather trousers and primped men in wide lapels and tight leopard-skin strides. A race of Rod Stewart doppel-gängers and Britt Ekland lookalikes. It was as if the new music had never happened, Ray thought, as if the Western World did not exist. He watched them marching on the red carpet outside the Speakeasy with what seemed like a curious mix of pride and shame, because although they were preening in front of a mob of photographers, nobody thought it was worth taking their picture.

But Ray could feel the random electricity that always surrounds one of the greats. He had experienced it just once before, when *The Paper* had sent him to cover a Keith Richards drug bust back in January in the little town of Aylesbury, and Mick Jagger had suddenly strolled into the tiny public gallery. That same wild mega-wattage now ebbed and flowed through the night. The pack of picture-grabbers, the ageing showbiz kids entering the Speak, and Ray himself – they could all feel it. The proximity of greatness.

'Is he in there? Is he in there? What's he doing? Who's he with?'

There was a carnival atmosphere, a party mood, but with an overcoat of tension. It was a special night for all of them. A night to never forget. But there was the chance you could miss something. Ray stared around, uncertain where to go, feeling the gin and tonic giving everything a sickly haze. One of the photographers was singing what at first sounded like a sea shanty. No – something else, chanted merrily to the tune of 'What Shall We Do With the Drunken Sailor?'

> *What shall we put in the daily paper?*
> *What shall we put in the daily paper?*
> *What shall we put in the daily paper?*
> *Early in the morning?*

Ray stepped on to the red carpet. That was the way to go. If he had little in common with all the old Rod Stewarts, he had even less in common with the hardened pros of Fleet Street. And John was in there. John was so close now. Ray could feel himself shaking.

Ray walked across the red carpet and the young woman on the door looked at him as if he was dancing on her granny's grave. She was flanked by two large skinheads in black Crombies. They frowned at Ray as if he had posed a question that needed thinking about.

> *Scroungers on the dole who guzzle*
> *Union chiefs who need a muzzle*
> *Plus the winner of our crossword puzzle*
> *Early in the morning.*

'Hello,' Ray said, smiling shyly. 'Ray Keeley of *The Paper*.'

'No press.'

'I'll pay,' said Ray, pulling out a handful of change. Usually it was enough being with *The Paper*, but not always. At the Marquee you sometimes had to fork out your seventy-five pence just like everyone else. How much was it here?

The woman's face twisted with a withering smirk.

'Oh, I don't think so,' she said.

> *Awful international crisis*
> *Idiot reader wins three prizes*
> *See how the public rises*
> *Early in the morning.*

Ray retreated, his face burning, spilling a few coins on the red carpet as he went. He stopped to pick them up and dropped Terry's tape recorder. It landed with a clunk. He was afraid the photographers might laugh at him, but it was as if he didn't exist. Nobody existed for them apart from the thirty-six-year-old man inside the club. Ray sloped to the back of the pack – he could see now that some of them were standing on ladders – and examined the dent in Terry's tape recorder.

Some of it's truth and some of it's lying
What's the odds if the public's buying?
We're the lads never leave off trying
Early in the morning!

And then it all happened at once. The flashlights going off, the voices raised, the surge of excited bodies. The bouncers pushed forward and were pushed back, almost overwhelmed.

'JOHN! JOHN! OVER HERE, JOHN!'

'ONE THIS WAY, JOHN! ONE THIS WAY!'

And then Ray's eyes were widening and his pulse was racing because there he was, glimpsed through the frantic crowd – John Lennon in the bewildering flesh. John! His hair was shorter than Ray had expected, almost like a grown-out crop, and he was thinner – maybe thin for the first time in his life. Ray felt himself falling forward, caught an elbow in his face, and shoved back. He wasn't missing this.

Through the camera flashes and flying arms, there he was, there he really was – round wire-rim glasses, denim jacket and jeans – like me, Ray thought! – the small woman with a riot of black hair bustling by his side. Oh, that was definitely John Lennon. Ray Keeley didn't breathe, and he had one foot on the first step of a ladder, and he could see quite clearly now. The glasses on the man's face were round golden orbs in the glare of all those flashbulbs.

'WHAT ABOUT ELVIS DYING, JOHN? ANY COMMENT ON THAT?'

Elvis – dead?

Through the flashing lights and over the heaving shoulders of the photographers, Ray saw something beyond the lenses, he truly did, but just for a moment and then it was gone, the glasses impenetrable once more in the shine of the flashlights, John and Yoko hustled into the back of the Rolls-Royce purring by the pavement. But Ray had seen it in his eyes, and he couldn't mistake it for anything else. It was . . . anguish.

Before Elvis, Lennon had said as a young man, *there was nothing*.

Now John's hero was gone, and he hadn't known about Elvis, Ray was certain of that, John had not known until now. And Ray Keeley's hero was gone too, the Rolls pulling away fast with a couple of the madder photographers chasing it, firing without aiming into the windows, like they do for some celebrity prisoner, thought Ray with revulsion, somebody on trial – and the rest of them were already turning away, laughing and complaining, the mood jolly now that the prey had been found, and even the woman with the clipboard was smiling with the bouncers as if they had all been presented with a few seconds that they would talk about for ever. Only Ray felt as if he had failed.

He stood on the red carpet trembling, and nobody cared. He had found him and lost him. And he had been nuts to think he could get closer than these proper newsmen. It was all over.

'Ray? It's you, isn't it?'

A woman had come out of the Speakeasy. Slim, pretty, long black hair. Tight pink jeans and a leather jacket and high heels. Funky but chic. Maybe ten years or so older than Ray. Late twenties. She was smiling at him. 'You don't remember me, do you?'

He nodded. 'I do, I do.'

And he did. She was the wife of the manager of one of the biggest bands in the world. She was nice. A Rolling Stones fan, Ray remembered. One of those women who think that the important one was Brian Jones.

Her husband's band had made a little go a long way. They had started out as a pub rock band, banging out souped-up rhythm and blues in the Nashville and the 100 Club and Dingwalls, but a couple of big hit singles had sent them through the roof.

Ray had done a piece on them at the end of a triumphant tour of America, in front of basketball stadiums full of college kids screaming *'Whooh! Rock and roll!'* and solemnly holding their cigarette lighters above their heads, as if it meant something more than a faked sense of community, a Seventies parody of the Woodstock spirit.

The woman looked rich, and Ray knew it was because the new music had arrived too late to swamp her husband's band. Their small, pugnacious manager had told Ray at the end-of-tour party that he saw his band's career on the college circuit of the USA. England was dead, he said. Johnny Rotten could have England.

Ray had met his wife at the same party, on the roof of a hotel overlooking Central Park. At an event that was awash with cocaine, tequila sunrise and self-satisfaction, she had seemed friendly and bored. They had talked about music, but not her husband's band. They talked about the Stones. Standing outside the Speakeasy she seemed distracted and agitated, as though she had just had something stolen.

'Mrs Brown,' Ray said. 'How you doing?'

She nodded, ignoring the question. 'Did you see Lennon?' She was pretty but there was a hardness about her, and Ray thought that maybe all rich people got that way. You would think that money would soften you, but as far as Ray could tell it seemed to do the opposite. Her husband had it too.

'Yeah, I saw him,' Ray said. He looked wistfully down the street. 'Thought I might interview him.' He looked back at her, and she seemed amused. 'Anyway,' he said, dismissing the idea.

'Don't know what all the fuss is about,' she said. 'He hasn't done anything for years, has he? And the Stones were always the better band.'

'Well,' Ray said, not wanting to get into it, and he realised what it was that stopped her seeming beautiful. She was just too pissed off. 'Well, I don't know about that.' He laughed nervously. 'I better get going. See you around, Mrs Brown.'

But she laid her left hand on his denim jacket. She was wearing a fat gold wedding ring and the biggest diamond ring that Ray had ever seen.

'Have one drink with me,' she said, smiling but with a strange note in her voice. Almost like she was shy about saying it. And she wasn't a shy woman.

Ray hesitated. Shouldn't he be – what? Chasing the Rolls-Royce? Staking out the VIP lounge at Heathrow? Clearing his desk?

'Go on – one drink,' she urged. 'Do you know what day it is?'

He thought about it. 'The day Elvis died?' Ray said. 'Is that true? Is Elvis really dead?'

She pulled a face, as though he was a waiter who had got her order wrong. 'Apart from Elvis dying,' she said. Then she smiled. She had a good smile when she gave it a chance, Ray thought. 'Today's my birthday.'

Ray wished her happy birthday, but she was already on her way, and he found himself following her to the door. The woman with the clipboard and the men in Crombies stepped aside. Ray saw that everyone stepped aside when Mrs Brown was coming. He looked around with interest. He had never been here before.

'This place is getting really tired,' she said.

But Ray was impressed. The Speakeasy was much plusher than the clubs he usually went to. It was much bigger, for a start, with red velvet chairs and sophisticated lighting and waiters asking you what you wanted to drink. But there was a large empty stage and an unmistakable feeling of anti-climax now that Lennon had gone. There were plenty of free tables. They found one. A waitress came over, this Linda Lovelace type that you never saw in the places Ray went to.

'What do you want?' Mrs Brown said, removing her jacket.

Ray mumbled his order, and the Linda Lovelace frowned, shaking her head, as if Ray was a kid who was out past his bedtime.

'What's he say?'

Ray cleared his throat. 'Scotch and coke, please.'

'I'll have the usual,' Mrs Brown said. She was smiling at Ray. 'You're going to have to speak up when you interview John Lennon, you know.'

Their table was lit by a red light bulb in the shape of a candle. Her long, bare arms were resting in front of her. Ray peered at her watch in the darkness.

'What time is it anyway?'

She glanced at her watch, and it flashed gold in the gloom.

'Who cares?' she said.

Linda Lovelace brought the tray. Ray felt that he should really get going. But he remembered his manners, and lifted his glass.

'Well – happy birthday, Mrs Brown.'

She laughed, nodded. They clinked glasses.

'Thanks for having a drink with me,' she said, and he was embarrassed. She seemed like the loneliest person he had ever met. But she was pretty and rich and her husband managed one of the biggest bands in the world. How could she be lonely?

'No – you know I'm happy to,' Ray stuttered, lost for words. 'Very happy to have a drink with you on your birthday.'

She lit a cigarette, exhaled through her nose, narrowing her eyes. She pushed the pack across the table to Ray. Marlboro. He helped himself.

'You know my husband, right?'

Ray nodded. 'Sure. I mean, not very well.'

'But you know him,' she said, keen to get to her point. 'Do you know what my husband bought me for my birthday?'

Ray shook his head. He had no idea. How would he know? 'Go on – have a guess,' she said, and it sounded like an order.

Ray shrugged. He knew it would not be the kind of present his father bought for his mother. It would not be bath salts and a box of Black Magic chocolates. He knew that much.

'I don't know.'

She stubbed out the cigarette as if she had never really wanted it. 'Well – guess.'

Ray racked his brain, sipping his Scotch and coke. She ran a hand through her long dark hair and her wrist and fingers glittered.

'A watch?' Ray suggested. He knew it had to be something expensive. That was for sure.

'A watch? Did you say a watch?' Her face was pretty and angry. Ray didn't understand what was going on. 'No, he didn't buy me a watch, Ray. A watch would have been nice. No – you're never going to guess it, so I'll tell you. My husband bought me a vibrator for my birthday. What do you think about that?'

Ray didn't know what to think. He had never even seen a vibrator. But somewhere inside him he knew it was a hateful thing to give to your wife. Especially on her birthday. Maybe Black Magic chocolates and bath salts weren't so bad after all.

'Say it with flowers,' Mrs Brown said. 'Isn't that what they say? They say you should say it with flowers.'

Ray stared at the ice in his drink. 'I don't know. I guess so.'

Mrs Brown laughed, truly amused. She finished her drink and signalled for the waitress. 'Let me tell you,' she said. 'You can say it a lot better with a vibrator. That should be the catch phrase, Ray. *Say it with a vibrator.*'

Linda Lovelace appeared.

'Another round,' Mrs Brown said, ignoring Ray's half-hearted protests. The waitress nodded and left. Ray hurried to finish his drink. He didn't know if he could keep up with this woman. He suspected not.

'And what is he saying?' said Mrs Brown. 'What is he saying – this husband of mine who bought me a vibrator for my birthday?'

Ray knew an answer wasn't expected. So he just waited, sipping his Scotch and coke, staring at the wife of the manager of one of the biggest bands in the world, wondering how someone that lovely could ever be so sad.

'I do believe,' said Mrs Brown, as their drinks were laid before them, 'that my husband is telling me to go fuck myself.'

TEN

The security light died and there was the factory's ancient care-taker, PJ, grey and wispy, rolling himself a cigarette in a wooden cubbyhole the size of a coffin.

'Didn't expect to see you again,' he said to Terry, running the tip of his tongue over a Rizla.

PJ had changed into his stripy pyjamas. That's why they called him PJ. Get past the witching hour and PJ would put his jammies on, bring out the Old Holborn, and get ready for what he called a good old kip. 'Thought you'd be flying all over the world with those drug-taking weirdos.'

'That was last week,' Terry said. 'Are they up there?'

A thin smile. 'Where else they got to go?'

Terry went inside the factory, and it was strange to be here after the best part of a year on *The Paper*. He looked around at the great expanse of the bottling plant, silent and still now, the conveyor belts snaking all over what looked like a giant aircraft hangar. He had thought he would never come back. But being here was oddly comforting.

The place was in darkness, but one floor up he could see fluorescent lights blazing. The data-processing department never closed.

Everybody else – in the bottling plant, in the offices – was given free gin at the stroke of six and told to bugger off home thirty minutes later. But the young people who attended to the needs of the factory's monolithic computer worked around the clock, pulling twelve-hour shifts, eight at night to eight in the morning. And all of it done on a bellyful of gin.

Computer operator – it had sounded modern and intellectual to Terry, but it was just manual work for kids who had left school with five O Levels and a certificate for swimming their width. Kids like Terry – restless, reluctant to work in a normal office, wanting the world to shut its mouth and leave them alone.

Being a computer operator meant staying up all night changing giant spools of tapes, swapping disks as big as dustbin lids, and feeding payroll cheques, invoices and inventories into a metal printer the size of a car. The best thing about the job was that you were totally unsupervised. You could do what you liked in here.

He sprinted up metallic steps to a tiny office littered with kitbags, half-eaten food and drinks, and there they were behind the glass, the white banks of the computer looming above the three of them. Peter, a good-looking boy with bad skin and long, lank brown hair, the one who was in a band, the music nut, his first friend at the factory.

Kishor, the Pakistani lad who wanted to be a programmer but couldn't find a firm who would give him a chance.

And Sally Zhou – real name Zhou Ziyi – her face frowning as she stood with Kishor staring at a message that was chattering out of the teleprinter on the keyboard. He had forgotten how much he loved her face. How had he ever forgotten that?

She looked up and saw him, shook her head and turned away,

folding her arms across her small breasts. Then Peter was bounding out of the room, lank hair flying, laughing with disbelief.

'I can't believe it – what are *you* doing here? You should be – I don't know – on the road with Springsteen or Thin Lizzy or something.'

Kishor came out of the computer room, grinning shyly, and then Sally was there, reluctantly, her arms still folded across those breasts, looking like Terry had let her down once and was never going to get the chance to do it again.

'You've been plucking your eyebrows,' she observed coldly. 'Looks ridiculous.'

How did he let this girl go? And how could he have been so strong, and so stupid? 'Hello, Sal,' he said.

'Girlfriend got the night off?' she said. Her accent was classic British-born Chinese. Pure Cockney, but with a hint of Kowloon in some of the vowels.

Terry shrugged, wanting to be cocky but feeling too sorry for himself. Like poor Rocky Balboa, misunderstood by the world.

'What girlfriend?' he said.

'Maybe she dumped you,' Sally ventured.

'I'm right off women,' Terry said.

Peter laughed excitedly. 'All those groupies! Mate, you must be worn out!'

Sally smiled, her teeth shockingly white, her eyes like molten chocolate. 'Yes, she dumped him,' she said knowingly.

'The things you must have seen!' Peter said. He sat on the desk and clapped his hands. 'Concerts in America! Exclusive playbacks in studios thick with dope! Backstage rows! On the tour bus, with the Cuervo Gold and pure Colombian being passed around! Groupies! Groupies! Groupies!'

'Don't be blooming disgusting,' Sally said. She always was a bit of a prude, Terry remembered. At least in public.

'Oh my goodness!' Kishor said, blushing furiously, and Terry recalled how any talk of sex always embarrassed him. But Peter was dirty enough for all of them. He shuddered with delight, rubbing his hands together. 'I want to hear all about it,' he said.

'Well,' said Terry, 'I saw a woman take a leak.'

Peter smiled uncertainly.

It had been during his first weeks on *The Paper*, when he was on the road with Lynyrd Skynyrd. He had been sent on the road by Kevin White as a punishment for taking speed in the office – or rather for letting one of the cleaners catch him at it. His first misdemeanour at *The Paper*. But he had liked the music – bar band boogie on an epic scale – and he had liked the musicians – a hard-drinking family of southern boys and girls. He still couldn't believe the life he was leading and every day brought some new adventure.

Terry had been in someone's hotel room, one of those crowded, boozy hotel rooms that you get on the road, talking to one of the boys in the band in the doorway of the bathroom because there was nowhere else to stand.

One of the backing singers – the short, good-looking one – had barged past them and pulled up her skirt, pulled down her pants and peed like she really needed to go. Terry's jaw dropped, although he tried to act as if he had seen many women pee. And it probably wasn't even her bathroom.

Peter looked confused.

'But . . . you must have met all the stars. But . . . you met – I don't know. Mick Jagger. Keith. Rotten. Springsteen. The Clash. Debbie Harry. *Debbie fucking Harry.*'

Terry conceded that he had indeed met all of these people. 'But you feel that you sort of know them already, don't you?' he said. Peter looked blank – no, he didn't know. 'You've spent so long thinking about them, listening to them,' Terry said. 'So when you meet him, Jagger is sort of familiar. But I had never seen a woman pee before.'

Peter punched Terry's arm playfully, as if he was a big kidder.

'Someone get this man a cup of tea,' Peter said. He picked up a can of soft drink. 'Or there's some G and T left in there, if you want something stronger.'

Terry smiled. That was what they always loaded up on before they came to work – gin and Tizer. Numbing themselves for the twelve-hour shift ahead. They wouldn't understand that up at *The Paper.* They would never understand that this was another kind of work. It wasn't fulfilling, or rewarding, or any of that middle-class stuff. You worked here to pay your way in the world, and that was the only reason you did it, and sometimes the tedium was so great that you needed to deaden a part of yourself just to get through the shift.

It was hard staying awake until eight in the morning, especially when you knew that other people your age were out on the town, or tucked up in bed, and it was even harder with a bellyful of gin and Tizer.

Terry remembered what else made it hard – the soporific jingles the radio played in those long hours before dawn. There was one jingle in particular that always made his eyes close and his head drop and his spirits sag, a jingle that sounded like it was sung by session singers who had just been buried under an avalanche of Valium.

'*Cap-it-al . . . helps you make it through the night,*' went the

203

jingle that always knocked them out. *'Cap-it-al . . . helps you make it through the night.'*

But tonight the radio was different. Tonight there was wall-to-wall Elvis. 'King Creole' was playing on a tinny transistor radio. Peter turned it up.

'You hear about Elvis?' Peter said.

Terry shook his head.

'Died in Memphis,' Peter said. 'Heart attack, they reckon. Forty-two years old. Bloody tragic, mate. He started it all, you know.'

Terry was shocked. Being invisible to the mourning Teds suddenly made sense. He had never imagined that Elvis Presley was dead. Elvis was one of those figures that had always been there at the back of your life, and you assumed they would be there for ever.

When Terry had been growing up, Elvis had always been slightly corny, a bit of a rock-and-roll Shirley Bassey, all grand showbiz gestures and big empty ballads. But now, listening to 'King Creole' on Capitol Radio the night he died, he felt the raw greasy magic in the music. Terry felt an unexpected surge of grief. Tears sprung to his eyes and he quickly wiped them away. Maybe it was just the speed.

'How's Land of Mordor doing?' Terry said. 'Got any gigs lined up?'

Land of Mordor was Peter's band. Terry had seen them once at the factory's Christmas disco. With their twenty-minute guitar solos and songs about elves, Land of Mordor had almost killed the party stone dead. Only food poisoning in the cocktail sausages could have been more of a downer.

Peter looked gloomy. 'Nobody wants prog rock any more,' he said. 'Look at the way they talk about Clapton. They want the new stuff.' He looked at Terry's spiked, dyed hair accusingly. 'The kind of crap you like. You know – two-minute songs about riots and pensions.' He brightened. 'But if you could get us a review . . .'

Terry pretended to be giving it serious thought. 'I'll have a word with the editor of the live pages,' he lied.

Kishor handed Terry a polystyrene cup of scalding brown liquid and he smiled gratefully, even though he knew it was undrinkable. He remembered how everything that came out of the vending machine looked exactly the same. And the boiling hot swill reminded him of other things – like half-filling a can of Tizer or Coke or Tab with gin as he argued with Peter about the merits of *Harvest* and Pink Floyd and Jimmy Page, and Kishor telling him about the things that were pushed through the letterbox of the newsagent's run by his parents in the East End, and the nights spent with Sally curled up inside her sleeping bag in one of the empty offices, her body slender and warm against him while Peter and Kishor took their half of the shift. That's what he remembered most of all. Gin-flavoured kisses and brown eyes shining and the feel of those slim limbs.

'Here,' she said, handing him the cup from the top of her thermos. A few leaves floated in perfumed water. 'It's not the kind you like. It's not Brooke Bond PG Tips. It's Chinese tea.'

He set down the polystyrene cup and took Sally's drink.

'My favourite,' he said, and she looked at him as though she didn't believe a word of it.

Then they all looked up as the keyboard thundered out a message. The tapes had stopped revolving. 'Those payroll tapes need changing,' Sally said. 'Come on, Kishor.'

They went back into the computer room. Terry had been waiting for them to go.

'Got any stuff?' he asked Peter.

Peter smiled doubtfully. It was as if everything Terry said was not what he was expecting.

'You don't need me to give you stuff, man,' he said. 'Do you?'

'I'm right out and I need a bit of a lift,' Terry said. 'A bit of speed. Some blues, black bombers, anything you got.'

Terry knew that Peter bought the odd half-gram of amphetamine sulphate for six quid when Land of Mordor were rehearsing in his parents' garage. But Peter clearly thought that Terry should be getting his gear from Keith Richards' dealer. Or Keith Richards himself.

'But . . . what about all those rock stars, all those bands you hang out with?' Peter said. 'There must be stuff all around them. I mean – sex and drugs and rock and roll, right? That's what it's all about, right?'

'Cap-it-al,' sighed the radio. 'Helps you make it through the night . . .'

Terry felt his head drop. That fucking jingle! Beyond the glass, Sally and Kishor were spooling fresh tapes on to the great white slabs. He sighed wearily.

'There's a bit of a drought in my neck of the woods,' Terry said. 'Haven't you got anything?'

Peter looked bashful.

'All I've got is some Pro-Plus,' he said apologetically. His face lit up. 'But what we could do is, we could crush it up and snort it.'

'Pro-Plus?' Terry said, unable to disguise his distaste. 'You can buy that in any chemist. You don't think Keith Richards and Johnny Rotten score their stuff in Boots, do you?'

Peter's face was a mask. 'I haven't met Keith and Johnny. You tell me.'

Terry took a long pull on the Tizer can. He tasted the sweet red sugar drink, and the mule-kick of the gin close behind it. Pro-Plus! How low can you go? He would be smoking banana skins next.

But he said, 'Come on then,' and he helped his old friend to start crushing the little yellow pills to dust.

Sally and Kishor came back into the office. She stared at them with disbelief. 'Please don't tell me you're thinking of putting that stuff up your nose,' she said.

But Terry didn't tell her anything, and he didn't look at her, and he watched his old friend carefully pummel the Pro-Plus to yellow powder with the bottom of his thermos flask.

'Ah, sex and drugs and rock and roll,' Peter said wistfully. 'Tell me all about it, Terry.'

Ruby Potter.

Her name sent Leon into a rapture where he saw fleeting visions of future possible lives.

Ruby Potter. Ruby Peck. Mrs Ruby Peck. Mrs Ruby Potter-Peck. Leon Potter-Peck. The Potter-Pecks. Look, there go the Potter-Pecks.

But away from the swirling lights of the Goldmine and in the unforgiving glare of the doughnut shop, Leon learned that the most beautiful girl in the world already had a life of her own.

'You can call him if you want,' said her fat friend, picking a custard doughnut from the box on the table, and sending Leon's heart tumbling. 'There's a phone booth at the end of the road. Go on – why don't you call him?'

'But I don't *want* to call him,' said Ruby, her lovely face fierce with defiance.

Dunkin' Donuts was lit like an interrogation room and, sitting at a Formica table that was bolted to the ground, Leon was forced to ask himself some tough questions.

Like, who the fuck were they talking about? And what was this bastard to Ruby? And how, oh how could Leon have been so dumb as to imagine that a girl like Ruby Potter could ever really be interested in a boy like him?

But when he looked at her face, none of it mattered. Leon looked at Ruby, and she smiled at him over a chocolate doughnut, and the world made sense. The bad stuff slid away and he lived in the blissful moment.

'Well, I don't know why you don't call him,' Judy said, removing a dab of cream from her lips. 'You know you want to.'

Leon saw it as a good sign that Ruby had a friend with a weight problem. What a wonderful heart she must have, thought Leon, to have a fat friend. How sensitive and deep Ruby must be, to not care about something as trivial as physical appearance. Beautiful on the inside as well as the outside, he sighed, poking a finger into his jam doughnut and then sucking the raspberry goo.

They didn't ask him what he did. That was strange because in the world of his parents, and even at *The Paper*, it was the given icebreaker. And what do *you* do? But not to Ruby and Judy. They came from a different kind of working world. He found out she was a hairdresser only after she had made a long speech about the merits and drawbacks of Autumn Gold.

'I write about music,' he told them, hoping to impress. 'In fact, I'm working tonight.' Trying to sound important now. Do you have any idea how busy I am? 'I'm meant to do this thing,' Leon said. 'Do you want to see a band? There's this band I'm meant to see.'

'A *band?*' Ruby said, frowning, making Leni and the Riefenstahls sound like Joe Loss and his orchestra. He was hoping that she might come with him. He was hoping that they might make a night of it. But his career just seemed to perplex her. Going to see *a band?*

'So can you get tickets for Queen at Wembley?' Judy said, suddenly more interested.

Leon tried to hide his contempt. He failed. 'Probably,' he said. 'But why would I want to do that?'

'Because Freddie Mercury's great,' Judy shouted angrily, 'you butt-fucking queer.'

Ruby slammed down her doughnut. *'Judy!'* There was a grace about her, Leon thought, and somehow it illuminated her perfect face. She had no doubt left school at fifteen, and never had any of what Leon's father called his 'advantages'. But Ruby Potter had more natural grace than anyone he had ever met.

'Who have you met then?' Judy said.

Leon drew a breath. 'Bob Marley. Patti Smith. Joe Strummer. Paul Weller. Pete Shelley. Phil Lynott. Johnny Thunders. The Sewer Rats.'

'Have you met Abba?'

'No, I haven't met Abba.'

Judy turned away with a sneer. 'He ain't met nobody.'

And then Leon saw them. Dagenham Dogs. Two of them, one on either side of the street. Shaven heads gleaming. Coming towards Dunkin' Donuts, playfully tossing a dustbin lid at each other. Leon watched one of them catch the dustbin lid, stagger into the road, and hurl it back at his mate with full force. The dustbin lid went sailing over the head of the second Dog and clattered into the window right by their table.

Judy was on her feet screaming abuse, and Ruby dropped her doughnut. The two Dogs guffawed with delight and approached the window, rubbing the front of their trousers and making obscene gestures. But by then Leon was under the table, on his hands and knees, watching Judy's foot stamping with fury. He didn't come out until he heard the Dogs retrieve their dustbin lid and go cackling off into the night.

'Found it,' he said, sheepishly coming back up. 'My contact lens. It's okay. Found my contact lens.' The two girls watched Leon putting the imaginary contact lens into his eye. Then he blinked at them furiously. 'That's much better.'

'Look, Ruby,' said Judy.

She was indicating a car full of neat, well-shaven youths that had pulled up outside. A stocky youth in a cap-sleeved T-shirt and Prince of Wales check trousers got out of the car and walked into Dunkin' Donuts. Grinning broadly, he saw them and came over, sitting on the edge of their table.

'Well, well, well. Little Ruby Potter. As I live and breathe.'

There was a half-eaten chocolate doughnut in front of Ruby. The youth in the capped T-shirt plucked it up and popped it in his mouth.

'Oy, you mucky pup!' said Judy, punching his pale, hairless arm. The youth made a great show of enjoying the doughnut, smacking his lips and rubbing his flat belly.

'You suck,' Judy said.

'You blow,' snarled the youth.

'You *wish*,' said Judy.

'I *know*,' said the youth.

'Ignore him, Judy, and he'll go away,' said Ruby, all imperious.

The youth laughed, and leaned closer to Ruby.

'Where's Steve tonight then?' he said in a stage whisper.

Ruby took a small round mirror from her handbag and made a great show of staring into it and rearranging a few strands of hair. 'Don't know, don't care,' she said.

The youth chuckled, as if he knew the awful truth. Leon smiled weakly. The bozo had not even bothered to acknowledge his existence.

'You want a lift back?' the youth said. 'We got the Escort outside.' He leaned on the table, leering in her face, oozing phoney sympathy. 'Don't worry – Steve will understand.'

'I don't care what Steve understands!' Ruby said, her voice rising.

Leon felt like crying. I should have known. *Steve*. Probably all the really good ones have a boyfriend called Steve who can kick your head in.

'Who's *we?*' Judy said. Leon could tell she was quite interested in the prospect of a lift home.

'You know,' the youth said. 'Ron. Alfie. Lurch.'

Ruby and Judy rolled their eyes at each other.

'Those creeps,' Judy said.

'We don't need a ride,' Ruby said. 'We got one already.'

Leon realised she was smiling sweetly at him. He wondered what it could possibly mean. Panic fluttered inside him. She didn't think he owned a car, did she?

'Suit yourself, darling,' said the youth, still cocky, although Leon could tell he was disappointed. 'We're right outside if you change your mind.'

He eased himself off the table, still acting as though Leon was invisible. And Leon thought – why is she surrounded by all these horrible people? I must save her. They show her no respect, they do not cherish her the way she deserves to be cherished.

'He'll tell Steve he saw you,' Judy warned darkly.

Ruby laughed, her eyes sly. 'He can tell Steve what he likes, can't he?'

Judy was all doom and gloom. 'Steve will go crazy . . . you down

211

the Goldmine on your own . . .' A knowing look at Leon here. 'Having a good time . . .'

'Do him good,' Ruby said, and Leon saw that she was capable of being ruthless. The beautiful must be like that, he thought. They do what they want.

Then he was scrambling after the girls as they traipsed out into the street where a canary yellow Ford Escort was parked right outside Dunkin' Donuts. There were four youths inside, all of them wearing capped-sleeve T-shirts, all leaning out of the windows and grinning. None of them had cut their hair yet. Donna Summer's 'I Feel Love' was turned up on the radio. Leon quickly checked the street for Dagenham Dogs. But they had gone, no doubt off to join the mayhem at the Western World. There was an abandoned dustbin lid in the middle of the road.

'Oooh, it's so good, it's so good, it's so good, it's so . . .'

'Any more fares, please,' the tallest one shouted. 'Ding-ding!' He had to be Lurch. Judy leaned her head into the window but Ruby held back, waiting for Leon to say something. He stared at her helplessly.

'Where's your motor?' Ruby asked him.

He spread his arms. 'I don't – I haven't . . .'

Judy turned on him, hands on hips, icy fragments of doughnut still on her lips. 'You haven't got a car? Then how are we meant to get home?'

He turned to Ruby, his head spinning. He would probably never see her again. 'I'm sorry,' he said.

Judy was already climbing into the back of the yellow Escort, squeezing herself between the two youths on the back seat. They all cheered. Donna Summer came closer to orgasm.

'Come on, Ruby,' Judy shouted.

But Ruby shook her head and turned away, her arms folded across her chest. They waited for a moment, making sure she really meant it, and then the Escort took off in a blur of burned rubber and 'I Feel Love'. Leon caught a glimpse of Judy on the back seat, giving him a two-fingered salute.

'What are we going to do?' Ruby said. 'How am I going to get back?' And then she noticed his bruise for the first time. 'What happened to your face?'

'Oh,' he said, touching his cheekbone. 'I got this on Saturday. Down at Lewisham. You know – the riot.'

'Oh,' she said. 'Lewisham. Yeah, my dad was there too. Protesting and that. He feels strongly about these things. Just like you.'

And Leon didn't dare ask. He didn't dare ask the most beautiful girl in the world which side her dad was on.

Nothing. Not a thing.

Just nostrils caked with crushed Pro-Plus and nerves clattering with caffeine. Terry and Peter stared at Sally and Kishor on the other side of the glass, swapping reels of tape, the pair of them as busy as dockers with a ship in.

'It's all been done before, anyway,' Peter said.

Terry looked at him. What was he going on about?

'All this new music,' Peter said. 'All this blank generation bollocks. The Stooges and MC5 did it first. Even before that. On the first Hendrix album. "I Don't Live Today" – that's about as blank as it gets. And then he *died*. Jimi *died*.' Peter took a swig of flat Tizer and warm gin. 'What these bands are doing – it's all been done before.'

Terry exploded.

'Not by us! Not by me! Fuck! I hate it when people say that!' He was on his feet. He was tired of hearing this stuff. He was tired of being told that everything was shit and nothing had happened since the Sixties. He wasn't young ten years ago – he was a kid. And he wouldn't be young in ten years' time – he would be an old man. *This* was his time. Now. Tonight. Right here. And it felt like some fucker was always trying to spoil it.

'I'm sick of having to bow down to all these old bastards in their thirties! You think Johnny Rotten's going to live to see forty? You think Rotten's going to turn into Des O'Connor? It doesn't matter what anybody else has done – *we* haven't done it!'

Peter snorted. 'Tell you what – shall we nick some gin?' he said.

Terry only had to think about it for a moment. 'Yeah, all right. Let's nick some gin.'

There were always odd bottles of gin stashed at the bottom of desks in the office. It was the only thing to steal in the factory. Terry and Peter wandered through darkened rooms trying desk drawers until they found something. It was already half-empty. Some poor little clerk wiping himself out at elevenses. Peter unscrewed the cap on the bottle and took a long pull.

'Got any Tizer left?' Terry said.

Peter shook his head, taking a swig from the bottle, and grimacing with disgust. 'I hate this stuff,' he said.

'Yeah,' Terry said, taking the bottle. 'Worst drink in the world.'

Leon stood outside the locked doors of the Red Cow, quietly cursing, and hours late for Leni and the Riefenstahls.

'It looks shut,' Ruby called from the back of the black cab.

Leon peered through the dusty glass of the Red Cow, knowing it was pointless. He had missed the gig. Because of a girl. Because he was dancing.

And he knew this was serious. As long as the cleaners or the straights at *Country Matters* didn't see you, nobody cared what you did at *The Paper*. Kevin White didn't care if you shot up with Keith Richards, shared a spliff with Peter Tosh, or snorted sulphate with Sid Vicious. Nobody cared – as long as you *did the work*.

But whatever drug was in your system, and whatever rock star was turning blue in your bedsit, White and the older guys expected you to get your copy in on time. Among the chaos and chemical excess of *The Paper*, a steady work ethic endured. Clean copy, the correct length and on time. The only things they took seriously at *The Paper* were music and deadlines.

'You getting out or what, mate?' said the taxi driver.

But the good thing is, thought Leon, I already *know* what I think about Leni and the Riefenstahls. I don't really need to see the silly cow strutting about in her jackboots to know I don't like her. So what's to stop me writing about an event that I didn't actually see? It's just as true – isn't it? *I know what I am going to write before I even start writing.*

Leon turned back to the cab and Ruby's perfect face, happy again, and feeling like he was becoming a real journalist at last.

The big problem was Dag Wood's penis.

Terry had seen it – an enormous, barnacle-encrusted todger that would not have been out of place in a porn movie. That giant knob haunted Terry's dreams, and filled his Pro-Plus reverie with anxiety and dread.

Terry had gazed upon the great beast, its helmet with the appearance of a monstrous lychee, not long after meeting Dag for the first time. The great man had been at the head of a long table at a restaurant in West Berlin. He was doodling on the linen tablecloth with a black felt-tip.

After being introduced to Terry, Dag had challenged him to a race through the streets of Berlin. Terry stared at him, wondering if he was serious. And when he realised that Dag was dead serious, he accepted. He knew he had no choice. So the pair of them left everyone else at the restaurant and ran through the empty streets at midnight. They ran as fast as they could, but halfway to the Hilton, Dag told Terry it was okay – they didn't have to run any more, and Terry knew he had passed some sort of test.

Then Dag asked Terry about the new music, what was happening in London, what he could expect and what the audiences would expect from him. It was only later, when Terry was a bit older, that he realised Dag Wood had been frightened – afraid he would not be able to live up to all those great expectations, afraid he would disappoint all those feral children waiting for him in London and Glasgow and Liverpool.

'Must be great though,' Peter said, staring into the gin bottle. It was almost empty. 'Hanging out with rock stars . . ?'

Terry and Peter were sitting on the desks of the tiny office, watching Sally and Kishor work, listlessly passing the bottle between them. Elvis was on the radio, threatening sudden violence. It was the one about being a hard man. Trouble.

Maybe it was true, Terry thought. Maybe there was nothing new under the sun, and every generation dressed up and struck poses and thought they were too cool for school, but in reality it had all been done before.

'Free records, free gigs,' Peter said. 'What a life you lead, Tel.'

Terry laughed bitterly. 'You're better off here, mate.'

Peter glared at him. 'Oh, bollocks.' He stood up, swayed and slurred. Pushed his face into Terry's so that he could smell the metallic stink of the gin. 'Great big hairy bollocks.'

'The truth is,' Terry said, knowing it was the last thing he wanted to admit and the last thing Peter wanted to hear, 'the truth is, it's not all it's cracked up to be.' He took the bottle, swigged, felt his stomach rise and wondered if he was going to throw up. 'These rock stars – they pretend they're your friends.' He thought of Billy Blitzen taking him to one side at the sound check in Newcastle. He thought of other good ones – Joe Strummer, Johnny Thunders, Phil Lynott. 'Maybe one or two really are – if you're lucky. But mostly they just . . . they use you. They want to be in *The Paper*. That's all. What do we sell? A quarter-million every week? Of course they're fucking nice to us! But it's all bullshit. And you think they're happy? The musicians? The bands? They're all terrified! The young ones are afraid they're never going to make it, and the old ones are afraid it's all going to end.'

The lead guitarist and main songwriter of Land of Mordor looked devastated.

'Then it's all . . . rubbish,' Peter said finally, taking the gin bottle and tipping what was left down his throat. When he saw it was all gone, he contemplated the empty green bottle for a moment and then hurled it at the glass that separated the office from the computer room. Sally and Kishor jumped back in alarm as the glass collapsed, and Elvis sang on, jittery with joy.

Peter had someone's thermos flask in his hand, and was hammering at the remaining glass panels until they broke, collapsed, shattered. Terry was chuckling with disbelief, Sally was shouting Peter's name and Kishor looked on the edge of tears.

Then Peter was in the computer room, ripping off spools and throwing them through the smashed windows, the streamers of

217

shiny brown tape trailing behind them like toilet rolls at a football match, lashing out at the great white obelisks with his sandals, making Terry laugh harder as he hobbled with pain.

Sally had her arms around Peter's waist, trying to drag him away from the computer, while she shouted at Terry to stop him.

'We'll all lose our jobs!'

Kishor was in the office, babbling something about the step up to programming, the step that he was never going to make now, and Terry stopped laughing because suddenly it was all over, and the storm inside Peter had blown itself out, and he was lashing out at the monolithic tape stacks and only hurting himself, and it wasn't as funny as it had been before. And he couldn't stand to see Sally that upset. Then PJ was standing in the doorway, blinking in his pyjamas, a broom in his hands.

'You stupid, stupid little bastards,' he said. 'You better get this cleared by morning, or you're all out on your earholes.'

'Clear it up?' Sally said. 'How can we clear it up, you silly old sod?' She threw a broken spool at PJ, and glossy brown tape spilled out behind it. 'He's smashed the place up! Look at it!'

Peter came back into the office, using the door – although there was no need to, he could have stepped right through where the glass used to be. He looked sweaty and shocked.

'Well,' Terry said, jumping off the desk and taking the broom from PJ, 'let's get cracking.'

They all stared at him.

Sally laughed, shaking her head. 'You can't come back here just because your new life hasn't worked out. Don't you know that?' She placed her hand on Kishor's shoulder. 'Don't cry, Kish. We'll tell them – well, I don't know what we'll tell them. Burglars did it. Vandals.'

'But they'll never believe it!' Kishor said, wringing his hands. 'They'll know it's us!'

Peter sat on the floor and covered his face.

Sally gently prised the broom from Terry's fingers. 'You should go now,' she said.

ELEVEN

The meat market froze Terry's bones.

All around the great roaring cavern men in white coats smeared with blood loaded slabs of meat on to two-wheeled carts that looked like rickshaws and, with their breath steaming, transported their loads out to the waiting caravan of lorries and vans lining the perimeter of Smithfield with their engines idling. The freezing air was ripe with profanities as the men roundly swore at life and each other. It was hard work, and a long night. Terry's head reeled at the fact that his father had worked here since leaving school at fourteen.

He turned up the collar of his Oxfam jacket and stuffed his hands deep inside his pockets. The cold air made his eyes fill with tears and his breath come in short cloudy gasps. He walked down the central aisle, looking for his dad.

Terry found him hauling a giant side of beef on to his back, a great carcass of meat and bone that made his knees buckle for a moment before he recovered and staggered upright, face contorting like a weightlifter.

'My boy's here,' he gasped, his sweat-smeared face cracking into a smile at the sight of his son. He was wearing a hat that made him look like he was in the French Foreign Legion – a canvas cap with an expanse of white material coming out of the back, as if to keep off the desert sun.

'Help you with that, Dad?'

The old man laughed. 'That'll be the day.'

Terry followed him through all the men in their bloody white coats and out of the market, the old man bow-legged with the burden on his back. Shuffling behind him, all Terry could see of his father were the grubby tails of his white coat and the worn-out heels of his boots. When he had deposited the meat in the back of a refrigerated lorry, he wiped his hands on his sleeves before slapping Terry on the back.

'My boy's here!' he shouted to no one in particular. 'He goes all over the world, interviewing film stars!'

'Dad,' Terry protested. 'They're not *film* stars.'

'Look at you,' the old man said happily. 'You're all skin and bone. You hardly touched your tea, did you? Let's get you something to eat.'

Even at these hours in the dead part of the night, the pubs around Smithfield meat market were doing good business. In fact, trade was picking up now that the porters were nearing the end of their graveyard shift.

Behind foggy glass windows, red-faced men in white knocked back pints of brown ale and drenched freshly made pies in HP sauce or sucked hungrily on cigarettes. Terry's dad ordered pies and pints and found them seats at a table surrounded by loud, exhausted-looking men. Terry was the only one not wearing a white coat.

'My boy,' Terry's dad explained. 'Goes all over the world interviewing these showbiz types.' His barrel-like chest expanded with a pride that made Terry blush. 'You could say he's a bit like Michael Parkinson, I suppose.'

The men looked moderately impressed. 'Who you interviewed, then?' one of them asked.

'Well,' Terry said, taking a mouthful of beef-and-onion pie. He paused, his stomach recoiling from the taste of hot food. When was the last time he had eaten? He remembered being on the plane back from Berlin, pushing away a foil tray of something that may have been chicken. And, with a stab of guilt, he remembered being unable to make a dent in the special meal that his mother had cooked for Misty. Take enough speed and your appetite seemed to fade away. 'I just interviewed Dag Wood,' he said, putting down his knife and fork. Blank faces around the table. 'And I've interviewed Grace Fury.'

Nothing. Terry's dad was still smiling proudly.

'The Clash? The Jam? The Stranglers?' He was struggling now, but he didn't want to disappoint his dad. 'I did one of the first pieces on the Sex Pistols – and I wrote something when they did that secret gig at the Screen on the Green . . .'

The name pressed a nerve. 'The mob that called the Queen a moron?' said one enormous porter. 'They don't want to come down here on a dark night. We like the Queen round here.'

The other men chuckled at that, and made enthusiastic predictions of a 'good hiding' for any of the Sex Pistols that dared set foot in Smithfield. But their interest had been piqued.

'What about the birds in Abba? You meet them?' Lewd laughter and rolled eyes, pieces of pie dropped and retrieved. 'I wouldn't mind doing something in-depth with that blonde tail!'

Terry had to concede that he hadn't crossed paths with Abba.

'What about the Beatles?'

'Elton John and Kiki Dee?'

'What about Disco Duck?'

Some of the more sophisticated music lovers chortled at that. 'The song's called "Disco Duck", you daft cunt. The singer's Rick Dees and His Cast of Idiots! Listen to him with his Disco Duck!'

Terry had to admit he hadn't met any of them.

'See,' Terry's dad said proudly. 'All the stars. Travels all over the world, he does.'

His smile didn't falter until they were outside the pub.

'You don't eat,' the old man said. 'You don't sleep. And you're skin and bone. What's wrong with you? What's going on?'

Terry said nothing, filling himself with the chilled night air, glad to be out of the pub and away from the smell of cooked meat.

His father picked up the handles of a two-wheeled cart, and began pulling it behind him. They walked back into the great freezing cavern of a market, where the old man rested his rickshaw.

'Your mum liked that girl. Young Misty. Serious about her, are you?'

Terry looked away. 'Not really.' How could he tell the old man about Dag Wood? How could he tell him any of that?

His father shook his head, eyes blazing. He had never raised a hand to Terry in his life. But he had a way of looking at his son that hurt as much as any slap. 'One of these days we're going to find out what you *do* like, Tel,' he said. Terry knew that the life he was leading was unimaginable to his father. But the old man was not stupid – he knew that whatever his son was doing, he couldn't go on doing it for ever. Without being asked, Terry's dad produced a worn-out wallet from his back pocket, and started peeling off the notes.

'Twenty-five quid do it?' This said without a hint of reproach. 'It's the best I can do until Friday.'

Terry hung his head. 'Dad, I'm sorry – I'll pay you back.'

Terry's father stuffed the money into his son's hand and dragged his cart over to a line of showers. WASH ALL TRUCKS HERE, said the sign.

'I don't care, I'd give you the shirt off my back,' Terry's father said. He began hosing down the rickshaw. Blood streamed in the gutter. 'But you can't even eat.'

'Help you with that, Dad? Help you with that?'

But Terry's old man shook his head, and continued hosing down what the porters in Smithfield called a truck, and he wouldn't even look at his son.

Mrs Brown swung the canary yellow Lotus Elan left at Marble Arch and gunned it down Park Lane, hitting the brakes as they passed the Dorchester and then the Hilton. Ray scanned the big hotels for packs of photographers. But the only sign of life was a lonely doorman in a top hat. Ray nervously rubbed his bare wrist.

'Do you want to try the Ritz?' she said, hitting the floor. She was a good driver, and the Elan just flew, and when she put the pedal to the floor, Ray thought it felt like some new kind of drug.

'Where's the Ritz?' he said.

She looked at him to see if he was joking. Then she said, 'The Ritz is on Piccadilly, just round the corner from Park Lane, he might be there. Or the Savoy, down by the river. Or Claridges – that's probably even more likely. They're all pretty close.'

'I know Claridges,' Ray said. 'I know that one.'

She chuckled. 'Yeah, what did you do at Claridges? Have tea and buttered scones?'

'No,' Ray said. 'I interviewed Bob Dylan.'

She raised her meticulously plucked eyebrows. She was impressed, he could see that. People were always impressed when they heard who he had met, although Ray couldn't understand why. It wasn't as though genius was contagious. And he had hardly got a coherent sentence out of Dylan – Ray had been sick with nerves, and Dylan had been monosyllabic. This beardy, middle-aged guy who clearly wanted to be somewhere else.

White had stuck it on the cover, because Acid Pete had a good concert shot, and because Dylan still warranted a cover. But it had been a crap piece. People thought they would be changed if they could just breathe the same air as the biggest stars. Ray knew it didn't work out like that. John Lennon wasn't going to save him. John Lennon wasn't going to save anyone.

'Well,' she said. 'If you interviewed Dylan, you shouldn't have any problem with John Lennon.'

'That was different,' Ray said. 'It was all set up for me. It's not so easy when you have to do it alone.'

'Ah,' she said. 'You're not alone.'

They smiled at each other. It was true. She had been a big help. If he had tramped around the five-star hotels by himself, John Lennon would have been at Heathrow before Ray had seen half of them. But as she expertly threw the Lotus around the empty West End streets, Ray felt a creeping despair. This was never going to work. Who was he kidding? He had never been a real journalist, just another kid who loved music.

'Anyway,' she said, when they had driven by the deserted entrance of the last hotel, 'the Beatles were thugs pretending to be gentlemen, and the Stones were gentlemen pretending to be thugs.' She got this funny smile, and looked at Ray sideways. 'Did you know I had a thing with Brian? I was just a kid. Did my husband ever tell you that?'

'Brian Jones?' Ray said. He was dumbfounded. Beautiful Brian, playing his sitar. Beautiful Brian, floating dead in his swimming pool. He was a part of history. Now Ray was impressed. It was like hearing that she had slept with Napoleon.

'Met him at that club where they started – the Station Hotel.' She laughed softly at the memory. The Elan was flying the other way up Park Lane. She seemed to like this road. She could really get up some speed. 'The Station Hotel, Kew Road, Richmond. Sunday nights. Back in 1963. I was – what? Fourteen! He had lots of girls, of course. My husband never mentioned it to you? It drove him crazy for years. The thought of me with Brian.'

Ray shook his head. 'Your husband never mentioned you to me.' He tried to soften the words. 'I mean, all we ever really talked about was his band and how they were doing. He didn't really talk about you.'

She laughed sourly.

'Of course not. When the sexual jealousy wears off, a woman knows she's on her way out. The next thing you know, they're giving you sex aids for your birthday.'

She said these things and he didn't know how to respond. He was aware that Mrs Brown wasn't asking for his opinion. So Ray said nothing. Then she sighed, as if she had had enough for one night.

'I can drop you home, if you like. Where do you live? Do you share a flat?'

Ray shook his head. 'I might just wander about for a bit.'

She pulled a face. 'Not in a squat, are you?'

Ray looked embarrassed. 'I'm still living at my mum and dad's place. At least, I was until I left home.'

'When was that?'

'About two hours ago.'

She laughed, and Ray realised how much he liked her. Under all that hardened frost, she was lovely. It all got mixed up for Ray – her kindness in helping him look for Lennon, the way her face lit up when she laughed, and the feeling of driving through London in the middle of the night in a yellow Lotus Elan. He didn't want to be walking the streets alone.

'Then I guess we are going to have to go back to my place,' she said.

In the moonlight the squat reared above them like a derelict Xanadu. There had been wealth here once, years ago, but now the façade of the great white house was scarred with gaping black cracks. Lights flickered in the bare upper windows – candles, open fires, the fiery glow of a bar on an electric heater. A baby was crying.

'Who lives here?' Ruby said. 'Dossers?'

'They're not dossers,' Leon said, counting out his change to pay the taxi driver. 'They're homeless. Can you help me out here? I'm a bit short. Sorry.'

Ruby frowned at him.

'Girls don't pay. *Boys* pay.' She sighed. 'How's fifty pence?'

There was a phrase he remembered from somewhere – something about new strategies needing to be devised to bring the wage of the female workforce in line with that of their male counterparts. But he couldn't keep this girl in his life by parroting stuff he had read in books. After Evelyn 'Champagne' King, that wasn't enough. So instead he said, 'Fifty pence would be brilliant. I've got the tip.'

She pulled out her purse and counted out the rest of the fare. Leon found a Luncheon Voucher in the sticky bottom of a pocket in his Lewis Leather, and slapped it on the driver's palm. The taxi driver shook his head.

'Bleedin' gypos,' he said, and drove away.

Ruby was reading the graffiti. '*Cats like plain crisps . . . No drugs in here . . . pull the other one.*'

'No, it's true,' Leon said. 'The people who run this place don't believe in drugs. People take drugs to make themselves free. And we think that – you know . . .' He felt embarrassed talking to her this way. 'We're all free already, I guess.'

'But *you* were taking drugs.'

'That's because I was with my friend. He thinks he needs them.' He smiled at her in the moonlight. 'And he sometimes leads me astray.'

She smiled back. 'Easily led astray, are you?'

Leon took out his key. 'Sometimes. How about you?'

She shook her head. 'My dad would kill me.' She looked up at the squat. 'Steve would kill me.'

'Then it's lucky Steve's not here, isn't it?'

Ruby looked back at him, not smiling now. 'Lucky for both of us.'

She held on to the back of his leather jacket as they negotiated their way across the planks. Leon let them into the darkened hallway and Ruby immediately smashed her shin against a bicycle.

'Careful,' Leon said. 'There's light upstairs. Sorry.'

Shadowy faces appeared on the first-floor landing, and then

were gone. Leon and Ruby climbed the stairs. In the main room candlelight and bare bulbs lit a circle of young men sitting cross-legged on the floorboards. They glanced at Leon and Ruby, nodded, and went back to their council. Voices murmured in the tongues of northern Europe.

'There are some people here who were in Paris,' Leon said. 'Paris in '68.'

'I went to Calais once,' Ruby said. 'With the school.'

They moved through the house. There was almost no furniture. You could smell mildewed wood and unwashed bodies and something cooking.

'It don't half pong,' Ruby whispered.

Faces peered out of the darkness, suspicious at first and then accepting and friendly, in a vague, unfocused sort of way. Leon felt Ruby relax. This wasn't such a bad place to be. They passed through a small kitchen where a huge pot of soup was simmering on a grease-encrusted cooker. Unwashed cutlery and scraps of food were scattered around. A longhaired young woman was washing a naked baby in a plastic bowl in the sink.

They went into the unlit bedroom where his father had stood. There had been new arrivals. Rucksacks were spilling their contents and half a dozen sleeping bags covered the floor. Most of them were occupied. A couple were making grunty love, the floorboards creaking beneath them. Ruby took Leon's arm and pulled him outside, giggling.

'They don't mind,' Leon said.

'I mind,' she said.

She shook her head and led him back to the kitchen. The woman and her baby were gone. Ruby made him sit in the only chair. She looked around for a moment, located half a lemon, a bottle of bleach and a teacup celebrating the wedding of Princess Anne and Mark Phillips. Then she faced Leon. She was very serious. She had her professional mask on.

She pulled off his hat, helped him out of his Lewis Leather, and then finally pulled his old Thin Lizzy T-shirt over his head.

He made a movement towards her but she shook her head, no, that wasn't what she wanted, at least not now, and got him to position his chair in front of the sink. He stared at himself in a cracked mirror.

Leon kept watching his reflection as Ruby washed his hair with cold water and hand soap, then squeezed the juice of half a lemon on it, and finally rinsed it with the Anne and Mark teacup containing a spoonful of bleach, more cold water and the remains of the lemon.

Leon watched his reflection as Ruby turned him into a blond, and he watched her face in the cracked mirror as she performed this magic.

For the first time in his life, Leon felt like he was possibly good looking, although he knew this had less to do with the changing colour of his hair than the feel of her fingers massaging his scalp, and her face considering his head with total concentration, and the warmth of her breath on the back of his neck.

He felt like she really cared about him, and his heart did somersaults.

Later, when the foreign voices in the big room had stopped, and the couple making grunty love were snoring, Leon and Ruby crawled into his sleeping bag.

Then Leon and Ruby made love as close to silence as they could, the only sounds their breathing and the bare floorboards beneath them and his delirious, babbled whisper.

'I love you,' he moaned, his eyes filling up at the terrible truth of it. 'Oh, I love you so much!'

Ruby giggled beneath him, and then sighed, and held him, and drove him wild.

Leon came a bucket.

How many nights without sleep?

Almost three, Terry thought, the darkness of Covent Garden all around. When morning came it would be three full nights without sleep.

He counted them off.

The last two nights in Berlin. One spent running round the backstreets of the city with Dag, watching him and the band borrow instruments from a beardy jazz quartet, banging out a ramshackle version of his greatest hits, Dag throwing himself around like a lunatic, at one point swinging from a lampshade and doing a belly flop on a table of middle-aged jazz fans.

And then the next night locked up in Dag's hotel room, doing Christa's coke, talking until the maid was banging on the door because she needed to service the room and it was time for Terry to wipe his nose, pack his bags and catch a cab to the airport.

And now this night, this dying night, with only hours before it was gone. That would be the three nights without sleep, the killer three nights in a row, and Terry knew too well what always happened on the third morning.

On the third morning you started seeing things.

It could be anything. After three nights without sleep, Terry had once seen a sparrow jiving. After a different three nights he had seen a crashed plane, a jumbo jet peeled open like a can of sardines, tilted on its side outside his bedsit. Mad stuff. Insane stuff. The jiving sparrow, the crashed plane – they weren't there – Terry knew that, and he tried to hold on to that knowledge. But it was hard.

After three nights, the speed in your liver turned to mescaline – a hallucinogenic – and you saw visions and they seemed so real. You swallowed your terror, and you tried to tear your eyes away, because you couldn't help believe in them. After three nights without going to bed, it seemed so real.

And as Terry saw the lights of the Western World coming out of the blackness, he wondered what slice of madness he would have to see tonight.

In the hours since he had left the Western World, the club had gone berserk. Stark raving berserk.

It was as if all the psychosis and frustration and violence that had been storing up in the Vortex and the Marquee and the Roxy and the Red Cow and the Nashville and Dingwalls and the Hope & Anchor had descended on this hole in the ground in Covent Garden.

Terry fought his way downstairs and saw that there were Dagenham Dogs everywhere.

They had annexed the dance floor. Smashing into each other, lobbing cans and spit at the stage, shoving aside anyone who didn't belong to their little tribe, taking over the place and loving it. Terry thought about Leon and hoped his friend was far away from here.

There was a Union Jack jacket right in the middle of the mayhem. Brainiac was out there with the Dogs, doing his mad piston dance, like a cross between a mascot and a punch bag, and Dogs twice his size pummelled into him, knocking him back and forth like a red, white and blue shuttlecock.

Brainiac saw Terry and grinned his dopey grin, as if they were all pals together, but Terry couldn't manage to smile back.

He thought there was a good chance the Dogs were going to do the thing that they had threatened all year. They were finally going to go all the way and kill someone.

Terry pushed his way upstairs to the toilets. It was tough moving around this place tonight. No one gave way. Strangers scowled and snarled at him. There seemed to be more and more faces that he didn't recognise, and he felt like fucking crying.

It's just the speed, he thought. It's just the three nights and the speed and the fear of what I will see.

He entered the men's toilets. Dub reggae shuddered the splintered white tiles and fractured mirrors. The toilet was crowded with men and women and boys and girls taking drugs, selling drugs and applying dollops of make-up. Nobody was using the place for its intended purpose, but somehow it still managed to stink with the trapped excretions of a thousand and one nights.

Terry found the bespectacled longhair he was looking for, hawking his gram and half-gram bags from a toilet stall. The dealer. By his side was a hippy chick with a paralysed smile. His burnt-out girlfriend. They all nodded in recognition and Terry forced a smile, slipping into the etiquette of scoring, which mostly meant looking interested while the dealer jabbered about whatever scrap of lunacy was floating around his badly fried brain.

'Terry – I was just saying – you have to live on a boat, right?' the dealer said, his bright eyes gleaming behind thick glasses. 'Because – if you live on a boat – right? – they can't trace you – you're not on the electoral, you know, roll call. The register. Registrar. Hmm?'

The dealer cackled at his cunning plan to outwit the authorities. He had been selling his wares out of the lavatories of various music venues for ten years, but suddenly he had this burning need to explain his retirement plans to Terry.

'And, like, no Rates,' smiled his dazed-looking girlfriend, 'No Rates on a, like, boat.'

'So you save money right there,' cackled the dealer.

The babble, thought Terry.

The babble and the prattle and the bullshit that a man has to listen to, just to buy some drugs. Terry wanted to be out of there, but the politesse of scoring obliged him to listen to a speech of speed-addled insanity. The dub thundered on, and Terry felt his brain begin to swell.

'It's a good idea,' Terry said, watching Warwick Hunt walk into the toilet. 'Live on a fishing boat.'

With a flicker of contempt, Terry saw that the A&R man was the only fat person in the Western World – all those expense-account lunches and flying first class to LA, New York and Tokyo. All those perks of the job.

The man who had been responsible for signing some of the biggest bands of the last ten years looked like the brother of someone who was in ELO. He took a fastidious pee at a cracked urinal, zipped up his pressed Levi's and looked around for some kind of personal-hygiene facilities. Terry smiled grimly. Where did he think he was? The fucking Marquee? In the Western World, all the sinks were smashed and the water had been turned off long ago. Sighing with irritation, Warwick Hunt removed a small silver snuffbox from his short leather Budgie jacket, snapped it open and dipped in the silver spoon that he wore on a chain around his hairy neck.

'You *got* to get a fishing boat, man,' said the dealer. 'You *have* to get a bo-bo-boat.'

At moments of great excitement the dealer developed a high-pitched stutter.

'Makes sense to me,' Terry said, wondering if every drug salesman inevitably sampled too much of his own stock.

He was distracted. A small adoring crowd had already gathered around Warwick Hunt. Hunt may have been the only man in there with love handles and a mullet and glasses that had smoky lenses, but he had the power to make dreams come true. A girl with a ring through her nose and a nappy worn over ripped black tights was giving him a cassette that Terry knew with total certainty must contain her band's demos. Warwick Hunt smiled patiently, enjoying himself now he had the world at his feet and the coke up his nose. Nothing has changed, Terry thought. We thought that everything would change, but it's the same old rock-and-roll showbiz.

'You don't – you don't – you don't,' said the dealer, 'you don't buy fish that swim in filthy water – do you, hmm?'

Terry nodded emphatically, and he was rewarded with two fat little bags of amphetamine sulphate. At last. Two grams for £24. As the notes his dad had given him slipped into the dealer's pocket, an image of his father came to Terry's mind. The old man staggering across a frozen landscape, his legs buckling beneath him, and carrying his only son on his weary back.

Billy Blitzen swaggered in and a jolt of electricity ran through the toilet. He ignored Warwick Hunt, who watched him with an ingratiating grin, then came over to Terry and smiled. Billy had a way of smiling that made you feel like you were the most important person in the world.

'Hey, man,' Billy said in his soulful murmur. Then he turned to the dealer, and his voice became brisk and businesslike. 'I'll take a G of your good stuff.'

The dealer held up his hands, as if surrendering. He looked embarrassed.

'As soon as you pay me for the last time,' he said, his grin so fixed it seemed nailed in place. 'And the time before that.' Trying to turn it into a joke now. 'And the t-t-time before that.'

Billy Blitzen's handsome face clouded with fury.

'You fucking drug-dealing scuzzball – you talk to me like that in front of *my friend?*'

There were tears of rage in Billy's eyes. The dealer raised his hands higher, saying they could possibly come to some arrangement, but it was too late.

'I'll tan your queer limey ass!' Billy thundered.

Terry watched his dapper little friend unbuckle the elaborate cowboy belt that was holding up the trousers of his destroyed Italian suit. The dealer cowered back into the toilet stall, hiding behind his girlfriend, as Billy lashed the belt at thin air.

Terry wrapped his arms around Billy and dragged him away. The crowd parted for them as Terry pulled his friend from the toilet. It was surprisingly easy. Billy weighed next to nothing, and Terry felt some unnameable grief well up inside him.

He thought – what's going to happen to us all?

Terry put his arm around Billy and led him to the club's tiny dressing room. Terry was always shocked at the size of the place. Legends had begun here, but it was just a broom cupboard with a bench on one side, the walls covered from ceiling to floor with posters of countless bands, and a layer of graffiti on top of that. Terry sat Billy down.

The P45s were shuffling around, drinking beer and tuning up for the show. They regarded their leader with supreme indifference.

'Now are you going to be okay?' Terry asked.

He had never seen Billy so far gone. His mouth gaped, the lids of those huge brown eyes seemed too heavy to stay open, and in the yellow light of the dressing room the suit was stained and frayed.

'Just need a little lift,' Billy Blitzen said.

A tall man with cropped hair stuck his head around the door. 'Showtime,' he said.

Suddenly Billy seemed aware of the moment, and his eyes opened wide.

'Big gig tonight, man. That guy's here. That guy from the record company.'

Terry stuck his hand in his jacket, palmed one of the bags of sulphate and clutched hands with Billy. He knew that Billy wouldn't want to share any of this with his backing band. When his friend took a peek at what he had in his hand his face lit up with a smile.

Terry would do a lot for one of those smiles. Because Billy Blitzen had been in a band he loved. And because he had more natural charm than anyone Terry had ever met.

'My buddy,' Billy Blitzen said, patting Terry's face, and Terry felt this strange brew of pride and sorrow.

'Just go easy on it, okay? His stuff is pretty pure.'

Billy pulled a face. 'That scuzzball. That fucking scuzzball. Talking to me about money.'

The P45s had strapped on their guitars and were heading out of the dressing room.

'Just have a good show,' Terry said, pulling Billy Blitzen to his feet. He watched him strap on his guitar and start to turn into someone else.

'The shows are all good,' Billy said. 'Ain't they?'

Terry nodded, and laughed, and felt himself fill with feelings that he couldn't blame on the speed or the three nights.

It was true. The shows were all good. It was always worth watching Billy Blitzen.

You never knew when it would be the last time.

In the shadows at the back of the Western World, Terry climbed on a chair to watch the show.

He took out his remaining gram, untied it and dipped in his key. He had always loved watching Billy Blitzen through the alert reverie of amphetamines. The Dean Martin of rock and roll in front of you, and the man-made euphoria pumping through your veins – it was Terry's idea of happiness.

But as he stared out across the terrified spaces opening up around the Dogs, and he felt the days and nights without rest pressing down on him, it was impossible to feel anything but a kind of exhausted melancholy.

Tonight didn't feel the same. Tonight everything was falling apart. It had begun with Misty, and he could feel it spreading to every corner of his life. Everything he loved was slipping away from him.

Billy and the P45s filed on stage, plugged in and contemplated the teeming madness before them. Billy's trousers seemed to be falling down. Terry saw that Billy had neglected to put his cowboy belt back on.

Then Billy was counting them in – one! two! three! four! – and they tore into their signature tune, 'Shoot Up, Everybody'. Almost immediately things started to go wrong, and Terry thought of the older guys at *The Paper*, and what they said about seeing Jimi Hendrix at the Isle of Wight, how it was like watching someone you loved dying right in front of your eyes.

Billy forgot the words to 'Shoot Up, Everybody', and filled the gaps with obscenities about the Dogs who were spitting their beer at him. Then he mimed jamming a syringe into his arm and somehow the gesture suddenly seemed pathetic instead of thrilling.

Under the stark stage light, Billy Blitzen's face no longer seemed rakishly handsome. Even in the heat of the club near closing time, Terry felt a chill run down his spine. Billy looked like he belonged in a morgue.

And Terry remembered something that his dad had told him about the real Dean Martin – how it was all an act. Dino just pretended to be loaded on stage because he knew Mr and Mrs Suburbia lapped it up, just as their grandchildren loved seeing Billy Blitzen play at rock-and-roll suicide. But Dean Martin was always in control and it wasn't like that with Billy Blitzen.

This was the real thing, and Terry felt like a ghoul for watching it.

He saw Billy attempt to duck walk, trip over a cable and almost fall flat on his face. And he had to look away. Everything was collapsing. But the P45s, those wizened old musos, were holding it down, slashing out those shoplifted Eddie Cochran riffs, and the crowd was going out of its collective box.

Even the spaces around the Dagenham Dogs seemed to have closed up. Terry looked back at the stage. Maybe it would be enough for Warwick Hunt and his team of rock-and-roll bean counters.

You never knew, Terry thought. Even when bands were good, you never knew. You never knew if it was all going to melt away, and they were going to have to find real jobs, or if you would one day see them walking through Soho, unsmiling and proud, all new clothes, thinking about getting their teeth done, veterans of the *Top of the Pops* green room, treating the record company advance like spending money they would never have to return.

And even as he watched Billy Blitzen struggling to remember the words of songs he had played a thousand times, and even as Billy fought to keep his balance, Terry believed that there was still a possibility that his friend could survive this night, and pull himself together, and record an album that went triple platinum. As he led the P45s through a ferocious rendition of 'Summertime Blues', Terry thought that maybe it wasn't too late for Billy Blitzen after all. Then why did Terry still feel so bad? Because something had spoiled.

He bleakly watched the crowd going mental in front of the stage, raining spit and beer down on his friend, and it felt like a private party had been thrown open to the public and they didn't know how to behave. The days of walking in off the street and paying seventy-five pence to see an unsigned band who would turn out to be the Clash, or the Jam, or the Buzzcocks were passing. Billy Blitzen, he could see, had peaked with the Lost Boys. Peaked when he was nineteen years old.

Terry caught sight of Grace Fury across the crowded floor, imperious and unsmiling among the mayhem. She had her back to the stage, trying to move through the bouncing mob, and she looked up at Terry and smiled with what seemed like real pleasure. A friendly face, he thought. He knew how good that felt.

Then she suddenly turned angrily on a leering Dagenham Dog who had decided to stick his tongue in her ear. Terry saw with a shudder that it was Junior, the wolfish grin on his face out of kilter with his three-teardrop tattoo. It looked like a tribal scar under the lights. Grace lifted a contemptuous middle finger. Junior and the Dogs howled with delight. Terry looked back at the stage where Billy had stopped the music and was lecturing the crowd about spitting.

'Stop gobbing you motherfucking wankers,' he slurred, and Terry felt a pang of affection. Nobody mixed up New York and London swear words quite like Billy Blitzen.

'Where's the girlfriend?' said a voice level with Terry's groin. He looked down at Grace Fury. You could tell why men were crazy for her. Even in this madhouse she looked like sex in a tartan mini-skirt.

'There's no more girlfriend,' Terry said.

There was something about Grace that he had always liked – he didn't feel the need to be cocky with her. Maybe because he thought he would never have a chance with her. Maybe because he thought that she was way out of his league. She was famous.

She held up her hands and he helped her climb on to the chair. They stood facing each other, still holding hands. Like kids in *Happy Days*, he thought.

'Went off with Dag, didn't she?' Grace said, and he looked over her shoulder at the stage, his face burning with humiliation.

Grace shook her head.

'Misty – fucking Misty – she really makes me laugh. Goody-two-shoes in her white frocks. Miss-butter-wouldn't-melt. Then she does that to you,' Grace said, turning around so she could watch Billy throwing beer at the crowd. She pitched forward and Terry caught her, slipping his hands around her waist.

He left them there, like a pillion rider on a motorbike, and he felt himself getting hard. Her waist was nothing, his hands almost encircled it. Her skirt was the shortest he had ever seen. And he admired her – she was a tough girl from New York City who dared to walk through the Dagenham Dogs dressed like that.

'What do *you* think?' she said.

Terry was lost for words.

He felt Grace's palm rubbing the front of his trousers. 'About Billy, I mean,' she laughed. 'Has he blown it?'

She took her hand away. Terry took another breath.

'The guy's still watching,' he said, indicating the mullet-head of Warwick Hunt that clung to the perimeters of the crowd. 'Billy's smashed out of his box, but maybe he's doing enough.'

She half-turned her head. A hand on his face. He liked the way she touched him. Just a touch and it got him bone hard.

'You scored, didn't you?' she said, and he nodded. Her eyes half closed. Grace was a girl who loved her drugs.

'Then let's get out of here,' she said.

He watched Warwick Hunt turn away, having seen enough, and he knew there would be no happy ending for Billy Blitzen.

'There's too many outsiders,' Grace said, facing the stage again but reaching around to give his buttocks a friendly squeeze. 'If I'd wanted beer-swilling jerk-offs, I'd have stayed in New Jersey.'

The band abruptly stopped. Billy was angrily pointing at someone in the audience, screaming at them to stop throwing things. It was a perfect cue for glasses, cans and chairs to rain down on stage.

Billy picked up a pint glass resting on an amp and threw it with all his remaining strength into the crowd. Terry watched it sail through the air and strike Warwick Hunt on the side of the head. He collapsed in a shower of blood and broken glass. The cans and bottles rained down like arrows at Agincourt. Billy Blitzen and the P45s fled the stage.

'Yeah, let's go,' Terry said. 'This is so fucked.'

They were meant to be breaking down the barriers between performers and the audience. They were meant to be different to other generations.

And it was true in the early days – there had been a kind of wanton democracy about the Western World. But rebellion had become the excuse to act like a cretin. He used to love this place. Now what he had loved was gone. He wanted to get away, and he wanted to take this incredible girl with him.

He jumped down off the chair. She jumped down after him and fell into his arms, the red slash of her lips on his mouth, and he was hungry for her, but then she was pulling away, laughing, saying, 'Take it easy, tiger.'

He took her hand and she followed him, smiling, looking sexy and coy all at once, and he thought about Misty in somebody's room, he thought about Sally and the chance he had missed, but here he was going home with the girl of the moment, here he was about to make love to one of those women that men fantasised about, and Terry felt like the world would be made good again once he had this woman in his bed.

But first he had to see his friend.

Billy was slumped in the dressing room, his nose buried deep in the bag of speed. He came up looking like Frosty the Snowman. The P45s were bruised and angry and arguing with the manager about money.

Billy was beyond caring. He licked the white powder from his lips and chin.

'My man,' he laughed, seeing Terry, then his eyes were rolling back into his head and he began tearing at his suit, his shirt, his skinny tie. Suddenly his clothes seemed to be suffocating him. 'My London mate.'

'Jesus Christ,' Grace said, looking away.

And Terry saw that it was always going to be this way. Billy Blitzen had that New York thing, and if you meant it – that New York thing – if you truly meant it, then you didn't sign with Warwick Hunt and go off to record an album with Phil Spector in Nassau.

If you meant it, if you really meant it, then you destroyed yourself. You died, Terry thought, and a great sob rose up inside him.

All those Billy Blitzen songs that they had loved at the Western World – Terry saw now that they were all suicide notes, and it broke his heart.

'Got to do one more set . . . maybe you review . . . fuck that Warwick Hunt . . . then we party.'

One of the P45s, the drummer who had throttled Brainiac earlier that night, light years ago, abruptly turned on his leader. Terry could see that beyond the dye job and the zippy clothes, he was really old.

'Party's over, you fucking dickhead,' he shouted in Billy's befuddled face.

Terry took two steps across the dressing room and shoved the drummer against the wall.

'Leave him alone, you bastard,' Terry said, then he was with his friend on the bench, his arm around his skinny shoulders, a cloud of white dust between them.

'I got to go, Billy,' Terry said, and he hated to see the look in those eyes, and when he thought about that night years later, when the news of Billy Blitzen's death had just come through, Terry thought that of all the betrayals of that night, deserting Billy Blitzen in the dressing room of the Western World was the worst.

'Let's go, Terry,' Grace said, and so they did, leaving the Western World with their arms wrapped around each other. There was a strange sound in the air and for a long second Terry couldn't work out what it was. And then he realised. There was no music. Nobody on stage, the dub all gone. The music had stopped.

Grace expressed no surprise at the car that Terry had parked nearby.

These Americans, he thought.

A Ford Capri is nothing to them.

Ray slid out of bed, looking for the bathroom, and everything seemed new.

There was an egg-shaped lamp on a coffee table big enough for ping-pong. Never seen one of those before, thought Ray. There were silver ashtrays as big as dog bowls. That's new. Gold records in glass frames. Only seen those on the walls of the record labels, never in someone's home. Long, low furniture still in plastic covers like giant condoms. What's all that about? A bookshelf with a wooden ladder, believe it or not, the books curiously uniform, their spines unbroken, as though they had been bought by the yard. Well, I'll be blowed, thought Ray.

And a married woman warm beneath the sheets.

That was the newest thing of all.

There had been girls. There had been lots of girls. Because they liked him – and men too, he knew that, although that had never been his thing. And because he had started young, a fifteen-year-old virgin who only cared about music when White first gave him a gig on *The Paper*. But there had never been a married woman before, and the thought excited and frightened him.

Where was the manager of one of the biggest bands in the world?

Where was her husband tonight? Where was that vibrator-buying bastard? And what would he do to Ray if he found him here?

Ray moved through the house, aware of his nakedness, alert to every noise, but still with the space to be dead impressed. He had never seen such luxury.

He padded across the living room, his bare feet sinking into the shag carpet, and beyond the wall-to-floor windows he could hear the gentle flow of the river.

It was hard to imagine that this was the same river that ran by their office, the timeless river where they smoked their mid-morning spliffs in the shadow of a tower block and the tugs chugged by the sad, dying docks.

This was the suburban Thames, the river that ran past the huge houses of men who had made their money, bought their mansions to store their gold records and their bored, ignored wives. Like the one Ray could smell on half a dozen places of his sticky skin.

She was bossy, Ray thought with a smile. Bossy but nice. 'Don't make love to me,' she had told him, not that impressed by his leisurely technique. 'Don't make love to me – fuck me.'

The things she said! But he liked it. He liked her. A lot of the sex he had had felt mechanical. As though the girl you were with could have been doing it with anyone. But Mrs Brown cared. Ray felt like it meant something to her. And he didn't mind being told what to do. He wanted to learn.

He located the bathroom and spent a while gawping at all the bottles of perfume. How could anyone ever get through all that stuff? And that's when he heard the noise.

Holding his breath, Ray wrapped a white towel around his waist and stepped outside. A strange, shorthaired cat rubbed against his bare leg and he gasped with fright. Then he heard her call his name.

Back in the bedroom, her mouth wandered across his face as though she could never get enough of it, her hands pulled him down, and they both laughed with delight that they still wanted more, and then they rocked on the waterbed, their skin slick with their exertions, hair in their faces, her long dark hair and his long fair hair mingling. Doing it on a waterbed, Ray thought proudly. That's new. He couldn't believe his luck.

Then Ray must have fallen asleep because he found himself coming awake with a start, and knowing he had to go, as much as he hated the idea. Somehow sex with her had convinced him that he could find John Lennon. Sex with her made him feel like he could do anything. And as he pulled on his pants, he thought for the first time how great it would be to live with her.

She sat up, resting on an elbow, then sunk a little. He smiled at her. It wasn't easy sitting up on a waterbed.

'Oh, don't go,' she said, her voice husky in the darkness, losing that hardness he had noticed in the Speak. 'Stay the night. He's not coming back tonight.'

Ray pulled on his Levi's. 'It's not that. I've got to do this interview. Or I'm out.'

Silence for a moment. 'If you liked me, you'd stay.'

He laughed. 'Of course I like you.' He got back on the bed so he could see her face. And so she could see his face. 'I'm mad about you.' She pouted, looked unconvinced. He got up, pulled on his T-shirt. 'I've been thinking about it – you're not happy here, are you? It's a terrific place, but it doesn't make you happy.' He worked up the nerve to say it. 'So maybe we should find somewhere. To live. You and me.'

She laughed at that and he was stung. 'What we going to do?' she said, and some of the old hardness crept back. 'Live with your parents?'

He shrugged. He hadn't really thought about that part. 'Get a flat somewhere. A room.'

'A room? What – like a bedsit?' She rummaged in the bedside table, then there was the flare of a match and a cigarette's glow. 'You really don't have a clue, do you?'

Ray pulled on his boots. It was true. He didn't have a job, he didn't have a flat, and he didn't have a clue. 'No, I guess not.'

But the thought gnawed at him – how great it would be to be with her every night. Yes, she was married. But she didn't love her husband. And he didn't love her. Anyone who could give you a vibrator for your birthday didn't have a shred of love in their heart. So what was keeping her here? Just all this . . . stuff? Was that what happened when you got old? You developed this desperate need for stuff? But he knew she was angry with him for going, and so he said nothing.

He sat on the bed, his bottom swaying on the waterbed as he pulled on his cowboy boots. She sighed, sitting up in bed, her small breasts uncovered, and then there was a faint jingle and the phone was on her lap, and she was dialling a number she knew by heart. And suddenly he was angry with her. For not wanting to live with him. For needing all this fucking stuff. For getting on the phone before he was even out of the bedroom.

'It's me,' she said, and she used that voice she had used with him. Ray watched her, his face a mask. He shut down. That's what he did. He knew people his age flew off the handle. But not him. He found it easier to show them nothing. 'No, I don't – I'm not wearing a watch,' she laughed into the receiver, her eyes flicking on to Ray's face and then away. 'What? Nothing, actually, nothing at all.' Ray walked to the bedroom door, and he felt her watching him. He wasn't going to cry in front of her. 'So why don't you

come over?' she said. 'Yes – now.' Laughter in the dark. 'Come on –
you know you want to . . .'

Ray watched her from the doorway, touched his hand to his
lips and let it fall away, a sad little wave. His fingers were still
sticky. He could still taste her.

'Yeah – no – well,' she was saying, 'that's what you get from the
likes of her, I'm afraid.'

Ray let himself out of the house, quietly closing the front door
behind him, so he didn't see the expression on her face change.

'Listen,' Mrs Brown said when she heard that he was gone.
'Listen – I tell you what – I'll call you next week, okay? It's late
now. I tell you what. I think I'll just sleep.'

He stood by the road that led back to London, holding out his
thumb for an approaching lorry. It didn't even slow down.

A police car cruised by, checking him out, the two cops grinning
at him – a harmless hippy who missed the last train – before moving
on. Then nothing, just the mist on the river, and everyone in their
beds, and his eyes scanning the sky for the first light of dawn.

A sports car came by. A yellow Lotus Elan. She threw open the
passenger door.

'I'm not sleepy anyway,' she said. He'd never seen her looking
shy before. He smiled at her, and it felt like his face would ache
with the smiling.

She hit the floor and they sped away from the suburbs, and
when she had nothing but the open road to the city ahead, she
rolled down the window and threw out something stuffed inside
a bag from Harlequin Records.

Ray didn't have to ask. He knew it was the birthday present.

*   *   *

Terry's bedsit wasn't much.

A mattress shoved up against a crumbling bay window where the rain came in, a two-bar electric heater and records everywhere, and on the wall the classic poster of *Enter the Dragon*, Bruce Lee naked to the waist, holding up his Nanchuks, everything about him perfect, even the claw marks on his face and torso.

The roadie upstairs was playing Motorhead at top volume – something he always did when his girlfriend went home to her mother. The carpet was stained with the memory of a hundred residents. There was a pile of white towelling bathrobes in one corner that said Glasgow Hilton, Newcastle Holiday Inn and Leeds Dragonara. And Misty's stuff scattered around – the dresses, the piles of photographic books, the rolls of film and contact sheets, her change of boots. A room untouched by domesticity.

But Grace was a rock and roller. She had worn her torn stockings on the Lower East Side, and given a middle finger to the Bowery bums who had something to say. She was used to squalor. He pulled her skirt up around her waist, their tongues wrestling, his desperate hands wanting to be everywhere at once.

'You got the stuff?' she said.

He nodded, found his mirror with the razor blade and pulled out his stash. Grace sat on the bed, crossing her legs, and he had to tear his eyes away to concentrate on chopping out the lines. His heart thumped with anticipation. Terry was minutes away from the fuck of a lifetime. Grace lay back on the bed. The razor blade frantically chopped out the four lines of sulphate.

The nice thing about the room was that you couldn't see it very well. It was lit by a bare, dusty 40-watt bulb, the fiery glow of the electric heater, and the fairy lights that Misty had strung around the bedstead when she moved in and never taken down. It was

251

only a £6-a-week hovel in Crouch End, rented from a Greek land-lord who told Terry that he was moving to Melbourne because England was finished, but those fairy lights made it feel special – like home. Or maybe that was just because Misty had put them up.

Terry found a red-and-white plastic straw and did two of the lines on the mirror. Then Grace was sitting up, reaching for the mirror and Terry crushed his mouth against her mouth and went down the hall to throw some cold water in his face.

He was excited and nervous, wanting it to go well, wondering about Grace's boyfriend, the singer in her band. Did they sneak around behind each other's backs? Did they have some kind of arrangement? Terry was discovering that there were more shadows between men and women than he had ever imagined. And would she be his girlfriend after tonight? That would show Misty, that would show them all – Grace Fury as his girlfriend. She was the one they all wanted, and the drumbeat in his chest told him that he was about to have her. He threw water on his face and smiled at himself in the bathroom mirror, ready for the one he would never forget.

She was waiting for him when he went back to the room. She was in the pose that was designed to inflame him, the position that he would have favoured, if there had been any choice in the matter. On the edge of the bed, her clothes off, her legs crossed, leaning back.

But the thing that made Terry's blood freeze was that she was shooting up.

Grace had not hoovered the white lines up her nose as he had expected. She had produced her works – the needle, the belt tied tight around her upper arm – and as he came into the room to see his fantasy made flesh, his dream girl was searching for a vein, then finding it, and gasping – panting – with pleasure at the act of penetration, the spike entering her vein, the cooked-up speed quickly finding her bloodstream.

In a daze, Terry declined the mumbled invitation to join her shooting up, to share the dripping needle, as if he was refusing an extra ginger nut at tea, and he watched her writhing with pleasure – arching her back, closing her eyes, exhaling with a kind of euphoric disbelief – and he knew it was far more pleasure than he could ever give her.

He didn't really want anything after that – not the drugs, not the girl, and certainly not any part of the act before him. Needles scared the shit out of him. But he was young and it was too late to stop and he had always wanted to get the girl that everyone wanted.

So he tore his clothes off and fell upon her on that lumpy mattress in that leaky bedsit, more in desperation than enthusiasm, her thin white body still and doped beneath him, her needle sharing their bed and glinting in the Christmas lights, almost festive.

PART THREE:

1977 – LOVERS OF TODAY

TWELVE

The night was almost over.

From the window of the editor's office, Terry could see the sky above the old dying docks streaking with light. Somewhere a tug made its mournful sound. Twenty-one storeys below, beyond the hermetically sealed, suicide-proof windows, he could see the river black and glittering, most of the city still sleeping, but already there were the lights of the first cars on the Embankment.

Not long now.

Terry went back to his office and did a line of speed at his desk. He liked being in White's office, but he didn't want to take drugs in there. It would have felt disrespectful. He rocked in his swivel chair, staring at the images on their three walls. High up on his own wall, Norman Mailer's battered face caught Terry's eye.

He had heard this story about Mailer on the eve of his last wedding, and it had stuck with him. Mailer was depressed about walking down the aisle the next day. His future wife asked him what was wrong, and Mailer said that he had never wanted this – marriage, monogamy, fusing his life with one other life. All Mailer had ever wanted was to be a free man in Paris. And his future wife said – now look, Norman. If you were a free man in Paris you would eventually meet one special girl and end up exactly where you are today. And Norman Mailer saw that this was true. And so did Terry. In those brief moments of freedom that came your way, you were always looking for a way to *not* be free, to belong totally to someone. You went looking for new worlds, and then you found them in just one face. Terry found Misty. Now he had lost her, and now he was free again.

He did another line, and then he got up and wandered through the dark empty rooms of the office, and he was soon rummaging around in the filing cabinets, thumbing through photo files and bound back issues, soaking up the incredible history of the place. *Jimmy Savile says 'Hi there' to all readers of* The Music Paper *and wishes one and all a Merry Xmas and a great 1968 – 'See you in* The People *every Sunday, guys 'n' girls.'*

It was like being locked in a museum after hours, he thought. During the day *The Paper* was a constant round of work, play and music, of spats, spliffs, and strange new sounds blaring from the review room. Kevin White and the older guys shouting for the dummy. A constant procession of faces old and new – freelancers, musicians, PRs – looking for feature work or publicity, who were often willing to settle for free drugs or lunch or a gig doing 300 words on the Vibrators at Dingwalls.

During the day maybe you would walk into someone's office and there would be Joan Jett sitting on a desk, batting her eyelashes and asking you for a light. Or maybe a couple of writers would be arguing about the merits of a record that came out years ago – on Terry's first day, he had seen two of the older guys almost come to slaps about *Sgt Pepper's Lonely Hearts Club Band*. Or maybe some female freelancer and one of the older guys would be having a quick joint, cuddle or debate about the new Steely Dan record in the stationery cupboard. That was the day. But at night everyone was gone. Well, almost everyone.

Terry looked in the window of the review room. Skip Jones was still in there, writing in his agonised, left-handed longhand, surrounded by that strange garden, the small forest of forgotten cigarettes resting on their filter tips, the cones of ash long and wilting but curiously undisturbed. Terry tapped lightly on the glass. Skip looked up, smiled shyly, nodded.

'Terry Warboys, wild,' he said, dog tired now, the night nearly gone, and with hours of writing behind him.

Terry came into the review room. Shy too. Skip Jones still meant so much to him. Because, because – Skip was just the best there had ever been.

'Not going home, Skip?'

Skip shook his head, looking at a point somewhere above Terry's shoulder. It occurred to Terry that Skip had no place to go tonight.

'Might as well stick around,' Skip said. 'It's going to be a busy day.'

Terry nodded. 'Because of Elvis, right? I guess White will want some sort of special for the new issue.' He was shocked to see how pale-faced and frail Skip seemed. But then again, Terry knew he probably didn't look too rosy-cheeked and hearty himself. 'You going to write something about Elvis, Skip?'

Skip shrugged. 'Maybe. Might write something about the early days at Sun. Sam Phillips and the boy in the red shirt who wanted to record a song for Mama. "Good Rocking Tonight" and dreams of being a truck driver. All that.' Skip smiled at a point above Terry's shoulder. 'Not sure I want to be part of the whole, uh, *canonisation* process. Not sure it's right. We haven't had a good word to say about Elvis since he went into the army. Now we're going to turn him into – I don't know what – Lenin's preserved corpse in Red Square or something. Know what I mean?'

Terry nodded, pulling out his Marlboros. He had no fucking idea what Skip meant. Rock stars died and then you loved them more than ever. Brian Jones. Jimi Hendrix. Jim Morrison. That's the way it had always been. But he thought of Billy Blitzen, alone and strung-out in the Western World, and for the first time Terry glimpsed something beyond the eternal glory of rock-and-roll martyrdom. He saw the waste.

'Thanks, man,' Skip said as Terry offered him his last cigarette. Skip lit up, dragged deeply and then carefully set the Marlboro on its filter tip, immediately forgetting it. Terry stared at it hungrily. 'Rock and roll is turning into museum culture now,' said Skip. 'Like jazz or painting. You know? The canon exists, and all we can do is stand back and admire it. When Miles Davis and Picasso have come and gone – or Elvis and Dylan – what more can you say?'

Terry picked up the album cover in front of Skip. 'What about this lot? Television?'

'A footnote,' Skip sighed. 'A glorious footnote, a magnificent footnote, but a footnote all the same. Who's going to be on the cover next week?'

Terry scratched his head. 'Elvis? Got to be Elvis.'

'Young Elvis. Elvis in 1956. Elvis with the sap rising. White's not going to put the Elvis of 1977 on the cover. No fringed jump-suits. No Las Vegas glitz. No middle-age paunch. It's going to be Elvis when he was a skinny kid with everything before him. It's going to look like something great, but it will be just another nail in the coffin.'

Terry thought about it. 'What coffin?'

'The coffin with our music in it,' Skip said. 'The coffin of rock and roll.' The Marlboro standing upright on the desk was glowing red. Skip picked it up and inhaled deeply, running his bony fingers through matted bird's-nest hair. 'Don't get stuck in rock and roll, man,' Skip told Terry. 'People are starting to treat it like the civil service – a job for life. It was never *meant* to be a job for life.' Skip smiled, glanced at Terry then looked away. 'But I thought you were hanging out with Dag tonight.'

'Ah,' Terry said, attempting to laugh off his mangled heart. 'That didn't work out so good.'

Skip nodded thoughtfully. 'Well, Dag can be hard to handle. He takes whatever he can get his hands on. Starts acting crazy.'

'It wasn't that,' Terry said. 'Nothing to do with taking stuff.' He paused, studied the cover of *Marquee Moon* that was still in his hands. 'Well, in a way. Misty – she sort of went off with him.'

Skip thought about it. 'Okay,' he said. 'Okay, man. Dag and Misty. Wild.'

'I thought he was my friend,' Terry said, trying to laugh and finding it choke somewhere halfway up his throat. 'In Berlin –'

'He's not your friend, man,' Skip said, suddenly full of feeling. 'Dag's not your friend. Doesn't matter how well you got along with him when you were on the road. Dag's a *rock star*, man. You could know him for twenty years and he still wouldn't be your friend. Not really. Not the way that Ray and Leon are your friends. Or even Billy. Because you give Dag one teeny-fucking-weeny bad review, and you would be *out*, man, and you would *never* be allowed back in. You can be *friendly* with these guys – especially guys your own age, who start out when you do. Bit harder with someone like Dag, who's been around the block a few times already, but you can still be friendly with him. You can be friendly with the guys your own age because when it all changes, and it stops being about loving music and starts being about other stuff, about egos and limos, and blow-jobs from skinny models, part of you still remembers when you were all just starting out and all you wanted to do was talk about music and meet girls and you couldn't even get into the fucking Speakeasy. But sooner or later you have to decide if you're a writer, man, or just a groupie who can type.'

Skip sounded bitter now, and Terry thought of the file on him in the photo library. There were photographs of all the writers on *The Paper*, pictures used to accompany their by-line mug shots mostly, but Skip Jones had a file all to himself. Terry had often pored over those pictures on his nights wandering the deserted office, because Skip was the reason he was here, Skip had lived the life he had dreamed of when he was a music-mad kid working in a gin factory, rushing out with his eighteen pence every Wednesday to buy *The Paper* a day early.

Pictures of Skip. There was Skip with Keith Richards in a sun-drenched villa in the south of France. Skip with Iggy Pop in a destroyed hotel room in Detroit. Skip with Dag Wood in the dingy gloom of the dressing room at the Roundhouse. And here Skip was tonight – friend of the stars, the finest music writer of his gener-ation, of any generation – killing time in a little review room, no place to rest his brilliant head, his famous friends all gone. Then Skip chuckled to himself as if it was all a bit of a joke after all.

'Wild. Old Dag doesn't change. Tried to fuck your girlfriend, did he?'

'Well, I think he probably has by now,' Terry said, his smile faltering, his spirits sinking at the thought of that enormous barnacle-encrusted todger being unleashed from Dag's leather trousers and pointed at Misty. 'More than once.'

'I wouldn't be so sure,' Skip smiled, setting down his cigarette so that he could fish around in his pocket. 'You never know with Dag if he is going to shoot you up or bugger you sideways or just fall asleep.' His smile vanished. 'But we have to be realistic, man. That chick has probably just had the best loving of her life.'

Terry's spirits sank twenty floors. The best loving of her life? How could he compete with that?

Skip stared Terry right in the eye. It was only for a moment, and the eye contact jolted Terry, but it was real. He hadn't imagined it. Skip Jones had looked him in the eye.

'The question is,' Skip said, 'what are you going to do about it?'

Terry shuffled his feet. 'Well, I don't know. What *can* I do?'

Skip pulled out an assortment of pills, and began rifling through them. When he held out his hand to Terry, there were a dozen different-coloured capsules in his palm.

'You give these to Dag,' Skip said. 'With my compliments.'

Terry stared at the pills. 'What are they?'

'You give these to Dag and it will be a while before he fucks your girlfriend again. Or anybody else's.'

'Ex-girlfriend,' Terry scowled. 'She's not my girlfriend any more. Are you kidding? She's nothing to me.'

But he took the pills from Skip Jones, and stuffed them in the pocket of his dead man's mohair jacket, as if perhaps she was still something after all.

Leon dreamed of Bambi.

Strange, he had always thought, that the world considered the little deer to be Walt Disney at its most saccharine. To Leon, *Bambi* had always seemed like the first snuff movie.

He had been taken to see the film at the Swiss Cottage Odeon when he was five years old, and he had found it such a deeply traumatic experience that his mother had to lead him trembling and tearful to the lobby well before the final credits.

How could the other boys and girls just sit there chomping on their choc-ices? *Bambi* was a film where a child loses its mother, where a world bursts into flames and – the part that haunted Leon's dreams as he lay tossing and turning and sweating inside his sleeping bag – that made tangible the horror of the moment when paradise is defiled.

He awoke with a gasp, already sitting up, and he realised immediately that it was all true. They were here at last. Bailiffs were kicking down the front door of the squat, the windows were caving in, there were men shouting, women screaming, the baby crying.

Man had entered the forest.

Ruby was still sleeping by his side, a thin arm thrown across his waist. Leon shook her, unzipped the bag and was on his feet, the bare floorboards like sandpaper beneath his toes, pulling on his clothes. The other couple in the room were already half-dressed and stuffing meagre belongings into rucksacks. It still looked dark outside, but the room was bright, lit by moonlight and the headlights of a dozen cars.

'Get up now,' he said, ducking as a half-brick smashed through the window. There were voices in the street. Men shouting about dossers, stirring themselves for the fight, pumping themselves up. 'They're coming in.'

Except they were not coming in.

It was worse than that.

From downstairs Leon could hear nails being pounded into wood. Voices from inside the house being raised in anger. Curses and threats and cries of fear. He went to the window and saw burly shadows carrying thick planks of wood to the house.

'The bastards,' Leon said. 'They're sealing us in.'

He had known that one day the bailiffs would come, but he had always imagined it would be to throw them into the street. Many times Leon had envisaged the final battle for the squat to be a glorious siege – Leon standing shoulder to shoulder with veterans of the barricades of Paris in hand-to-hand combat with hired thugs and the boys in blue. Room to room fighting – like the battle for Stalingrad. Now he was faced with the choice of staying inside a boarded-up squat until the landlord decided they'd had enough, or legging it. If he had been alone, it would have been different. But he didn't want anything bad ever to happen to Ruby.

He took her arm and they fled for the bedroom door, still pulling on their clothes. At the top of the stairs he glimpsed her long pale legs in a wash of moonlight and it made him catch his breath. He stopped her, and gave her a chance to pull on her dress. He even zipped her up, allowing his fingers to rest on her shoulder blades for just a moment. His hands were shaking. She patted him reassuringly and gave him a smile. Her hand was cool and still.

One floor below he could hear the sounds of scuffles and the staccato pounding of hammers. Most of the downstairs windows were already boarded up, and slashes of headlights came through the slats in the wood. But the front door was half-open and either side of it a scrum of heaving bodies fought for control. Leon and Ruby headed in the opposite direction, to the back of the house, where they had just started sealing the kitchen door.

Leon cursed them and threw himself at the door, shoulder first, and a plank flew away and caught a bailiff flush in the face. Then they were out into the garden and into the night, tripping over the step, obscenities being screamed behind them, something heavy thrown at their heads, maybe a hammer, but whistling past and lost in the grass. They were not followed, but Leon helped her over a dozen garden fences before they stopped, sprawling exhausted on a manicured lawn and panting for breath next to an ornamental pond and a garden gnome with a fishing pole. You could still hear the voices and the hammering and the fighting in the distance. It made him shudder. Squatting was all right when you were young and on your own. But what about later? What about when you found someone?

'Sorry,' he said. 'I didn't expect them to come tonight.'

'Now you really are homeless,' said Ruby, and it made him laugh, and his mouth was on her mouth again, and the dew was soaking his knees, and she was laughing too, his hands on her fabulous face, and he was mad for her, alive for her, for she was all that he ever wanted.

The first tube train was still hours away.

They held hands and started walking west down the Marylebone Road, with the early birds singing in Regent's Park to their right, and the sky behind them just beginning to smudge with the dawn. He was going to walk her to her door. That was the plan, although they didn't feel the need to discuss it much. Leon was going to make sure she got there. Home and dry. Safe and sound.

He wished he had money for a hotel. Wouldn't it be great to have money for a hotel and just crawl into bed and stay there all day long? To kiss and cuddle and fuck until their strength was gone? Wouldn't it be great to have some money for a change? Still, if he couldn't get back into bed with her, at least he could take her home.

But a Ford Cortina full of boys pulled up alongside them just beyond the great dome of Madame Tussaud's. Leon looked at them with distaste. They were the kind who were always threatening to kick his head in.

'Darling, do you want a lift?'

'Where you going, love? Acton? Ealing? Greenford?'

Ruby looked at Leon, almost apologetically. Greenford, yes. She was going to Greenford and back to her real life.

They were depressingly familiar – capped-sleeve T-shirts showing off pale, meaty biceps, hair still worn in sub-Rod Stewart feather cuts, short leather jackets that seemed one size too small. But they didn't seem particularly drunk. And Leon couldn't deny that they were going her way. He couldn't deny that.

'It's okay,' Ruby said, touching his arm. She sounded a little sad and very tired. 'They're not going to do anything to me. Just drive me home and ask me for my phone number. And I'll give them a fake one. Okay, baby?'

He nodded, not risking words.

The sun peeped over the dome of Madame Tussauds. After the storms of the night before it was a shock to see the blinding light of an August dawn, to be reminded that it was still summer. Sunlight glinted on Leon's newly blond locks. She touched his hair – proud of what she had done, and he had to smile. For the very first time in his life, he felt he looked just about okay. Maybe even more than okay.

'Well,' he said. 'Sorry about – you know. Everything.'

'No, I had fun,' she said. There was a real warmth and sweetness in her, Leon thought. She was beautiful, and she was tough, but it was that warmth and sweetness that had him hooked. She laughed, and Leon thought – the beautiful ones. They have it so easy. 'It was . . . different,' she smiled.

The boys waited patiently in the car.

'I had fun too,' Leon said. He couldn't describe what the night had meant to him – how he had been lost in her, and the music, and the sex. He couldn't put that into words. For the first time in his life, words failed him.

'And you're a good dancer,' she said.

'Come on,' he said.

'Sure you are,' she insisted. 'You just need to – I don't know. Relax a little.'

Then the sky was full of sound, and at first it seemed like another storm, but it was louder than any noise Leon had ever heard, louder than any storm, and it grew louder still until suddenly it was directly overhead and he looked up to see the new plane, the one that resembled a giant white bird, Concorde, just one year old and slim as a rocket and gleaming white and gold in the dawn, losing altitude as it prepared for landing west of the city, not far from her home. It was beautiful.

When he looked back, the Ford Cortina was pulling away and Ruby was waving from the rear window. He waved in return, knowing he had meant what he said in bed, what he had said in the middle of the heat and madness, when the words were meant to be just for the moment. Leon loved her.

He really loved her, it wasn't just the sex talking. He loved her although he didn't even know her. How did he manage that? How can you love someone who you don't even know?

He was twenty years old, and it was easy.

THIRTEEN

'You should leave him,' Ray told her.

This wasn't his way. His way was to be cool. Three years at *The Paper* had taught him that it was the only way to be. You were cool when you didn't care, and you were cool when you did care. But this was different. He couldn't be cool with her.

'Your bloody husband,' he said. 'Mr Love Muscle.'

She smiled politely and he knew it was hopeless. Where would she go? With him? In a few hours he wouldn't even have a job. He saw himself through her eyes – a dumb kid still living with his parents, smitten after one night of good sex. But you don't walk away from the kind of life she had. Even Ray knew that much.

She looked from his face to the lightening sky, smiling slightly. 'It doesn't feel like there was a storm last night, does it?' she said.

They were sitting in her Lotus Elan in Hyde Park, by the curve in the lake where the Serpentine meets the Long Water. The sun poured through the great trees and coated the water with a sheen of molten gold. On the far side of the Serpentine there was a small wooden jetty with blue-and-white boats clustered around it.

'We should go rowing sometime,' she said. 'I haven't been rowing for years.'

They watched twenty horses from the barracks of the Household Cavalry lazily clop down a wide sandy track, their riders in full uniform, gleaming breastplates and red Spartan cloaks, the white horsehair tails swishing on their white-and-gold helmets, and yet the soldiers were clearly off duty, carelessly yawning and rubbing the sleep from their eyes and talking among themselves. It was a good moment. But something in Ray seemed bound to spoil it.

'I mean,' he said, 'if you're really so unhappy, if you're really as unhappy as you say, then why don't you just get a divorce?'

'Are you going to bang on about this?' she said, not smiling now.

'Yes,' he said. 'I'm going to bang on and on about it. I'm not even talking about you and me. I'm talking about saving yourself. Getting the fuck out of that loveless place.'

She was silent, still considering the lake, and for a while he didn't know if she was thinking about getting divorced or going rowing. He wasn't just frustrated with her. He was angry with himself. He was meant to be with John Lennon, not some married woman whose husband was too rich to leave.

'It's not so easy,' she said finally. 'You sort of get stuck with each other. I don't know how to explain it.' She stifled a yawn, and he could see she was very tired. She shook her head. 'It's hard to make the break. Hard to face all the changes. You're scared of the unknown, I guess. Scared of being alone.'

He didn't know what to say. Everything he knew about marriage he had learned from his parents. Which possibly meant that he knew nothing. He tried to imagine why his father and mother had once loved each other, and why it had changed. Impossible to ever really know, Ray thought, but although he had grown to hate his father, he could understand how his mother would have been attracted to the old man's strength, his physical certainty, that manly bearing. Women seemed to love that crap.

And how could his mother ever have known that his strength would curdle into shouting and bullying and violence? That the things she loved about him would be the weapons he turned on her and their children? Who could have seen that coming? This woman beside him, the woman he was urging to leave her husband – they must have loved each other once, they must have been mad for each other at the start. People changed. He saw that now. They changed in ways that you could never imagine.

It was not difficult for Ray to see why his father had fallen in love with his mother. All the evidence was there in the smiling black-and-white photograph of their wedding day, the fair, delicate beauty of his mother's youth, and that heartbreaking gentleness she had about her, an almost child-like vulnerability, guaranteed to bring out the protective instincts in a man like his father, who was so old fashioned that he considered combing hair effeminate (you were meant to just use your fingers until it all fell out).

But his mother had also changed with the years, and the changes had been accelerated and soured by the death of Ray's older brother. The girlish softness had turned into a kind of timidity, a net curtain-twitching, kitchen-dwelling neurosis, a fear of life. A love of home had degenerated into a form of agoraphobia. It seemed to Ray that the reasons his parents had fallen for each other were the same reasons that they now drove each other insane. Perhaps every marriage was like that. It wasn't true that you killed the things you loved. It was far more likely that they would kill you. And could he imagine his mother walking out on his dad? Of course not. Where would she go?

'But you don't love him,' Ray said, sounding outraged now, and unable to do anything about it. 'And he can't love you, can he? I don't see how he can love you and give you that . . . thing.'

He couldn't speak of the birthday present. The idea of it appalled him.

'I told you – I'm too old for bedsits and grotty one-bedroom flats,' she said. 'Someone stealing your milk from the fridge. Arguments about who does the washing up. The sound of shagging in the next room. Someone playing bloody Wishbone Ash upstairs. I've done all that. Ten years ago.'

Ray hadn't done any of that. 'How old are you anyway?' he said.

'Twenty-eight today.' A knowing smile. 'Too old for you.'

His heart sank. It was all hopeless. 'But too young for what you've got,' he said bitterly.

He was upset, working himself up for an argument, loathing the thought of her going back to that life – the big house, the flash car, the husband with a wallet where his heart should be. He felt as though he could only stand to say goodbye to her if harsh words had been exchanged. But she was not going to let the night end that way.

'Don't be so angry with him,' she said gently. 'Who do you think pays for everything? Who bought my clothes, this car, the bed you slept in last night? Besides – he likes you. He told me so.'

He thought of her husband's band. The packed basketball arenas of the Mid West going ape shit – 'Whooh! Rock and roll!' – for their souped-up R&B. They were all right, Ray thought. Nothing special. A good bar band, writ large, pub rock to fill stadiums. Nothing more. And Ray thought of their manager, her husband, who had always been pleasant enough to him, but who in the end was just another record industry lifer who happened to be standing in the right club when the right band came by. He would never get married, Ray decided. It robbed you of yourself.

'You think you're nothing,' Ray told her. 'But I think you're terrific.'

She looked at him for a while, and then she kissed him quickly on the mouth.

'Come on,' she said, getting out of the car. She took his hand and they walked down to the boathouse, the grass still slick and glistening with the apocalyptic rains that came down the night Elvis died.

It was far too early to hire a boat, but they agreed that nobody would mind very much if they just borrowed one for a while. Giggling now, their shoes sopping wet from the grass, and afraid of falling into the lake, Ray stumbled to the sharp end of the boat – the bow, she insisted on calling it – while she settled herself facing him, slipping the oars into their worn metal rings.

They pushed off, gliding over the still glassy water, and she began to row with a slow, lazy motion. She was good. He had to admit it. Far better than he would have been. They smiled at each other, and didn't feel the need to talk. A few black swans followed them until it was clear that they were not going to provide breakfast, and then they peeled away and squawked back to the shore, their wings tucked up beneath them.

The sun was already dazzling and in the distance Ray could hear the muffled roar of the traffic on the Bayswater Road and Park Lane, heralding the day to come. But Hyde Park still seemed to be sleeping, and it was a thousand shades of green.

When they were in the middle of the lake she pulled in the

oars and let the boat drift. Ray trailed his hands in the water as the boat lazily traced a half-circle, at first pointing south towards the Albert Memorial, then drifting round to aim at the statue of Peter Pan on the west bank.

Ray watched her tugging at the gold ring on the third finger of her left hand, frowning with the effort for a few seconds, unable to get it off, and then pulling it over her knuckle and free.

She held the ring between the thumb and index finger of her right hand, regarding it thoughtfully, as if she couldn't quite work out how it had ever got there. Then she threw it into the air as far as she possibly could.

The ring hit the water with a soft splash that made the black swans stir for a moment, anticipating breakfast again, flapping their wings towards the boat, and then turning away when they realised that it was nothing.

As Leon took the lift up to the twenty-first floor, he worked on his review.

Leni and the Riefenstahls. A dumb name for a dumb band. Leon didn't regret missing their gig. He was glad he had missed it. Nothing would ever be better than meeting Ruby and dancing to 'Shame' with Ruby and having sex with Ruby in a sleeping bag. Nothing would ever be better than the night he had just had, the first night of his life when he felt like he had escaped the confines of his own skin.

Leon entered the office, dawn streaming through the windows now, and noticed a light on in the review room. Skip Jones was in there, surrounded by upright cigarette butts and records.

'You got any smokes?' Skip said, looking somewhere over Leon's shoulder.

Leon fumbled in the pocket of his Lewis Leather, always a little nervous in the presence of Skip, and pulled out a crumpled pack. There were still a few in there. Leon realised with a twinge of pride that he hadn't had much chance to smoke.

'Wild,' Skip said, glancing at the pack and then briefly at Leon's face. Leon offered him the pack, but there was something wrong with Skip's hands. They were shaking so badly that Skip dropped the cigarette he pulled out, and he had to hold his hands as if to stop the trembling as Leon picked up the cigarette from the stained and pock-marked carpet. They both pretended that nothing had happened.

'You review somebody last night?' Skip said.

Leon lit two cigarettes, took a long drag from both and passed one to Skip. 'I was meant to review the Riefenstahls,' Leon said. 'But, to tell you the truth, I got a bit sidetracked.'

Skip studied the tip of the Marlboro. His hands were still shaking, but holding the cigarette seemed to calm them. 'What kind of sidetrack?'

'I met a girl,' Leon said. 'I met this great girl. This unbelievable girl.'

Skip smiled shyly. 'Well, I missed gigs for worse reasons than that. Don't worry about it. The older guys are going to have their hands full with Elvis. They won't miss your review.'

'Oh, I think I'm going to write it up anyway,' Leon said, grinning. 'But don't tell anyone.'

Skip looked concerned. 'Wild,' he said, sounding worried.

'It'll be all right,' Leon said reassuringly, more to himself than Skip. 'I've seen Leni and the Riefenstahls plenty of times, and they were always rubbish. What's the point in us writing about a band like that anyway? Bunch of posers. They're not going to change the world, are they?'

Leon spoke with his usual total certainty, but inside he was confused. He thought about Ruby and Evelyn 'Champagne' King and how he had felt when he had worked up the courage to dance. Being at Lewisham last Saturday seemed to show him the road he had to take – fighting Fascism, being committed, awakening the masses. But last night suggested that the masses were already more awake than he would ever be.

'Skip, do you think that people can love black music and still be racist?'

Skip Jones shrugged. 'I don't know, man. Unfortunately, yeah, I guess so – people can love black music and hate black people – but maybe not if they listen to enough of it.' Skip carefully placed what remained of the cigarette on its filter tip with all the rest. 'Hey, you're right to make a stand. If you don't care at – what are you now? Twenty? – then you never will. And it's good to get these bits and pieces into *The Paper*. Fuck, man, Nazis are a complete bummer.'

Leon thought of the faces contorted by hate at Lewisham. The total, all-consuming loathing on the other side. The jeering *sieg heils* and Nazi salutes. Which one of them was her father?

'But they are never going to be more than bits and pieces,' Skip said. 'If this was the *Daily Worker* then no dude would buy it, no dude would advertise in it, and you, dude, would be selling it on a street corner and outside factory gates. And frankly, the number of dudes buying would be few.' He rubbed his eyes, dragged fingers through his oily Keith Richards hair. '*The music isn't there to save the world*,' Skip told Leon, and the words struck him like a bolt of lightning. '*It's there to save your life.*'

Skip smiled, looking exhausted now, but the trembling in his hands was subsiding. Leon realised that he should start writing soon if he wanted to finish before they all began arriving at the office. But he loved talking to Skip. Even though he still felt confused about what he should expect from music, and what the world should expect from him, somehow it made him feel better.

But the morning was coming fast now, so Leon said see you later to Skip, went to his desk, threaded an A4 sheet of paper into the red plastic Valentine typewriter and stared at the empty page. And then he thought.

There were many things that annoyed him about Leni and the Riefenstahls – their toying with Fascist symbols, their po-faced stage demeanour, their clumping three-chord songs dressed up as something profound. But it was their patronising smugness that really infuriated him. If you knew that Leni Riefenstahl was the director of *Triumph of the Will*, that chilling celebration of Nazi Germany on parade, then you could be in their gang. And if the reference flew over your head, then you couldn't. Leon began to type.

Ever heard of Triumph of the Will, *dear reader? When Leni and the Riefenstahls played the Red Cow on a wet Tuesday night, it was triumph of the wankers.*

Not brilliant, but pleasantly abusive. The sun was coming up strong now, streaming through the Venetian blinds and smoked glass, making him squint, and his mind and body were suddenly aware that they had been up all night. Leon numbed himself with scalding vending-machine black coffee and didn't stop pounding the typewriter until he had a 500-word hatchet job. Then he rose from his desk, stretched his aching limbs, and deposited the review on Kevin White's desk.

On his way to the lifts, he glanced through the window of the review room. Skip was resting his head on the table, his face turned away from the door, surrounded by old cigarette butts and new vinyl.

He appeared to be sleeping, so Leon didn't say goodbye.

Ray left the park and started walking east down Oxford Street, the sun directly ahead of him, hurting his eyes, coming up over the miserable concrete slab of Centre Point. The night's broken glass crunched beneath his feet like ice.

The day was coming on but the armies of the night were still abroad – stragglers reeling home from the night before and bleary-eyed workers returning from the graveyard shift, all sharing the rubbish-strewn streets with the first of the day's commuters.

Ray increased his pace, wanting the chance to clear his desk at *The Paper* before the working day began. The fact that he had not found John Lennon got all mixed up with the woman he had met who could not leave her husband. His heart felt like it had been kicked down the street, but he wasn't sure what had kicked it the hardest. If only he could have been with her. If only he could have tracked down John. If only he could have done one thing right.

It was too late now. The night was dead and gone and there was nothing left to do but grab the few souvenirs he had collected from the last three years – an Emmylou Harris promo T-shirt, a C-90 cassette of his interview with Jackson Browne, an 8x10 photo Misty had taken of Ray smiling shyly next to James Taylor – and get out before there was any need for goodbyes. That was the thing that would really break his heart. Having to say goodbye to Terry, and Leon, and the old life. No goodbyes, he thought. Just go.

The sun was temporarily lost behind the department stores of Oxford Street and suddenly he could see clearly. Ahead of him a larky pack of shaven-headed lads shoved and jostled each other. They were dressed in the latest revival style – number one crops, Ben Sherman shirts, thin white braces, white Sta-Press trousers and highly polished DM boots. You were starting to see them all over the city – the new skinheads, who were never going to deck themselves out in Vivienne Westwood T-shirts and bondage trousers. Ray swerved towards the road, planning to give them a wide berth.

He saw that there was an Asian kid with glasses and a plastic Adidas kitbag walking towards them. There were a few jocular greetings, and someone chanting, '*Oh, Doctor, I'm in trouble – well, goodness gracious me!*' and then suddenly they had the Asian kid's bag in their hands and they were tossing it between them, the kid playing piggy in the middle as they easily held him at bay. On their fingers gold signet rings flashed with the sunlight.

The bag must have been open because the next thing Ray knew the filthy pavement was covered with the kid's pitiful belongings. Some foil-wrapped sandwiches, a thermos flask, a book called *Computer Programming for Beginners*. The kid was on his hands and knees, retrieving his stuff, as the skins – tiring of their game now – tossed his kitbag into the middle of the road, and began kicking around the foil-wrapped sandwiches.

'They think it's all over,' one of them shouted, booting the sandwiches so hard that the foil split open and shreds of white bread and cheddar cheese and tomato flew everywhere. 'It is now!'

They were still good humoured, pretending to be football commentators or Peter Sellers, and their mood only changed when Ray passed to one side of them and just couldn't keep his mouth shut. He picked up *Computer Programming for Beginners*, the sole of a size-ten boot imprinted on the cover, and gave it to the kid. Those happy skins – they were everything he loathed.

'Why don't you leave him alone?' he said.

They were immediately on him. Fists flying, boots lashing out, so engorged with rage that the wild blows seemed to skim off his head and legs or miss him completely, and it didn't even hurt very much at first. Then one of them had him in some kind of head-lock, and Ray could smell the sweat and Hai Karate aftershave, and he caught a glimpse of the Asian kid retrieving his kitbag just before a big red number 73 bus crushed it under its wheels.

Then the Asian kid was running away and Ray was flat on his back, the toes of the boots catching him in his ribs and head, not missing now, hurting him now, and he was curling up on the pavement, covering his eyes and his balls, gasping at the stabs of pain. Then, as abruptly as it began, they were backing off.

When Ray looked up he saw Terry lash out with the side of his foot and drive it deep into a midriff that was adorned in Ben Sherman blue-and-white gingham. There were three skinheads around him and Terry smacked one in the face with a right hander and, as his momentum spun him around, kicked another up the arse of his Sta-Press. Then they were running, shouting that Terry had better keep looking over his shoulder, telling him that their brothers would kill him, and Ray saw that they were just weaselly little nothings, all swagger and spite and sixteen at the outside, lousy rotten bullies who folded as soon as someone hit them back.

Still, he was impressed, and shook his head with wonder as Terry pulled him to his feet.

'Who the fucking hell taught you –?' Ray began.

The words died in his throat because Terry had struck the pose of his hero – a boxer's stance, wide legged and left side on, but with the hands relaxed not clenched, watching the pack of skinheads go out of the very corner of his eyes while moving his head from side to side – slowly, snake-like, as though he had a mild nervous disorder – and Ray knew the answer to his question before it had even left his mouth.

Bruce Lee.

Bruce Lee taught Terry how to do that.

Terry had the Ford Capri with him.

He was a poor driver, hanging on to the steering wheel as if it was a life belt, constantly drifting either too close to the centre of the road and making other drivers hoot with alarm, or so near to the kerb that the Capri's wheels sometimes hit concrete with a screech of rubber and metal.

But Ray was so exhausted by now that he dozed in the passenger seat, a new song on the breakfast show coming out of the radio. 'Dancing Queen' by Abba, the Hairy Cornflake said, and it was full of yearning and youthful nostalgia, as if it was about this kid who was already missing some lost golden age. *Having the time of your life – oooh, oooh.* Terry went over a bump in the road and Ray was jolted awake. He expected to see the bleak towers of the South Bank. But they were somewhere in the backstreets of the West End, just north of Marble Arch, where the Arab cafés and restaurants seemed to go on for miles.

'Are we nearly there?' Ray said.

Terry pulled the car up. 'Something I've got to do first.'

They were outside a hotel. Ray rubbed his eyes and realised that it was the Hotel Blanc, the place that had almost been his first stop of the evening. It felt like a lifetime ago.

Ray watched Terry walk slowly towards the main doors, and saw him disappear into the lobby. Ray must have fallen asleep for a moment because the next thing he knew the fire alarm was ringing and Terry was coming out of the main doors.

Halfway to the car Terry paused, and waited, holding his right hand, which seemed to have been cut somehow. Soon the guests began to stream out of the hotel, blinking in shock in the dazzling daylight, like the living dead woken from some timeless slumber, unsure where to go, in their night clothes or half-dressed or in the kind of white towelling bathrobes that were scattered all over the floor of Terry's bedsit.

Then there was Misty and Dag Wood, coming through the main doors, walking towards Terry, while he just stood there holding his hand, and trying to stop the blood.

Misty was in the white dress of the night before, but with a robe draped over her shoulders and carrying her biker's boots. Dag was barefoot, naked from the waist up, the fly of his leather trousers unzipped, his face hollow with years of abuse but his body muscled and toned.

More than ever, Ray thought, Dag looked like the freshly deceased corpse of Charles Atlas.

And then Ray forgot about Terry and his girl troubles because there was a small woman in hotpants with hair like a black haystack coming quickly through the doors of the lobby, and behind her was a hawk-faced man in round wire glasses, taller than Ray had expected but unforgettable and unmistakable. A face that Ray felt he knew better than his own. The face of John Lennon.

Somehow the school satchel was still hanging from his shoulder. Somehow it still contained the clunking great tape recorder he had borrowed from Terry at the other end of the night. Somehow he was breathing the same air as John Lennon.

And somehow, despite being almost paralysed by exhaustion and fear and love, Ray got out of the car.

'For you, Dag,' Terry said, the words stalling in a mouth that was suddenly bone dry with nerves and anger and this terrible grief. He couldn't even look at her. 'From Skip.'

Terry held out his fist, palm down, and Dag's corrugated features split in a reptilian smile. He seized Terry's fist, for all the world as if they were old pals shaking hands, and Terry palmed him the pills.

Then he pulled his hand away. He couldn't stand to touch the old bastard.

'I'll save these for the Rainbow,' Dag said, referring to the gig in Finsbury Park later that night. It would be the highlight of his tour. 'Thank the Skipper for me.'

Terry nodded, poker-faced and trying hard to keep it neutral. He still hadn't looked at Misty. Then Dag was talking to her, casual as can be, making sure she was okay for tickets to the Rainbow, right under Terry's nose.

'Terry's name will be on the door,' she was saying. 'Plus one.'

Dag yawned and stretched like an old tom cat, as if it had been a long night and he was ready to turn in. They were letting people back into the hotel by now, and Dag smiled farewell at the pair of them with a sickening kind of intimacy.

As if he fucking owns us, Terry thought.

They watched him go.

'I've got this for you,' Misty said, slipping the hotel bathrobe off her shoulders.

Terry shook his head. 'I don't collect those things any more.'

She looked surprised.

'I mean, what's so special about those things?' Terry said, letting his eyes rest upon her now. Forcing himself to look at her. 'Everybody's used it, haven't they?'

She looked exasperated. 'Don't freak out.'

'I'm not freaking out.'

She rolled her tired eyes. 'Nothing happened, okay?'

Words failed him. For about two seconds. 'Fuck off, you slag,' he said.

She flinched. 'Terry – I didn't have sex with him, okay?'

He shook his head. 'I don't believe you.'

The crowd was melting away. She noticed the Ford Capri for the first time.

'Is that my father's car?'

He looked at the car, expecting to see Ray. But his friend had gone.

'You're a fucking liar,' he said, turning away.

She grabbed his arm.

'Look – he didn't want to do anything, okay? And neither did I. Okay, Terry? We just talked all night.' Misty got a dreamy look in her eyes. 'Well, until he passed out.'

Terry turned his back on her. But he wasn't walking away now. He wanted to hear it. He wanted to believe her. He wanted things to be the way they were.

Misty was babbling, name-dropping, still dizzy from the experience. 'We talked about Byron, Jim Morrison, Nietzsche. It was fascinating, actually. *He must have chaos within him, who would give birth to a dancing star.* Dag has a mind the size of a planet.'

Terry snorted. 'Yeah, and a knob the size of a donkey.'

She gave him that cool look. 'Well, you would know more about that than I do.' Then she smiled. 'He said this thing, and I thought it was rather sad – he said, *I prefer drugs to women.*'

Terry stared at her. Dag had said exactly the same thing to him. And it was true – that's what he was like. Dag Wood was from the old school. He would fuck anything and he would take anything. But he would much rather take everything than fuck everything. Perhaps it was because in his world drugs were harder to come by than women. Or maybe they just made him feel better.

Terry immediately knew two things beyond any doubt. Misty was telling the truth. And Dag Wood was doomed. Not the same way Billy Blitzen was doomed. Dag would probably live to be a hundred. But he was doomed all the same.

Terry almost felt sorry about giving him all those laxatives.

Everyone was so nice. That was the thing that shocked Ray. Once he had got over that first paralysing second when he knew he was going to actually open his mouth and talk to John Lennon, everyone seemed to go out of their way to make things easy for him.

At first it was just the pair of them, this magnificent, vilified couple, a man and a woman who'd showed Ray the way a marriage could be. Standing there, outside the Blanc, seeming almost shy as he stumbled towards them. In a daze, in a dream, strung out with exhaustion and excitement and the realisation that it was all true, it was really happening.

Ray said the name with a question mark – *John?* – as if they were old friends, as if Ray had known him all his life – and of course that's exactly how it felt – and then he said his own name – *Ray Keeley* – and the name of his magazine – *The Paper* – and John, the man, John Lennon in the flesh, was saying how he knew *The Paper* from way back, when the group were just starting out the group! Ray knew what group he was talking about! – and how they played *The Paper's* annual poll-winners concert a few times before the madness forced them off the road.

And Yoko was smiling at him, and John was smiling, and Ray wasn't quite sure what to do next, but then there was some assistant person, not someone from the record company but some permanent assistant there to smooth their way through the world, and she was tired and wary, but John was inviting Ray to come and have a cup of tea, and Ray thought – what a wonderful world.

This was his world, and this was his time, where a kid from a music paper could just walk up to the biggest rock star on the planet and then get to hang out with him for a while.

And Ray saw that it was still true – that sense of community that he had glimpsed in the playground where they sang the songs of the Beatles, that world of shared feelings. It was *real*. It wasn't bullshit, it wasn't hype. Everything he had heard in the music was true.

Walking through the lobby of the Hotel Blanc, Ray was aware of the dumbfounded stares – what must it be like? To be stared at in every room in the world? – and Yoko was asking him a question about the B-52's, this new American band that Ray knew nothing about, nothing at all. Terry could have given her chapter and verse, but it didn't really matter because it wasn't a contest, you didn't have to pretend to be cool, or clever, Ray could just be himself. And as they rode the lift to the top floor – John and Yoko and Ray and the woman who was some kind of personal assistant – Ray felt a joy like nothing he had ever known rise up inside him, and it obliterated the nerves and the fear and the embarrassment that he couldn't answer Yoko's questions about the B-52's. He had held out his hand and John Lennon had taken it. And Ray knew he had been right to believe in the music. He had been right to believe all along.

And then he was inside the hotel room – although it seemed more like a house, it was nothing like the thousand other hotel rooms that Ray had seen occupied by musicians. The room went on for ever. There was even a piano in it.

And then sitting on the sofa, facing John, warm and chuckling, happy to talk about music with this kid, this strange kid who had refused to cut his hair, Yoko sitting beside him, that great black haystack in her face, but that was okay, that was to be expected, and the permanent assistant was phoning down for some tea, and Ray could do this thing, because he had actually done it many times before, and it was what he lived for, the music was what he lived for, the best thing in his life, the only thing that had always made perfect sense.

And there it was – John Lennon's voice – the talking voice no different from the singing voice – droll and wise and full of soul, kind and mocking and just the way it should be. They talked – how could Ray ever have imagined that there would be nothing to say? And after a while, just after the tea had been placed before them, John Lennon reached across and pressed the *start* button on Terry's tape machine.

'You should turn that thing on, Ray,' John Lennon said. 'I don't want you to lose your job, man.'

There was a radio behind the counter of the café. Leon didn't notice it until he was counting out the coins for his tea and bacon sandwich.

'. . . *swamped by people with a different culture,*' a strange new

voice was saying. A woman's voice, somehow transparently arti-
ficial and yet full of conviction. A voice that was fake and genuine,
all at once. '*We are not in politics to ignore people's worries.*' Nagging,
strident, wheedling. '*We are in politics to deal with them.*'

Leon's jaw dropped. He stared at the radio and kept staring even
when 'Don't Go Breaking My Heart' replaced the woman's voice.

'Who's that?' Leon said, desperate to know.

Behind the counter was a fat man in a washed-out Silver Jubilee
T-shirt. 'Elton John and Kiki Dee,' he said.

'No, no – the woman. The woman who was talking. The one
going on about being swamped.'

The man handed Leon his bacon sandwich. 'Maggie Thatcher,'
he said. He looked at the radio with naked admiration. 'About
time we had someone to stand up for us,' said the man in the
Silver Jubilee T-shirt.

Leon gripped his bacon sandwich like someone in shock. He
had not foreseen this. He had not seen this coming. The relevance
of the major political parties had seemed to melt away in recent
years and as he had sold his copies of *Red Mist* and attended
anti-racist rallies and pogoed to the Clash, the woman who had
led the Conservatives for the last eighteen months had barely
registered on his radar. Why should she?

Leon had assumed that the government of the day was an irrel-
evance now and would be irrelevant for ever. He had imagined
that the fight for the future would be decided on the streets.

But as he gripped his bacon sandwich, he suddenly saw an
alternative future in a parallel universe, where a mainstream
politician told the country – or a large part of the country –
exactly what it wanted to hear about immigration, the unions, law
and order, counting the pennies, keeping your net curtains clean.

No screaming skinheads and *sieg heils* and Nazi fantasies. Nothing so crass. Just a different kind of mainstream, steamrolling everything in its path. And he knew with total certainty that Ruby's father would happily vote for the owner of the voice that was both fake and genuine, a voice that seemed designed to speak for the nation. How had Leon failed to see it coming? How had he been so blind?

And then Leon suddenly had something else to worry about. Because Junior was entering the café, followed by his henchmen.

In the growing daylight, the Dagenham Dogs were a grotesque sight. The clumsy home-made nature of their face piercings, all those safety pins penetrating the flesh of nose, lip and cheek, the assorted stains of beer, blood and dirt on the front of their sleeveless T-shirts, their eye make-up a complete mess. In the harrowing light of dawn, the three-teardrop tattoo under Junior's right eye looked as if it had been done by a monkey with a welding iron.

The café was packed with builders getting the goodness and grease of a full English breakfast under their belts before going to work. Hard men who would normally allow themselves a few smirks at the freaks who were walking the streets these days. But even the builders looked down at their fried eggs and red-top tabloids as the Dagenham Dogs passed by.

'I don't want any trouble,' said the Maggie Thatcher fan behind the counter, and Leon thought that the man sounded like a bartender from a Western.

'Outside,' Junior told Leon.

He slowly got up from his chair, his bacon sandwich untouched, and followed them out of the café, with nobody daring to look at him, the condemned man.

In the street Junior faced Leon, Dogs to the left of him, Dogs to the right of him, a terrible fraternity of pierced ugly bastards.

Junior took Leon's head in his hands, almost lovingly, and then seized his ears. Then he crashed his face into the windscreen of the nearest car. The shock was greater than the pain, although the pain seemed to double with every passing second. Something was torn on Leon's forehead, and there was something warm and wet trickling in his eyebrows. As Leon's head was yanked back up, he saw he had been bashed against the windscreen of a rather beautiful car. A gold Buick, all tail fins and chrome and black-and-white piebald upholstery. Like something from a Buddy Holly song, Leon thought, or a car that Elvis might have bought with his first royalty cheque from Sam Phillips. Leon's head felt as though it had been kicked by a horse.

'You lot make me laugh,' Junior said, still gripping Leon's ears. 'All you middle-class wankers at *The Paper*. REBELS WITHOUT A COCK, is it? So I don't have a cock, is that what you reckon?'

'I was speaking metaphorically,' Leon gasped. The pain, the incredible expanding pain, made it difficult to think straight.

Junior seemed unconvinced.

'You think you can say what you like and there's no comeback. You think you're in some kind of student debating society. You think –'

A high-pitched voice cut in from out of nowhere. 'That your car, mate?'

Junior turned to look at the speaker, not relinquishing his grip on Leon's ears. It was the biggest Ted that Leon had ever seen. Leon's mouth dropped open, stunned with recognition. It was Titch himself, the giant among Teds.

Titch was surrounded by a dozen of his greasy-quiffed tribe, young Teds in their violent prime, all of them weighing up the Dagenham Dogs.

'What?' Junior said, his train of thought interrupted.

Titch had a surprisingly gentle voice. Like Elvis singing one of his devotional hymns, Leon thought. 'There Will Be Peace in the Valley', perhaps.

'I said – is that your car, mate?'

Still very reasonable, but indicating the windscreen of the gold Buick. Leon's head had left a smear of bloody grime on the glass.

Junior shook his head. 'I got the bus,' he said. 'It's not my car.'

The mountain of a Ted nodded, seemingly satisfied with the answer. Titch turned to look at his friends, sharing a chilled smile before once again facing Junior.

'I know it's not your car, you tattooed tit,' Titch said. 'BECAUSE IT'S MY FUCKING CAR!'

Then Titch swung a meaty right hook and it sent Junior flying, and then sprawling. Like George Foreman smacking Joe Frazier, Leon thought, the blow that lifted Smokin' Joe right off his feet in the hot Jamaican night. Junior let go of Leon's ears.

Titch stared down at Junior's prone form for a moment, as if examining something he had stepped in, and then brought down the sole of a size-thirteen brothel creeper. Junior howled, his eyes bulging.

The Teds were first to attack, sweeping into the Dogs with the practised fury of their warrior tribe and driving the Dogs back into the road, forcing a milk float to swerve and a crate of gold-top to fall off the back and shatter. But the Dogs quickly rallied, all those away matches on the terraces behind them, accustomed to scrapping on uneven ground, soon finding their footing on the spilt milk and broken glass beneath their boots.

Leon crawled away on his hands and knees, surrounded by

flying DMs and brothel creepers, through the puddles of blood and milk and glass, with Mrs Thatcher's bossy, ingratiating voice still ringing in his ears.

'. . . swamped . . . swamped . . . swamped by people with a different culture . . .'

Up and on his feet, he jumped on the platform of a passing bus, the pole almost ripping his arm out of its socket. Ignoring the protests of the conductor he went upstairs, staring out of the rear window, dabbing at the cut above his eyebrow, looking back at the gang fight that had now sprawled right across the road receding behind him.

The Dogs had staged an impressive comeback, but the superior fighting ability of the Teds was proving decisive. Titch had two of the Dagenham Dogs by the scruff of the neck, and Leon watched him bang their heads together as if they were cymbals. Junior was crawling away, now with real tears on his face. He disappeared under a pack of Teds. Then the bus took a left on to Blackfriars Bridge and the fight was gone.

The bus crossed the river and Leon stared at the dome of St Paul's without seeing it. He was pale-faced and shaking with an emotion that threatened to overwhelm him.

'Swamped . . . swamped . . . swamped . . . we are not in politics to ignore people's worries . . . we are in politics to deal with them.'

Shaking because he had just narrowly escaped a good hiding. And because he had just seen the future.

FOURTEEN

There was no real traffic.

A young man at the wheel of a Ford Capri could get up a real head of steam as he headed south to the river – barrelling down the long sweep of Regent Street, taking a sharp left round Eros at Piccadilly Circus, then down Haymarket, and almost one long straight run all the way to the Embankment.

'Can you slow down a bit?' Misty said.

Terry swerved to miss a Lotus Elan. 'Had enough excitement for one night?'

He increased his speed, zipping through a red light. There was a rage inside him. In a way it would have been a lot easier if Misty and Dag had been fucking their brains out. Then it would have been simple. Then it would have been over.

But what do you do when your girlfriend has spent the night talking about Nietzsche, Byron and the first Doors album with another man? Terry didn't know quite what to do. Increasingly, he felt that way – life was more complicated than he had ever imagined, and he was struggling to keep up.

'Will you *slow down*,' she said, with that cold edge of steel that she could always summon up at will. 'This is not even *your car*.'

'What's your old man going to do? Sue me?'

'Terry,' she said. 'Oh, Terry.' A long sigh. 'You really don't get it, do you?' So she said it very slowly, as if she was light years ahead of him. 'I'm having a baby.'

He stared at her, wondering if this was a joke, or a trick, or a lie, but she was looking straight ahead through the windscreen of her daddy's car, and in an instant it all made sense.

He remembered the pills on the first night. The pills she could no longer take, and he remembered their cavalier attitude to contraception, the blithe disregard of a pair of rutting youngsters.

They had briefly contemplated condoms, but packets of three seemed so ridiculously Fifties that they had ended up laughing at the very idea. Condoms went out with banana rations, Billy Fury and the hula-hoop.

They had been banging away for months, and because nothing happened they had believed that it never would. And then it did. And now it had. A baby. He hadn't even thought about it. The possibility had never crossed his mind. It seemed like the stuff of some other, grown-up life. A *baby*.

She screamed just then and Terry turned his head in time to see a police car stopping to let an old lady in a Morris Minor out of a side road. He slammed on the brakes, and then practically stood on them, almost rising out of the seat, and the cop car was hurtling towards them in a rush of shrieking rubber and Misty shouting. Terry held his breath, waiting for the mangling of metal and glass, tears in his eyes.

A baby, he thought. A little baby.

*　　　*　　　*

294

The crash never came. The Ford Capri screamed to a halt inches from the bumper of the law. The tyres howling, the two cops already turning in their seats to see what kind of maniac had almost driven up their backsides.

Terry sat at the wheel, gasping for breath, trying to take it all in – a *baby* – and watching the policemen get out of their car and start walking towards him. He knew he was going to be stopped and searched. And he knew there was no time to hide the drugs he was carrying. He looked at Misty and laughed. A *baby*. A cop stuck his head in Terry's window. There was an old one and a young one, just like at the airport.

They made him get out of the car. Then they breathalysed him, telling him to blow harder, to blow properly. It was neutral. Then they made him empty his pockets, and one of them read his driving licence while the other patted him down. The cellophane bag of amphetamine sulphate was in the ticket pocket of his dead man's jacket. And they missed it.

'Sir,' said the younger one, 'may I ask why you are driving like such a fucking cunt?'

Terry shook his head. The world seemed to have changed. He couldn't put it into words, but it seemed like the world had changed for ever. Or at least his little part of it.

'I just found out I'm going to be a dad,' he said. He let the words settle, fill the space between them. The cops looked at each other. 'I took my eyes off the road – took my eyes off the road for a few seconds there.'

The two cops dipped their heads to take a look at Misty, all demure and blonde in the passenger seat, and then they looked back at Terry.

'She's a lovely lass,' said the older cop, holding out his hand. 'Congratulations.'

The younger cop slapped Terry on the back. 'I remember when my missus told me about our first,' he laughed, as the old cop crushed Terry's fingers. 'I nearly choked on me Rice Krispies.'

Then both of the policemen were smiling and laughing and patting Terry on the back, and they went off feeling slightly better about the world, or maybe young people. As if, Terry thought, they had just learned that the younger generation were really no different to all those who had gone before, despite their strange hair and clothes from Oxfam. And maybe they were right.

But Terry watched Misty's impassive face with a sinking feeling, as something occurred to him for the first time.

What if she didn't want this baby?

They parked up on a side street and sat by Cleopatra's Needle, watching the boats on the river, the tower block containing *The Paper* the tallest building on the skyline.

'We're young,' she said. 'Young to have a baby.'

'That's true,' he said. There was no bad feeling between them now. There was only this bond, this incredible bond between them, as though they were more than lovers, and more than friends. As though they could never be this close to anyone else.

'It's a big responsibility,' she said.

'I know,' he said. 'It's a huge responsibility. A baby. Jesus.'

Misty bristled. 'And I'm not going to be one of those mothers who stays home making jam or whatever the fuck they do all day.'

He laughed with genuine amusement. 'That's for sure.'

Misty relaxed. 'But it doesn't have to change anything,' she said, excited now, and it allowed Terry to be excited too. 'And what a great experience – to bring another human life into the world.'

They were laughing together now. 'Imagine what it will look like, Misty. A little bit of you, and a little bit of me. All mixed up.'

Then she was suddenly all serious again. 'I don't want to get rid of it, Terry. I don't want an abortion. Of course I'm pro a woman's right to choose and everything, but I just don't want to get rid of it.'

He shook his head. 'No,' he said, 'no, that would be awful.' He already loved their baby.

Then they were both quiet for a while. Something magical had settled on the day, and they sat there by the river, feeling it, trying to understand what it all meant. Their baby.

'It doesn't have to change anything at all,' Misty said, trying to work out how things would be. 'We can take it with us. When we work. When we go to gigs.'

Terry thought about it, furrowing his brow. Concentrating. Trying to be a responsible dad. 'Maybe we should put some cotton wool in its little ears. To protect them while they're still, you know, growing.'

Misty nodded thoughtfully. 'That's a really good idea. Cotton wool for its ears.' She laughed, and her face seemed to light up. 'What if it's a *girl?*'

Terry laughed too, and he took Misty's hands and kissed them. 'What if it's a *boy?*'

Then they were both silent for the longest while, letting it all sink in, watching the boats on the river without really seeing them, and feeling the heat of the sun as it came up on their adult lives.

Leon held the second bacon sandwich in his hands, savouring the moment.

Against all odds, he had somehow contrived to meet the girl

of his dreams, review the band of his nightmares, and avoid the kicking of a lifetime.

Not a bad night, all in all.

After fleeing the battle between the Teddy Boys and the Dagenham Dogs, he had jumped off the bus at London Wall in the heart of the financial district, which was already filling up with men in suits and their young female helpers. Leon walked among them, thinking – what was it that Engels said about the relationship of men and women in the nuclear family? Something about man being the bourgeois and his wife the proletariat. Well, Friedrich, my old mate, Leon thought, it's exactly the same in the City of London.

Unable to face eating a bacon sandwich so close to the heart of capitalism, Leon walked east to Charterhouse Street and the Smithfield meat market, deciding that he would prefer to eat his breakfast in a café full of real workers, not a bunch of chinless paper pushers sipping their weak tea and nibbling their cheese-and-Branston toasties.

Terry had taken him here once, when he was trying to borrow money from his father, and Leon had been much taken by the place.

Almost in the shadow of the Bank of England and the Stock Exchange, a market of sweating, shouting men toiled through the night with animal carcasses as big as they were, and then went off to sink pints of beer and nosh enormous fry-ups in the countless greasy spoons and smoky pubs surrounding Smithfield before staggering off home to collapse in bed. That's the place to be, Leon thought, trying not to touch the bloody scab on his forehead.

The market was winding down now, and the small café Leon chose was full of porters in filthy white coats tucking into plates piled high with fried eggs, bacon, beans, sausages and toast.

Good, honest working men at the end of their labours, Leon

thought warmly – real people! – although of course he deplored the way they leered over young women displaying their pert young breasts in the tabloid newspapers. He paused with the sandwich halfway to his lips, as his eyes drifted to the paper of the man next to him, and the girlish smile above the womanly body of Mandy, sixteen, from Kent. It made him remember the heartbreaking springiness of Ruby's body inside the sleeping bag, and he felt himself stir with love and longing.

He wondered if he would see her at the weekend.

He wondered if he would ever see her again.

He wondered if he could compete with Steve.

Leon put the bacon sandwich back on its plate and murmured an apology as he reached across an elderly porter for the HP sauce. He pulled back the top layer of bread on his sandwich and considered the bacon, fried to a crispy brown, nestling on butter that had already melted into the thick slice of Mother's Pride. His tummy rumbled, ravenous after the exertions of the night, and his mouth flooded with saliva and hunger.

Then he shook the sauce bottle as hard as he possibly could and – as the top was merely resting rather than screwed on – a projectile of thick brown sauce shot into the air like something hurled into space out of Cape Canaveral. It came down on the table directly behind Leon and from the shocked intake of breath all around the café, he knew the landing place wasn't good news.

Leon turned to see a meat porter with violence in his eyes and HP sauce on his shaven head. He was as broad as he was wide and the muscles in his arms were thick and knotted from a quarter-century of heavy lifting.

Leon could see the muscles in his arms quite clearly because, as the man rose from his seat, making no attempt to wipe away the HP sauce that was dripping into his eyes, he was rolling up the sleeves of his blood-splattered white coat.

And that was when Leon Peck stopped worrying quite so much about the workers.

Terry's father was an old man now.

Terry watched him coming down the street from the window of their front room, coming home from the night shift, and he looked like he was dragging the weight of the years behind him.

Worn out by work, worn out with worry about his son, worn out by the unforgiving toll of the years. An old man at forty or fifty or whatever he was.

Terry's mum smiled at her son as they heard the key in the lock. She indicated that they should all be very quiet, all three of them. And then the old man was standing in the doorway, still in his white coat and his French Foreign Legion hat, blinking at his wife and his son and his son's girlfriend, young Misty.

'Guess what?' Terry's mum said, as if she had been saving this up for a long time. 'Guess what, Granddad?'

Yes, his father looked ancient these days. But when he heard the news and it had started to sink in, that kind, exhausted face lit up with a smile, and it was a smile that Terry knew would last the old man for years.

The editor's office was crowded but the only sound was the metallic limp of a spool on Terry's tape recorder and the singsong voice of John Lennon.

'I've been through a lot of trips – macrobiotics, Maharishi, the Bible . . . all them gurus tell you is – Remember this moment now. You Are Here.'

The editor swooned. It was the kind of moment that Kevin White lived for. Everybody would go crazy when they heard this stuff. The Fleet Street boys would be banging at the door.

'The break-up of the band . . . the death of Brian, the selling-out of Paul . . . Ringo makes the best solo records . . .'

Kevin White thumbed through Ray's handwritten notes, shaking his head, a slow smile spreading across his face. Lennon kept talking. He was the great talker. And he seemed to have this need to get it all out, to get it all down, to confess to everything. He was the great confessor, talking about the whole mad trip as if for the first time, as if for the last time.

'We were pretty greasy . . . outside of Liverpool, when we went down south in our leather outfits, the dance-hall promoters didn't really like us . . . they thought we looked like a gang of thugs. So it got to be like Epstein said, "Look, if you wear a suit . . ." And everybody wanted a good suit, you know, Ray? A nice, sharp, black suit, man . . . We liked the leather and the jeans, but we wanted a good suit to wear off-stage. "Yeah, man, I'll have a suit." Brian was our salesman, our front. You'll notice that another quirk of life is – I may have read this somewhere – that self-made men usually have someone with education to front for them, to deal with all the other people with education . . . You want another tea? You sure?'

'You know what you've got here, don't you, Ray?' White said. 'A world exclusive.'

Ray nodded, smiling weakly. He was suddenly spent. He felt like he could sleep for a thousand years. He wished he were curled up under clean white sheets with her – with Mrs Brown, although he no longer thought of her as Mrs Brown. Now she was *Liz* – her parents had been to see Elizabeth Taylor in *National Velvet* on their first date – because now she was no longer just some other

301

man's wife, because that was her name. Liz. It was a good name for her.

And then there was Yoko.

'I'm not somebody who wants to burn the Mona Lisa. That's the great difference between some revolutionaries and me. They think you have to burn the Establishment. I'm not. I'm saying make the Mona Lisa into something like a shirt. Change the value of it.'

'Turn the Mona Lisa into a shirt,' White chuckled. 'I love it.'

Was it a good interview? Ray couldn't tell. Turning the Mona Lisa into a shirt – that was just mindless babble, wasn't it? That was plain nutty. But it had happened. That was the important thing. And in the end it had all been so easy. And everyone had been so nice. And with hindsight it seemed perfectly natural to walk up to the biggest rock star in the world, introduce yourself, and then sit down and have a talk. That world of shared feelings – John Lennon believed in it too.

Ray Keeley had approached John Lennon with love in his eyes – a supplicant, a fan, a true believer. How could his hero refuse him? And Lennon was kind. He was more kind than he had to be.

'It can't be the cover,' said one of the older guys, unable to keep the resentment out of his voice.

Kevin White had been treating Ray like the prodigal son ever since he turned up with his Lennon interview, but the older guys seemed curiously put out, as though Ray had got something over them.

The editor nodded. 'Any other week it would be the cover,' White said, almost apologetically. 'This week – well, there's only one cover.'

'I was thinking Elvis in '56,' said one of the older guys, tapping a pencil on his pad. 'One of the classic Alfred Wertheimer shots. The Memphis Flash in all his pomp. Headline – REMEMBER HIM *THIS* WAY. Italicise the "This".'

White nodded thoughtfully.

'Yesterday Elvis was a fat embarrassment who went on twenty years too long,' he said. 'Never the same after he joined the army, blah blah blah. Today he's a rock-and-roll martyr, a cultural god, immortal. And taken from us far too soon.'

'That's cruel,' Ray said.

'That's showbiz,' sneered one of the older guys. The tape played on.

'Our gimmick is that we're a living Romeo and Juliet. And you know, the great thing about us influencing in this way, is that everybody's a couple. We're all living in pairs. And if all the couples in the world identify with us and our ideas go through them, what percentage of the population is that?'

'Er ...'

Ray flinched at the sound of his own awkward voice.

'You know what you've got here, don't you?' White said to him, laying a loving hand on the tape recorder. 'A job for life. *A job for life.* You're the writer who interviewed John Lennon in the middle of the Summer of Hate.' White smiled proudly at Ray, as if he had never stopped believing in him. 'You're going to be getting free records when you're forty. Think about it.'

Ray could sense every eye in the room on him, and he could feel their envy. It was what they all wanted – it was what he had wanted at the start of the night. The promise that the circus would never leave town without him. Perhaps it was just nervous exhaustion, but he didn't feel as happy as he'd thought he would.

Free records at forty ... Why did the idea depress him?

This was the only job that he had ever wanted, because it had never felt like a job. And yet the prospect of growing middle-aged within these walls filled him with dread. Maybe it was that he needed to sleep now, needed it urgently. Or perhaps it was because his generation, and the one that came before, had made such a big fucking deal about being young that the thought of growing old was unthinkable. Even if you still got free records when you were forty.

'Life's too short,' said John Lennon, and then there was a click as the cassette ran out. 'Life's too short,' and then he was gone.

Then White's secretary was bursting into the room, and she was doing something that you were never meant to do in the office of The Paper, where beyond everything else, you were expected to be cool.

She was crying.

'It's Skip,' she said.

There were green shoots pushing through the crushed rubble of Covent Garden, like the promise of a better season, or possibly an early warning of chaos ahead, all the old wildness breaking through.

No, thought Terry Warboys. Call it a better season. That's what you have to believe.

He was standing outside the Western World. It looked so different in the daylight. Little more than a hole in the wall, the extinguished neon sign bleak and filthy. It looked as though it had been closed for years, not a few hours.

Suddenly Terry was aware that there was a crumpled figure curled up in the doorway. His red, white and blue jacket was in tatters now. He blinked at Terry as if he had just emerged from some enchanted sleep.

'Is that it?' Brainiac said.

'Yeah,' Terry nodded. 'I think that's it, Brian.'

Terry was nostalgic for this place already. He thought about the nights he had gone through those doors and down into a cellar full of sound, the speed pumping in his veins, the faces of old friends and beautiful strangers coming out of the darkness.

Misty had gone on ahead to *The Paper* to deliver some shots of Dag Wood to the picture desk, and that was fine because Terry needed time to think. Before everything was different.

Misty said that the baby would change nothing. Terry suspected that the baby would change everything. But what would never change, he thought as he stood outside the Western World, was the way he felt about his girl. He would never stop wanting her, and the baby would make the bond between them even stronger. Everything else would have to take second place.

He knew he wouldn't be coming to the Western World quite as often as he had in the past. It wasn't just the audience that was changing, as word of the new music and the good times to be had spread out to the council estates and the suburbs and the faraway towns. The groups were changing too.

Bands were like sharks – they kept moving or died. You couldn't play a place like the Western World for ever. He looked at the fly posters for coming attractions and he realised he didn't know any of these bands, and he wasn't particularly interested in knowing them.

The bands he had started out with were on their way. Last year there had been a real camaraderie – the days of amphetamines and new friendships and a whole world opening up. Everybody escaping from their own private gin factory. Now it was all capped teeth, cocaine and bodyguards. The bands he had known and loved were either getting left behind or they were becoming famous, and struggling to remain famous, and they were changing. And Terry was changing too.

He took out the bag of amphetamine sulphate that the police

search had failed to find in the ticket pocket of his dead man's jacket. Then he tossed it as far as he could on to the wasteland that faced the Western World.

Brainiac looked up, sniffing the air, and then abruptly lost interest.

It seemed to Terry that the thing they had come here for had been better a year ago. During that blazing summer when it was all just getting started. They couldn't wait for that time to be gone, and for their real lives to begin.

But he saw now that was *it* – that was the special time, when you could walk into a club and hear the Clash playing 'London's Burning' or the Jam playing 'Away from the Numbers' or Johnny Thunders and the Heartbreakers doing 'Chinese Rocks', and you knew that you were in exactly the right place, the centre of the universe, and you could go out every night of the week and see a great band, a great band who didn't even have a recording contract, and you could take home a girl whose name you wouldn't remember in the morning, and there wasn't just one girl who you couldn't live without. That brief period when he had been Norman Mailer's free man in Paris.

He had not appreciated how good it all was at the time. Or maybe it was always like that, and you only noticed happiness when it was past. They all had more now – the bands had recording contracts, the writers had careers, and he had the girl he had always wanted from the moment he first saw her.

And yet somehow it felt like nobody was quite as happy as they were a year ago. There was a fragment of poetry running around his head, a snatch of someone – Larkin? – from an English Lit class of five or six years ago when he had been watching the clouds drifting over the playing fields and only half listening. And now he saw that the poem was about him.

He married a woman to stop her getting away
Now she's there all day.

Terry watched Brainiac slowly get to his feet and stumble across the wasteland of Covent Garden, a forlorn figure wearing what appeared to be a ragged old flag. The builders had started work for the day. They were cementing over their beloved bombsite. All this was going to change. Everything.

The sun had come up on a different world and Terry couldn't run around like a dumb kid any more. He loved their baby already. Yet it brought him down to think that he would never again go out watching bands with his head full of chemicals and ready for anything. It brought him down hard.

But he stopped outside a bakery on Neal Street, bought a bag full of bagels and started walking south, his fingers and teeth tearing greedily into the hot white bread, the smell the best smell in the world, his stomach rumbling with protest but somehow remembering what food tasted like, and by the time he reached the river and the bag of fresh bagels was gone, Terry was aware that he was smiling.

FIFTEEN

Terry burst into the review room full of news for Skip – about fatherhood, about how your life could change in a night, about revenge being a dish best served with laxatives.

But instead of Skip he found Misty drinking vending-machine tea with a tall, middle-aged lady. She looked kind and pretty and Terry felt that he had seen her somewhere before.

'This is Skip's mother,' Misty said, taking a quick, concerned glance at the woman. 'Skip – Skip's not very well.'

Terry shook his head, not understanding. These were still the days when he thought they were all going to live for ever. 'What happened to him?'

'He's in the hospital,' Misty said. 'They think he's had a stroke.'

The woman seemed to bow her head towards her plastic cup of tea. Terry stared wildly at Misty. He didn't know what she was talking about. He didn't understand anything. 'A stroke? What's that – like a heart attack?'

Misty took a breath.

'The ambulancemen said it could be a cerebral haemorrhage,'

Misty said. 'Bleeding from a weakened artery getting into the brain. If he survives the first week or two, he'll be fine.'

Terry took a step towards them, and words failed him. It was shocking enough to discover that Skip had a mum. The thought of his friend and hero dying was beyond his imagination.

How could your own body betray you like this? How could it just happen without warning? Where was the justice? Who could you complain to?

'I wouldn't be here without Skip,' he said, and it sounded pathetically inadequate to convey his feelings – who cared if he was here or not? What did it matter to anybody? But the woman smiled and nodded.

'The boss wants to see you,' Misty said. 'The pair of you.'

Terry turned and saw Leon standing in the doorway, pale-faced with shock and lack of sleep. One of his eyes was half-closed and purple. There was a black scab of blood on his forehead. And his hair was golden.

Terry took Leon's arm and stepped outside the review room, looking at his friend anxiously. 'Jesus, Leon – what happened to you?'

'I went dancing,' Leon said, and Terry had to smile. He gave Leon a shove and felt the mad, inappropriate laughter bubbling up inside him.

'You went dancing, did you?'

'Yeah, I went dancing.' Leon was smiling now.

'Did the Dogs catch up with you?'

Leon's smile grew wider. 'No, the Teds caught up with them.'

Terry nodded with satisfaction. 'And what about Skip? What's going to happen to Skip?'

'I don't know,' Leon said, tearing up. Terry placed a hand on his shoulder.

'Skip will be all right,' he said. 'He has to be. He's only – how old is Skip anyway?'

Leon bent his head, and for a moment it seemed to Terry as if his friend was not thinking about the question but about the articles they had all grown up reading – Skip Jones telling them about his adventures with Keith Richards and Iggy Pop and Dag Wood and Lou Reed and Jimmy Page and the New York Dolls, Skip's hard-earned wisdom and reckless appetites somehow co-existing, Skip ripping apart the pretentious, celebrating the good stuff in that cool, pristine prose. Terry watched Leon thinking about Skip, and he knew that Skip was a better writer than he would ever be.

'Skip's twenty-five,' Leon said.

They walked the short distance to Kevin White's office. White was staring out of the window at the traffic on the river. Ray was standing beside him. They turned when Terry knocked on the open door. White gestured for them to enter, and Ray smiled, and as they walked in Terry remembered the last time the three of them had been together, hiding from the Teds in that destroyed building at the start of the night. A lifetime ago.

'Boss, the three of us are going to the hospital,' Terry said. 'We've got to see Skip.'

White shook his head impatiently. 'Don't worry about Skip,' he said. 'They're taking good care of Skip. He's going to be all right. And we've got a big issue to get out.'

'A big issue?' Terry said. 'A big issue? Skip's in the hospital with a cerebral whatever-the-fuck-it-is, and you're talking about a big issue?'

White said nothing, just looking at them, letting the silence fill the room. When he eventually spoke his voice was very quiet.

'You boys are getting a little long in the tooth for this teenage-rebel stuff, aren't you?' he said, looking at Terry like he was a greaser on Brighton beach on a Bank Holiday Monday in 1965. 'I heard about the stunt you pulled at the Hotel Blanc.' Terry said nothing, but something in White's eyes made him look at his feet. He hated it when White was angry with him. The editor let his voice get softer. 'In future don't bring your personal problems to work. Okay?'

Terry nodded. 'Okay.'

White looked at Leon. 'And God only knows where you were last night.'

'I went dancing,' Leon said, but his editor didn't crack a smile.

'Look at the state of you,' White said, shaking his head.

'But – I thought we were meant to be wild,' Leon said. 'I thought we were meant to be a rock-and-roll paper.' He could feel his argument gaining momentum. 'I thought – I thought that's what it's all about!'

Terry noticed that White's desk was covered with pictures of the young Elvis Presley. And he saw for the first time that Elvis had been beautiful.

'You think that's what it's all about, Leon?' White was saying. 'Coming into work looking like you've been up all night, playing in the traffic? Maybe once. Maybe rock and roll was about being young and wild – once. But look at you two,' he said, nodding towards Leon and Terry. 'Now it's just an excuse to never grow up.'

'Whatever happened to anarchy?' Leon said.

'Yeah,' chimed in Terry, wanting to stick up for his friend, willing to risk incurring the editor's wrath. 'I thought anarchy was all the rage.'

But White just smiled at them. 'Don't make me laugh,' he said.

'If Johnny Rotten was a real anarchist he would be sitting in a pub in Finsbury Park with his thumb up his arse. He wouldn't be signing a recording contract with Richard Branson.' The editor shook his head with exasperation. He was almost thirty years old and tired of all this crap. Terry could see it. He was tired of arguing with them. 'You boys are going to have to decide if you're serious about what we do up here, or if you're just happy amateurs. Because there's no place for happy amateurs in the music industry any more. If that's what you want, go write a fanzine.'

'Boss, you're talking like some old businessman,' Leon said quietly. He did not want to row with White. He loved him. 'But I know it's more than that to you. I know you care about the music. I know you care about *The Paper*. I know you do.' Leon smiled triumphantly. 'You're just like us.'

'The times have changed,' White said, and Terry thought their editor looked more tired than any of them. 'We're not one step away from the underground press any more. This is a business. We have advertisers, management, subscribers – all that grown-up shit. I had them in here last night, the fucking suits – complaining about drug use, about loud music, about all these journalists swanning around like they're in a band. Complaining about you lot. There's no such thing as a free festival. Not any more. That's why, when he's better, Skip's going to take extended leave.'

The three of them were stunned.

'Skip's not coming back?' Terry said.

'Skip needs a rest,' White said. 'A long rest.' Terry and Leon looked at each other. Ray let his hair fall over his eyes. 'Look – I know you love Skip. So do I. Of course I do. Who gave him his first proper job? Who kept him on when he was frightening the old ladies on

Country Matters? But Skip couldn't go on like that for ever. Trying to keep up with Keith Richards? Going cold turkey in the review room? You think the men in suits don't *notice* this stuff?'

'I can't believe Skip's not going to be around,' Terry said, looking at Ray. But Ray's face betrayed nothing. It was as if he had already had everything explained to him by the editor. Terry watched his friend brush the hair out of his face.

'You know what it's going to be soon?' White said. 'It's going to be the Eighties. Think about it.' Terry thought about it. But he couldn't imagine the Eighties. They were unimaginable. Then White was grinning like a loon, happy for the first time, jerking a thumb at Ray. 'Guess who this guy interviewed for us?'

Terry and Leon stared at Ray for a moment and then they were all over him, slapping him on the back and laughing together and congratulating him.

'So Ray's going to be writing Lennon for the new issue,' White said. 'Terry, what are you doing for us?'

Terry played for time. He hadn't given any thought to what he would be writing for the new issue.

'Well – thought I might talk to Billy Blitzen. Get him to –'

'Forget it,' White interrupted. 'That's all over. Everybody's tired of the noble junkie thing. It's all played out, and the music is just too bad. I'll tell you what you're doing – you're doing the singles this week and then I'm sending you up to Sheffield next week. The Sewer Rats are on the road. Take Misty with you. Tell her to get plenty of pictures of the Dogs going mental and smashing the place up.'

Terry said nothing, but his face said it all. About the Sewer Rats, about the Dagenham Dogs, about Misty being around the likes of them.

White nodded, as if agreeing with him. 'Want me to get somebody else?' he said evenly.

Terry realised that the days of writing about his friends were over. 'No, I've got it,' he said.

'Good,' White said.

'What about me?' Leon said.

White searched through some papers on his desk until he found what he was looking for. Leon recognised it as his review.

'Leni and the Riefenstahls at the Red Cow,' White said, nodding thoughtfully. 'Good gig?'

Leon shrugged. 'The usual. Kraftwerk for dummies. It's all in the piece, boss. Not really my cup of poison.'

'Good piece, Leon,' White said. 'Funny, abusive – exactly the right word length. And you got it in on time. Well done.'

Leon beamed. One word of praise from Kevin White, and all of them felt their spirits soar. 'Thanks, boss.'

'Except it never happened,' White said, and Leon felt his heart sink to his boots. 'Leni called in sick. She had root canal treatment yesterday afternoon.' The editor dropped the review in the bin and brushed his hands. White looked at Leon. 'They didn't play the Red Cow last night.'

Ray and Terry were staring at Leon, suddenly aware of their breathing. They knew that there was no right of appeal. You could do almost anything in the offices of *The Paper*. But if you reviewed a gig that never happened, and you got caught, then you cleared your desk.

And then you walked away.

'Sorry, Leon,' White said sadly. 'You've written some good stuff for us. I'll make sure you get all the references you need.'

Terry put his arm around Leon and said nothing. He saw the

tears fill his friend's eyes and dug his fingers into his shoulder blade. Terry saw the shock on Ray's face. Leon hung his head.

There was a soft knock on the door. A thin boy with a red fringe drooping over huge, heavily made-up eyes glided into the room, carrying a fistful of typed pages. He was younger than all of them. Even younger than Ray.

'The think piece you wanted,' he said to White, smiling brightly. 'Berlin's influence on Bowie, and Bowie's influence on everyone.'

When the painted youth had gone, Terry stared at the editor.

'Who the fucking hell is that little bender?' he said.

'That's the new guy,' the editor said.

The three of them sat in Trevi, drinking endless cups of tea, and Terry and Ray stole glances at Leon, not knowing what to say. When one of them moved his feet, he could feel the cardboard box under the table containing the contents of Leon's desk. It had never crossed their minds. That one day there would be an end to it.

Leon felt he should say something. It was like being in the Goldmine when Elvis died and there had been that horrible cheering. He just had to *say* something. He wondered where he got it from, this urge to say something. He wondered if it was from his father.

'I just – you know,' he stuttered, 'I just want to say – it's been great.' His eyes filled up again. 'The best thing in my life. Being at *The Paper*. And working with you two . . .'

Ray bit his lip, staring hard into his tea. But Terry slapped his hand on the table, glaring at Leon.

'Bullshit,' he said angrily. 'Don't give me this Vera Lynn we'll-meet-again bullshit – this doesn't change a thing, Leon – you going – it *doesn't*.' Terry sniffed, wiped his eyes with dirty fingers.

'Do you know what today's going to be?' He smiled wildly. 'Today's going to be the best day ever. *The best day ever.*'

Terry took a gulp of tea and laid out the plan. Soon Ray, and finally Leon, were joining in. They didn't feel the need to talk about it, but it was quite clear – they were not going to let Leon's sacking put an end to what would be the last great friendship of their lives.

They would spend the morning in Rough Trade, looking at the new records and fanzines and talking to the two guys who ran the place about new music. Then maybe in the afternoon they would go over to Rehearsal Rehearsal in Camden Town, where they all knew Terry, and where maybe Subway Sect or the Clash would be practising, and everybody would talk at once, about music and politics and girls, and there would be a lot of bitching about other bands and other music papers, and there would be speed and spliffs for those who wanted them, and Skol and Red Stripe for everybody, and it would feel just like it felt at the start. At one point they might even have something to eat, to make up for all the meals they had missed. And when the night came they would be spoilt for choice.

Terry spread the live pages of *The Paper* out before them. He looked up at Leon and they smiled at each other. Terry gave him a shove and laughed.

'Look at this lot,' he said.

Dag Wood was at the Rainbow in Finsbury Park. That would be interesting, especially if Dag had really saved Skip's laxatives for the show. And Elvis Costello was at the Nashville Room, on the corner of the Cromwell Road and North End Road, tickets £1. Eddie and the Hot Rods were at the Marquee – £1 on the door, £1.20 for members – Slaughter and the Dogs were at the Roxy, 41–43 Neal Street, Covent Garden – support act the Varicose

Veins. The Tom Robinson Band were at the Hope & Anchor on Upper Street, Islington. And the Sex Pistols were on a secret tour – no billing, no advertising – and they had just played a date at the Lafayette, Wolverhampton, and kids were writing to *The Paper* complaining about the exorbitant £1.50 entrance fee. There were rumours the Pistols were going to play the Screen on the Green again in the early hours of the morning.

'So what do you want to see?' Ray said.

'Let's see all of it,' Terry said. Leon laughed, watching the pair of them working out their schedule, thinking about the logistics of doing it all, and he loved them like the brothers he had never had.

'I reckon we could just about do it all,' Ray said. 'Although we might have to miss the Varicose Veins set at the Roxy.'

'That new guy,' Terry said, making a jerking motion with his right fist, and Leon's heart flooded with gratitude. 'Give me a break. The whole Bowie thing has been done to death.'

Leon stared at the table. It didn't have much to do with him any more. The small cardboard box between his feet reminded him that he was out. He felt like something had gone wrong that he would never be able to put right. But he thought about the day to come and his mood lifted.

Then Misty came in. Leon could see she wanted to talk to Terry alone, and after a few uncomfortable moments Terry slipped outside with her, and then one of the older guys was there, oddly respectful, needing to speak to Ray about his piece on Lennon so they could start laying it out, and Leon said go ahead, don't mind me, and Leon sipped his tea while Ray talked to the older guy about the Lennon story, and Leon knew in his heart that, as much as they wanted to be with him for the best day ever, his friends had other places they needed to be.

The older guy left and Terry came back without Misty, but somehow the thing they called the vibe had changed. They paid the bill and left. They no longer talked about the day to come.

Outside the café they paused, the wind whipping around the tower as it always did, as if urging them to move on. Misty was at the wheel of her father's car, parked on a zebra crossing, engine running, the sound of Radio One blaring from the car's open windows. The DJ was saying that Elvis was going to sell two million records in the first twenty-four hours after his death. They were calling it his best day ever.

'It's too bad this is such a busy week,' Ray said apologetically. 'It's just a big issue, that's all.'

'It's fine,' Leon said. He didn't want them to feel bad. He didn't want them to make a big deal about it. He couldn't stand it if they were too kind. 'I'll call you, okay?'

'We can do it another day,' Terry said. 'We've got all the time in the world. Right?'

Terry hugged Leon and then he let him go, pushing him away with a rough shove. Ray placed a shy hand on Leon's Lewis Leather. Leon tried to smile. The three of them looked at each other for a moment, uncertain what would happen next. Then suddenly a few bars of Colonel Bogie blared from a car horn. They all turned to look at Misty, waiting at the wheel of the Capri.

She smiled and waved, anxious to get moving.

'So your dad's not really a lawyer then?' Terry said.

They were sitting in her father's car outside her home, which turned out to be a council house on a hill overlooking the ripped backside of King's Cross.

The front yard – it may once have been a garden – was buried under spare car parts. A couple of blackened exhausts, a grease-smeared engine, a solitary passenger seat, the rusty carcass of an old Mini Cooper, its wheels gone. The sound of trains filled the air like birdsong.

'A lawyer wouldn't drive a Ford Capri,' Misty said absent-mindedly. Then she looked at Terry with what he felt was infinite tenderness. 'You don't know anything, do you?'

It was true. He was so easy to fool. Here he was, about to become a father, and he didn't know anything. But he was learning.

'What does he do, then?' Terry said. 'Your old man?'

For some reason he half-expected her to say – exactly the same as your old man. He half-expected her to say – he's a porter at Smithfield. We are exactly the same, and we have been exactly the same all along. But instead she said, 'He's a mechanic. Self-employed. A small businessman.'

He thought about it for a while. Everything he had believed about her – the home full of Bach and books, the life of easy privilege, an upbringing of skiing trips and pony clubs – needed to be rethought. Many of the things that he had liked about her were receding fast.

'Where does it come from?' he said. He wondered what you would call it. 'This invented life.'

Misty sighed. '*Cosmopolitan*, I guess. All those beautiful people living beautiful lives. And the *Sunday Times* – especially the maga-zine, the colour supplement. And then all the people I met in the sixth form, after my real friends had left at fifteen.' She nodded thoughtfully. 'And then the people I met at *The Paper*.'

He still didn't get it. 'But you didn't have to lie to me.'

She laughed. 'Of course I did. I didn't do it for you, or anyone

320

else. I did it for myself. I lied so that I would feel more comfortable. Do you want to go inside? And meet them?'

He took her hands. 'But I don't want us to lie any more. Not if we're going to have a baby. Not if we're going to do this thing properly.'

Misty contemplated the scrap metal littering the front yard. 'Maybe only if we lie for a very good reason,' she said finally. 'Maybe only if we lie because we don't want to hurt the other one.' She smiled, running her fingers down the curve of his face. 'That's what marriage is all about,' she told him.

Misty's father laughed and clapped Terry on the back.

'You've had your fun and now you've got to pay for it,' he announced.

He was a large man in a vest, a thick mat of monkey hair on his broad back, and he poured two shots of Famous Grouse into filthy glasses. Ignoring Terry's mumbled objections, he forced a glass into his hand. 'I know how you feel – her mum was four months gone when we tied the knot.' He raised a glass. 'Down the hatch.'

Terry followed his lead and threw back the whisky, feeling it burn a path all the way down to his Doctor Martens. His head was whirling. Everywhere in the shabby little house there were images of Jesus and Mary. It felt like they were in every alcove, on the wall, all over the mantelpiece. Christ writhing on the cross, Mary's hands together in prayer. All these images of suffering and purity. Terry placed a hand on his sweating forehead, felt the whisky working its dark magic.

'You're a lucky bastard,' her father gasped, wiping his mouth on the back of a hairy hand. 'My wife's brothers gave me the hiding of a lifetime, even though I was always planning to do the right thing.' He waved a glass at the three sullen males contemplating Terry from the sofa. Misty's brothers, two bigger, one smaller. Vicious brutes, the lot of them, thought Terry.

'Seems like you're getting off lightly,' her dad said. Then he got down to business. 'I can get you and Mary the Scout hall on the cheap for the reception.'

Terry thought – *Mary?*

'And I know someone at the local Westminster Wine who will do the booze and then you and Mary can move in here with us until the council sort you out a nice little flat.'

It was all worked out. Tears sprung to Terry's eyes. It was partly the Famous Grouse, and it was partly the shock of learning the truth about Misty's family, and it was partly that he had been up all night taking drugs and having adventures. But mostly it was the feeling that his life had suddenly been taken away from him.

This family wasn't like his own. His mother would have gone mental if someone had knocked over a garden gnome in their front garden, let alone covered it in the greasy guts of an abandoned motor. Terry's parents owned the house they lived in, not the council. And Terry's father, for all his hard-man exterior, spent the weekends cultivating his roses, not stripping Ford Escorts. These people, Misty's family, were from the other side of the working class. Cash in hand, one step ahead of the rent man, ducking and diving, too many bodies in too little space. And Terry was an only child.

Misty's three brothers looked like the kind of mean, pogoing peasant who was suddenly turning up in all the places he loved, and ruining it for everyone. They still had long hair! The tail end of the summer of 1977 and they still had long hair! And not because they were like Ray, believers in another way of living, but because they were too slow and stupid to change. That hair – Terry recoiled from it. Hair that five years ago they would have beaten you up for having. Feathered hair, and flared baggy trousers, and stretchy, short-sleeve shirts so tight you could see their disgusting nipples. Their gaunt, gum-chewing faces disappeared behind the film of Terry's humiliating tears.

'Ah!' laughed the smallest one. 'Now the cunt's going to start crying!'

'None of that,' Misty's father barked, and while it didn't appear to have any effect on Misty's kid brother, it certainly made Terry jump. 'He's family now – or he will be soon – and I want him treated proper. Now, the lot of you – come on. Shake the cunt's hand.'

Nobody moved.

The old man's face was suddenly red with rage. 'Shake the cunt's hand!' he commanded, his rheumy eyes popping.

The brothers lined up to shake Terry's hand.

'God bless,' muttered the biggest brother, almost wrenching Terry's arm out of its socket with his meaty paw. Terry shook his hand in a daze, too far gone to feel the pain.

'God bless,' repeated the middle brother, squeezing Terry's hand as hard as he could, making his fingers sound like cracking walnuts at Christmas.

'God bless,' said the smallest brother, briefly touching Terry's palm and quickly pulling his hand away, muttering under his breath, 'and if you ever look sideways at my sister Mary, I'll fucking kill you.'

Terry could see that for the rest of his time on earth he would be known as the Cunt. What are we getting the Cunt for his birthday? Would the Cunt like a drink? Is the Cunt coming round for Christmas? Finally he understood why girls – women –

found the term offensive. No wonder Misty had been driven into the arms of Germaine Greer, after growing up among all these cunts.

Misty and her mother came into the room bearing tea and ginger nuts. Her mother was a willowy heartbreaking blonde with a soft Irish accent. Terry helped her with the tea and biscuits, half in love with her already. He wanted to rescue her from this place. He wanted to be rescued.

'Well,' reflected Misty's father, his mouth full of soggy ginger nut. 'They've had their fun, Mother.'

And although Terry smiled politely, sipping his hot sweet tea, blinking back the tears, inside he thought – oh no, no, no.

I haven't had my fun yet.

The new hair had yet to reach Greenford. Everyone still wanted to look like someone they had seen on television or at the pictures.

Leon peered through the steamed-up window of Hair Today at a world of Farrah Fawcett flicks, Purdey pudding bowls, Annie Hall centre partings, Jane Fonda *Klute* feather cuts and Kevin Keegan perms.

With instruments as complicated as any brain surgeon's tool box – styling wands that hissed steam, white-hot four-pronged forks, and all those egg-shaped spacemen's helmets hovering over Nescafé-sipping heads – hair was teased, twisted and above all burned.

You could smell it from the street – burning hair, singed into place and then held fast with clouds of sticky perfumed spray.

Leon reached inside the pocket of his Lewis Leather and felt the St Christopher's medal. After saying goodbye to Terry and Ray, he had walked to the West End and found himself staring in the window of the big Ratner's at the end of Shaftesbury Avenue, looking at the patron saint of travellers on a silver-plate chain and thinking to himself – oh, she would like that. At that moment he would have been happy to spend the rest of his life that way – finding the things that would please her.

He saw Ruby immediately.

She was standing behind a chair containing a girl with hair like Susan Partridge from *The Partridge Family* – very long with a centre parting, and curled gently at nipple height. Radio One was playing – Tony Blackburn talking, Carly Simon singing.

There were a few men in there too – working, or getting their elaborate locks trimmed and tickled for the weekend – hearty lads with their David Essex curls, Rod Stewart peacock cuts and white-boy Afros. Leon watched one of them, the good-looking one who made all the housewives laugh, the one with the Clint Eastwood quiff, cross the floor with a can of Wella spray held in his hand like a big purple phallus.

Ruby and the Susan Partridge fan were talking to each other in the mirror, so that when the man kissed Ruby lightly on her glossy lips, Leon saw it twice – once in the mirror, and once for real – as if he really needed to have it rubbed in, as if he might somehow fail to get the message.

'Steve?' someone shouted as Leon turned away, the St Christopher tight in his fist. 'Do you want normal-hold or extra-hold on this one?'

'Wait a minute,' Ray's bug-eyed little brother said. 'You're *giving* them to me? You're *giving* me your record collection?'

Ray stuffed his spare denim jacket into his rucksack. He looked at Robbie and smiled. He wanted to give his brother his records because he was leaving, and because they were all he had to give. But he couldn't say that to his kid brother.

'I can get all the records I want now,' Ray said. 'Just don't leave them out of their sleeves, okay? I know you always do that.'

'I *never* do that,' Robbie insisted, hopping from foot to foot with excitement. 'I've *never* done that in my life, actually.'

White socks, Y-fronts, Terry's tape recorder. The few shirts that hadn't been bought by his mum. As he was leaving the records behind, there wasn't much to pack.

'You've got two records and you leave them out of their sleeves all the time,' Ray said, but gentle now. 'Oh, forget it – they belong to you now. You can do what you like with them.'

'I'll take care of them,' Robbie said, reverently holding a worn copy of *Let It Bleed*. 'I'll take good care.'

Ray pulled the rucksack string tight and hefted the bag on his shoulder. 'Just don't destroy them the minute I'm out the door.'

'Can I even have your bed?' Robbie said.

Ray nodded. 'Sleep where you like, Rob,' he said, and it felt like there was suddenly something in his throat. He wanted to go now. But he stood there, watching his brother with the records.

Twelve inches by twelve inches, you had to hold them in both hands, and they were all you could see in front of you. Holding a record was like holding a baby, or a lover, or a work of art. Robbie waded through the collection with a kind of stunned wonder, like an archaeologist fingering impossible riches in a pharaoh's tomb. *Sticky Fingers* by the Rolling Stones, with the Warhol cover, the picture of the jeans with a real zip. *Led Zeppelin III*, with no words on the cover, no words needed, just the picture of the old farmer with a bale of twigs on his back, and then when you opened up the gatefold sleeve, you saw the picture was on the wall of a demolished house, and in the background were tower blocks going up and the old world being torn down.

Revolver and *Rubber Soul* and *Imagine* – John's head, lost in the clouds – and records that Ray had almost forgotten about – *First Steps* by the Faces, back when Rod was still being played by John Peel, and *Highway 61 Revisited* by Dylan and *Blue* by Joni Mitchell – Ray had laid in bed with that record on his pillow, and dreamed of kissing those cheekbones – and *Harvest* by Neil Young. And greatest hits by Hendrix and the Kinks and the Lovin' Spoonful – when he was trying to catch up, cramming in everything he had missed the first time around, when his head was still spinning with how much great music there was in the world. Ray envied his little brother, with that feeling still ahead of him.

And then Robbie was pulling out the records that embarrassed Ray now – *Band on the Run* by Wings, *Days of Future Passed* by the Moody Blues and *Chicago Transit Authority* by Chicago. But nobody's record collection could be cool all the time. And you never knew what you were going to grow out of, you never guessed that *The Hangman's Beautiful Daughter* by the Incredible String Band would one day wear right off while *Tupelo Honey* by Van Morrison would sound great for ever.

He crouched by Robbie's side, picked up a copy of the *Easy Rider* soundtrack, remembering when his mum had bought it for him. Then he looked at Robbie, kneeling by his side with a copy of *Sgt Pepper's Lonely Hearts Club Band* in his hands, and he realised that his brother was crying.

'Don't go,' Robbie said.

'Ah,' Ray said, a consoling hand on the boy's shoulder. 'I have to go, Rob.'

'But I'll be all alone if you go.'

Ray hugged his brother tight, both of them on their knees, the records all around them. 'You'll never be alone,' he said. 'Not now.' They pulled apart. Robbie wiped his nose on the sleeve of his bri-nylon school shirt. 'And you'll come and join me. In London. When you're big enough. Okay?'

His brother nodded, trying to be brave, and Ray left the bedroom where he had been a boy, and walked down the hall past his big brother's closed room. Already the house seemed too small to live a whole life in.

His mother was waiting dry-eyed at the foot of the stairs. She handed him a small crumpled pack of something wrapped in kitchen foil.

'Fish paste,' she said, by way of explanation.

'Thanks, Mum.'

He could sense his father's presence in the living room, shuffling about, that hard man always out of place surrounded by the knick-knacks his mother stuffed into every nook and cranny, the white Spanish bull and the *Greetings from Frinton* ashtray and a green-and-white model of Hong Kong's Star Ferry. Ray thought about leaving without saying goodbye, but something made him push open the door, and there was the old man in the curiously stiff uniform of the Metropolitan Police.

His father stuck out an enormous hand and Ray took it in the only way he knew how, like he might take a girl's hand in the back row of the Odeon, and he saw his father flinch with a quiet contempt before he pulled his hand away. Ray realised that their attempts at civilised formality would somehow always be worse than their arguments.

Then there came the noise from upstairs. This dirty, chugging riff on slide guitar, and then a singer who sounded as if he had been gargling with gravel. The old man's face clouded with fury and disgust.

'What the bloody hell is that racket?'

'That's the Faces, Dad,' Ray laughed. He stared thoughtfully at the ceiling for a second. 'Sounds like "That's All You Need". I'll see you around.'

The car was waiting for him on the street, and some children from the neighbourhood were gathered around it, boys and girls alike in flared denims, the hems of their jeans uniformly frayed by the adventure playground and filthy with muck from their bikes, all of them keeping a respectful distance from the yellow Lotus Elan, as if it had come down from some other planet.

'Turn it *down!*' Ray heard his father shout as she opened the passenger door for him, but Ronnie and Rod and the lads just seemed to get even louder.

These were the last days of hitching.

Lorry drivers and sales reps who had never heard of Jack Kerouac or *On the Road* would offer a lift to a young man with no money and his thumb in the air just for the company, or just to perform a good deed in a wicked world.

So it was that Leon was picked up on the North Circular by an oil tanker heading all the way to Aberdeen, and the driver told him that the English were stealing Scottish oil, just as the thieving English bastards always stole what they wanted, they would nick the coins off a dead man's eyes if you let them, and after driving all the way across the great sprawling expanse of north London, he dropped Leon off halfway up the Finchley Road, telling him to mind out for the traffic, and the thieving English bastards.

Leon walked up the hill to Hampstead, through the leafy streets with their huge houses where he had grown up, through the Village and across the Heath, the grass burned yellow by two burning summers in a row, and all of London spread out below him.

The squat would be gone by now. When the bailiffs had cleared the building, they would do what they always did. Rip out the plumbing and smash the toilets. There were other squats, thousands of them, but summer was almost gone and Leon knew that soon the squatters would be freezing their non-conforming arses off, wearing their greatcoats and Afghans inside their sleeping bags, too cold to think. Leon no longer had the heart for it.

So he went to the place where a young man goes when there is nowhere left to go. Across the Heath, over the fence that surrounded the grounds of Kenwood, past the great white house, and then the Suburb, and the clean, quiet streets of home.

He had thrown away his front-door key so he had to knock. His mother answered the door still in her dressing gown. His father was sitting at the big wooden breakfast table, surrounded by broadsheet newspapers, orange juice, coffee, bagels. Cream cheese and smoked salmon. Bach on the hi-fi – 'Sheep May Safely Graze'. Leon could smell real coffee and toasted bread, and it almost made him swoon.

'What happened to you?' his mother said, taking it all in – the fading bruise from last weekend, the cut on his forehead from Junior, the black eye from the porter with HP sauce on his head.

'He was at Lewisham,' his father said proudly. 'Bloody thugs!'

'Let me put something on it,' said his mother.

Over Leon's protests, his mother brought a pack of frozen Birds Eye peas and made him hold it against his wounds. His parents watched with a kind of affectionate amusement as Leon shovelled down bagels and lox with his spare hand. They didn't remember him having such an appetite.

'I haven't been reading your column,' Leon said, wiping crumbs from his mouth with the back of his hand. He gulped down some black coffee. He couldn't remember the last time he had drunk coffee that hadn't been the kind where you just add boiling water. 'What's your take on this Thatcher woman?'

'Never happen,' his father said emphatically. 'In this country? With Benny Hill and Page 3 lovelies and mother-in-law jokes? The British will never vote for a woman.'

'Oh, I don't know,' said his mother. 'I think it would be rather nice to have a woman Prime Minister.'

'She'll be burning her bra next,' his father laughed.

Leon's parents were still laughing when he undressed and crawled into bed in his old room, out of his mind with exhaustion, the room dancing around him.

It felt both cosy and ridiculous to be between these boyhood walls again, the embarrassing pictures of outgrown passions on the wall – *Jaws* and Jimmy Page and Jimmy Greaves – and a mad library where copies of *Jonathan Livingstone Seagull* and *Das Kapital* shared space with Anthony Buckeridge's tales of two larky lads called Jennings and Darbishire at Linbury Court Preparatory School — *Jennings Goes to School, Jennings and Darbishire, Thanks to Jennings* and maybe thirty more – whatever happened to Jennings? Leon had loved Jennings, he had wanted to *be* Jennings – *'That shepherd's pie we've just had was supersonic muck so it's wizard, but this school jam's ghastly so it's ozard . . . being a new chap's pretty ozard for a bit, but you'll get used to it when you've been here as long as I have.'* Silly really, but it didn't matter right at this moment, because – oh, Ruby – the sheets were soft and clean and his parents had taken him back without making him feel bad, without asking any questions, as if he had never been away, as if he had never thrown away his front-door key, and Leon knew it would be like that for as long as they lived, they would never turn him away, and also he could not feel too bad about sleeping under a *Jaws* duvet because he was so very tired, swamped – *swamped* . . . *swamped* . . . *swamped* by tiredness, his eyes closing now – and he knew that sleep would come the moment he laid his head on the pillow. And it did.

So Leon drifted away, a man in a boy's bedroom, the St Christopher around his neck feeling cool against his skin, and many miles to go when he awoke.

CODA:

1977 – ANOTHER GIRL. ANOTHER PLANET

SIXTEEN

Terry liked belonging. He saw that now.

Belonging to his paper, belonging to her. It was good. He was glad that he hadn't been sacked. He was happy that they hadn't broken up. Knowing he was getting married next month, knowing he was going to be a father next year – these things did not frighten him. They made him feel as though he belonged to this woman, and to this unborn child, and to this world.

But sometimes *The Paper* felt like just another job, where someone older than you was always telling you what to do, not so very different from the gin factory, except there was less freedom to run wild. And sometimes Misty really got on his nerves.

The two of them sat facing each other on the Inter-City 125 train, waiting for it to leave, and Misty was reading aloud from a paperback called *The Flames of Love* that she had just bought at W. H. Smiths. And Terry understood that the opposite of love is not hate. The opposite of love is irritation.

'Listen to this bit,' she said. '*She came through the French windows and suddenly felt his strong, manly, dirty fingers in her taffeta. Miles the gardener was on his knees before her, imploring with his heavy-lidded eyes.'* Misty guffawed. *'She gasped as he kissed the hem of her gown. "Valerie," he said, "do you understand how big this thing is?"'*

A gaggle of businessmen staggered down the carriage, smelling of smoky bacon crisps and shorts bolted down at the railway bar. They eyed Misty hungrily. Terry glared at them. She didn't notice. She was enjoying her Doris Hardman too much.

"'No one – least of all that cad Sir Timothy – is man enough to do more than kiss your gilded slippers.'" She was laughing so hard now that she struggled to get the words out. Misty shook her head, wide-eyed with disbelief. 'Isn't this just *fabulous?* Don't you *love it?* I'm going to read *everything* by her, she's so *mad.'*

Terry smiled politely. It *was* funny – he could see that – but was it quite as funny as Misty was making out? Was she planning to read the whole book out loud? Was it going to be like this all the way to Sheffield? Was it going to be like this for the next fifty years?

He could hardly stand to admit it, but it was suddenly all a little bit different. With Misty, and with *The Paper* too. He began leafing through the latest issue. It was a good issue. The kind of issue that would have had his heart beating faster when he was out there in reader-land, travelling up to the city to buy *The Paper* a day early with all the other true believers.

Young Elvis on the cover in all his greasy pomp. Pages of tributes and memories and reflections from some of the older guys. Ray's interview with Lennon. And the new guy tearing Dag Wood to bits for spending most of his gig at the Rainbow squatting behind the amps, his leather trousers down by his ankles, clutching his stomach and groaning.

And – who would have thought it? – the diary mention of a band called Electric Baguette who wore Italian suits and played synthetic dance music and said they were bored with politics, they just wanted to make pop music and money. Brainiac had finally formed his band, and everybody seemed to think they were going to be the next hot thing. Funny how time slipped away – it was no longer the Sex Pistols that filled the sky for the new groups, but Chic. How quickly the new music – the new anything – became old hat. There was a rumour that Brainiac had even had his teeth fixed. But Terry closed *The Paper,* feeling curiously unmoved by all of it.

Partly it was the ham-fisted, infantile quality of much of the writing – one of the older guys had compared Elvis to Jay Gatsby, 'the hero of F. Scott Fitzgerald's brilliant novel, *The Great Gatsby.*' As if everyone needed to be told who Jay Gatsby was, and as if everyone needed to be told that the book was one of the greatest novels ever written. As if, Terry thought, we're all just a bunch of dumb kids, waiting to be educated by our betters. There was nothing by Skip Jones in *The Paper.* For Terry, there was always something missing when Skip's by-line wasn't in there. He was happy that Skip was on the mend. But *The Paper* seemed almost ordinary without him.

'*His large hands were too powerful to resist,*' Misty giggled. '*His mouth fastened on her rosebud lips like a vice.*' She looked up at Terry. 'Now how can lips possibly be like a vice, you silly cow?' She shrugged. 'Oh well ... *She felt his desire rise up inside her –* that's a bit of a Freudian slip, his desire rising up inside her – *then suddenly he swept her up in his rope-like muscles and carried her to the waiting four-poster. "Damn you, Valerie!" he cried hoarsely. "Why should we wait another year?" And she knew in her beating heart that her reticence was only inflaming him still further.*'

The real reason Terry felt a little blue today was because for the first time he could see an end to the whole music thing. He thought it was changing. But it was more than that. It was dying.

One of his best friends had been kicked out, and the other one seemed suddenly to have a proper job, his future set in stone, the career of an adult. They had sent Ray off to New York to talk to Springsteen. His comeback was complete.

But for Terry this life was coming to its natural end – as if it was really just his version of going to university, or doing national service. A few years and you were out. You went in a boy and you came out a man. All grown up. Or at least on your way to being grown up.

You turned around and the bands were new, and a bit younger than you, and you didn't like them quite as much as the bands you kicked around with at the start, the bands who were now struggling to record their second albums, or trying to crack America, or arguing among themselves, or overdoing the drugs. Suddenly, just to seem interested, you had to fake it a bit.

And the faces in the clubs and at the gigs were changing too. Now every night he went out he was aware that he no longer knew everyone in the house. The familiar faces were thinning out.

The day after the Western World disaster, Billy Blitzen had gone back to New York, deported by the Home Office for not having the correct work permit. Legend had it that Billy went home to Brooklyn with his guitar full of Iranian heroin, which he sold at a rock-bottom price to his kid brother, who had never even smoked a spliff before. Terry had no way of knowing it as he sat on that train with Misty, but Billy was just a few years away from a date with a disease that none of them had heard of yet.

And whatever happened to all the other boys and girls that

Terry had known back in the summer of 1976? Where had they all gone? To drugs and nervous breakdowns? To marriage and babies? To real jobs and early nights? He would never know.

He knew he would miss the good stuff. He would miss coming down the stairs of some club into a world of noise, his spirits lifting with the music and the speed, the feeling of sweat inside his Oxfam jacket, and the overwhelming sensation of being a part of it all. But he couldn't kid himself. The life he had known was drawing to an end.

He tried to remember what Skip had said. He knew it was something about all art forms having their day. Like jazz had its day. Like painting had its day. Skip had said that there would probably never be another Miles Davis, and there would never be another Picasso. Skip had said that the music would never again be quite as good as the music they had loved, and so you were left with just another dying art form, and soon it would be ready for the museum.

But if their music was dying, wouldn't they die with it? It had been the heart of their world for as long as Terry could remember. Their music was more than a soundtrack – it was a life-support machine from childhood through adolescence and into what was passing for maturity. Perhaps they were all going to have to find other things to live for, and the music would be just something they came back to now and again, like the memory of someone you had lost.

As he waited for the train to leave the station, Terry felt lucky that he had a woman he loved, a baby on the way, and a little family of his own. Things would be easier after the wedding, wouldn't they?

'*She felt the love she had for him burning inside her. He was all*

she wanted and all she would ever need. Her young body trembled
with a thrill that felt one step from sin. Soon she would be his wife
and be his forever.'

Terry walked down to the dining car to look for tea and bacon
sandwiches. By the time he came back empty-handed, Misty had
put down her book and was staring thoughtfully out of the window.

'They're on strike,' Terry said. 'This bloody country. Somebody
should do something.'

But she wasn't listening. She didn't care about bacon sandwiches and strikes on British Rail.

'What do you think is better?' she said. 'To never change – to
be the same person you always were as a kid – or to grow out of
all that stuff and grow old gracefully?'

'We'll never be old,' Terry smiled. 'They'll have invented a cure
for it by the time we get there.'

She stuffed Doris Hardman into her bag, and then paused when
she caught a glimpse of something. She pulled out her pair of
pink fake mink handcuffs.

'Remember these?' she said, as if they would bring the fond
memories flooding back. But all Terry remembered were silly games
where he didn't know the rules.

He watched her snap one of the pink fake mink cuffs around
her wrist and admire it, as if it were the finest bracelet in the
window of Ratner's. Then, with one of those aren't-I-a-naughty-
thing? looks on her face, she reached across the table separating
them and snapped the other cuff around Terry's wrist.

'I remember,' Terry said.

Misty rippled with laughter. 'I wonder if Doris Hardman would
approve?' she said. 'Can you believe that millions of ordinary
women fill their heads with that garbage?'

Terry nodded. 'Can you take it off?'

Misty fumbled in her bag for the key. Then she began to search more desperately, and it took a long moment for him to realise that she wasn't joking. Terry stared at the pink fake mink handcuffs around his wrist and then he looked away. He loved her but sometimes she drove him crazy. Was that real love? Or was that something else? Did true love really have room in it for irritation? Or was that kind of love a lesser kind, a love that was already on the way out?

The thing was, now that he knew he was definitely going to be with this one girl – woman – for the rest of his life, he sort of missed all the others he had known. And he couldn't help wondering how it would have turned out if he had gone with one of them instead.

He missed Sally, missed her goodness and decency, and he missed the way she didn't look like everyone he had grown up with. He missed that lustrous black hair, he missed those eyes like melting chocolate, and he missed her slim, golden body inside the sleeping bag on the night shift. He missed how straightforward she was, and he missed her friendship. He missed the way she never mentioned the suffocating tyranny of men.

And he even missed Grace Fury, despite the strangeness and the horror of her visit to his flat, because everybody wanted her, and because he loved it when they had that wildness inside them.

Terry could have been happy with any of them. At least for a while. They were all great women in their way, and they all liked him. Maybe more than Misty liked him. Because he knew he irritated her too. Loving someone – it wasn't the same as liking them.

And he wondered how much choice we really have in the person we end up with, and how much of it is down to pure chance. That was the big problem with loving someone. There were lots of other people that you could love, if the timing was right, and if you got the chance, and if you were not already promised to someone else. It all just seemed so random.

But Terry had built his dreams around the one in front of him, and there was a baby growing inside her, he had to follow those dreams through now. Then she winked at him, and smiled, and he was aware of the old feelings, felt them rising up inside him, as strong as they ever were. Maybe it would be all right after all. Maybe it would. He looked up as a whistle blew, knowing that, either way, it was too late to stop now. The whistle blew again.

The train lurched forward and began to move out of the station, the jewel lights of the city soon yielding to the soft dusk of harvest fields, and they headed north into what was left of summer with the pair of them still joined at the wrist, just like Sidney Poitier and Tony Curtis as runaway prisoners in *The Defiant Ones*, or the bride and groom on a wedding cake.